RECKLESS CRUEL HEIRS

OLIVIA WILDENSTEIN

RECKLESS CRUEL HEIRS
Book 5 of THE LOST CLAN series

Copyright © 2020 by Olivia Wildenstein
2ND EDITION Copyright © 2022

For information contact:
OLIVIA WILDENSTEIN
http://oliviawildenstein.com

Cover art by *Celin Chen @celingraphics*
Under the cover art by *Oksana @_alex_oxy_*
Art of Amara and Remo on train by *@artbySteffani*
Drawing of Ace and Cat by *@lasq.draws*
Character portraits by *@cir.arts*
Map of Neverra created by *@p.dulcis_*
Editing by *Jessica Nelson*
Proofreading by *Katelyn Anderson & Rachel Theus Cass*

DISCLAIMER

The Gottwas are an invented tribe, loosely inspired by the Ojibwe people. I did not want to cause offense to Native Americans by writing about customs that aren't mine.

GOTTWA GLOSSARY

aabiti: mate

abiwoojin: darling

adsookin: legend

bagwa: jackass

baseetogan: fae world; Neverra; Isle of Woods

bazash: half-fae, half-human

bekagwe: wait for me

chatwa: darkness

debwe: truth

gajeekwe: the king's advisor, like a minister, *wariff*

gassen: faerie dust

gatizogin: I'm sorry

Gejaiwe: the Great Spirit

geezhi: day

Geemee: Uncle

gingawi: part hunter, part fae

giya: daisy

golwinim: Woods's guards, fireflies; *lucionaga*

gwe: woman

Iba: Dad

ishtu: sweetness
kwenim: memory
ley: light
ma kwenim: my memory
maagwe: come with me
maahin: come forth
Makudewa Geezhi: Dark Day
manazi: book
mashka: tough
mawa: mine
meegwe: give me
meekwa: blood
Mishipeshu: water faeries, *Daneelies*
mika: beauty
naagangwe: stop her
Neenee: Aunt
nockwad: mist
nilwa: defeater
Nima: Mom
pahan: faeries
tokwa: favor
twa: men
zava: love
zavagingwi: I love you

FAELI GLOSSARY

adamans: glass flowers as tall as wheat stalks

alinum: rowan wood

amoo: darling, my love

astium: portal, door

calidum: lesser fae; *bazash*

caligo: mist

caligosubi: one who lives below the mist, aka marsh-dweller

caligosupra: one who lives above the mist, aka mist-dweller

calimbor: skytrees

capra: slithering Neverrian creature with rubbery skin that can paralyze prey for days

captis: magnetize

clave: portal locksmith

cupola: cage of nightmares

Daneelies: water faeries, *Mishipeshu*

daffos: tall trumpet-headed flowers that grow in shrubs

dias: day

diles: venomous Neverrian creature, a cross between a frog and a crocodile

draca: first guard; *wariff*'s protector (dragon form)

drosa: type of Neverrian rose

duciba: council made up of a member from each faerie race

duobosi: coupling ceremony

enefkum: eunuch

fae: sky-dwellers

forma: underground-dwellers, bodiless, *Unseelies*

fias: child

gajoï: favor

gladeberry: sour berry that grows beside the Glades.

hareni: grotto

kalini: fire

lucionaga: faerie guards

lustriums: clusters of stars

lupa: wild dog

mallow: an edible plant, faerie weed; doesn't affect humans the same way it affects faeries, and Hunters are immune

Massin(a): Your highness

Massini: your highnesses

mea: mine

mikos: Neverrian snake coated in sharp quills

milandi: marvelous

Neverra: baseetogan; Isle of Woods

octas: octopus-like Neverrian creature with eyes at the tip of each tentacle

obso: please

pistri: shark

plantae: plants

potas: I can't

Prinsis(a): prince(ss)

quid est: who is it?

quila: Neverrian eagle with sharp talons and curved beak

runa: Neverrian gondolas carried by faeries

Seelies: light faeries, *Fae*

sepula: ceremony of the dead

stam: giant flat shells that bob in the Glades

ti ama: I love you

tigri: striped wild cat that lives in the jungle beyond the Glades. Medium-sized. Exist in a variety of colors.

Unseelies: dark faeries, bodiless, *Forma*

vade: go

valo: bye

ventor: Hunter

Wariff: equal to *Gajeekwe*

wita: faerie dust, *gassen*

Sometimes you must fall
to know where you stand.

HUMAN

PROLOGUE
CATORI

EARTH YEAR: 2034 / NEVERRA YEAR: 806

A hand stroked up and down my trembling arm. "Cat, we need to stop. This needs to stop."

"I . . . can't."

"You also can't go through this again, *amoo*. It's too much. For your body, but also for your heart." The mattress dipped and then Ace's body curled around mine, his arm falling over my empty abdomen. Weeks had gone by yet the pain lingered. "And for mine."

Five months. This had been the longest a child had held on.

A sob raced up my chest and spilled into my damp pillow. Outside our bedroom's sliding glass doors, steel clouds coiled over Neverra, darkening our kingdom, muting its beautiful colors. At this rate, I would drown our people in my sorrow.

"I'm so sorry, Cat."

A slash of lightning painted the floating garden upon which we'd built our stone and glass nest garishly bright.

"Why?" I whimpered.

Ace sighed. "You know why."

I turned in his arms. "I wish I could give up all my powers and just be human."

He slid a lock of long black hair behind my ear, his turquoise eyes raking over my tearstained cheeks. "And deprive Neverra of its weekly sound and light show? How dull."

In spite of my smashed heart, I smiled. "The farmers are complaining that your wife's temper is ruining their crops."

"My wife has a temper?" His features were taut with grief and yet his ability to pluck humor from terrible things hadn't waned.

There were many things I loved about this man, but it was his wicked humor I loved best. Perhaps that was why we kept losing our babies. Not because their tiny bodies couldn't bear the combination of so many powers, but because we'd somehow reached our quota of happiness and weren't permitted more blessings.

I attempted to push away my longing, but as the Pink Sea raged beneath our hovering bungalow, its whitecaps scudding across wood, I knew I wasn't ready to give up. "One more time, and then I promise, *never* again."

He kissed the tip of my nose and tucked me closer. "Cat . . ."

"Please."

"Willful wife." He released a resigned sigh. "Fine. Use me for my body."

I swatted his chest, then climbed onto one elbow to better see the glorious man who'd walked into my life three Neverrian years ago, armed with unrelenting humor, irresistible charm, and an inordinate amount of patience. He traced the sharp ridges of my face with one finger before weaving his hand through my hair and towing my head back toward his.

"You know I would do anything for you, Kitty Cat."

When our lips touched, the storm fuming outside our walls and inside me finally abated. I wasn't done grieving for those tiny souls stolen from my womb. How could I when they all still existed inside my heart?

But love and hope crawled back into my chest and pushed away the residual anger. Perhaps I'd never have a child to cradle, but at least I had a man who cradled me.

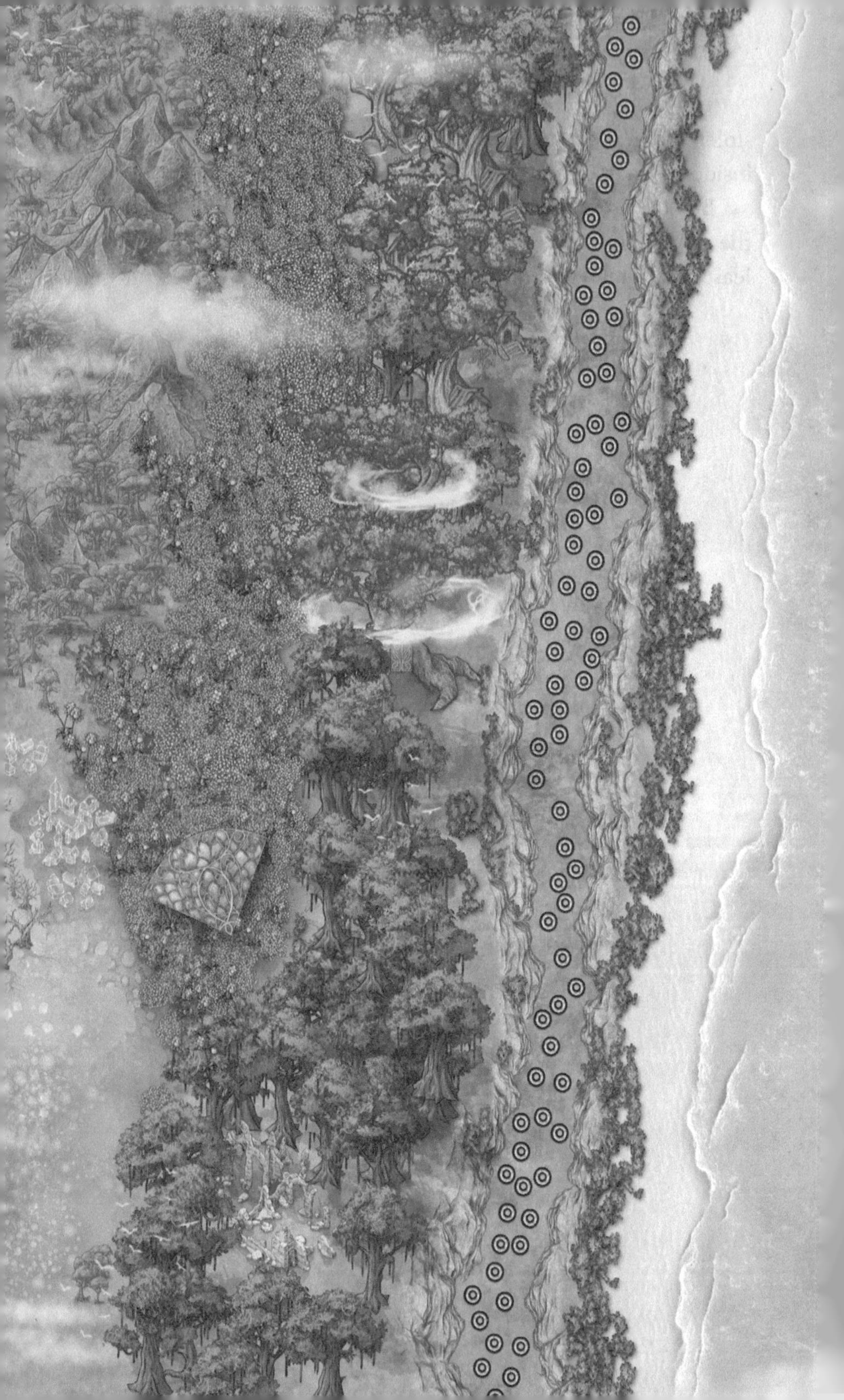

I

YORK HOUSE

AMARA

EARTH YEAR: 2124 / NEVERRA YEAR: 824

The security-bot scanned my biometric bracelet to make sure I was of legal age to enter the bar. Since I wasn't, I conjured up my dust to create interference and wrapped it around the piece of human technology faeries had adopted four Neverrian years ago.

The Infinity was brilliant. With a swipe of my finger, I could control my outfit and footwear, beam and receive objects to anyone outfitted with a similar band, as well as pay and comm people in the human world *and* in Neverra. Plus it never needed charging. Our pulse created an electromagnetic field that fueled its battery. So long as we were alive, our little piece of technology was too.

As the security-bot blinked and splashed red light over the line of humans forming behind me, I checked the sidewalk for my personal guards. I'd managed to give them the slip back on Neverra by pretending to go for a swim in the depths of the Pink Sea, the only place in the kingdom where they didn't follow since they were

Seelies, aka air fae, and not Daneelies, aka water fae. Before surfacing, I'd disguised my appearance with a heavy dusting of *wita* and soared toward the portal for Old York before my two assigned guards had even noticed I was out of the water.

A woman with turquoise hair tapped her spiky-heeled boot behind me and muttered something about how bots could be so useless. At least she didn't fault me for the defective machine. "Any humans around?" she yelled. "Hello? A little help out here."

A man dressed in head-to-toe denim finally emerged from the dusky interior of the bar and silenced the whirring machine. He glanced at me. After a slow sweep of my leather-clad body, he tipped his oval face to my wrist. "Try again, baby."

I wasn't a fan of being called *baby*, especially by men twice my age, but since I needed to get into York House, and fast—my guards were bound to grow impatient and look up my location—I clamped my lips shut and lifted my wrist. The bot emitted a shrill beep, followed by some more crazy red blinking.

Denim-man cursed the machine under his breath. "Stupid contraption." Sighing, he made it stop screeching. "Just display your ID for me."

Three rapid clicks on the shiny black surface, and my face along with detailed information about my physique leaped off in 2D.

"Um, sweetheart, you're sev—"

The second his eyes locked on mine, I said, "Nineteen tomorrow. I know."

The man's dark eyebrows writhed, but his pupils swelled as he absorbed my false statement. Nodding, he scanned his own wristband, and the glass doors of the bar slid open. "Go right on ahead."

"Thank you," I said sweetly.

As I sidestepped him, the man inhaled a long whiff of air. My heart came to a standstill, worried he was fae and had smelled my deception, but fae couldn't be influenced, so he had to be human. Still, I hurried through the short, mirrored corridor that reflected my waist-long black hair, blue-gray leather jumpsuit, and turquoise eyes from a hundred different angles.

Being the Neverrian king's daughter afforded me privileges, but skirting human laws wasn't one of them. My parents were always on my case about setting an example, to which I always rolled my eyes, because I'd heard plenty of stories about them. Most from Neenee Cass.

When Cassidy had a little too much faerie wine—a typical occurrence—she would tell me all about my mother and the trouble she got into. Nima would of course deny deny deny, but her tipped black eyes would always tilt a little higher, and eventually, so would her lips. However much she insisted my aunt loved story-telling as much as she loved sampling the casks of fae wine delivered daily to her Neverrian bar and club, I knew my mother wasn't the goody two-shoes she claimed to have been.

And my father. Well, Iba never pretended to be good. The only thing he ever declared being good at was infuriating my mother and loving us *ut Rowan e retri. From Rowan and back.*

Rowan was where my mother grew up. Smackdab in the middle of a cemetery filled with human and Hunter graves. My uncle Kajika spent two centuries in one of those graves, preserved by magical rose petals born of faerie ashes. According to his daughter, Giya, this still bothered him to no end.

My bracelet beeped with an incoming call.

"Speak of the Unseelie," I murmured before tapping the wristband twice to deny the call.

My cousin wasn't a tattletale, but if I picked up the call and she caught sight of my surroundings on the holographic feed that would rise from her band, she'd ask where the heck I was. Unlike my guards and my parents, she didn't have access to my Infinity's GPS.

GIYA: *I'm at your house, but you're not.*

I touched the implant behind my ear to convey the answer

scrolling through my brain, which appeared like magic on the holo-chat: *I'm on Earth. Running an errand. Why are you at my house?*

GIYA: *Your father's organizing a big revel tonight, so I came to get ready with you.*

ME: *Another revel? In whose honor this time?*

GIYA: *Have no clue, but apparently, the whole family's convened. Maybe they have an announcement?*

ME: *You think?*

GIYA: *No clue, but hurry back. Veroli is chomping at the bit to do your hair and makeup.*

ME: *OK.*

After shutting down our little chat, I squinted to discern the patrons seated at the bar that girdled a thick glass cylinder lined with every alcoholic beverage imaginable. The color-changing bulbs that floated like jellyfish within the wide tube didn't afford much light, yet it took me mere seconds to spot Joshua Locklear.

The Earthly-born Daneelie, who'd moved to Neverra at seven years old and misbehaved almost every day since, was a big man, with a head of hair so blond it looked almost white. Said head was currently bobbing to a beat layered over sultry female vocals. As though sensing my approach, it turned in my direction.

"Hello, little princess." He raised a tumbler of something green to his lips. "Saved you a seat."

I climbed onto the stool and crossed my legs. "Call me that again, and I walk out of here."

He shot back the green stuff, then tapped his index finger against his glass.

The barmaid, whose flexible screen dress lit up with moving images of the various cocktails on York House's menu, gave him a refill. "What can I get you, hon?"

"Just some water, please." I stared at the patrons closest to us. Although more than a few stared back, all were strangers. Still, I regretted having dismissed my earlier disguise of a bald septuagenarian.

"You do realize you're old enough to have alcohol. I mean, according to human standards, you *are* eighty-n—"

"What is it you want, Josh?"

"Straight to business, huh?"

"I agreed to meet you here because I owe you. However, I need to get back to Neverra soon, so make it quick."

"Have you ever owed anyone a *gajoï*?"

Not for the first time, I regretted asking Josh to take the downfall for my little illegal dealings. "No. You should feel privileged."

"I do. I feel *very* privileged."

The barmaid came back with my water.

When she left, he said, "A person, who'd rather remain anonymous, recently told me about a supernatural prison Gregor and your grandfather Linus created centuries ago."

My eyebrows drew together.

"Apparently, it's only accessible on Neverra through a portal that magically relocates every month."

I let out a disbelieving grunt. "I may be gullible, but come on."

"I'm not pulling your wing, Amara."

"I don't have wings."

Smiling, he spun on his stool until his broad body was angled toward me. "Figure of speech." Josh's shoulders, like most Daneelie shoulders, were wide, and his biceps bulged from hours spent in water. My arms weren't as defined, but that probably had to do with the fact that my preferred means of locomotion was flight.

Josh was pure Daneelie; in other words, he couldn't fly.

I was a mix of everything: Seelie, Unseelie, Daneelie, and human. Which meant I had blood, fire, iron, and water coursing through my veins. I was a lethal faerie cocktail who could live underwater, in the sky, and on Earth.

"I swear. No joke." Josh's freckled face puckered. "My source tells me the portal's presently located in the ceiling of the Duciba, more precisely in one of the leaves of the golden circlet mural your aunt Lily painted. Since I'm locked out of Neverra, I can't check it out myself."

"Wait. This source of yours actually saw it?"

"Yeah." He speared his freckled fingers through his nose-length bangs and shoved them off his forehead. The rest of his hair was buzzed close to his scalp. "If you look long enough at the leaf, the paint ripples. Like a faulty projection."

"*Okay* . . . And what does this prison have to do with our *gajoï*?"

"I believe Kiera might be in there."

"Kiera?"

"My sister. The one who didn't make it into Neverra."

Didn't make it was putting it nicely. Kiera had tortured my aunt and uncle when they'd visited the Daneelie camp back in Michigan a little over an Earthly century ago.

"Um. You do realize that if time in this prison moves like it does around here"—I gestured to the bar but obviously meant Earth—"her chances of being alive are extremely slim."

He shot back his drink. "Time doesn't move the same in there as it does in the human world. 'Parently doesn't move like on Neverra either."

Instead of asking how it moved, I said, "So, you want me to ask my father about it?"

"Hell, no. He and Gregor will zip up the portal."

"So what do you want me to do?"

"I want you to go check it out."

"You want me to go through a prison portal?"

"Just to take a peek, then jump back out."

Even though the air wasn't cold, and I was made of fire, Joshua's suggestion chilled me. "If it's a real prison, I doubt I can get in."

"All you need is a handful of salt to gain entrance. Then again, you're the Trifecta—"

I hated that nickname even more than I hated the boy who'd come up with it.

"—you could surely get in with a drop of your potent blood."

"Josh—"

"Or I can tell our dearest king about your little transaction."

I pressed my lips together, ruing the day I'd struck a deal with this man whose criminal record ran the gamut of peddling Daneelie scales on the Earthly black market to arms dealing.

"Amara Wood, take one look inside, and then we'll be fair and square."

The use of my full name, combined with the firmness of his demand, locked in the repayment of his favor. I'd heard of the pain associated with *gajoïs* but had never experienced it first-hand. As an invisible fist gripped my gut, I swore I would never again strike a faerie bargain.

Never.

I flung my palm against my abdomen. "Fine." Not that I had a choice.

The pressure inside my body vanished instantly, but it would return if I tried to renege on the claimed *gajoï*. There was no messing with fae magic.

Smiling, Josh knocked back his drink. "Oh, and, Amara, get to it quick. The portal changes location in five days."

I sipped my iced water, wincing when I swallowed, expecting pain that thankfully didn't come. "Have you considered the possibility that I won't be able to get in, salt or no salt?"

"Yes."

Why, oh why, had I let Joshua Locklear take the blame for my mistake? I tapped a button on the countertop to get the barmaid's attention. "Can I get two shots of tequila, please?"

"Tequila?" Josh whistled. "Damn, *Prinsisa*. Here I'd pegged you for a prosecco girl."

"I don't like bubbles." The same way I didn't like the idea of peeking into a supernatural jail. "Anything else I should know about this place?"

"It's a prison, so don't expect rainbows and unicorns."

I rolled my eyes as two shot glasses filled with clear liquid appeared in front of me. I lifted the first and tossed it back, the alcohol singeing my tongue and throat. Josh tried to grab the other, but I made the glass levitate to my mouth, sprinkling some *wita* to hide my little magic trick from human eyes. After pounding it back, I floated the glass back down to the counter. Unseelie mind control might've been one of my favorite powers.

"Showoff." He signaled the waitress for some refills.

I longed for the alcohol to loosen the dread clinging to every organ in my body. *A supernatural prison. Geez.* I'd rather he'd asked me to kiss a *dile*, poison and all.

"I'll try to do it tonight." I licked the bittersweet dregs of alcohol from my lips.

The Plexiglas stool squeaked as he crossed one foot over his opposite knee. "I almost wish I could take it back."

"Take what back?"

"The *gajoï*."

I grunted. "You're telling me . . ."

He raised a shameless smile. "I should've locked you into spending a whole night with me, naked and horizontal. Or vertical."

Whoa. Nasty. I wrinkled my nose. "You did not just suggest that."

He laughed. "Don't look so appalled. I'm a very good lay."

"You're gross."

"Never thought I'd agree with Trifecta on anything." The familiar voice made my spine tighten and my eyes close.

How I wished I could open a portal and jump into it. Why couldn't portal creation have been part of my arsenal of superpowers? Remo Farrow—aka my worst enemy—had joined the party. This was shaping up to be the worst night of my life.

"Propositioning your princess gives me grounds for immediate arrest." Even though my eyes were still closed, I could imagine Remo's golden ones, all shiny and smug. There were a few people

Remo disliked more than me, and Josh was one of them. My mother was the other.

To this day, Remo was convinced that she'd killed his grandmother for her dust. Remo's mother, Faith, shared her son's belief. Neither mother nor son believed Stella Sakar had attacked my mother first—and not even once, but twice.

"Sorry to interrupt your little *date*," Remo all but spit, "but the *wariff* and your father need to speak with you before dinner, *prinsisa*. They've tasked *me*—since your guards proved extraordinarily inefficient—to bring you back to Neverra immediately."

My eyes flew open. First Giya, now Remo. Maybe this wasn't just another silly revel. "I can bring myself back." I asked the waitress to beam over my bill. After I wired the money, tagging on a hefty tip, I stood, careful not to brush up against Remo and the three *lucionaga* he'd brought along—two males with inflated muscles, and a female guard, whom I'd heard was lethal with blades. "Worried you needed backup to get me home, Farrow?"

Remo's face darkened, turning the same burnt-copper shade as his hair. "Actually, my desire to protect the women in your family is so very lacking I thought it sounder for you to have others around if anything were to *happen* to you."

"More like you're worried about your own safety around our *prinsisa*," Josh lobbed in good-naturedly.

"Careful, Daneelie," Remo growled.

Josh rolled his shoulders back, the tendons and joints rippling underneath his short-sleeved white tee. He reclined against the bar, propping his elbows on the black glass. "Are you going to gas me for voicing what everyone else is thinking?"

Even though I disliked Remo, I disliked bullying more. "Stop it, Josh."

"I'm merely defending your honor."

"I can defend my own honor," I said.

Remo's fingers flexed. "So can I, Trifecta."

"Whatever." I started to walk away, when Josh called out, "Don't forget our *date* tonight."

My stomach rolled from the reminder—a mix of nerves and magic. Had he needed to use the word *date*? Actually, it was probably better everyone considered my meetups with Josh that way so they didn't question my true motive.

Denim-guy, who was still hanging around the entrance of York House, looked on as we left.

"Eyes off her ass. She's not legal," Remo snarled before lengthening his strides to catch up to me.

Not that he actually cared if people ogled me. He just enjoyed throwing around his weight and power on Neverra and on Earth. Power he got from being Gregor's favorite grandson and the *draca*'s stepson.

I'd had many talks with my father about having Remo demoted, but he'd said that unless Faith's son committed a grave mistake, he couldn't lawfully have him kicked out of the guard. He'd even told me to prepare myself for Remo becoming the next *wariff*, and then he'd warned me that certain enemies made excellent allies in politics. I didn't understand how he'd put up with Gregor, and told him that if I ever became queen—I was in no hurry to take my father's place—and Remo was *wariff*, I'd have him fired. My father had sighed and reminded me that I was young and naïve and had so much to learn about running a kingdom. I'd stomped out of his chambers.

That was thirty Earthly years ago—I'd been eleven years old. I'd never brought up Remo Farrow since, even though I watched the *lucionaga* like a *quila*, waiting for him to slip. Unfortunately, Remo was extremely careful, as though he knew I was paying attention to his every move.

"Is your father aware of the sort of men you're dating?" Remo asked.

"It's none of Iba's business who I date."

"I beg to differ. Who you date reflects on the crown."

I slanted him a look. "Spare me the unsolicited advice."

"If your father asks, I won't lie."

I rolled my eyes. "Knowing you, Iba wouldn't even have to ask; you'll volunteer the information."

"If I suspect your tryst endangers the crown, then I'll share my concerns."

If the elevated Old York sidewalks weren't crawling with people, I would've run back to the portal to avoid enduring a single more minute in Remo's presence. "Enjoy your days of power, Farrow. Once I'm crowned, you'll be lucky if you get a job taxiing a *runa*."

Remo smirked, obviously not taking my threat seriously. Why would he? He didn't take *me* seriously. "How did you even get into York House, Trifecta?"

If he was trying to get a confession out of me, a confession that could lead to a hefty fine and an argument with my parents, he could hold his breath. I masked my annoyance under a plasticky smile. "I promised the owner I'd hang out with him after my date with Josh."

Remo's nostrils flared. I could tell he was thinking vile thoughts about me, probably lining up some new rumors about the princess' loose morals and limbs. There was nothing the petty tyrant enjoyed more than smearing my good name.

I used to care but didn't anymore. Or at least, I cared less. "And my name is *Amara*. Use it."

He smirked. "You'll always be Trifecta to me."

"Technically, Trifecta's wrong since I'm also part human."

"I'm aware, but Quadfecta doesn't roll off the tongue as nicely."

I stopped walking so suddenly that Remo ended up a couple feet ahead of me. Keeping my voice low so that the three *lucionaga* trailing us couldn't hear, I said, "I wish Nima hadn't stopped at your grandmother; I wish she'd eliminated every last one of you."

Remo's lips thinned, and a vein pulsed at his temple, underneath his raspberry-shaped birthmark.

I almost felt guilty, but the Farrows—Gregor, Faith, Remo, and even his little brother Karsyn—were all hateful and manipulative. The sort of family who felt like they were owed the crown, and whom I suspected one day would try to steal it. Not that I'd let them.

I conjured up my dust, cloaked myself in it to make humans believe they were looking at a flock of pigeons, then pushed off the sidewalk and flew over the passing magnetic train. When I reached the traffic light, I pressed my palm against the green bulb. The stamp on my wrist—a rosette—flared, and then my body was sucked through and spit back into Neverra.

2

THE POLITICAL MATCH

I emerged from the dark, gelatinous tunnel into the Gorge of Portals located in the heart of Neverra, between the forest of *calimbors*, trees so thick and tall their crowns seemed to kiss the purple sky, and the Pink Sea that resembled a plum-tinted mirror at night and glistened rose-gold in the light of day.

When red hair began rising from the slender disk under my boots, I dove off and bobbed in the air, waiting for Remo to tell me where the meeting was taking place. Was my father in the *calimbor* that housed the Duciba, or in the hovering palace he'd built over the Pink Sea from *volitor* fronds and stone quarried from the Five, the gray cliffs that cinched the Valley of Hunters?

After the *Caligo Dias*—the Day of Mist—Negongwa's tribe had finally been invited to settle on Neverra. The Hunters, along with their bodiless Unseelie brethren (most of them had claimed human forms since, but the older ones had chosen to remain specters, unwilling to constrain their spirits to flightless, aging bodies), had chosen to live in the valley.

Giya and her twin brother Sook lived there with their parents, in a palatial stone wigwam. I stayed over whenever I could, not so much because I didn't like my cottage on the sea, but because my cousins were my best friends.

My *only* friends.

Remo hopped off the portal, his *lucionaga* uniform, a black bodysuit made from a coated, laser-proof weave, contorting around his solid frame.

"Where is my father?"

"In the Duciba." Remo's tone was as frigid as his expression.

As the three *lucionaga* popped out of the portal in their golden firefly forms, I flew toward the base of the great tree that had once lodged Neenee Lily's favorite candy shop. Iba had requisitioned the first five floors of the *calimbor* after the Woods' palace had slipped off the mist and shattered into large chunks of pink quartz and clumps of moss-flecked stone.

The remnants of my grandfather Linus's legacy had been transplanted to the middle of the forest of *calimbors* and had become a playground for young fae. As a child, I'd spent afternoons hopping from one eroded chunk of quartz to the next with Giya and Sook. We'd pretended prickly *mikos* and poisonous *capras* slithered in the mossy space between.

Before the Year of Flight, the year Seelies learned to harness their fire, our game had been particularly fun because I could still fall. Unfortunately, my Year of Flight had come early. Right after I'd turned four, I'd slipped but failed to tumble, levitating instead. My cousins had gaped, then told me I wasn't allowed to play with them anymore. That night, Nima and Iba called the family together and sat us all down. Our four parents reminded us that we all had different powers, but that deep down, we were all the same—all of us faeries.

Even though Giya and Sook apologized, their ostracism intensified when my parents threw a huge banquet to celebrate my achievement. Iba was particularly proud, because most Seelies learned to fly in their fifth year and had to be taught. I'd picked it up without anyone's help an entire year early.

It took my cousins several days to come to me and admit they'd been jealous and missed me in the playground. They'd hurt me, but I'd forgiven them because I wasn't the type to hold grudges. Except toward the Farrows. I held a massive grudge against that family for sullying Nima's name with their false accusations.

After I landed on the mossy ground, I pushed my curtain of black hair behind my ears and glanced over my shoulder. Sure enough, the recipient of my grudge landed beside me. "Are you going to stalk me the entire way?"

Mouth as tight as his shoulders, he gestured toward the dark entrance at the base of the *calimbor*. "My orders were to deliver you to your father."

"I'm not a package."

His golden eyes narrowed. I tried to remember what color they'd been before he was made a *lucionaga* but couldn't. Oh no, wait. Poison green. That was how I'd described them to Giya the afternoon we'd watched Remo and his friends play Floatball, the Seelie version of basketball—the nets were crafted from hovering *volitor* fronds, but the ball was human-made, and when it fell, it fell fast. The players spent more time divebombing after it than scoring points.

I spun away from his venomous glare, speed-walking toward the giant tree edged in silver starlight. As I walked, boots squishing the moss, bobbing faelights overhead illuminating the path that led into the council house, I wondered what was so urgent. Did Iba need to coach me before I met with our illustrious revel guests? I was already well-versed in regal manners thanks to the etiquette classes I'd been subjected to since I'd popped out of my mother's womb. The only upside to those classes was that Giya and Sook had to take them with me, so when we were bored, at least we were bored together.

Not that we were ever bored long around Sook.

The minute I stepped inside the Duciba, a hush fell over Gregor, Silas, and my father. Curiously, they were the only three people present. Usually there was a representative from each fae faction, but apparently, this wasn't a Neverrian matter . . . this was an Amara matter. I raised my gaze to make sure no one else was there, but not a single *lucionaga* hovered. My eyes snagged on the gold circlet mural five stories up from where I stood. I studied each leaf in search of the one Josh had described, but then remembered I wasn't alone, and staring at the ceiling would raise some eyebrows, eyebrows I definitely didn't want to raise. I snapped my gaze back to my father, to the leaf circlet glimmering atop his gelled-back, golden-blond hair. I'd gotten Nima's hair and most of her features, but my eyes were all Iba, a sandy-blue ringed by a stroke of teal.

"You wanted to see me?" I said, approaching.

Silas smiled at me. Even though he was Remo's stepfather, and Faith's husband, Farrow blood didn't flow inside the *draca*'s veins, so I liked him.

"Shut the door behind you, Remo," Gregor said, hazel eyes flickering in the twinkling faelights gathered over his white hair like a swarm of gnats.

The hinges on the great door groaned as Remo and two fellow guards started to pull it shut.

"Remo," Iba called out, "this matter concerns you, too."

I frowned, searching my father's face for a hint of why this matter concerned Remo. Skies, I hoped this wasn't some sort of parent-kid sit-down to force us to be nice to each other, because that was *never* happening.

My heart quickened, my fiery, iron-loaded blood swooshing around my body. "What's going on?"

Iba looked at Gregor.

Dread hardened my stomach like Josh's claimed *gajoï*. I didn't like the solemn look that passed between both men.

Remo came to stand between the *draca* and *wariff*. If our parents hadn't been present, I might've asked him if he felt so

22

threatened by me that he needed to be bookended by a dragon and the prime minister.

He must've gleaned my thoughts from the tipped corners of my mouth, though, because his scowl turned positively searing, as though, any minute now, some of his fire would leak right out of him.

"Amara, I know I promised to never force your hand or heart, but you're almost eighteen, and unless you've been extremely discreet," Iba said, "I don't believe you have a boyfriend."

All the blood in my body converged inside my cheeks. "Excuse me?"

"A boyfriend? Do you have a boyfriend?" Did Gregor really mistake my embarrassment for a lack of understanding? "A fae one. Human ones don't count."

Remo's murky stare brightened. If he mentioned Joshua Locklear, I'd toss a handful of dust in his face, not enough to kill him, but more than enough to make him gag until the morning.

I folded my arms, on my guard now. "I don't see what my age has to do with me having a boyfriend."

"Tradition wants Neverrian women to bind their essences in the Cauldron before their eighteenth year," Gregor explained.

"That was in the olden days," I volleyed back. "This tradition no longer applies. Right, Iba?"

The crow's feet bracketing my father's eyes deepened as though he were in pain. Since his health was fine, I assumed the pained look was for what he was about to say. "You're the *prinsisa*, Amara. Even though we're no longer enforcing this tradition among common Neverrians, we believe the royal family needs to uphold this custom."

Was he saying what I thought he was saying? After feeling overwhelmingly warm, a chill tiptoed down my spine.

"Therefore if you have a boyfriend, you'll need to end things promptly." Gregor's hazel eyes shone as brightly as the faelights spangling the dark hull. Had he put this heinous idea into my father's head? "At least until after the wedding. What you do once you're married is entirely up to you."

I opened my mouth to ask if this was some practical joke, but only trapped air puffed out. I looked around the circle of men. My gaze lingered on Remo, who was positively gloating, before sliding back to Iba. The tightness between his eyes tempered my anger but in no way my docility.

"Nowadays, most people get engaged at thirty," I said. "I don't see why I need to rush into this."

Gregor looked down his hooked nose at me. "Stability appeases people."

Iba sighed, then rubbed his jaw, smooth from a fresh shave. "It would be a political match to reassure the people, Amara. As the future queen, you need to understand that politics will always play a role in your life." His hand arced back toward his black tunic hemmed in gold thread. "Besides, this is an engagement, *amoo*, not a marriage."

I understood what he was saying; I'd heard the story of how my parents ended up being married a thousand times. "So, I won't have to marry whoever it is you want me to get engaged to?"

He didn't respond. I wasn't sure how to interpret his silence.

"Who's the unlucky candidate?" I deadpanned, which made Gregor guffaw.

He tried to school his cheery features into his usual imperious mask, but his smile wouldn't flatten. "You inherited your mother's humor."

"I also inherited her poisonous blood." I directed my taunt at Remo, who didn't even have the decency to flinch. What had I expected? That he'd suddenly grow a conscience and apologize for the rumors he'd spread when I was thirteen? "So, who?"

Gregor slid his arm around Remo's shoulders. "My grandson."

The ice inside my body expanded. "No way." I shook my head and stepped back. "Absolutely not. Anyone but him."

Remo raised twitchy fingers to his remarkably pale forehead, thrusting his amber bangs aside. Good. At least he'd been blind-sided too. For some reason, that reassured me. Not much. But enough not to declare *wita* warfare.

Outside the great tree, thunder cracked.

Iba strode toward me and laid a palm on my shoulder. "Amara, please calm down. I'd like to avoid Neverra getting pummeled by a hurricane tonight."

"I'll get engaged, just not to him." I was shaking as hard as every leaf on the *calimbor.*

Iba angled himself so that his back was to the three others. In a voice that barely carried over the rolls of thunder, he said, "Please, *amoo.* I need you to do this for me. Please." Then, lowering his voice even further, he added, "I promise you won't have to marry him."

Tears of indignation stung my eyes. "It's not fair."

"Unfortunately, you can't rule a kingdom with your heart; you must rule it with your mind."

"You married the love of your life."

Iba dropped his mouth to my ear. "And you will too one day. This is an alliance. Nothing more." He pressed a lock of hair behind my ear as he pulled up to his full height, then gripped the back of my head and kissed my forehead, imprinting his apology on my skin.

Ugh. Remo Farrow. Out of the thousands of Neverrians, why did I have to braid my essence in the Cauldron with my wickedest enemy?

"Maybe he has a girlfriend?" I shot out, snatching at one last shred of hope.

"He has many," Gregor said. "*Had* many. He'll convene them all tonight and end things."

Many? I wrinkled my nose. What girl in her right mind would voluntarily date the arrogant *bagwa*?

Remo's face pinkened. Since I hadn't called him the Gottwa

word for jackass out loud, I assumed his high color was due to disgruntlement.

He cleared his throat. "I'll behave appropriately during our engagement."

Lucky. Me.

<h1 style="text-align:center">3</h1>

THE PREPARATIONS

Although the downpour had thinned, my discontentment hadn't. As we flew back toward the royal gardens, raindrops plopping on our bodies and hissing off instantly, Iba apologized for forcing my hand. I didn't say anything because guards were trailing us, and I didn't want to give them fodder for gossip. Their barracks were surely filled with enough juicy court tales as it was.

The moment my boots made contact with the garden moored to the Pink Sea by hundreds of anchors, our guards scattered to the different lookout points of the maritime castle. Only two hovered over our heads, *high* over our heads. High enough to afford us privacy.

My father's undereye circles marred his tanned skin, somehow making his eyes appear darker, as though his fatigue had leaked into his irises.

"Iba, can I ask why we need this alliance at least?"

"Let me worry about that."

"I'm not asking for details."

Iba glanced around him, then tipped his head toward the

gazebo he'd had built to celebrate my Year of Flight, an architectural gem of white wooden lattice and powder-pink *drosas*.

"Make it rain again, Amara."

Once we stepped inside, I lifted my hands, curled my fingers, and visualized a downpour. Threads of liquid magic swam through my fingers, making them glitter blue. I slashed the air vertically, and needles of rain followed my hands' path, creating a din that would veil our voices from neighboring ears.

"This is about Kingston." Iba's voice was barely audible over the rustling petals jeweling the gazebo.

I hated Remo, but when Iba's half-brother had been alive, I'd hated him more. "He's dead . . . isn't he?"

Back in my grandfather Linus's day, it was fine—*normal*, even—for married fae to have multiple partners. What wasn't acceptable was to bear children out of wedlock. Bastards were unequivocally put to death, even royal bastards, which had spurred Linus to lock my father into a marriage with his pregnant consort. Thankfully, the Day of Mist happened, and Iba was spared marrying Angelina, Kingston's mother.

After Linus's death, Iba changed the law about bastards, which had not only benefited Angelina, but also Gregor since his daughter had been born out of wedlock, and even though Faith was an adult by the time the fae world found out about her, the *wariff*'s child would nonetheless have met a cruel end.

"I've heard disquieting rumors, Amara. Rumors that he wasn't executed."

I blinked, the images of Kingston's coup spooling through me like barbed wire, catching on the leftover scabs fear and horror had scored over my heart that day. Iba had been flying, and then he'd been falling, trailing smoke like a crashing rocket, while Nima and I had watched, powerless, from the Pink Sea.

Four years had gone by, yet the memory was still fresh and raw.

"I think Gregor hid him somewhere and is grooming him for a second coup."

My heart came to a violent halt.

"Silas is trying to find out more. In the meantime, he thought an alliance with his son could keep us safe since Gregor's affection for Remo surpasses his hatred for me."

"Why doesn't Silas look into Gregor's mind?" One of the *draca*'s powers was to read what hid inside our heads.

"Gregor would know we were onto him and would either move Kingston before we could get to him, or launch an attack of his own. I might be the king, but I don't delude myself into thinking that I have all of my subjects' votes." My parents' regime had the full support of Unseelies and Daneelies, but these two castes of faeries together only made up a quarter of the Neverrian people. "When Linus fell, many fae wanted to see Gregor on the throne."

I chewed on my bottom lip, finally grasping the necessity and urgency of this engagement. "Do you think Remo knows anything? Has Silas read *his* mind?"

"Even though Remo looks up to Silas, the boy's loyalties lie with his grandfather. But, Amara, I don't want you to worry. I'm handling this, okay?" Iba stroked my cheekbones, which were prominent like Nima's, a remnant of our Native ancestry. "Let me pretend to be a good father and keep the weight of the kingdom off your shoulders while I still can."

"Pretend? You're the best father, Iba." When I was a little girl, and it was bedtime, Iba would put everything on hold and sit by my side, armed with patience and an endless collection of stories. My favorite was the one about the day he'd agreed to be linked to Nima through a brand that still flared on Nima's hand and Iba's palm every time her pulse accelerated. It was my favorite because it was the night he realized he was "a goner" as he liked to say.

"Even though I broke my promise to you?"

I sighed. "With good reason."

"Come here." He pulled me into a hug.

"Does Nima know about . . . *everything*?"

A soft snort rumbled from Iba's chest into my ear. "I haven't been turned into a houseplant yet, so no."

I pressed away from him. "Nima would never kill you."

"She might try once I break the news Faith will become your future mother-in-law. Promise to keep me safe?"

I shook my head, a smile playing on my lips. "Gregor was wrong."

"About what?"

"About my sense of humor; I got it from you."

Pride made his chest puff out a little. "Damn right, baby girl. Now, put a stop to this drab weather and go get ready."

Nodding, I slashed the air vertically again, but this time from moss to sky. The raindrops froze before steaming away.

"Amara Wood?" A high-pitched voice carried over the frolicking Pink Sea and through the latticework of the gazebo that stood on the edge of the garden like a lighthouse. "Are you playing with the weather again?"

Iba smiled, and I grinned back.

I peeked through the cage of *drosas* at the deck of my hovering bungalow where Nana Vee stood with her hands on her hips.

"You better go before Veroli fords the bridge to yell at me for keeping you away." Iba's eyes glinted with humor.

Not many people could give Iba an earful, or call him by his first name, but Nana Vee, who'd raised him before she'd raised me, had that privilege.

"Coming!" I stepped out of the gazebo but paused. "Will you tell Nima *before* dinner?"

Rubbing the back of his neck, Iba glanced at the acre of landscaped shrubs and trees upon which he and my mother had built their cozy nest of glass and stone.

When Iba still hadn't answered, I asked, "Want me to come with you and hold your hand?"

He chuckled. "I promised Gregor I'd wait until dinner to tell her. He wanted Cat to hear the news at the same time as Faith."

"Fun times ahead."

"Oh, yeah. I'll be the one with the crooked crown and the half-empty bottle of whiskey welded to his palm."

"Save me some?"

"Hmm. Aren't you underage?"

I cocked an eloquent eyebrow. "If I'm old enough to get engaged, then surely I'm old enough to drink, don't you think?"

He relented with a smile. "Fine. Fine."

"Amara!" This time my name was accompanied by rhythmic thumps against the wooden bridge.

"Uh-oh. She's coming for me."

"Better run."

I spun around and all but smacked into a cluster of tall, green *daffos*. I pressed away their trumpet-faces, then rounded the thick trunk of a mallow tree, its cloud-like violet crown injecting the air with a treacly scent that turned my stomach. Many fae smoked or ate the purple fluff on a regular basis. Not me. And not even because my parents had warned me against drugs, but because the one time I'd tried mallow, I'd been convinced my skin had grayed and fissured.

"Amara Wood, you are very late." Nana Vee sounded winded, as though she'd paced my bedroom for hours before plodding over the bridge.

"Yes, Amara Wood. You are *very* late." Giya was leaning against the back wall of my bungalow, arms folded in front of a gown made of so many layers of white chiffon she resembled a Glade pearl.

"Dinner's in thirty minutes. Thirty minutes!" Nana Vee's red cheeks puffed. "And you aren't even bathed."

"I'm sorry. I was talking with Iba."

Giya's gray eyes sparked silver in the purple dimness. I could tell she was dying to ask what about but refrained from doing so in front of Nana Vee.

Harrumphing, Veroli cut her eyes to the opposite side of the garden as though ready to march over to my parents' private rooms and bang on their glass door. If dinner hadn't been in a half hour, I bet she would've done just that. "Your bath must be cold."

I smiled down at the short fae, whom I considered my grandmother and not my nanny, the same way I considered Pappy's wife my grandmother, even though I shared no blood with her. I'd never known Nima's real mother. She'd died long before I was born. Apparently, Gwenelda had siphoned her soul by mistake. Sometimes when Nima watched Giya's aunt, her wistfulness was so strong it felt almost solid.

I dropped a kiss on top of Nana Vee's graying hair, which she always kept pinned into a poufy bun. "I'll warm it up."

She pivoted, leading the way back across the short bridge and around the deck girdling my bungalow.

Giya fell into step beside me and whispered, "Did you find out what the dinner was about?"

"Yes."

"And?"

I flicked my gaze toward the *lucionaga* hovering in their firefly form. "Later."

She trailed me through my open sash windows and into the bedroom, which had once belonged to her mother but became mine the day I turned twelve. Like my parents' home, it was fashioned from glass and gossamer-white, but instead of stone, my bungalow was made of lacquered wood and shiny copper.

I plunged my hand into the bath scented with crushed beetle shells and honeysuckle. The water beaded around my fingers and knuckles as it warmed, and my submerged skin began to glisten with tiny copper scales, courtesy of my Daneelie heritage.

I had a love-hate relationship with my reptilian skin—love because it tied me to Nima and allowed me to swim underwater for hours without needing to come up for air, and hate because it had landed me a *gajoï*. Although my engagement to the devil's spawn sucked, having to repay Joshua Locklear sucked harder.

As though he'd felt me thinking of him, my wristband beamed a message.

JOSHUA: *So?*

Sneaking a glance at my cousin, who stood in front of a mirror, smoothing the brown hair Nana Vee had turned into lustrous waves, I touched the chip implanted in the bone behind the back of my ear, and my sentence appeared beneath Josh's. *Something came up. Won't get to it until a few hours from now.*

JOSHUA: *Don't forget.*

ME: *I'm sure you'd remind me if I did.*

JOSHUA: *You know me well.*

I straightened and pressed on my wristband to make all my clothes blink out of existence.

Giya turned toward me. "At least tell me if it's good or bad."

I sank into the bath, releasing a little hiss of pleasure. "It's not good."

"Shit . . ."

"Giya Geemiwa, your mouth is much too pretty for such an ugly word," Nana Vee chided her, bustling around the bathroom for the soap. "And what's not good?"

Giya rolled her eyes at me the second Veroli's head was turned, and I smiled.

"My love life, Nana Vee." I leaned my head back against the mint-green quartz and shut my eyes.

"You have a boyfriend?" Nana Vee exclaimed.

I almost snorted at her shock. Almost, because the fact that my having a boyfriend surprised her so much painted a pitiful picture of my amorous life. "Would I keep it from you if I had one, Nana Vee?"

"You better not, dearie. Because I'll need to investigate the man you set your heart upon."

I smiled. "You and Iba both."

Although I was plenty capable of washing my own hair, Veroli loved the task, so I let her untangle my long locks and rub an oily soap made of the same musk-scented beetle shells and aromatic white blooms that fragranced my bath.

As Giya told me about Sook's most recent business venture—her twin was always inventing something . . . most recently, *volitor* surfboards—I scrubbed my scaly skin quickly, then rose, the fire in my veins lifting the water from my body like mist. I was dry before I even set foot on the bathmat, but my skin still glimmered and would continue to do so for an hour or so. The scales would smooth in a matter of minutes, though.

"Here." Veroli swiped her finger over her Infinity and beamed over the dress I was to wear. "Your aunt sent it over this afternoon."

When our biometric bracelets had become standard accessories on Neverra, Giya's mother had gone to Earth to take a digital fashion design class. She'd returned soon after and had opened the first boutique that didn't sell physical clothes but digital ones, outfits that could be stored inside our wristbands, then beamed onto our bodies.

Giya worked with her mother during the long Neverrian summers, but what my cousin truly wanted to do was become a kindergarten teacher—she had an endless supply of patience and was as sweet as I wasn't. So Neenee was presently training Veroli's daughter-in-law, Magena, in the art of digital couture, and Magena loved it. Their customers, too, because the Huntress from Geemee Kaji's clan injected her designs with tribal patterns and beadwork that had become all the rage on Neverra.

I accepted the beamed dress from Nana Vee, then slashed my index finger over its holographic image to apply it on my body.

Giya studied her mother's creation—stretchy and opaque on top, gauzy and sheer on the bottom—and then her eyes flicked to mine, and a small gasp flitted past her lips. "It's purple!"

Faeries got engaged in purple and married in red. Although you could wear both colors year-round in regular clothes, no one wore gowns of such shades unless they had something to celebrate.

Or *not* celebrate in my case.

The brush Nana Vee had been clutching clattered against the pale-green quartz. "I thought you didn't have a boyfriend!"

I shrugged. "I don't. I have a fiancé. Well, soon I'll have one."

Giya's eyebrows gathered over her nose. "You're getting engaged?" Hurt. She sounded hurt. Like I'd purposely kept this a big secret from her. "To whom?"

I pressed my lips together so as not to grumble his name. "It's a surprise."

Forever the romantic, tears surged from Nana Vee's eyes. "Oh, Skies, another one of my babies is getting engaged." Since she was half-fae, she didn't have a lot of fire, so her tears didn't plume right off her cheeks.

Nana Vee grabbed both my hands and squeezed them so tightly she stopped the flow of blood and fire to my extremities. "Which boy stole your heart?"

"Oh . . . no one stole my heart," I replied, a bite to my words.

Nana Vee's eyebrows quirked. "Wh-what?"

"I'm not allowed to discuss it, but in fifteen minutes—"

"Fifteen minutes?" Nana Vee screeched before jerking me into the chair.

She crouched to grab the fallen brush and yanked it through my hair. After drying the damp ends with her palms, she braided the lengths into a crown which she pinned to the top of my head. And then she applied a line of kohl to my bottom lashes, swiped mascara over my top ones, and slicked on a nude lipstick that tamed the fullness of my lips.

"Giya, grab the jewelry I laid out on the bed."

My cousin, who'd stayed silent as though trying to make sense of my sudden engagement, pushed off the wall and strode into my bedroom, her white dress whispering around her willowy frame. She returned holding a pair of dangling earrings fashioned from amethyst cabochons sprinkled through with rose-cut diamonds.

Nana Vee speared them through my lobes, then told me to hurry, that I was already five minutes late. Sighing, I got up, beamed high-heeled sandals onto my feet, and followed Giya back onto the deck.

Before we took to the skies to join the family, and the people who thought they were about to become our family, Giya asked, "Please tell me who."

I leaned over and whispered Remo's name into my cousin's ear.

Her eyes and mouth rounded in shock. "No . . ."

"Yes."

"Why?"

I tipped my head toward the field of purple *adamans* shimmering like cut glass beyond the forest of *calimbors*. Even from the distance, I could see bodies milling over the fan-shaped pavilion built for regal functions. "Politics."

And then we both soared upward, two newly appointed sentinels tailing us. My guards were swapped around so often I never learned their names. Remo's fault. After he'd become a *lucionaga*, he'd insisted familiarity resulted in sloppiness and had advised the Council never to assign the same person to me twice in the same month. Oh, and he'd also instructed the guards never to address the princess . . . for propriety's sake.

Safety and propriety, my ass. It was simply another way to ostracize me from Neverrians and show off his control.

"Maybe it'll make him nicer," Giya said as the pavilion came into view.

I slanted her an extremely dubious look. I didn't think binding my essence with the man who took such pleasure in ostracizing me from the people in our world would make him any kinder. If anything, he'd probably get a bigger power trip out of it.

It's just an engagement; not marriage, I reassured myself as we landed on the bow-shaped terrace of the pavilion.

4

THE MOTHERS

Giya and I were surprisingly not the last to arrive in the fan-shaped Adamans Pavilion. Nima and Iba were still absent.

As we stepped past the curved strip of windows facing the Glades, my gaze zeroed in on Geemee Kaji, who stood stiff as a *calimbor* beside his wife and Remo's mother. Where Faith and Nima were perpetually on the outs, Faith and Lily had remained tentative friends. If a war broke out between the Farrows and the Woods, Lily would side with Iba and Nima. Since there hadn't yet been any war, just sporadic skirmishes that led to cold fronts, she'd never needed to pick sides. Giya, though, had always picked a side—Nima's. Unlike her mother, she had no affection for the Farrows, and Giya was a very affectionate person.

I was glad for my cousin's presence tonight, as well as my maternal grandparents', my great-aunt Aylen's, and her daughter Shiloh's. The more non-Farrows, the merrier.

When my grandfather spotted me, he called out my name and opened his arms, and I strutted into his embrace. He had no Daneelie blood, no faerie blood for that matter, yet he always smelled briny and mineral like the sea. After he released me, Aylen spun me in a circle, gushing about how gorgeous my dress was, how the shade made my eyes seem almost violet, while Nana Em interrupted her soap-making discussion with Shiloh to kiss my cheek.

As Aylen fingered the chiffon, I caught Faith glancing at me through the web of bobbing service fae passing around twinkling golden orbs. Her blue eyes widened before they snapped back over to Neenee Lily. My aunt rolled her fingers into fists, probably to keep herself from signing the reason for this strange dinner—which I assumed she was privy to since she'd designed my dress.

Clutching her goblet of faerie wine, Faith's eyes cut across the room toward her eldest son, who had his head bent next to his grandfather's, probably discussing the cleverness of their crown embezzlement venture. If they actually thought I would go through with the wedding, they had another thing coming.

The air churned as powerful wings propelled Neverra's one and only dragon onto the glass deck beyond the curved glass wall. Remo's little brother Karsyn, who'd been riding on his father's black-scaled back, hopped off and traipsed through the open sash windows toward his mother, leveling a serrated little glower my way.

A cloud of shimmery smoke billowed around the *draca*, blurring his dark contours, shrinking him back into human flesh. Tightening the leather tie binding his shoulder-length brown hair, Silas entered the pavilion, inclining his head toward the assembled crowd. As he strode toward Remo, Faith intercepted him, shackling his wrist. Her hissed words were lost amidst a fanfare of loud stomps.

A line of *lucionaga* climbed up the sweeping glass stairs, forming an aisle through which Nima and Iba walked arm-in-arm, sporting matching golden leaf circlets and decorous smiles. Nima's grin lost some of its power when she noticed Faith, and then it wilted entirely when her black eyes landed on me. Her body grew so stiff so fast that when she whipped her face toward Iba, I worried her head would unscrew itself from her neck. Iba winced, even though Nima hadn't even opened her mouth.

The dust locked in the tattoo wreathing her neck seemed to pulse harder. So hard that for a second I actually worried for Iba's safety, but for all her temper, my mother possessed unrivaled self-control. Iba placed his glowing palm atop Nima's forearm, above her second tattoo, spoils from the battle she'd waged to free our kingdom of the cloying mist. Anguish lit up her dark features and made the W on her hand flare like a beacon.

"Thank you all for coming on such short notice." Iba's knuckles whitened as though he was physically restraining Nima. "Some of you might have guessed the occasion from the color of my daughter's magnificent dress."

He winked at his sister, whose face was much too drawn to register the compliment.

"Tonight, I called you over to celebrate a momentous event in my family's life—the engagement of my beautiful Amara to a loyal subject of the crown, Remo Farrow."

The vein at Remo's temple fluttered his birthmark. I suspected he hadn't appreciated being referred to as a loyal subject of the crown.

Nima turned the same shade as Giya's dress, which made her tipped eyes appear black, and then the veins in her hands ignited, a luminescent blue.

Oppressive silence ensued after Iba's short speech, but it didn't last long. Soon it was punctured by one *long* roll of thunder that had everyone looking at the incoming clouds. The *lucionaga* who'd remained on the deck filed into the pavilion to slide the glass doors shut. Neverrians were surely wondering why another storm was forming when the last one had just abated. Or perhaps they were too busy running to find cover to wonder about the weather, and which Daneelie was causing it.

Aylen clapped. She'd loved Stella, and even though she'd heard Nima's stories, her fond memories of Faith's mother made it impossible for her to hate the Farrows. Shiloh and Nana Em clapped along politely and so did Pappy, although he wore a big frown that pleated his suntanned brow.

"Is this my niece's choice, or yours, Ace?" Geemee Kaji's voice cut through the applause.

"She is the crown princess, brother," Iba answered.

A look passed between the two men. A look that made Geemee Kaji's corded arms tighten in front of his massive chest, the myriad of confiscated Seelie dusts writhing in their tracks. Unlike Nima, he couldn't use the dust he ensnared. Merely stored it until he felt the misbehaving Seelie deserved their power back.

Where Gregor and Silas governed the royal guard, Geemee Kaji, along with a handful of other Unseelies, ran the Neverrian police. He was trying to get his twins to join, but Giya had zero interest in patrolling the kingdom, and Sook was much too passionate about his inventions.

As I watched my uncle's inked forearms, I wondered if I'd be like Nima—able to use the dust—or like the rest of the Hunters— merely a storage unit. I'd come close to seizing a Seelie's dust once, but Sook had beat me to it, slashing his skin and exposing his blood. That was how we Hunters magnetized *wita*. Our iron-rich blood attracted the dust and trapped it in the form of dark whorls.

Lost in thought, I'd missed Remo walking up to me.

"The Cauldron has arrived, *Amara*," he gritted out, as though my name were the most detestable word in the Faeli language. Considering *amara* meant love, I bet it *was* painful for Remo to utter.

I glanced at his proffered arm. "What? Not Trifecta?"

His pupils distended, almost entirely obliterating the gold surrounding them. Was he worried someone might ask the meaning of his unpleasant nickname, which he employed as a substitute for freak? He raised his arm higher as though to hurry me to take it. I shot him an icy smile, scanned the pavilion until I spotted the black cauldron hovering between Gregor, Iba, and

Nima. Refusing my future fiancé's escort, I strode toward the vessel of fae essences that magically materialized for betrothals and weddings.

Remo's boots banged against the copper floor, the weight of his anger striking the nape of my neck. Not only had I openly demeaned him by refusing his arm, but I'd done so in front of his fellow *lucionaga*.

Go me.

When I reached my parents, Nima who hadn't spoken a single word since her arrival, broke away from Iba and clutched my elbow. "I need a minute with my daughter." She towed me away from the men and the Cauldron spitting up glittery tendrils of smoke, her fingers cool and firm. When we were far from prying ears, she threaded a fugitive tendril of hair back into my braided crown. "Why?"

One tiny, loaded word.

"Because Iba asked this of me."

"Why would he ask you to . . . to . . .?" One of her eyes spasmed from the mixture of worry and annoyance she was surely trying to contain before the clouds she'd called forth ripped.

I placed my hand over hers. "It's okay, Nima."

"Okay? How is it okay that you're being forced to tie your essence with a boy you don't love?" Her eye twitched again, her thick black lashes flapping. "You don't love him, do you, *abiwoojin*?"

"Skies, no."

Lightning slit the sky, this time cleaving the steel clouds. Raindrops fell in droves, clapping the flat copper roof like mallets.

"But it's just an engagement, Nima, not a wedding."

Her eyes darted toward Iba, who watched us steadily, even though he was discussing something with Gregor and Remo.

"Did you marry the man you were engaged to?" I whispered just as Faith stomped toward us, curly red hair bouncing violently against her shoulders.

"I object," she bellowed over the deafening cacophony of my mother's anguish, "and I'm guessing you do too, Catori."

Nima schooled her features back into her sovereign's mask. "I might not be *fond* of the union, but I trust our king's judgment, as should you."

Faith set her hands on her waist, crinkling the emerald satin of her floor-length gown. "The king is your *husband*. Of course you'd trust his judgment."

Nima seemed to grow a few inches taller than the full head she already had on Faith. "Everything my husband does, he does for Neverra."

"Well, I don't want my son marrying into a family of murderers." Spittle flew from Faith's mouth, smacked Nima's chin.

"Murderers?" Nima growled. "Because your family's so much better? Would you like a list of the fae and humans your father snuffed out?"

"How dare you compare what he does to what you did! My father punishes criminals." Faith poked Nima's collarbone, right under Stella's captive dust. "You killed my mother! An innocent!"

"Your mother was *not* innocent. When are you going to take off those ridiculous rose-colored goggles of yours and see her for the viper she was?"

"Stop lying."

"I never lied." Nima balled her hands into tight fists. "Besides, you didn't even like her!"

"That's not the point!"

I grabbed one of Nima's fists, trying to pry her fingers apart, but they seemed fashioned from steel. I beseeched Iba with a frantic look, and he soared toward us, Silas in tow. The *draca* wound his hands around his wife's biceps and eased her away.

"Daughter, please behave." Although Gregor's tone was dulcet, it was sharp. "Now, can we please get on with this union? I wouldn't want the Cauldron to grow bored and disappear."

Faith narrowed her eyes on her father. "We wouldn't want that," she hissed, tearing her arms from Silas. "But I won't stand here and watch my son defile Mom's memory by tying himself to this harlot." She flicked her chin to me.

I jerked back. Harlot? I'd never even dated a boy, much less slept with one.

Iba shoved in front of Nima and got in Faith's face. "How dare you disrespect my daughter! She's never done anything to you."

Silas's nostrils flared as though he were about to shift back into his dragon form. "Faith, please apologize."

His wife's mouth remained cemented shut.

"Mother, I'd appreciate it if you didn't talk about my future bride that way." Remo's voice rang over the wild thunderstorm and wilder heartbeats pounding in the pavilion.

I glanced over my shoulder at my intended, who hadn't left the Cauldron's side. I didn't delude myself into thinking he was defending me because he cared. All the overgrown firefly cared about was his status, which would automatically improve once we got engaged.

"How could you want this, sweetheart?" Faith whined.

"It's a great honor that's been bestowed upon our family, Mother."

Faith's brow pinched. "Marriage shouldn't be a badge to add to your uniform, Remo." And with those words, she broke free of her husband, strode out to the soaked deck, and soared into the wet night.

5

THE ROYAL DINNER

Even though I wished I could've left at the same time as Faith, I played dutiful daughter and stayed.

"*Prinsisa* Amara?" Gregor tilted his head toward the Cauldron.

Sighing, I returned toward the big black vessel, Nima and Iba close behind me. Gregor raised his fist in the air and stretched out two fingers. A low chant vibrated out of his men's chests, matching the cadence and volume of the raindrops splattering against the window before overtaking both as it grew and resonated against the glass.

If it had been any other event I would've associated the goosebumps popping over my bare collarbone with awe, but there was nothing awe-inspiring about tonight. Regret prickled my breastbone as I stared into the Cauldron's foaming belly. I'd dreamed of this moment for years. Of how it would feel to don purple and link myself to a person I loved. To a person with whom I'd want to share my heart, my body, and my kingdom. Remo was *not* that person.

As the chant slowed and quieted, I noticed the rain had abated too. I glanced over my shoulder at Iba and Nima, who stood hand-in-hand, regal and calm. Iba's lips flexed in apology—or was it encouragement? Perhaps both. Nima's mouth was immobile, but her expression encompassed as much worry as the sky encompassed clouds.

I squared my shoulders and steeled my spine, swearing to myself that the day I'd wear red, I'd wear it for a man I loved, and nothing about the ceremony would be fake.

Gregor nodded to the Cauldron. "Please place your hands inside, children."

Heat snaked behind my lids. I blinked furiously to prevent any tears from falling. I wouldn't show weakness tonight. I'd be an example of stoicism. I'd make my father proud.

For you, Iba, I thought as I dipped my hand inside.

I'd asked Nima to tell me the story of her wedding so many times that I knew what to expect: the Cauldron would lock my hand in place until the rite was complete.

From the corner of my eye, I saw Remo bury his hand beside my own. When his fingers closed over mine, I murmured, "Don't."

He jerked, but the Cauldron had snared his hand.

Our hands needn't have touched for the Cauldron to link us, but apparently the mechanics hadn't been explained to the *lucionaga.* So now, until the Cauldron released us, his hand was in contact with mine.

Ugh.

Scintillating strands of magic rose from the dark depths and scampered into both our arms, irrigating our veins with its otherworldly light. The chanting grew anew, a more sonorous and lively tune that seemed to egg the magic on, make it flow faster, fill us harder. My heartbeat quickened, thumping in time with the song that palpitated into every corner of my being.

Remo's fingers twitched against mine, his pulse nipping my knuckles. At least it wasn't only *my* heart which was about to rocket out of my chest. For some reason, knowing that Remo was also disquieted made me feel better. I didn't want him to delight in this moment, not even nefariously. I wanted it to be as uncomfortable and alarming for him as it was for me.

Before my next breath, the chanting ended, and the Cauldron recalled its magic now twined with our essences. Like the tentacles of a skittish *octas*, the glittery green threads receded into the rotund vessel, which puffed into oblivion, leaving behind wavelets of black smoke.

I snatched my hand away from Remo's and cocooned it against my frenzied heart. My skin prickled, cold and hot, numb and over-sensitive. It reminded me of the time I'd grazed the reptilian body of a *dile*, and it had shot me with a dose of venom so potent my heart had stopped for five entire minutes. When I'd come to, Giya and Sook were weeping, convinced I was dead, while Remo—who hadn't been there when I'd lost consciousness—was assuring them I'd be fine, that a little venom couldn't possibly kill the Trifecta. When our eyes had met, his had seemed garishly bright. Since their shine hadn't been due to tears, I'd imagined it had been hope . . . hope that he'd be wrong, and the *dile* venom would do away with me for good.

The same gleam animated his eyes tonight as he inspected his hand. Cauldron binding was thankfully not like fae marking—no outward trace showed up on our skin. I would've hated having an F light up every time my pulse quickened.

He finally lowered his hand along his navy tunic that shone like satin in the twinkling faelights bobbing around our heads. "Well, that was surprisingly painless."

I was still cosseting my hand. "For you, perhaps."

His reddish-brown eyebrows almost collided over his nose. "You're in pain?"

"Touching a *dile* was more pleasant than touching your hand." I spoke low so my parents and Gregor couldn't hear the snark dripping from my tongue.

A faerie dressed in a gown that looked sewn from butterfly

wings landed beside us, extending two glowing orbs. "Congratulations on your engagement, *massini*. May the Skies bless you both."

"Thank you, Lydia," Remo said.

I surmised he knew her name, because she was one of his many girlfriends. Why else would Remo Farrow learn the name of someone so far beneath his station?

I plucked the orb from Lydia's hand and squeezed it until it morphed into a goblet of faerie wine. I wasn't fond of the stuff because it was full of bubbles, but I wanted something to sweep my mind off my predicament, however fake it all was.

Since Lydia was still staring at him as though he'd invented faelight, I leaned toward him and whispered, "You should take Lydia back home to celebrate."

His eyes swung to mine so fast I had to pull my head back so our noses didn't bump.

When he glowered, I smiled, then dipped that smile into my wine glass. I might've given off naïve fumes, but I wasn't naïve. My eyes were open, and I was watching him. Waiting for him to stumble and commit a faux-pas that would take him out of the running for the crown. Sure this was a sham, but wouldn't it be lovely if he lost my hand by his own fault? It would paint me as innocent—which I was—and him as wicked—which he was. I'd love nothing more than for Neverra to see Remo Farrow's true colors instead of the bright, young, disciplined *lucionaga* he made himself out to be.

Lydia offered him a golden orb. "Wine?"

He slowly looked back at her. "Thank you, but I don't drink."

"Since when?" I asked.

"Since forever."

Gregor approached, and Lydia flitted upward, out of his path. He held out his goblet to mine, and even though I didn't want to clink with him, I docilely lifted my cup.

When metal met metal, he said, "You know, back in my day,

when a woman was unbound, she could be claimed by any man superior in rank."

I wrinkled my nose. "How savage."

"Could unbound men be claimed by higher-ranked women, or I guess, men?" Remo asked.

"No." Gregor's thick white hair flounced as a faerie flew over our heads bearing a platter of lettuce-wrapped fried *octas*. "The world didn't work that way." He grabbed two wraps and chucked them both into his mouth.

"I'm so glad our world has evolved," I said.

Remo didn't say anything. Knowing him, he probably mourned our new customs.

Gregor's eyes settled on something behind me. I turned to find Iba's mother, Addison, walking arm-in-arm with Angelina. As I watched them air-kiss the other guests, I wondered if Angelina was aware that her son might be alive.

The day Kingston had supposedly been put to death, Angelina's dark hair had become streaked with white and her eyes had turned perpetually glassy. I'd thought it was because of heartache but learned, from overhearing the adults talk, that after Kingston's failed coup, Addison had consoled Linus's consort with copious amounts of purple fluff. Now, they spent their days cooped up in my grandmother's living room, lounging about the velour boudoir, inhaling the hallucinogenic plant, and bonding over their disappointment in men.

"Granddaughter, don't you look ravishing tonight!" Addison proclaimed much too spiritedly.

Her breath and pale lavender hair reeked of mallow—sweet and pungent with a side of nauseating. I tried to step away, but this would cause me to bump into Remo. I chose the better of two evils and stayed close to my loopy grandmother.

"Doesn't she, Angelina?" Addison asked.

Angelina's eyes rolled in their sockets. I wasn't sure my image was even registering on her pupils, but she cooed and whispered.

"Your eyes look violet." Her nostrils flared. "You even smell purple."

My grandmother's eyes widened in wonder. "Oh, but she does!"

Behind her, Nima shook her head, murmuring something into my father's ear that pulled him away from Silas.

"Addison, you've arrived!" He took his mother's elbow and guided her to the bow-shaped wooden dining table weighted down by the prepared feast. "Why don't I get you settled?"

Angelina, whose arm was still wrapped around my grandmother's, stumbled as her feet caught up with my father's brusque movement.

"Lost her mind when she lost her son, that one." Gregor grabbed a handful of paprika-flecked *panem* leaves.

Usually the buttery scent of bread that wafted from the heart-shaped leaves made my stomach growl, but my insides were twisted into too many knots to produce sound. "I'm guessing it would haunt any mother to birth an evil child, and then watch that child be put to death. She did witness the execution, didn't she?"

Gregor turned his autumn-leaf eyes off the backside of a passing faerie waitress. "We no longer subject families to executions."

"Your consideration knows no bounds." I sipped my wine, even though the taste was souring my stomach.

His mouth curved. "Your tongue is as sharp as a *quila*'s beak, little Amara."

A warm hand wrapped around my forearm, dimpling the ultra-violet fabric of my dress's three-quarter sleeves. "Dinner. Come." Nima pulled me away from Gregor and Remo. "Please don't anger the *wariff, abiwoojin.* Your father and he are already not seeing eye-to-eye these days. Which is probably why he wanted you to get engaged . . ." She trailed off, as though considering what she'd just said.

I itched to explain all Iba had told me in the gazebo, but this was neither the time nor was it my place to tell her. He'd share his reasons soon enough. Nima clutched my arm until we reached the banquet table carved from a single *calimbor* trunk, then went to join Iba at one end.

"Amara." Iba gestured to the chair beside my grandfather's and across from Giya's.

My grandfather rose and wrapped one sun-spotted hand around the copper twig rung, scooting it back for me. "How lucky I am to be seated next to the prettiest girl on Neverra."

How I adored this man. "I'm the lucky one."

He tucked my chair in, then regained his seat beside my grandmother, who was fingering one of the *adamans* blooms tied into bouquets by sprigs of wild chives and scattered down the length of the table.

When she retracted her hand, the petals tinkled. "I still can't get over the fact that they're made of glass, and how long have we been living here, Derek?"

"Almost an Earthly century." Wonder lined Pappy's tone.

After my parents' wedding, Nima sat her father down and explained what she was and where she needed to live. Pappy hadn't believed her at first, so she'd shown him. Apparently, when he'd popped out of the portal, he'd blacked out. Iba had caught my grandfather as he'd toppled off the thin disk and had lain him on the mossy ground. To make a long story short, when Pappy had come to, he was still convinced it was a dream. It had taken him days of wandering through the land and passing through portals to believe it was real. And then it had taken him almost an entire Earthly year before he'd talked to his girlfriend Milly about the faerie isle.

Oddly enough, Nana Em believed faeries existed right off the bat and had been delighted by the magical land, and had grown even more so when Pappy had asked for her hand on the beach bordering the Pink Sea. Although Pappy and Nana went back to Earth each year, they never spent more than a week away from Neverra, because nothing was more important to them than family, and because all of their human friends had eventually died.

Pappy leaned forward to look at the person who'd taken the chair next to mine. I didn't have to turn to know the identity of my neighbor; the coppery glint of hair in my peripheral vision all but blinded me.

"Your father told me you've recently been promoted, Remo," Pappy said. "Congratulations."

"Promoted? What an achievement." I seized my goblet of water and gulped down its contents. "Was it thanks to your grandfather's name or your new fiancée's?"

He stiffened. "I didn't earn the promotion because of any blood or Cauldron relations, *prinsisa*."

"Of course not. Why would your relationship to the *draca*, *wariff*, and now the *prinsisa* facilitate your rise in *lucionaga* ranks? I'm certain you're a wonderful firefly."

Remo shifted on his seat. "You're just full of kind words tonight, fiancée."

"I'm sorry, but did you think the glittery smoke that traveled through my body earlier gave me amnesia?"

Giya made a sound at the back of her throat that she stifled with her palm.

"Skies forbid anything made you forget how deeply you hate me," Remo said under his breath. "Wouldn't want our time together to be boring."

"Indeed." The luminous *adamans* petals reminded me of when I'd scraped my leg on the flowers while flying too low over them. The sight of my blood had made most Seelies flee, including the two *lucionaga* assigned to me. They'd shot into the sky, supposedly to call for help.

Remo, who'd been swimming in the Glades with a few of his friends at the time, had sidled up to the side of the copper basin and had watched me bleed with unabashed amusement. It was only when one of my guards returned with Geemee Kaji and Sook that Remo had plunged back into the water to continue his game of water polo or whatever it was they were playing.

As though thinking of him had conjured him up, Sook sauntered in, brown hair so wet it looked almost black, and flopped into the empty seat beside his sister. He was panting, as though he'd run all the way from his house, and his coppery skin glistened with sweat and rain.

"Sorry I'm late. So, what are we celebrating?" His black eyes darted around the long table before returning to me. When he caught sight of my neighbor, he did a double-take, and his black eyebrows shot into his silky bangs.

"My engagement to your dear cousin." Remo slid both his elbows onto the table and aligned his forearms with his gold cutlery.

"Say what now?" Sook whipped his gaze toward the head of the table where Nima and Iba sat. "What did you do to deserve that?"

"Adsookin Geemiwa," my uncle boomed. "Be nice."

"Sorry, Iba." He flashed his father an apologetic look.

"It is not to me you should apologize. It is to your future cousin-in-law."

Sook's square jaw worked, as though he were chewing on a piece of dehydrated *panem*. "My deepest apologies, *golwinim*."

Remo flipped his knife over and over. Was he thinking of tossing it at Sook because my cousin had used the Gottwa term for *lucionaga*? Even though it was the appropriate terminology, most Unseelies—even half-Seelie ones like Sook—employed it solely to get underneath a Seelie's skin.

When Remo didn't send the knife hurtling across the table, I came up with a new hypothesis: Gregor's heir was uncomfortable. Even though he'd never struck me as someone ill-at-ease in social situations, tonight, his family was heavily outnumbered by mine. Not to mention his mother had left.

Clinking arose from the end of the table opposite Nima and Iba. Gregor stood and tapped his fork against his wine goblet. "I want to propose a toast to the newly betrothed. Amara, it is my honor to welcome you into my family, and it will be an even greater honor to share the Farrow name with you soon."

I almost choked on my spit. Even if I were to marry Remo—which so wasn't happening—I would *never* take his family name.

Gregor raised his glass higher. "To two families becoming one."

I was tempted to keep my fists on the table to display how I felt about Gregor's toast, but one look at Iba had my fingers clenching around my goblet and lifting it high.

"Skies lend me strength," Remo mumbled so low it sounded as though he were clearing his throat. He traded his knife for his golden goblet and raised it.

"Ditto," I said sweetly, knocking my glass so hard against his, wine sloshed over the rim and soaked the sleeve of his tunic.

His fire steamed away the damp spot but failed to lift his thickening displeasure. After the toast, I turned my back on Remo and spoke exclusively with my grandfather, who explained the origin of toasting—a way to check if drinks were poisoned—before sharing tons of other fun human facts, which had my cousins leaning closer.

Even though I was focused on Pappy, I couldn't help but overhear pieces of Remo's conversation with Shiloh, who sat on his other side. They mostly spoke about her bath products company, and how doing business with humans was so much easier than with faeries, which led them to talking about Earth, and did she miss living there?

My bracelet vibrated with an incoming message: *So?*

Joshua was relentless.

ME: *I'm in the middle of dinner.*

JOSH: *Don't forget,* prinsisa. *But in case you do . . .*

My stomach spasmed as though someone had just punched me.

JOSH: *I'll remind you.* ;)

I quickly shut down our chat. How unfortunate that faerie

bargains could be claimed from such a distance. I looked around the table. Now was as good a time as any to check Josh's suspicions. Since Iba, Nima, Gregor, and Silas were here, most of the *lucionaga* in the kingdom were, too. Which meant the coast was somewhat clear.

6

THE LITTLE BROTHER

Faelights bobbed like luminous raindrops around me as I made my way down the glass stairs and past the slender wooden pillars that supported the sides of the pavilion. I'd thankfully gotten rid of my guards, insisting I needed no escort to use the bathroom, which rose from the soft earth like a mushroom stalk, bearing most of the weight of the fan-shaped cap. I skirted the structure's moss-coated walls, hoping no *lucionaga* lurked amidst the tall, jagged flowers ringing the fence of artfully crisscrossed stilts at the far end.

Right as I peeked between the crisscrossed slats, a thin voice called out my name. I turned to find Remo's ten-year-old brother trotting toward me, one hand held behind his back. Although he shared certain facial traits with Remo, like my fiancé's straight nose and thick, low eyebrows, his coloring was entirely Silas's.

"What is it, Karsyn?"

"My brother doesn't like you. He'll never like you."

One of my eyebrows jolted up. "And?" I stared impatiently toward the *calimbors* that stood like giant sentinels against the violet sky. I had minutes left before someone upstairs questioned my toilet break.

"And I can't let him ruin his life."

I gave the kid my full attention now. "Ruin *his* life? Because you think *I* want to marry your brother?" I flapped my hand to shoo him off. "Go back to the party, Karsyn, and mind your own business."

"I love my brother," he said, advancing toward me.

"Lucky Remo."

"And that's why I need to do this." He whipped a long dagger from behind his back and aimed it at my ribcage.

My shoulders banged against wood as I caught the blade with my bare hands. Karsyn gave a hard shove, and the tip snagged my dress's bodice. Smoke curled around my knuckles, and blood dribbled through my fingers.

"Karsyn, put your dust away before I magnetize it!" I barely moved my lips as I yelled, afraid to inhale the *wita*. Although it wouldn't kill me, breathing in too much would make me black out, and this was really not the moment to become unconscious.

"My dust?" He laughed. The kid *laughed*. "I may be young but I'm not stupid, *prinsisa*. My dagger isn't made of *wita*."

I gaped down at the blade I was holding, my fear receding. Obviously, Karsyn wasn't the sharpest *adamans* in the field if he thought he could kill me with a normal weapon. Jabbing my heart with metal would hurt but it wouldn't end me.

Ticked off now, I said, "You're gonna be locked up, Karsyn."

"I don't care. As long as you're dead, I don't care what happens to me."

I didn't even think Remo hated me as much as this boy, but perhaps he did. Perhaps he'd sent his little brother after me. The fact that no *lucionaga* came to my rescue solidified this theory. I had screamed, hadn't I?

Grunting, I pushed hard on the dagger, trying to drive back the little brat. How had I let myself get cornered by a ten-year-old? The answer was that I hadn't deemed him a threat. Stupid me. I tried to toss the blade sideways, but the kid's arms were steel. Had Silas trained him or had Remo? Or maybe it was Faith herself. Maybe she had cutouts of my mother and me, and made her kids use them as target practice.

Karsyn jerked his arms, managing to nick my breastbone and pierce skin.

"*Enough!*" I screeched. I called forth my own dust and was about to slap it into the boy's puckered face when something glimmered at the edge of my vision.

Something shiny . . . and golden. Through the tendrils of smoke leaking from my chest, I made out what it was—an axe. If it was made of *wita* and came in contact with my open wound, I'd die.

Instead of shoving through the fence of stilts at my back, or fashioning a shield with my own dust, my muscles seized. Karsyn's brown eyes widened, which made me realize two things: it wasn't his dust coming at me and whomever it belonged to wasn't working with the kid. The axe chopped the dagger's blade from its hilt, and the blood-soaked metal slid from my trembling hands, clattering noiselessly against the soft dirt at my feet.

Karsyn's brown hair fluttered as he whipped around. Remo was advancing toward us, his mouth moving. His words pinged off my eardrums without registering.

Had he come to save me? I could hardly believe my fiancé's desire for the crown exceeded his desire to rid the worlds of me, but he'd ruined his brother's weapon, so perhaps it *was* stronger. Karsyn spun back toward me. He punched through the air, palm flat and sparkling.

Shielding my punctured chest with my injured palms, I rocketed sideways, toward the wall of curved moss. His dust followed my trajectory. I tried to coax my own out, but the cut in my palms stung so harshly I couldn't grasp the threads of my powers.

What was the point in controlling every single element if they all went into hiding the minute I needed them? The bobbing faelights illuminating the dark space caught my attention. I summoned them, then sent them careering toward the villainous kid.

"Karsyn!" Remo yelled in warning.

The lit globes met their mark and bowled the boy over. Unfortunately, they didn't smash into his ribbon of *wita*, and the noxious scent of it crept into my nostrils. I spread my fingers wider and pivoted, hugging the wall of moss to get my vital organs out of harm's way.

Come on, wita . . . I flexed my knuckles. *Come on.*

My fingers burned. I hadn't reached my dust, but at least, I'd gotten ahold of my *kalini*. I peeked over my shoulder to see where I was directing my flames only to realize no fire leaped out of my smarting palm.

7

THE FILIGREE

I stared at my left palm, then raised it and flipped it over.

And over.

Even though there wasn't much sound, the world around me grew even more silent. I no longer heard the heated whispers of the Farrow brothers or the tinkle of *adamans* petals beyond the barrier of stilts. All I heard were my softening breaths and cadenced heartbeats.

Under the drying blood and thin wafts of smoke drifting from the zippering wound, a filigree design had appeared on my palm. The inky tracks of captive dust wrapped around the base of my fingers and coiled all the way up to my nail beds.

I'd seized Karsyn's dust.

Or was it Remo's?

I finally looked up, meeting my fiancé's agitated stare. He yelled something my buzzing ears failed to catch. Sobbing, Karsyn shook his bruised head, no longer the cruel little warrior who'd wanted to gas me out of existence.

Thoughts of his brother's fate were surely careening around Remo's mind. Would I have Karsyn condemned to death? After all, the proof of his attack was inscribed on my hand. And on my chest.

Even though the cut would heal, a pale scar would remain for a few hours. Possibly, days, depending on the metal he'd attacked me with.

"Amara?" Remo spoke my name so loudly I blinked. "Are you okay?"

I frowned. "Like you actually care."

"Can you put your loathing for me on hold for a second? I need to understand what happened down here. Why were you and my brother fighting?"

"Fighting?" I gave a bark of laughter. "You mean, why did your brother just try to assassinate me?"

Remo flinched.

"Sh-she said she w-was going to k-kill you." Karsyn picked up one of the fiery globes that had hit him and flung it back into the air. "I was just pr-protecting you." He picked up another faelight and squeezed it between his shaky fingers like a stress ball.

I gaped at the boy, at his reddened eyes and tear-slicked cheeks. Was he kidding me? Was he really putting the blame on me? Little *lupa* turd. "Why don't you tell your brother the truth before I call over your father and ask him to read my mind? Or yours?"

Karsyn blanched.

"Karsyn." Remo sounded his brother's name without shifting his lips. "The truth."

"You said you hated her."

So much white appeared around Remo's irises that I thought he might pull a muscle. "I didn't ask you what *I said*; I asked you what *you did*."

He squeezed the faelight so hard it separated into two smaller gummy orbs that drifted out of his hands and up into the air, high-lighting his already fading shiners. "You shouldn't have to marry her."

"Did you try killing her? Yes or no?"

"If I say yes, will you gas me, Remo, or will you ask Dad to do it?"

"No one's gassing anyone right now."

The brothers looked long and hard at each other before Karsyn finally admitted, "Yeah. I was trying to kill her. And I don't regret it. I just regret that you came and ruined it all."

"Tell me how you really feel," I mumbled.

Remo's chest rose and fell, rose and fell. And then he clasped his lids shut as though he couldn't stomach the sight of his brother. "Go home, Karsyn."

My shoulders jerked back. "Shouldn't I have a say in where the kid goes?"

Remo snapped his gaze to me, his forehead scrunched in an emotion I had never spotted on him before . . . despair. "Have mercy."

"Mercy?" I laughed a tad bitterly. "Your brother tried to kill me, Remo." I gestured to my chest.

Remo winced as though a sword were slicing through *him*. "And he will be dealt with."

Had it been anyone else, I suspected the *lucionaga* would've let me pick the person's fate, but this was personal. Still, I didn't fully trust Remo to *deal* with it.

"Your brother admitted he'd do it again in a heartbeat."

"I know, Amara. I heard. I saw. But he's just a kid. Please. I'll do anything."

"Anything?" *Anything* was a dangerous word in our world. "Even strike a bargain with me over your brother's fate?"

His jaw hardened in time with the rest of his body. "Yes."

"Remo, you don't want to owe a Wood," Karsyn said.

"Shut up. *Prinsisa*, do we have a deal?"

Without hesitation, I said, "We do." I was going to kill two *quila* with one arrow: I would force Remo to sever our engagement, which in turn, would make the Cauldron lock him out of Neverra . . . for good. "Speak the words, Remo."

"Words are unnecessary. I already agreed."

He was right; I'd felt a little stitch form between our bodies when he'd said yes. Nothing uncomfortable. More like a strand that linked us, that I could pluck once the time was right. "I still want to hear you say them."

His jaw worked. "You shouldn't kick a man when he's already down."

I wanted to savor my little victory over his outsized ego, however petty that made me. "Speak. Them." Perhaps he'd never kicked me when I was down, but he'd always stared and did nothing. Indifference was just as cruel.

If looks could kill, his would've turned me into flickering dust motes. "I *fucking* owe you, Trifecta. Are we done?"

"Yes."

"Karsyn, home. Now. We'll talk as soon as this dinner is over."

The ten-year-old pursed his lips as though he'd bitten down on a tart gladeberry. Casting one last hateful look my way, he threaded himself between the stilts and soared upward, toward his home at the top of one of the *calimbors*.

I sighed, sensing too much time had passed and my family would wonder where I'd gone. Operation *check-if-prison-portal-exists* would need to be postponed till the end of the meal. I composed a quick message to Josh to wait another Neverrian hour.

"*Prinsisa*?" Remo's voice jolted my gaze away from the holographic texts. Why hadn't he flitted back to the dining room yet?

I vanquished my conversation with Josh out of existence with the swipe of a finger. "What?"

He stared at the stubby shadow spilling from his tall body and darkening the ground between his shifting boots. "You need to change." A blush mottled his jaw. "Your dress." Keeping his gaze averted, he gestured briskly toward me. "*And* your hand."

I glanced down and found that the stretchy purple bodice was torn and had retracted, displaying more of my breasts than the skimpy red bikini Giya had gifted me for my seventeenth birthday.

I raised my Infinity and swiped through my digital wardrobe until I found the outfit I'd been about to change into to ford through the field of *adamans*—a black bodysuit made of flexible carbon scales that was impenetrable like armor but flexible like spandex. Neenee Lily had developed the fabric for Daneelies who desired clothing suited for their amphibian lifestyle. Nima and I had become the proud owners of the very first edition.

Once my body was cloaked in the compressive material, I exchanged my strappy sandals for knee-high boots, then searched through my closet for a pair of gloves but found I owned none. "You can stop blushing now, Remo."

"I wasn't blushing."

I smiled, enjoying his discomfort immensely.

"You forgot the gloves." His voice was a low growl.

"I don't own any."

Remo swiped through his Infinity furiously, then slashed through the beam emanating from the bangle. A pair of black leather gloves materialized on his hands. He plucked them off and tossed them at me.

"I won't be returning your brother's dust for a long *long* time. Perhaps forever. So people are bound to notice my new tattoo."

He squeezed the bridge of his nose and closed his eyes. "Just hide it tonight. Please?"

Something occurred to me then. "Wait. Did I confiscate his *wita* or yours?"

His gold eyes snapped open, and his hand slid off his face. "Mine? Why would you think it was mine?"

"Because you sent yours at me too."

"To stop you from being skewered. Now put on the damn gloves."

"I thought you were trying to help your brother."

"Wouldn't expect you to think anything but the worst of me."

"Have you ever given me a reason to think otherwise?"

He held my gaze, and I held his, playing a game of tug-of-war with our eyes. When I was younger, shyer, I might've looked away first, but I was no longer the introverted little fae Remo Farrow got a kick out of intimidating.

"I pity the man who will stand at your side the next time the Cauldron appears." His tone was as abrasive as the stone wall beneath the moss. And with that, he backed away, soaring around the heavy pillar and through the gap between the stilts.

I ran his words through my mind, feeling my eyebrows dip and rise, before dipping again. Didn't he think he'd be the man standing at my side? Did he sense I would use my *gajoï* to kick him out of the kingdom?

Slowly, I put on the gloves, the material molding around my fingers, adjusting to their narrowness and shorter lengths, then circled around the bathroom just as Aylen and Shiloh appeared at the bottom of the glass staircase. Both stopped chatting at the sight of me.

"You've changed out of your dress," my great aunt remarked.

"Sauce stain."

Shiloh arched a brow. "That your fire couldn't remove?"

I let them assume changing out of my purple garb was my way of showing Neverra what I thought of my engagement. "Surprisingly, yes. I'll see you upstairs."

When Shiloh's nose twitched, probably catching a residual whiff of dust on the air, I sidestepped them, then slalomed around the hovering faelights and up the flight of stairs. Silence settled over the guests when I landed in the dining room.

"Snagged my skirt on one of the stilts," I told my aunt Lily.

Her dark, expressive eyebrows writhed. *I'll fix it for you tomorrow*, she signed.

I was tempted to tell my aunt not to waste her time, but instead, I smiled and said, "Great," and conversations resumed.

I felt Nima's black eyes on me. Pert smile pasted on my lips, I looked up. She inclined her head to the side and mouthed, *Are you okay?*

No, I wasn't okay, but I didn't want to worry her. Not yet.

Besides, I'd struck a bargain. If I didn't keep quiet, I'd lose my leverage over Remo.

"You wore the gloves." My fiancé was watching Lydia, the faerie waitress, serve Sook wine with such attentiveness it strengthened my belief that something was going on between them.

"Not for your sake," I replied quietly.

Lydia's mouth stretched into a wide smile at something Sook said. *Gejaiwe*, how many men was she after? Her lips were so red and glittery it looked as though she'd dragged them over a hedge of crimson *drosas*.

"Woods never do anything that doesn't benefit themselves," he muttered, glowering at Lydia and Sook.

I shook my head, making my earrings dance and cast tinsels of light over the table. I steadied them but regretted lifting my hands when Remo's scent leaped off the gloves and assaulted me. The desire to pluck them off and toss them back at him was strong, but I tamed the urge.

Patience wasn't one of my virtues, but I couldn't afford to ruin my *gajoï*, so patient I would become. I simply hoped it wouldn't take Iba too long to uncover what had become of his bastard brother.

8

THE LEAF PORTAL

When digestives and dessert were served, I excused myself to go to the bathroom.

"Did you eat Glade kelp again? That stuff gives me the runs every time," Sook said between mouthfuls of coconut pudding and spice cake.

Giya elbowed him, but I grinned. "You know me and my love for kelp." I hated the stuff with a passion. It was slimy and bland, and according to Aylen, prodigious for weight loss. "I'll be right back."

Several sets of eyes tracked my progress around the table, but it was Nima's I felt most intensely.

Please don't follow me. Please don't follow me.

When she pressed away from the table, I beelined toward her and placed a hand on her shoulder. "Has Neenee Cass commed you yet?"

Nima frowned.

"Didn't she have a date with that old actor who won an Oscar?"

"Old?" Iba pinched my waist. "He's younger than yours truly."

"Ancient, then," I shot back.

He pinched me again, and I giggled. He smiled, and it shooed away some of the worry lines around his mouth and eyes.

I squeezed Nima's shoulder. "Why don't you comm her up? I'm dying to know how it went."

She regarded me with that deep, dark stare of hers. The same she'd used on me when I was younger and she was trying to decipher if I'd had a good day in school. More often than not, my days weren't good. Especially after Remo warned the Seelie students that a drop of my blood could turn them into a pile of ashes. Giya, ever the righteous fae, had tried to dismantle the rumor. When that hadn't worked, she'd told Nima, who'd come to school with my father to demonstrate that Remo's claim was false. An assembly had been called in the *calimbor*'s gymnasium. Surrounded by the entire student body, my parents had cut their hands and pressed them together. Although it had veined Iba's arm a little gray, the Unseelie magic in Nima's blood had eventually receded and his skin had turned nice and golden again.

I crouched and whispered, "I promise I'm okay. Just period cramps."

"Do you need some medicine? I must have some in here." She swiped through her Infinity.

"Nima."

She kept swiping. Had she uploaded an entire pharmacy into her band? *Probably.* Even though she'd never become a human doctor, she had become a skilled fae healer.

The words: **20 mg of Drosaniol**, appeared on my Infinity.

"Take it. It'll help."

A long press on the medication's name released it straight into my bloodstream. "I feel better already."

No medication worked that fast, so of course my comment made Nima tilt her head to the side. "You'll tell me the truth later, right?"

A faerie lie detector, that's what my mother was. "Right." I kissed her cheek, then returned to the dim space beneath the pavilion—again, guard-free.

I considered dusting my face to hide my identity, but what if I brought out Karsyn's *wita* instead of my own and asphyxiated myself with it? That wasn't possible, was it? If I stayed low to the ground, no wandering fae or *lucionaga* would notice a figure cloaked in black snaking through the tall stalks of *adamans*. I'd be like a spy from one of the human movies my cousins and I had watched at the cineplex Iba had created sometime after his coronation. Apparently, no human pastimes had been allowed under my grandfather because they'd been deemed propaganda.

I unhooked the heavy earrings, beamed them back to my bedroom using my Infinity, then threaded myself through the slats and rocketed, belly to the ground, around the slender stalks, the jagged purple petals tinkling overhead.

Guards hovered high above the field, but most were conversing or scanning the humid air instead of looking downward. A hiss had my breath catching. I lurched backward and swore as a *mikos* darted its ridiculously long forked tongue in my direction.

If I hadn't been on a covert mission, I would've roasted the snake with my fire, but flames would attract attention. So I changed course and flew more carefully around the stalks, on the lookout for other reptiles. Neverrian snakes weren't venomous, but *diles* were, and they loved nothing more than thick vegetation.

Thankfully, I encountered neither. Still, my heart pounded, and kept pounding long after I'd crawled out of the field and bolted into the forest of *calimbors* where I became one with the shadows. Faeries were out and about—some flew, some walked. I gave them all a wide berth, reaching the Duciba without incident.

Insects droned around the thick branches. I squinted to make out if any of them glowed. I really didn't feel like answering to *lucionaga* about why I needed to visit the government facility in the middle of the night. Since sensitive files weren't stored inside, the place was neither locked nor guarded. Which led me to believe there was no secret portal. Wouldn't Gregor employ at least one person from Neverra's vast army to protect it?

I twisted the handle, and the heavy latch clicked. I dragged it out just enough to slip inside, then summoned up shallow flames that danced over the smooth surface of my borrowed glove. As quietly as the striped *tigri* that prowled the uninhabited jungle beyond the Glades, I jumped into the darkness, rising through the hull cautiously. When I reached the ceiling, I circled the golden crown, holding my fiery palm up to illuminate the painted leaves.

Josh's source had told him the paint rippled if you stared long enough at it. None of the leaves seemed to undulate. They were all perfectly flat and golden. I drifted down and conjured up a brighter flame, then leaned back until my body was parallel to the ceiling. I stared at the mural till my eyes watered. Josh's informant was either a liar or crazy, perhaps both knowing the type of people the Daneelie frequented.

For good measure, my gaze cycled around the crown of leaves one last time. I was about to draw up my Infinity to inform Josh that if a portal existed, it wasn't here, when something shifted in my peripheral vision. Something golden. I blinked and focused on the spot, then rose up to inspect it more closely. The paint was static. Hesitantly, I touched it, but the surface was grainy and hard and stayed grainy and hard. My weary mind must have imagined the movement.

I grazed the spot behind my ear and commed a message over to Josh, then started to fly back down when my Infinity beamed his answer.

JOSH: *Touch every leaf. And don't forget the salt.*

ME: *Feeling up the Duciba's ceiling wasn't part of the bargain, Locklear.*

JOSH: *Wasn't it? :)*

Out of nowhere, a pang so violent cramped my stomach that I muttered, "*Bagwa*," before drifting back up. I suddenly hated Josh more than Remo but less than Karsyn. Karsyn's homicidal tendency had won him top place on *Amara's Most Loathed Fae* list.

I purchased a packet of salt on my Infinity, which materialized in the beam of my band, then sliced it open, grabbed a handful of grains, and ran my knuckles along the paint. Halfway around the circlet, something moved again in my periphery, something that glittered, not on the mural but lower. Had I loosened a fleck of paint?

Keeping my gaze affixed to the space that had sparkled, I continued my slow loop. Suddenly my knuckles sank into something gelatinous, as though the ceiling's consistency had morphed from wood to sea sponge. Before I could snatch my hand back, the leaf slurped it up.

"Shit shit shit," I whispered.

My wrist went in and then my forearm. Releasing the packet of salt, I shot my legs up and pressed the soles of my boots into the ceiling, trying to fight against the suction, but the pressure almost dislocated my shoulder. My feet skidded off the ceiling and dangled uselessly beneath me. My stomach squeezed as tightly as my heart, and cold sweat beaded on my forehead.

The dot of gold I'd mistaken for flaked paint transformed into a human body. Relief that I'd been unstealthy, and thus followed by a *lucionaga* in firefly form, vanished the moment I saw mussed red hair. Out of all the sentinels in the kingdom, the one to trail me had to be the one who wanted me gone.

Today really wasn't my day.

Fate, you cruel lady, you saved me just to curse me.

When the portal sucked in my shoulder, I shut my eyes and damned the day I'd struck up a bargain with a Locklear. If I'd known my ticket out of trouble was a trip into a supernatural jail, I would've owned up to my mistake instead of allowing Josh to take the blame.

The gelatinous portal molded around the top of my head, then my face, neck, and chest. I swore that once I climbed back out of the dimension I was about to enter, I would *never* find myself indebted to anyone. Maybe I'd even abolish *gajoïs* altogether.

After I used mine.

Mine...

I'd wanted to make Remo break up with me, but if for some reason I couldn't find my way out of Gregor's magical lockup, I'd make Remo tell my father where I was. The solution appeased me, but that lasted all of two seconds.

The moment my head popped out the other side of the magical doorway, I knew I was screwed.

Oh, so very screwed.

9

FAERIE JAIL

Either I was dangling upside down, or Gregor landscaped the ceilings of his prison.

I realized when the portal spit me out, and brutally so —*Skies damn you, Wariff*—that my first assumption had been the correct one.

Even though I tried summoning my fire to break my fall, it didn't answer me fast enough, and I tumbled out of the magical doorway head first. I squeezed my eyes shut and coiled my body into a tight ball, somersaulting as I fell.

My lower back connected with the ground, which squelched like mud. Surprisingly, the impact didn't shatter my spine. I grunted and little stars crackled at the edges of my vision. Slowly, I opened my lids and unrolled my limbs, sprawling out onto the sticky ground while I waited for my heart to peel itself off my lungs so they could fill with air again.

Air.

What if it was tainted with noxious gasses, or what if it wasn't air at all, and I would suffocate? I cautiously sipped some in. After a few breaths, which didn't kill me, I concluded it was safe to breathe.

Brain ringing, I didn't attempt to shift out of my starfish position. How far had I fallen? I stared at the mirrored disk floating over my head. Far *far* over my head. At least fifty feet up.

How had I not passed out?

I twitched my toes and fingers to make sure they were still connected to my spine. Everything wriggled. I was the luckiest unlucky person.

Sure, I would've healed—*eventually*—but entering an unknown dimension as a paraplegic wouldn't have been efficient. I twisted my neck to look around, which was a feat considering the damp ground sucked at my skull and back like a starved mouth.

The sky was the color of cotton and the cacti circling the muddy yellow field were gigantic, bulbous things decked with fluted pink blooms and spiky needles that gleamed as though made of steel wool. I'd never seen a species as large, neither on Earth nor on Neverra.

I was about to yell *hello* when I thought better of announcing my presence.

The damp chill of the ground penetrated my suit and licked my skin, sending a shiver through me. I hadn't felt cold since before my Year of Flight when the fire in my veins was still just smoke.

I started to raise my gloved hand to test my fire when a grunt made my attention pitch upward. A body was hurtling straight for me. Adrenaline flooded me. Gritting my teeth, I snapped the right side of my body off the soggy ground and flung myself sideways, managing to roll onto my side just as the fleshy missile went splat where my leg and arm had lain, showering me with more brown glop.

Even though I should've hopped to my feet and sprinted away from the portal's second human ejection, I sat up and swiped two fingers over the clump slithering down my cheek, sniffing it tentatively. *Priorities.* It smelled mineral and green even though it was entirely brown—ochre actually. Now that I knew I wasn't covered in dung, I checked out what unlucky soul Gregor had pitched through the portal.

My pulse batted my ribs anew when I caught sight of the flaming tuft of hair atop the navy tunic-clad body. "You've got to be kidding me," I mumbled, until I realized Remo couldn't possibly be here as Gregor's prisoner.

Which meant he'd come for me, and my outrage converted into relief.

Unlike me, Remo had neither rolled himself into a ball, nor managed to land back-first. It probably shouldn't have made me smile, but Skies, how I grinned at the sight of the *lucionaga* buried in mud to his ears. He twitched, and his palms crawled up to his shoulders, then flattened. He began to lift himself, the suctioning sound like a sloppy kiss. When he managed to pry himself up and prop himself onto his ass, I threw my head back and laughed. His face was yellow and caked with more mud than Shiloh and Aylen used on their customers when demonstrating the rejuvenating properties of fae sediments.

Remo grumbled, rubbing his hands down the sides of his face, only managing to heap more wet earth onto it.

Tears formed in the corners of my eyes. "I will never let you live this down, Farrow." I laid my hand on my belly that was still vibrating with the dregs of my laughter.

He glowered at me.

One glance at his face, and my wild giggling resumed. I didn't laugh often, but when I laughed, I laughed hard.

He muttered a medley of unsavory Faeli curse words under his breath. "Where the hell are we, *prinsisa*?"

That knocked the laughter from my lungs and the smile off my lips. "What do you mean? Didn't you come to break me out of here?"

"Break you out? No. I followed you in, because . . . because I'm obviously an idiot."

"What?"

"I'm an idiot."

"That's not why I said *what*, Remo. Although I agree that you're an idiot, on *many* levels. I said *what* to you not knowing where we are."

Remo's eyes seemed to shoot out the same lethal laser beams used in human warfare.

"You really don't know where we are?"

"Why don't you enlighten me, Trifecta?"

"Wait, does that mean you didn't come to get me out . . .?"

"Get you out? It's a portal. I'm sure the princess of Neverra can get herself out."

He was right. I could surely get myself out. Unless the portal was locked. I decided to keep worst-case scenarios at bay.

"So, you really didn't know about this place?" I asked, even though his severe exasperation showed through his facemask.

"No, I really didn't." He swiped more muck off his face and flung it aside.

A new shiver coursed up my body, this time not from the bite in the air, even though the air *was* really cold. "It's a prison. Created by your grandfather. And mine."

His pupils shrank. "A prison?"

I bit my lip but tasted moist earth, so I released it. I wanted to wipe my mouth on my sleeve, but my black suit was as ochre as the faerie glaring at me.

Remo's gaze skated over the field we'd landed in, taking in the ring of green cacti and cloud-filled sky. When his eyes returned to me, they seemed somehow darker and sharper, less trusting . . . not that they'd ever seemed that trusting before. "How do *you* know about this place?"

I flicked a clump of mud off my leg. "Joshua Locklear."

Remo's skin color rose in the few spots he'd wiped clean.

I sighed. "I owed him a favor, and he claimed it. Asked me to look into the rumor he'd caught of a supernatural prison. He thinks his sister might be in here." I gestured around me.

There was no wire fence, no magical barrier either, as well as no doom-colored structure that remotely resembled a prison, so I doubted anyone actually lived here.

I hugged my arms. Why wasn't my fire kicking in? "Are you cold?"

"Cold?" Remo's eyebrows dipped toward his nose. "No, I'm not cold. What I am is fucking pissed off. A prison! You fucking led me into a prison?"

"Led you?" I asked indignantly. "*You* followed *me*. I didn't sprinkle salt into your palm and hold it to a portal." My tone held all the heat my body craved.

I got to my feet, my legs heavy with mud. I needed to burn the gunk off and get the hell out of here. I raised my palms and conjured up my fire, then held my hands over my thighs, waiting for them to ignite and burn off the pounds of grime clinging to my suit's carbon scales.

Neither flame nor smoke appeared. I concentrated harder. After what felt like a full minute, my gloves were still flame-free. I looked at Remo, who'd also gotten to his feet. "Do you have fire?"

He flipped his palms over. "Of course I have fire." He turned much less vehement when he too failed to produce flames. "What the hell?"

My heart picked up speed, going almost as fast as the magnetic subways that crisscrossed every large city on Earth.

I focused on my feet, trying to drive fire into them, but unless our *kalini* felt more icy-needle than flame in here, then my veins were all out of heat. My pulse quickened, and the chill permeating my skin sank deeper. "Can you fly?"

His forehead was so furrowed it created trenches in the thick mud glazing his brow. He didn't answer me for so long that my dread turned to full-fledged panic.

I stared at his feet, willing them to lift. When they didn't, I wrenched my neck back to look at the portal. "If we can't fly up there, then how the hell are we supposed to reach it?"

"If this really is a prison, then my guess is we're not."

I ripped my gaze off the slender disk hovering in the white sky and focused on my Infinity, swiping the tip of my gloved index over it. *Please please please be functional.* No beam appeared. "My Infinity's not working. What about yours?"

Remo rubbed his bangle against the back of his thigh, the only clean spot on his body, then held it up and swiped his finger over the glossy black surface. His grim expression told me his was offline too. Which was crazy because Infinities were powered by our pulse, and mine was beating. Galloping even.

"Whatever's blocking our fire is also blocking our technology," I whispered.

"Well, we *are* in a fucking prison. What exactly were you expecting? Bare-chested men fanning you and feeding you gladeberries?" Remo's sharp, mocking tone made my shoulders snap back.

"Can you put your dickish attitude on hold for a second? It isn't helping!" I expected a stroke of lightning or at the very least a roll of thunder, but the air was still. Did my Daneelie power not work here either? "Did you tell anyone where you were going?"

He glowered. "Considering I wasn't aware of my destination, *no.*"

I disregarded his sarcasm and stared up at the portal again, willing someone else to pop out of it, preferably Gregor. Hope suddenly streaked through my chest. "The packet of salt. I dropped it. They'll find it!"

"No. They won't." Remo gestured to the mud . . . and my packet of salt.

Crap. Although perhaps it wasn't such a bad thing that he'd taken it with him. Maybe we'd need it to get out. "Wait. Josh knows where I went. When I'm reported missing, he'll tell someone."

Remo grunted, running his hand through his clumpy hair. "Locklear's banned from Neverra. There's no way he's going to fess up to sending you in here. He'd be locked out of the isle for life *or* turned to ash."

"Unless he uses it as a negotiation chip. He's pretty smart." Like a weasel was smart.

"Yeah, a real genius."

"You really hate the guy, huh?"

"I really do."

"More than you hate me?" I wasn't sure why I asked him this, but since the words were out, it was too late to take them back.

For several heartbeats, his lips didn't flex, and it gave me hope that I wasn't stuck in Gregor's jail with someone who might try to strangle me in my sleep. "Amara Wood, there is no one on Earth or on Neverra more rankling than you."

"Wow." I took a step back, one of my eyes twitching with annoyance. "You could've just said *no*. You didn't have to drag out your declaration and use big words."

His name overtook his brother's on my mental list of loathsome fae. I whirled around, then clomped away through the sticky field toward the giant cacti and the arid ground beneath them. I wasn't sure where I'd end up, besides away from Remo Farrow, which was my current goal. Goal number two was finding shelter—preferably one with a roaring fire—to get my thoughts in order so I could devise a plan to escape.

Alone.

Remo could find his own way out. Better yet, he could stay stuck in here forever. It wasn't as though I'd tell anyone where he went.

10

THE FANGED FLOWER

As my boots crunched over the cracked ochre earth, I loosened my unraveling braid and sang. Not loudly. Skies, I wasn't trying to attract attention or put on a show. I sang because silence spooked me. I must've gone through at least ten songs before I finally emerged from the sea of prickly green.

A round valley stretched below. More of a crater than a valley considering how steep the belt of mountains surrounding it was. Keeping a safe distance from the ledge, I squinted to make out the barracks that lined a single dusty road. All were flat-roofed clapboard houses with the exception of the brick building at the end of the street. Were those old-timey dwellings supposed to be jail cells? I watched for movement, but found neither prison guard nor prisoner wandering below. However, something cheeped and fluttered in my peripheral vision. Nerves popping, I summoned my dust but no honeyed strands of *wita* shot out from my fingertips. Maybe they were there, just invisible. Unless this place jammed my dust, too.

Goosebumps danced over my skin as I scanned the desert of cacti and the baked earth below them. The high-pitched sound came again, accompanied by a beating of wings. I whirled, my heart spinning in time with my torso. Another shrill peep, this time from behind me. I whipped my head toward the sound, my mud-soaked hair flogging my cheeks. What was making that—I sucked in a breath when a fluted blossom detached itself from a bulbous green trunk and soared toward me, screeching.

Oh . . . Great . . . Gejaiwe . . .

Even though every cell in my body wanted to force my knees into a crouch, I balled my fingers and swung my arms. My fist connected with the shrieking flower. Yelping, I scrambled backward but lost my balance. My tailbone slammed into the ground with such force, birdies flew around my head.

Not birdies.

More pink blossoms.

I flung my arms out, batting the animate flowers away. One nipped at my ear, and I screamed.

What the hell! It had fangs?

Sweat drenched the back of my neck. The front of my neck too. Unless that was blood.

"What is wrong with you, Gregor Farrow?" I yelled up at the white sky, hoping my voice would carry through the portal and boom across Neverra. "When I get out of here, I will murder you with my *wita*. Then set fire to the thorny weed you'll become again and again until nothing ever rises from your damn ashes!"

Another flower flew at my head. This time I punched it before it could make contact. More dove off the green cacti and launched themselves at me. One thumped into the back of my skull and flapped there.

Horror spiked through me as I realized it must've gotten stuck in my hair. I wanted to cry and cursed myself for not taking Aylen up on her offer to chop off my locks in a fashionable bob. Sweeping one arm continuously in front of my face to shield it from the harrowing flux of winged flowers, I bent my other arm and dragged my gloved hand through my hair, thanking the Gottwas's Great Spirit and the Neverrian Skies that Remo had lent me gloves. When I got back to Neverra, I'd purchase an entire collection.

I finally managed to wrangle the flapping bloom. Although it pecked and poked and fought my hold, I squeezed. After several thunderous heartbeats—mine and the creature's—the thing stopped moving. I kept squeezing it for good measure. Gritting my molars, I swung my other arm faster, shaking my head from side to side.

Something whizzed over me, something thick and green. I ducked, one hand still tangled in my hair, clamped around the (hopefully) asphyxiated creature. My stomach heaved at the thought that something dead dangled in my hair, and a cry escaped me.

More than one.

I sobbed out of frustration and fear, out of disgust and exhaustion. But then I remembered the green bat that had brought me to my knees, and I cranked my neck back in search of what had vanquished the swarm of rosy fiends.

Face still yellowed with mud, chest rising and falling as fast as mine, stood Remo, armed with a cactus branch. Blood beaded around his bare fingers, probably where the plant's needles had punctured skin. While he scanned the cacti minefield for a new skein of evil flowers, I rubbed my face on my forearm, trying to dislodge the tears clinging to my lashes and curving down my cheeks before he could spot them.

Show no weakness, Iba was always telling me, *or your enemies will use it against you.* If we ever got out of here, Remo would probably start breeding these fanged flowers and train them to assault me.

When no new attack came, he lowered his makeshift weapon. "Are you okay?"

"Do I look okay?" I growled, still trying to untangle the inert bloom dangling in my hair.

New tears leaked down my cheeks. I was failing so hard at staying stoic. *What a queen I'll make.* A sob grew and grew, expanding in my chest like a storm cloud. I would not let it out. I clamped my teeth. Instead of plaintive, my cry came out as a hiccupy squeak.

I sat back on my heels and lowered my eyes to my knees as I pried strand after strand off the unmoving thing, yanking out so many hairs that my skull stung. Remo's boots crunched over the cracked earth before vanishing from my line of sight.

Even though I didn't want him to witness how low I'd sunk, I also didn't want to be alone. What if more of those things dropped from a cactus?

"Please don't leave," I murmured.

His knees clicked and then his warm breaths hit the shell of my ear. "I wasn't going to." He pushed my shaky fingers aside, then gently began disentangling the trussed beast.

I pressed my trembling lips together and focused on calming down. "Is it dead?"

A soft snort ruffled my hair. "Yes."

Thank the Skies.

"Were you picturing my neck when you strangled the life out of it?"

The corners of my lips ticked up. "Maybe. Was your improvised weapon meant for my face?"

"Maybe." I heard his smile.

Slowly, the weight tugging on my scalp vanished. I turned, wanting a closer look at it. The creature's pink wings were fuzzy and its pistils were hooked and tinged red from my blood. A bead of cool sweat slithered between my shoulder blades.

"Thank you, Remo."

The faerie's green eyes lifted off the fanged flower. "Did a Wood just thank a lowly subject?"

My gratitude seeped right out of me, and I climbed back to my feet to glare down at the crouched Seelie. "What did I *ever* do to you?"

Lobbing my tiny assailant aside, he rose. I hated that he was taller, even by a few inches. "Woods think they're so much better than everyone else. Your *diverse* blood doesn't make you superior to any of us, Trifecta."

I would've spit on him if I'd been the type to spit. "Me and my diverse blood say screw you, Remo Farrow." I added the middle finger to drive my point home before stalking off. I'd never flipped anyone off and felt cheap for having succumbed to the vile human gesture, but I was *so* angry. And tired. And annoyed. I was pretty sure that if anything attacked me right now, my aura would electrocute it.

Down the steep flank of the mountain I went. Instead of sticky mud, the vertiginous ground beneath my feet was bone-dry. Would've been too convenient otherwise. Even though I almost lost my balance twice, the crumbly surface made getting away from Gregor's cruel heir faster.

Little rocks skidded against my boots as Remo fell into step beside me.

Without turning, I snapped, "Leave me alone."

"A second ago, you begged me to stay, and now you want me gone?" He released a humorless snort. "Did it ever occur to you that I'm not following you? The world doesn't revolve around you, Amara Wood."

I spun and lashed out at him with my fist. My knuckles grazed his jaw as I fell backward, my arms windmilling.

Aw, crap.

Remo launched himself at me, probably to shove me in case I miraculously managed to recover my balance. One of his arms snaked around my back, and he squatted so hard I toppled forward. His back slammed into the ground, and I slammed into his front. I shut my eyes as our fall and subsequent skid down the steep slope lifted dust and rocks that came at us like sharp projectiles.

I wasn't sure how long we fell, but it was too long. Then again, a single second pressed against Remo, inhaling the musky scent of his sweat tempered by the mineral smell of wet earth, was too long.

As soon as we stopped, I picked my head off his chest and rolled onto my back. In between pants, he groaned.

"Serves you right for trying to push me down, Farrow."

He twisted his head to the side, shooting me an impressive glare. "Push you down? I was trying to stop you from falling, Trifecta." He glowered a couple seconds longer before turning his head back toward the dirty sky and shutting his eyes, his nostrils flaring as though he'd just played a grueling game of Floatball.

"Why would you do that? I punched you."

"Was that what that was? A punch?" A corner of his mouth tilted.

I sucked in a long breath, then pressed it out. "What did you think it was?"

"Not a punch."

I pushed myself up onto my forearm and stared down at Remo. "My fist connected with your jaw."

His smile grew, which fed my desire to smack it off his face.

I took the high road, though, and rolled myself up, dusting the back of my legs, even though at this point, I didn't think the fastest cycle in a human washing pod with an entire bottle of detergent could help the state of my clothes and body.

I started walking. "Next time I punch you, you won't be smiling!"

He laughed.

The *bagwa* actually laughed.

I'd show him.

After I found a prison guard to help me out of this godforsaken land, I'd show him.

II

THE GHOST TOWN

It took several minutes to reach the first house, minutes during which I scanned each window that lined the street. Curtains hung crookedly in some, but most were bare, made up of panes of glass in need of a thorough wash. A lot like my body.

The skid of little rocks and pounding on the hard-packed earth behind me made me look over my shoulder. It was just Remo. His gaze didn't meet mine, too busy surfing over the fronts of the houses. A huge white sign with BOARDING HOUSE in black block letters hung over the gaping door of the first building.

I glanced over my shoulder again.

This time, Remo met my gaze. "Want me to hold your hand, Trifecta?"

His belittling enquiry lent me courage. I pressed my fingertips into the worn wood, and the hinges groaned. "Hello?"

"Great idea. Shout out your presence," Remo muttered from across the road.

I shot him one of my best glowers. "I'm looking for a prison guard."

"What if you find a prisoner?" He ducked around an old horse carriage missing a wheel. The wooden thing was slumped against the weathered white siding. A sign indicating LIVERY swayed in a slow breeze, its chains clinking.

Humming softly, I entered the boarding house. I expected laser fences, cowering prisoners, or more homicidal pink-petaled creatures. The only thing I found in the old house was furniture painted an unfortunate grass-stain shade of green, open cupboards filled with piles of chunky plates and cracked bowls, and a lopsided round table surrounded by four chairs missing at least a rung or the entire seat. Dust motes glittered in the pale light slanting through the dirty glass. Yellowed wallpaper sagged against the walls that didn't seem quite straight. I walked over to a narrow staircase sandwiched between two walls and a ceiling I barely cleared.

I listened for footsteps on the faded boards or low murmurs, but besides the wind whistling outside, there was no sound. Humming a little louder, I started up the creaky stairs, keeping my gloved hand on the banister. The black material turned gray from the thick coating of dust. Rubbing my palms together, I made it to the landing that led to an equally narrow hallway with even lower timbered ceilings. I hunched a little as I stepped toward the first door, which gaped open. The bedroom was empty, save for a rusted bedframe, a three-drawer dresser topped with a chamber pot, and a speckled mirror. I strolled to the next door and the next. All ajar. And the rooms beyond them, vacant.

I returned to the ground floor and stared around me, my gaze locking on a blackened chimney where not even cinders or the scent of charred logs lingered. I exited the boarding house, shading my eyes. The sunshine hadn't pierced the dense cloud cover, but the light was still painfully bright, especially after the obscurity of the abandoned dwelling. I scanned the street, wondering if Remo was still in the livery. Had he found anything? Anyone? I almost crossed the street but decided not to seek him out.

I wasn't a coward. I could explore this world without his help. Without anyone's help. After all, I almost ended up here alone. Why he'd followed me in was still a mystery.

Even though I hadn't been particularly excited to meet Kiera, I almost wished I'd run into her, just to comfort myself that I hadn't dropped into a wormhole that killed off its inhabitants the same way it killed off their powers.

I walked to the next building, the front of which was curved like a horseshoe and cinched by a wraparound porch. The black sign nailed above it read SALOON in bold, chalk-white lettering. We had one of those on Neverra, modeled around an archaic human one, complete with squeaking swing doors, curled horns, and cowhide barstools. I pressed my fingertips into the swing doors and entered a space made of polished tawny wood. No decorations adorned the walls, not even black-and-white wanted posters. A varnished bar ran the length of the far wall, topped with a forest of green-glass bottles. Throat clenching for a drop of liquid, I strode over. Every receptacle was empty.

I went to flip a bottle over, but my gloved hand skidded right off its neck. *What the*—I attempted to pull it off the bar but it was stuck. I tried picking up another, but it, too, didn't budge. Frowning, I walked over to one of the tables and shoved it. Its feet might as well have been soldered to the wide planks for all it moved. The only thing not stuck was the dust. I was tempted to return to the boarding house to check if the furniture there was also wedged to the floor but decided to test this out in the next building instead.

I exited onto the dusty road. Again, no Remo in sight. He couldn't have gone far though, the valley was small and the town compact. He was probably exploring the . . . I lifted my gaze to make out the sign atop the building across the road from me. *How appropriate.* The BROTHEL. If Remo was anything like Gregor, and there were real women in there, I might never see him again.

Good riddance.

My next stop was the GENERAL STORE. There was no sign up front, but burlap sacks filled with grain trimmed the windowsill, a black iron register sat on a counter, and tall shelving units ran across the three other walls. The highest one was weighed down by porcelain canisters and brown medicine bottles with the words *witch-hazel, arrowroot,* and *ether* scratched across peeling labels. I poked one. Stuck. And empty. I climbed the ladder to check the canisters. The lids were screwed on too tight, but my guess was that there'd be nothing to see. The rest of the shelves were bare except for the dust.

I hopped back onto the wide-planked floor and crossed the store toward the burlap sacks. I lowered my hand inside, expecting my fingers to comb through the grains, but the seeds were pasted to one another. Were they even real? Edible? Although I wasn't hungry yet, if I didn't find a way out of here fast, I'd need food. My gaze snagged on the ladder I'd just climbed. Three of them were propped against the shelves. If I nailed all three together, I might reach the portal. Remo would have to hold it up. Would he work with me, or would he assume I was using him to leave and refuse to help?

I thought of my *gajoï* then. I could use it to *make* him hold up the ladder. Optimism flooded me until I went around the counter and gripped one of the ladders. Like everything else, it didn't move. Another decoy. If only I could get my hands on a saw. Unless the ladders weren't made of wood but crafted from a magical, unchoppable material. I wouldn't put it past the whackjobs who'd created this place.

As I retraced my steps to the glass door, I wondered what had gotten into the *wariff* and my grandfather to build a fake frontier town. What sort of twisted torture was this? It must've driven the prisoners mad. Oh, Skies, what if making fae lose their minds was the goal of their secret jail?

When I stepped out of the store, launching into a new tune, I squinted at the barren land stretching beyond the town, all gray dirt and clumps of glass. What if the vegetation was fake too?

I entered the bank next door. Or what I assumed was a bank from the teller windows and large vault in the back, which was gaping and empty. Pappy and Nana Em's favorite movies were

Westerns, so I'd watched plenty during our sacred Saturday night sleepovers, which coincided with my parents' weekly "date-night."

I walked back out, no longer on my guard. There was clearly nothing and no one around. Of course, the moment I thought this, a lace curtain fluttered in a second-story window across the street. My heart leaped right into my throat, interrupting my song. I grew silent and still, pulse rustling through my ears until the figure passed in front of another window, and I made out tufts of red hair amid caked ochre.

It's just Remo, I reassured myself, running a shaky hand through my own hair, weighed down by so much dried mud.

A new tune forming on my lips, I headed to the penultimate building on my side of the road—a small clapboard structure filled with desks and benches. A red apple was propped on the largest desk. Was this a schoolhouse? Had Gregor sent children to this supernatural prison?

I walked over to the apple. Expecting to be met with resistance, I almost took out my eye when the fruit came loose and my fist arched through the air and struck my face. I uncurled my fingers and stared at possibly the most perfect apple I'd ever seen—glossy and unblemished.

Since I wasn't hungry, and Gejaiwe only knew if I'd find any other source of food in this ghost town, I didn't bite into it. Just held it delicately and possessively. I called out another, "Hello," and was met with complete silence. Even though I hadn't *wanted* to run into prisoners, not running into anyone was downright eerie.

Singing softly, I backed out of the schoolhouse and scanned the road for footprints. Someone would've had to leave this apple not so long ago for it to be so fresh . . . I squinted, eyes stinging from the dust and white light. Unfortunately, the wind raking through the town had erased my own boot prints.

I returned my gaze to the brothel. No curtains undulated in any of the windows. I looked at the building next to it—BARBER SHOP. I doubted there was a barber, and if there were any scissors or razor blades, they were surely fake. Was Remo inside the shop? I waited for him a few minutes under the porch of the schoolhouse.

When he didn't emerge from the rustic parlor, I began to worry and reassess my decision to part ways. I despised his company but preferred it over *no* company. Especially once night fell. I checked the sky, still white as toothpaste with no hint of impending dusk. If night wasn't falling, was it too much to ask that the sun poke through the thick cloud cover and warm up the valley? I hugged myself and rubbed my arms to drive heat into my chilled skin, then plodded toward the last building—the brick structure.

In all of the Westerns I'd watched, there had been wild horses and coyotes. This seemed like the sort of place where herds of mustangs should be running wild. Then again, the grass was sparse and I had yet to spot a body of water. Could any animal, besides those freaky fanged flowers, survive in such barren wilderness?

I circled the brick wall, peeking through windowpanes caked with so much dust they distorted the details of what dwelled inside but not its shape or color—long, black, with a chimney and wagons. A vintage wrought-iron locomotive.

I sped up until I reached the opening, then paused on the platform to take in the wide trench filled with black tracks tunneling into the rocky mountain. Did this road lead to the prison barracks or more ghost towns? Unless this was it . . . One giant, derelict cell where nothing and no one could thrive.

Great Gejaiwe, what had I gotten myself into?

I discarded my pessimism and decided the railroad had to lead somewhere. Somewhere where there were people. Like Joshua's sister. I approached the deep trench, peering at the contraption parked on the opposite platform. To call it a locomotive would've been an exaggeration considering it consisted only of a closed blue carriage stamped *Property of the Scourge* and a black conductor car topped with a chimney.

My sense of adventure had always been tempered by a great sense of caution, unlike my cousin Sook who lived for exploring. I wished he were here and instinctively looked down at my Infinity to comm him before I remembered it wouldn't work. I stared at the glossy surface as though I could magick it to turn on, but however long and hard I stared, the band didn't reboot.

"I'd tell you to jump, but the train here seems to be as fake as the rest of this goddamn place."

I jumped, and my precious apple rolled into the trench.

12

THE PACK

Gritting my teeth, I lifted my eyes off my fallen apple and set them on the insufferable fae who stood on the opposite platform. "Go to hell, Remo."

His face, which was still streaked with dried ochre mud, swiveled slowly to take in our surroundings. "Pretty sure I'm already there."

I wouldn't agree with him out loud, but he was right. This place was the gold-rush version of human purgatory.

Even though I didn't want to engage Remo, I also needed to know what he'd found. Or not found. "Have you run into anyone else?"

"Nope." He stroked the massive nose of the black locomotive. It must not have been pure iron because his fingers didn't ignite and carbonize. Too bad. "So, do you always talk to yourself?"

My head jerked back. "What?"

He lifted his hand off the train car and inspected his palm, then flicked his fingers, making tiny dust motes spring into the chilly air. "You know, emit words when no one is around?"

I glowered at him, my hands finding purchase on my hips. "I wasn't talking to myself, you brainless firefly; I was singing."

One corner of his mouth ticked up. "Is that what that was?"

Had he not been standing on an opposite platform, I would've punched him, and this time, my knuckles would've done more than graze his jaw.

"Perhaps that's what drove the detainees away . . . your *singing.*"

Why was I even trying to have a conversation with him? He was obviously incapable of acting civilized.

His gaze returned to my fugitive fruit, which had settled against the black rail. "Didn't happen to bring a hydro flask from Neverra along with that apple?"

He thought I'd brought an apple with me? I almost laughed. Almost because I was really in no mood to laugh. If I'd brought anything with me from home, it would've been a chainsaw.

"I didn't bring the apple from Neverra." I gestured to my skintight suit, which made his eyes roam over my body. "Where the heck would I have put it?"

His eyebrows knitted, cracking some of the dried mud on his brow. "Where did you find it then?"

"In the schoolhouse."

A beat of silence echoed around us. "You didn't bite into it, did you?"

"No." My heart picked up speed. "Why? Do you think it's poisoned or something?" His answering silence made my throat tighten. As I stared at the perfect red apple, my stomach decided this was the right moment to grumble. "What if it's not poisoned, though?"

He tipped his head to the side and squeezed one of his eyes a little shut, sending me a *how-big-a-fool-are-you* look.

My stomach protested. Just because fresh produce was *improbable* in a place like this didn't mean it was impossible. Maybe it was some sort of gift to prisoners. A way to keep them alive so they could be tortured one more day.

"Does your father know this place exists?" Remo's question towed my attention off the apple.

"I don't think so." He'd never mentioned it to me. "Your grandfather really never mentioned this place to you?"

"Not once."

"Do you think anyone could actually still be alive?"

He pressed his lips together and slid them back and forth, as though mulling my question over. "Well, I've found zero traces of life, and no water, so my guess is that if anyone's alive, they've moved away from this quaint little town."

Little, sure, but there was nothing quaint about it.

He stared at the tunnel in the mountain. "Until we know the extent of—"

"*We?*"

"As much as it pains me to suggest this, Trifecta, it might be safer to travel together than alone." Must've pained him a hell of a lot because he couldn't even meet my eyes when he suggested it.

My hands slid off my hips. "If *we* travel together, then we need to lay down some rules."

"Rules?" His green eyes snapped to my face. "Shall I remind you that you are *nothing* here, Amara Wood? Neither princess nor queen. *Nothing*. There is no calling Iba or Nima for help." He pronounced the Gottwa names for Mom and Dad that I'd adopted over the Faeli designation with disgust. "There are no servants to do your bidding. No guards to protect you. And your little collection of powers . . . it doesn't work here."

And here I thought I'd reached the pinnacle of my aversion for this boy, but there was *so* much farther to go. "Screw you. You don't know the first thing about me. And as far as traveling, I'll make my own way because I'd rather have my own back than be followed by someone who wants nothing more than to plant a knife inside of it."

Had he brought one? *Lucionaga* usually carried weapons, but Remo was still wearing his formal engagement attire. "I wouldn't be *following* you. I'm not a dog."

"No. Dogs are devoted and kind. You don't know the first thing about kindness."

I jumped down onto the tracks, which were much lower than I anticipated. Ankles and shinbones smarting from my leap, I grabbed my apple, then straightened up. Chin raised high, I marched along the tracks toward the mountain, because like everything in this damn town, the locomotive was surely a useless prop.

"You walk away, and I shelve my offer!" Remo called out.

Like. I. Care.

"Don't count on me to save you next time you get in trouble, Amara Wood."

I spun around. "*Save me?* Why don't you shelve that hero-complex next to your stupid offer? I don't need saving. Besides, I never *asked* you to save me. Wouldn't want to waste our *gajoï* on something as silly as my wellbeing when I have *such* a great plan for it."

Remo's entire body seemed to expand as though he were flexing each one of his six hundred muscles.

I turned back around and walked. This time, I didn't sing. One, because my teeth were too firmly wedged together to let out anything other than huffs and grunts. And two, what Remo said had gotten to me. However much I wanted signs of life—if only to reassure myself that this place didn't kill fae off—I'd rather come upon them than they come upon me.

But mostly, I didn't sing because of number one.

Right before I reached the arched mouth of the mountain, a low growl had me stuttering to a stop. Instinctively, I tried to push off the ground to fly, but my boots didn't lift off the rails.

Crap crap crap. I squinted into the darkness, praying that whatever had made that sound wouldn't launch itself at me like the shrieking pink flowers.

Another growl sounded, this time louder, as though its source had moved closer. Heart blasting, I backed up.

Another growl, and then another.

Aw, fae. Did all animals travel in freaking packs here?

I edged closer to the embankment right as enormous, four-legged animals materialized from the entrails of the tunnel. I released a breath when I realized they were *lupa.* Neverrian wolves were harmless. Well, as long as you didn't pet them, because petting them opened a mind-link, and all they thought about was hunting small game and running. Something I'd learned first-hand.

A *lupa* pup had gotten dragged into the Pink Sea, and since fae wolves didn't know how to paddle to save their lives, I'd jumped in and saved the floundering fur ball. For the next two years, every time the animal was near, I was privy to its inner musings. It had been strange, at first, receiving thoughts that weren't mine, but then I'd gotten used to the strange little broadcasts and the day they stopped coming—my wolf had met an untimely death at the fangs of a *tigri*—I felt a twinge of loss.

I counted seven wolves. They were much larger than the ones back home but scrawnier, which confirmed the scarcity of food. Their ribcages poked against their white coats, which resembled their habitat—scant and filthy. Large patches of fur were missing on some; others were covered in so much grime, they looked like they belonged to another species.

One of them raised its head as though to sniff the air. As it leveled its face back on me, its tail came up, and then its fellow packmates' tails straightened too, poking out from their skeletal bodies. I held my breath, expecting them to start wagging.

"Amara!" My name was like a bucket of ice water waking me from a doze. "Get away from them!" Remo was moving down the platform in slow but long strides, as though worried that going any faster would spook the wolves.

"Is the *golwinim* scared of a few little *lupa*?"

A chorus of low growls reverberated over the corroded tracks, over every rock in the mountain and every brick in the station. *Good doggies.* I assumed they were growling at Remo and his palpable hostility.

Still moving fast, Remo growled louder than the wolves, his frustration traveling down the trench.

I turned back toward the pack, intent on proving I wasn't scared, that these creatures, although almost as tall as I was, were as sweet as creampuffs, but then a growl turned into a bark, which turned into a snarl.

I frowned. "Stop running, Remo." I spoke gently so as not to freak the animals out any more than they already were. "You're scaring them."

"I stop running, and you're a chew toy."

"Don't be ridi—"

The wolf, which stood slightly in front of the others—the Alpha, I surmised—let out a piercing howl before bounding forward. The others followed, their great paws pounding the trench. This wasn't normal *lupa* behavior. The wolves back home weren't aggressive. If anything they were skittish around fae.

"Amara! Get off the fucking tracks! Now!"

My body temperature dropped as fear flooded my veins. I backed up and then I spun and ran at the embankment, my legs not shuffling like they did back home. I launched myself at the steep wall, attempting to clamber up, but my foothold skidded, and dirt rained down. I landed on my ass but bounced right back onto my feet and jumped at the packed earth, attempting to claw my way up as the wolves galloped closer. Remo crouched and stretched an arm out. I slapped my palm into his, and he swung me up just as one of the beasts launched itself at where I'd been a second earlier, scuttling like an uncoordinated spider.

I shut my eyes as the force of Remo's pull had us both tumbling into the hard-packed soil of the platform. The ground shook, and I thought it was from our fall until it shook again and again as *lupa* after *lupa* slammed into the dirt wall, trying to reach us. The creatures snarled, the sound bloodcurdling.

I sat up, my head swimming, my blood thrashing. A wolf jumped at the embankment, its curved claws finding purchase on the ledge. For the longest second of my entire life, I thought it would manage to pull itself up. And probably so did Remo, because he shot to his feet and grabbed my arm, almost dislocating my shoulder in the process.

The wolf tumbled onto its haunches but got back up in the blink of an eye and snapped, globs of saliva dripping into the trampled dirt at his feet. The rest of his pack snarled and barked, scratching at the wall as though to bring it down.

Remo still clutched my arm. I was too terrified to shake him off, and he was too transfixed by the predatory beasts to realize he was still holding me. Unless he did realize it and had decided I couldn't be trusted with my own life.

"My apple," I said, suddenly realizing I'd dropped it.

Remo breathed hard but glared harder. "Seriously, Amara?"

The wolves growled and prowled and leaped but didn't manage to reach us. One of them sniffed the fruit, knocking it with its muzzle. The Alpha took interest in it next and shoved its packmate. After a long sniff, the mammoth wolf huffed and turned away.

"If that doesn't tell you there's something wrong with it, then I don't know what will," Remo said.

"Maybe they're fruitphobic," I blurted out because I didn't want to agree with him.

Remo stared at me, his jaw working.

The Alpha howled, its yellow eyes glowing. Tail and ears still erect, it galloped away, and I thought we were safe. Well, as safe as two powerless fae could be in a supernatural jail. But then the enormous wolf flipped around and sprinted down the tracks, gaining velocity. It was going for the platform at the end of the trench.

My heart held still as the animal lurched into the air, managing to dock the top half of its body. As its massive hindlegs kicked and pushed, Remo yelled, "We need to get to higher ground!"

My heart whizzed, hurtling against my ribs. "The train."

"The doors are all open."

"Maybe they close."

"Maybe they don't."

The wolf dragged itself farther onto the platform and then sprang onto its four paws.

"On top, then!" I ripped my arm out of Remo's hold, then took off toward the conductor car and swung myself inside.

Remo jumped in after me. He tried to shove the door closed but it was stuck. He punched the roof out of frustration.

"Up up up up!" I yelled, climbing out the window and pushing off the ledge to reach the top of the car.

Its rounded shape made scaling it a struggle, and I almost slipped right down onto the tracks where the rest of the pack had congregated, drooling and yapping. Finally, I managed to swing my leg over it. Remo's head popped out the window and then his torso. He heaved himself out, sweat dripping down the sides of his face. Just as the massive white Alpha sprang into the carriage, Remo tucked his dangling legs up.

My heart rammed into my ribs again. I was about to set a Neverrian record and become the very first faerie to die of a heart attack.

Latching onto the chimney, I scrambled upright, then offered Remo a hand so he could stand too. I didn't think the proud fae would take it, but his fingers gripped mine, and with my help, he heaved himself up.

The wolf's huge head popped out of the window. It snarled and barked. When it realized it couldn't reach us, it reared up. The carriage started to shake, and Remo, who'd been trying to keep some distance between us, circled his arms around the locomotive's chimney, sandwiching me between the cool black metal and his overheated hard body. I didn't push him away, because feeling like a burger patty exponentially diminished my chances of becoming one.

"I hate *lupa*," Remo gritted between clenched teeth.

The train shook and rattled so hard I thought the wolf would manage to topple it. When everything else was stuck in this damn town, why did we have to pick the only thing that wasn't? "You know what I don't get?"

"No, what don't you get, Trifecta?"

"Why you helped me get away from the wolves when you clearly hate my guts."

His hot breaths pulsed against the shell of my ear a half dozen times before he finally answered, "I've been trained to protect fae. Even the abominable ones."

Instead of my temper rising, it was my lips that did. I turned my head slightly, just enough for him to detect my mocking smile. "Is that why?"

His pupils spread, devouring their green backdrops. It hit me then that his eyes weren't gold anymore. This world had stolen his *lucionaga* magic just like it had stolen my *diverse* one.

I was about to say something about it in case he hadn't realized he couldn't transform into a firefly, when he asked, "Did you think I cared about you?"

"Cared about me?" I laughed, my chest shaking even though the carriage no longer did. "Oh no, Remo Farrow." My hilarity petered out as swiftly as it had struck, and I leveled a hard dry look on the faerie guard. "I assumed you cared about my crown, and it sitting on top of your head someday."

His lash line dipped, obscuring his eyes. "I don't give a shit about your crown."

Liar, I thought. "Then why did you agree to marry me?"

"To make my grandfather happy."

"Aw. Aren't you the sweetest?" My syrupy voice made him scowl. "You think you'll ever start thinking for yourself, or will you always let your grandfather and mother dictate your opinions and steer your life?"

The vein in his temple, the one under his birthmark, throbbed. "I should've let you get mauled."

Gratitude that he didn't abated my virulence. I gave him a close-lipped smile before directing my attention toward the tracks. "I think they're gone."

Remo peered over my head, twisting it to the right and then to the left. Slowly, he peeled his body off mine but kept one palm on the chimney for support.

"I think you're right, but considering they're smart as fuck, they probably haven't strayed too far. Did I mention how much I hate *lupa*?"

"A few times." I wrinkled my nose. "I've decided I'm no longer a fan. At least, not of the Frontier Land breed."

He snorted.

Gnawing on my lip, I added, "If you haven't shelved your offer, I'd like to take you up on it."

"My offer?"

I grimaced. "To stay together."

A smug smile tugged at his mouth. "Whatever changed your mind, *prinsisa*?"

I almost wanted to take it back. *Almost*. But a distant howl cemented my desire not to trek through this land alone. "I don't want to die, and if that means sticking to you for the next few hours"—or days . . . hopefully hours—"then so be it."

He studied me a moment before backing up some more. "Don't stick too close."

"Wouldn't dream of it. So what's the plan?"

"Not getting eaten by *lupa*."

"Besides that and reaching the portal?"

He took in the mountain and the tunnel running through it. "We need to see where the tracks lead."

How could we when a pack of rabid wolves guarded the entrance like some fae-version of Cerberus?

An idea surfaced. "The train. It shook."

"You don't say."

I rolled my eyes. "What I meant is, it's not stuck to the tracks, so maybe it works."

Surprise sculpted the line of his jaw. Ha! He hadn't thought of that. *Ten points to Amara. Zero to Remo. Okay, half a point for saving my ass earlier.*

"You might be onto something." He gestured to the platform with a flourish. "After you."

"Coward," I muttered.

"You mean, chivalrous?"

I glared at him, which just made his smirk grow.

"Fine. I'll go first." I kneeled and then slid myself back down toward the window, praying the wolf wasn't waiting quietly inside.

I probably should've checked before threading my legs through the opening. Apparently, my survival instincts were underdeveloped. Back in Linus's day, it was tradition for royal fae on the brink of adulthood to trek across Neverra alone and without the use of any of their powers. Although my aunt's account had made me grateful Iba had abolished the tradition, the initiatory voyage might've served me well.

Thankfully, the conductor wagon was empty. I tried the door again, but it was jammed open.

The train dipped as Remo vaulted through the window and touched down next to me.

There were two levers on the conductor's dashboard. Unfortunately, there were no plaques nailed beside either to explain what they did, and a scan of the cramped quarters revealed no instruction booklet. I sighed. They were probably just inoperable props. I wrapped my hand around one anyway, then gave a hard shove. The lever glided as smoothly as a Daneelie through water.

"Trifecta, don't touch—" Remo's command was interrupted by a deafening clank: the door smacking shut.

My heart fired up again. "At least, we know how to close the door now."

Remo grumbled something under his breath. Although I didn't make out his words, his incendiary stare gave me the gist of them. Before he could holler at me again, or grump out some more, I pushed the second lever up. A shrieking whistle tore out of the chimney, followed by a torrent of steam.

We were on our way! *Skies knows where.* All I prayed for was that it would be *livelier,* and by that I meant populated by humans instead of overzealous wolves or animate blooms.

The train shook hard, as though the wolves were throwing themselves at it, but didn't chug down the tracks.

Remo gripped the door lever and tried to shove it down, but it didn't move. Muscles bulging underneath his navy tunic, precariously stretching the fabric, he tried the second lever, but it, too, didn't budge. Perhaps the person who'd activated the train was the only one capable of stopping it? I gave both levers a violent tug. *Useless.*

"Did you think I wasn't pulling hard enough, Trifecta?"

"Don't bite my head off. And just because my arms aren't as big as thighs doesn't mean I'm weak."

He huffed and then turned toward the opening we'd come through earlier and gripped the sill to climb out, but a thick piece of metal rose like a window being powered up. "What the—" He snatched his hand back before the metal could saw it off.

I swallowed as the curved glass panel in front of us darkened and turned opaque.

Fear spread through me, and I backed up, my calves bumping into the conductor's bench. I sank down hard, and a bolt of pain shot up my tailbone. Oh, Skies, I was going to die in a metal box next to Remo Farrow. I wasn't sure what horrified me more: the claustrophobic nature of my death or the fact that Remo would be the last person I'd see before dying.

My fiancé rained punches on our wrought-iron casket and snarled like a *lupa* while I gathered my legs against me and pressed my eyes against my kneecaps.

I hadn't thought anything could beat sticking my hand in the Cauldron alongside Remo's, but then I'd dropped through a fifty-foot portal, was attacked by a swarm of shrieking pink blooms, explored a ghost town, and made the acquaintance of a rabid pack of wolves before getting locked into a clattering train car. The fact that I kept one-upping myself worried me to no end.

A sob lurched out of my mouth, but I managed to stifle most of it on my knees. Dust coated my wobbly lips, and my parched throat burned.

Remo's punching and swearing stopped. "Crying won't help, Trifecta."

I didn't pick my face off my legs, but I wedged my cracked lips tighter together to cry more quietly.

A hand landed on my tensed arm and gripped it gently. "Come on, don't cry." Remo's voice sounded strained. "You're not in this alone."

I lifted my head. "How neat. We can die together. Do you want to hold hands now?"

His green eyes flared, but I couldn't tell with what, because my vision was all blurry. "We're not going to die. I swear I'll find a way out of this thing."

I was about to shake my head at how naïve he was when the train stopped rocking and the darkened windows cleared. Both Remo and I watched the land develop beyond the window.

The rocky mountain was still there, but the terrain around us was ... it was different.

The train door hissed, releasing us into a brand-new cell.

13

THE GLASS CITY

"Look at that." Remo's voice sliced through the ringing silence. "I told you I'd get us out of here, and I got us out of here."

"Yeah. I don't think you had any hand in that."

"You'd be surprised by the power of positive thinking."

I side-eyed him. "Can you positive-think us back to Neverra?"

He smiled. "Trust me. Every few seconds, I'm sending brainwaves toward the portal."

I shook my head but smiled . . . a little.

He tipped his head toward the open door. "Ready to go explore?"

"I hate exploring. Maybe if we sit here long enough, the magical train will take us back home."

"If my grandfather designed this place, this train won't take us anywhere nice."

I slid my lower lip between my teeth and stared back out at the skyscrapers of glass rising from an endless slab of concrete. To say I missed the dry dusty town we'd left behind would be a stretch, but I wasn't looking forward to finding out what hid in this world.

Remo hopped out of the train, head swiveling as he scrutinized our new surroundings. Slowly, I rose from the bench and climbed out, too. The station had adapted to the environment. Instead of bricks, a single-paned dome of glass enclosed a platform fashioned from silver metal polished to a mirror-shine. The tracks consisted of the same magnetic strips humans used in their metropoles, and the train was sleek and bullet-shaped.

Even though this land looked more familiar than the last, it didn't feel any more familiar. It was cold, made colder by the blistering white sky and frosty air. I hugged myself as I took in the glass rectangles glittering like cut diamonds. They stretched so high that if the portal had been in the valley, we could've cracked open a window and easily hopped onto it.

Remembering something Josh had told me about the Neverrian prison portal, I whipped my attention to Remo. "You think the portal relocated?"

"I don't know." His gaze surfed toward the mountain we'd skidded down in Frontier Land.

Instead of a tangle of bulbous cacti, the forest that sprawled atop the cliff seemed made of pale blue trunks with glossy white branches—an ice garden?

"Does that mountain flank look steeper to you?" I asked.

"It does."

Was it to keep us from reaching the plateau? Did it mean the portal was up there?

"Your lips are purple, Trifecta."

"Well, it is freezing." My teeth chattered, but I wasn't sure how much of that was due to the biting air and how much was due to my mounting pessimism. "Aren't you cold?"

He shrugged. "Let's get moving. You'll warm up."

"Or we can hop back in the train and go someplace else?" Preferably somewhere tropical like a sun-drenched beach with floating hammocks and piña-coladas topped with cocktail umbrellas.

"We might end up right back with the *lupa*."

Sighing, I turned away from the train. My toes tingled in my boots, and the tips of my fingers throbbed. Thank the Skies for the gloves Remo had lent me. How I prayed he wouldn't reclaim them.

His dark eyebrows, which shone a deep auburn amidst the streaks of dried ochre, gathered a little closer together. "What?"

"What *what*?"

"You were clearly thinking something."

"Nope. I was thinking nothing."

He narrowed his eyes.

Before he could link my guilt to his gloves, I said, "Your eyes are green."

His forehead smoothed even though his gaze remained tapered. "And yours are blue. Shall we move on to hair?"

I snorted. "What I meant was, they're no longer gold."

His pupils shrank, then spread back out. "I figured as much when I tried shifting and didn't manage." He rolled his neck from side to side as though getting ready for a fight. Since for once, his fight wasn't with me, I worried what he expected to find in this place. Maybe mammoth polar bears or vampiric bunnies?

He started toward the curved opening in the glass dome, and I trotted to catch up. I'd promised not to stick too close to him, but there was no way I was letting him out of my sight. Our footsteps pinged off the metal and curved glass. Once outside, we circled around the modern station, coming to a stop on the cement road that stretched toward the cliff frosted with the ice garden. The setup of this world was the same as in Frontier Land—a single street bracketed by buildings. But the similarities stopped there.

"You think we'll find running water?" What I wouldn't give for a drink and a hot bath.

"Let's hope so." Remo tipped his head back, squinting at the buildings before heading into the tallest. "This one should afford us the best view."

"We're not looking for a piece of prime real estate, Remo."

He shot me an eloquent look. "The reason I want the best

panorama, Trifecta, is to peer into the rest of the buildings without having to climb them all."

"Bench the petulance, Farrow. It's unbecoming of an *almost* adult."

He punched me again with his neon-bright eyes. "And inanity is unbecoming of an *almost* queen." He didn't linger to watch the effect of his criticism.

"It's called sarcasm," I called out after him.

We entered the building through a large square opening that should've housed a revolving door. Thoughtless architect. The lobby was enormous, made more so by the bare, buffed white floors that reflected the winding, glass staircase.

I hugged my arms tighter. "You don't see an elevator by any chance?"

"Afraid of a few stairs, *prinsisa*?"

I set my teeth. Remo Farrow had the temperament of a *quila*. We'd surely end up murdering each other before any pack of zany animals found us.

"I'd offer to carry you but I might be tempted to drop you"—he dipped his chin into his neck—"and not from the first floor. Even though, considering the height of the first floor, it would surely hurt."

My arms fell from their tight knot and swung as I stormed ahead of him toward the stairs. "Like I would *ever* trust you to carry me."

"Would you honestly have trusted an elevator in this place, though? It would probably take you to the top and then drop down."

Goosebumps of fear sprouted over my goosebumps of cold.

"Plus, walking up a couple dozen flights of stairs should warm you right up."

"Hating you is already helping with that." My heart pumped harder, allocating heat to my extremities.

I caught his smirk in the shiny handrail.

The equivalent of four floors later, we reached the first landing, and I pirouetted to take in the expansive space. Nothing. There was *nothing*. No fake furniture. No fake people. No crazy animals. The next two floors were identical to the first. Instead of heading up another flight—I'd exercised enough to last me a decade—I crossed the gigantic space toward the floor-to-ceiling window that gave onto the street below, bumping the tip of my nose against the impeccably clean glass that must've been made from a special material, because my breath didn't fog it.

Inside the skyscraper across the road, apartments made of steel, pale stone, and cream drapes filled each floor. And the building next to that one was littered with office furniture. "Is it just me, or did you pick the only vacant building?"

Remo, who'd come up next to me, frowned.

"What?" I asked.

"When I looked up, I didn't see anything in those buildings."

"Maybe you should get your eyes checked?"

He turned said eyes on me. "Did *you* see anything?"

"I was too busy scanning the street for mutant mice."

He cocked up an eyebrow, which told me he couldn't tell if I was joking; I wasn't. I really was more worried about what lay in wait in the concrete wilderness. Now that I knew the buildings were missing front doors, though . . .

"Mutant mice," he grunted. And then, because he was glib like that, he spun around and pounded back toward the spirals.

"Careful. Glass breaks," I said.

"Probably not the magical kind. What the—Where the fuck are the stairs?"

"Seriously?" I gestured to where they . . . *should've been.*

Across from us, an elevator dinged.

He looked at the floor some more, then at the ceiling, and then back at me. "Next time, don't wish for something so loudly, Trifecta."

"Yeah. Because disappearing stairs are my fault." Muttering

bagwa under my breath just loud enough for him to hear, I crossed toward the elevator.

"You're not actually going to get in?"

"Do you see any other way out of this building?"

I stepped inside, then searched for the keypad to input Lobby, but the elevator's walls were black glass and devoid of buttons. I brushed my fingertips where the keypad should've been, hoping one would materialize. The doors began to slide shut. I jerked my attention to where Remo still stood by the missing spirals. Growling, he ran toward the elevator. I stuck my boot between the closing doors, which he seized and prized apart.

"I don't like this," he grumbled, squeezing himself through.

As the doors sealed shut, I said, "Can you help me locate the panel?"

His lashes hit his browbones, and then the color leached from his skin as the doors smoothed into a creaseless panel of black glass.

Crap.

Were we about to be transported like in the train? Claustrophobia clawing up my throat, I looked at Remo, but then the elevator darkened, and just like the stairs, my companion disappeared. A room materialized before me, with a bed and a table topped with a half-eaten burger.

A tall man with faded blond hair was lifting a chilled beer bottle to his mouth. After a long swallow, he moved closer to a young girl with hair the same coppery red as Remo's. *You're right, Faith. I do know the show's producer.*

Faith? I blinked. Remo's mother, Faith?

The blond man slid a knuckle down her cheek, and she flinched, her high ponytail swinging over her shoulder.

How badly do you want the part?

I . . . I—

Let me rephrase myself. It's a career-making role. How badly do you want an acting career?

Faith's tongue darted nervously over her lips. *It's my dream.*

The man smirked. *Then I'll make it come true.*

Relief wrought with some tension softened her stance. *Thank you. Thank you!*

She spun to leave when the man's voice rang out. *You're forgetting something . . .* She whirled back around and took in the room before her blue eyes landed on the man again.

The man who was now sitting on the bed, patting it.

The scene flickered then faded, and light flared, illuminating the elevator.

Relief to find Remo standing next to me mingled with confusion. "Was that your mother?"

Remo's mouth, which had been slightly agape, closed. "My mother?"

One of my eyebrows crept up. "Um. Didn't you just—Wait. What did you see?"

"Obviously not the same thing you did. So, you saw my mother . . . and what was she doing?"

"She was with this—" My words jammed in my throat as the man's face flashed behind my lids. There had been something so familiar about the shape of his smirk and the lines of his body. Oh, Skies, had I just gotten a glimpse of Remo's father? The man no one knew anything about?

Remo dipped his chin into his neck. "With this *what*?"

Did Remo know how he'd been . . . conceived? In case it was a secret—was it even real?—I countered, "Who did *you* see?"

"Finish your sentence, and I'll share what I saw."

I steeled my lips but then relented. "With a man."

"Not Silas?"

"No, but she was much . . . younger."

His eyes seemed to darken even though the light around us was still bright.

"So, what did you—"

Suddenly the elevator jerked, and my back rammed into the

wall. Heart in my throat, I braced for the black glass box to shoot up ...or down.

It descended. Slowly. And then it jerked to a stop. I imagined the doors would reform and release us—probably somewhere awful—but I was wrong. Whatever magic the black glass was imbued with made the air darken again and Faith reappear, older this time. She was crying, both hands clutching the front of Silas's black uniform. Silas whose downturned face was entirely unlined and whose dark brown locks was untouched by age.

He pushed a piece of red hair off her cheek. *Don't ask me to choose between my duty and my heart, Faith. Don't.*

Ace may not have murdered my mother, but he married Cat, which makes him complicit.

You have to forgive her. Your mother attacked her.

You know what? She released him. *You've obviously made your choice.* She flicked her hand toward the entrance of her apartment. *Leave.*

Faith . . .

Leave! Her large blue eyes glittered with tears. *And don't bother coming back.*

Brightness bled over the dark and whisked away Faith and Silas.

I blinked, found Remo already staring at me. This time, his lips were firmly wedged together, and his jaw ticked as though whatever had played out for him was deeply aggravating.

"You're seeing my parents, aren't you?" It wasn't such a wild guess. If I was witnessing chapters from his life, he must've been seeing episodes from mine.

He twitched.

"Tell me what you saw."

He thrust one hand through his hair, then averted his gaze. The elevator jerked before sliding down. This time, when it stopped, I was ready for my weird little show to begin.

Gregor was there and so was a younger version of Remo. If I had to guess, he was four, maybe five. And they were standing beside a floating crib. I couldn't see the baby inside, but I could hear it whimpering. Was it Karsyn? No … Karsyn was over a decade younger than—

What do you think of your future queen? Gregor asked.

I was in that crib?

She's a baby, Little Remo responded. *Babies can't be queens.*

Babies grow up.

She's ugly. And her cries hurt my ears.

Gregor guffawed, his thick, age-streaked hair dancing around his mirthful face. *Better get used to it, Remo.*

Used to what, Grandfather?

Women crying. That never changes.

My lips pinched together. Chauvinist.

Little Remo wrinkled his nose. *I don't like women.*

If you're anything like me, you will. You'll like them way too much. Maybe you'll even like this one. He nodded to my floating crib. *And if you did happen to like her, then you'd be king. Wouldn't that be just grand?*

Remo pushed up on tiptoe to look into the crib again, nose still wrinkled. *Do I need to like her to be king?*

Gregor sighed, and although he wasn't actually there, his piercing hazel gaze seemed to land on me—grown-up-Amara. *It'd be the easiest way … but not the only one.*

The air brightened, but my mood definitely didn't. My loathing for Gregor Farrow simmered and sank into my skin, curdling my blood. How I longed to launch my fire and dust into the *wariff's* face.

Remo and I didn't talk this time, even though our eyes met and held as the elevator dipped to the next floor. We'd gone up three stories. Did that mean there would be one more memory to wade through? Gripping my elbows, I readied myself. Right on cue, the elevator leveled out, and the air blackened.

A ball smacked into the side of Remo's jaw, which was slightly round and dusted with sparse stubble.

Get your head in the game, Remo, another boy called out to him.

My head's in the game, he grumbled.

Really? Because I could've sworn you were prinsisa-*gazing.*

The look Remo tossed his friend was full of venom. *She's a kid, Aaron. A kid, who thinks she deserves the world on a fucking silver platter because her father wears a crown and her mother can manipulate stolen* wita. His fingers were rolled into fists. Wita *she took from my family, by the way.* Wita *which I plan on setting free.*

Dude ... Aaron backed up.

What? You think our queen should be allowed to keep something that isn't hers?

Aaron raised his hands. *I don't want to hear this.*

When the boys faded, my fingers dented the skin over my elbows with such fury I was surely cutting off my blood circulation. "You planned on slicing my mother's neck open?" I yelled.

Remo's brow pleated in confusion. "Amara, I—"

The elevator dinged, snatching away the rest of his words— undoubtedly a lie—but the glass panel didn't split open. Instead, it lit up and four words appeared: "Welcome to the Scourge."

That word again. What did it mean?

The glass went dark, then brightened with a *dile* injecting venom into someone's foot, followed by a *quila* clawing through flesh, faerie bodies bursting into gray dust and human bodies being decapitated by laser beams, wounds oozing and bubbling with sores.

A wave of sickness slammed into my clenched teeth. The projection shut off and then a seam appeared in the glass wall that widened as the doors pulled apart. I scrambled out into the lobby, palms gripping my thighs, body hunched over. As I worked on swallowing back the vile taste of vomit, wind whistled through the gaping entrance, filling the lobby with an eerie silence.

"What's a scourge?" My voice was flat even though I brimmed with rage.

"A whip. One that causes immense pain."

I wondered how Remo knew this. It wasn't as though he could look it up on his Infinity. Maybe he owned one. That made sense.

"Maybe it's the name of this place," he ventured.

"It'd be suiting." Once I got my stomach under control, I straightened and turned to face Remo, who was standing near enough for me to touch him. Not that I *ever* would after what I'd just witnessed.

Unless it wasn't true and this place was trying to stir up trouble.

"Did you once tell a boy called Aaron that you would hack through my mother's neck?"

He blinked.

I took a small step back. It *was* true. "I hated you before, but now . . ." My hands locked into fists so tight my knuckles whitened.

His eyes turned stony. "Trust me, I got that from the episodes I was subjected to. I didn't know you had quite so many nicknames for me, and that my eyes were . . . how did you describe them to Giya again? Oh, right, the color of *dile* poison."

"I might've said unpleasant things about you, but I never plotted your mother's murder or your family's downfall." I backed up. "To think I was beginning to trust you."

Color rose to Remo's cheekbones. "I wasn't going to murder her."

"Like I'd believe you." I whirled around and stormed out of the building.

Footsteps sounded behind me. Too quick and too near. "That conversation happened almost four years ago."

"Just because it's in the past, it doesn't make it any less real."

He growled. "I'm sorry, all right!"

I halted my mad dash toward the train and spun back around. "Is Remo Farrow apologizing for something? *Wow.*" I looked up at the unremitting white sky. "I hope someone's recording this because I want to play it over and over after we get out."

If we ever freaking did!

I stared at the cliff. Was the portal somewhere beyond it? And then I looked up into the surrounding buildings, seeing furniture, even in the tower we'd just come from.

I'd been wrong about the glass being magical. It wasn't magical; it was evil, offering deceptive salvation and cruel truths. As I stalked off toward the train again, I rebaptized this cell Deception Central. I neither sang nor hummed, and not because I was afraid Remo would pick on me, but because I was so disheartened I couldn't find it in me to produce a single sound.

My stomach growled, but I doubted it was in hunger. I didn't think I could eat anything after the horrific movie in the elevator. However, if I remained in the Scourge much longer, I'd need to find food. I thought of the pack of *lupa*. I'd never eaten one before, and the idea was revolting, almost as much as the oozing sores from the video, but meat was meat. How could I hunt one down without a weapon, though? And how would I cook it without fire? Sure, there'd been a chimney in the boarding house, but without access to my Seelie power or to matches, I had no way of kindling flames.

The glare of white sky against glass made me blink my eyes closed. And then an idea made me blink them wide open. Sun through glass created flames. I'd seen it done in a movie. There had been windows in Frontier Land. I could surely punch one out.

I was about to share my musings when I remembered I wasn't talking to Remo. And then a spot of color made me forget all about hunting *lupa*. On a stair in the building closest to me rested a single red apple. I pirouetted to take in the silent city on the lookout for a shadow or some flicker of movement. Was someone leaving them for us? Were they our magically-allotted prison meal?

I decided to go retrieve it when Remo clapped his hand around my forearm and held me back. "Did the *lupa*'s reaction to it slip your mind?"

I plucked his fingers off my sleeve. "It showed up in *both* worlds, so it's got to be important. Besides, the wolves here might only like human flesh."

Remo stayed quiet as though mulling over my hypothesis.

"And holding it didn't hurt me."

He nodded to my hands. "Maybe because you're wearing gloves."

I waited for him to ask for them back; he didn't. Had he forgotten they were his? I didn't remind him. "Perhaps. Or perhaps because it's not poisonous." I trotted into the building and up the glass spirals, climbing fast, afraid the fruit might vanish or relocate. Thankfully, it wasn't on the first-floor landing. I didn't want to be caged inside an elevator again with one of Remo's or Faith's memories.

When I reached it, I was completely out of breath and had a stitch in my side. I really needed to exercise more when I got back to Neverra. I bent down and scooped it up. It was as unblemished and glossy as the one from the schoolhouse.

I brought it up to my nose to sniff it when Remo raced across the lobby, bellowing, "Don't eat it!"

I jumped, and the apple almost slid out of my fingers. "I wasn't going to," I mumbled, body vibrating from his yell. Clutching the fruit to my heaving chest, I took a step down.

A great, rattling rumble echoed around me. I thought the sound was coming from my stomach, but I couldn't be *that* hungry, could I? When another boom sounded, I stared out the windows, expecting to find the street darkened and slick from a thunderstorm. Instead, I saw fissures race through the enormous clear panes. Another rumble reverberated through the skyscraper and up my legs.

Aw fae, what now?

"Amara!"

Another loud quake rolled through the city, splintering the stair beneath my boots.

"Amara, the building's breaking apart! Get down here! NOW!"

Heart pinned to my throat, I ran, leaping from one stair to the next. Glass and stone cracked and crashed all around me. I wanted to yell at Remo to run to safety, but my voice couldn't get past my battering heart. If only I could jump the rest of the way down, but I was still much too high.

The stair beneath me gave way, and air replaced the sensation of shaking ground. A cry tore up my throat as I fell, arms flailing to latch on to something solid. I managed to seize the edge of a step, but the momentum of my fall sent a bolt of fire into my elbow and rent a scream from my lungs.

"Amara, let go!"

"I know you want me dead, but I don't want to die like this," I shrieked.

Could I die from a fall, though? Not on Neverra and not on Earth, but back home, when skin tore, it knitted; when bones ached, they mended. Here—I whimpered as the outside tremors breached my body and flowed into my veins.

"If you don't let go, we both die, so fucking let go already!"

The building shuddered, and my hold broke. I squeezed my lids shut, desperately seeking out my fire, even a wisp of it, but my veins were empty, and I tumbled through the air like the doll Nana Vee had made me when I was a baby.

Glass shards tinkled like tossed glitter around me, scratching my skin and poking through my suit. I almost wished a piece would just pierce my heart, because the anticipation of cracking my skull and every bone in my body was beyond horrifying.

I thought of Iba and Nima, prayed they assumed I'd run away. I didn't want them mourning me. And then I thought of Sook and Giya, and how they probably wouldn't stop looking for me if they believed me gone and not dead. I thought of Pappy and of my two favorite nanas. I even thought of Remo, the boy who hated my mother. I hoped he'd make it out of the Scourge and alert Neverrians to Gregor's atrocity.

Suddenly, I stopped falling, and although the landing was brutal, and the entire world around me seemed to be shattering, my body miraculously stayed in one piece.

The smell of sweat and blood hit me, and I wrenched my lids up.

The sight of Remo's tensed face rid me of breath. "You saved me ... again."

Glistening rivulets ran down his brow, and his cheeks puffed with ragged breaths. "Yeah, but not for long if we don't make it out of here."

A stair fell and exploded at his feet, bombarding us with sharp projectiles. Flinging his face to the side, he curled himself around me until the glass pellets stopped coming. And then his attention zipped to the exit, and cradling me against his pounding chest, he took off, zigzagging around the collapsing rubble. I tried to hook my hand around his neck, but a bolt of pain shot through my elbow when I lifted my arm.

I swiveled my head, trying to see around us. We were almost outside.

Almost—

A sharp gurgling cry tore out of Remo's throat, and his body pitched forward, sending me careering toward the road. I rolled and rolled, molars gritting from the knifing pain. The second I stopped, I dug my palms into the ground. The road might've been safer, but the tall buildings were bound to come crashing down over us. My left arm gave way, and I almost toppled back onto my face, but I gritted my teeth and heaved myself onto my good arm and then onto my knees. Slowly, I rose and turned toward Remo.

A scream, louder than the one which had escaped when I'd been pitched off the spiral, surged out of me. I sped toward where he lay and dropped onto my knees as the ground gave another violent shudder, obliterating more of the skyscrapers.

A shard of glass was lodged between his shoulder blades, and a pool of blood darkened the concrete beneath him. I didn't know whether I should pull it out or if that was the exact thing I shouldn't do. Nima would've known. She knew injuries, human and fae alike.

"Remo?" My voice sounded as broken as the world around me. I brought my face closer to his. "Remo, you can't leave me. Hang on. I'll get us to the train."

His lips were open, and yet no breath pulsed against my nose.

"Remo?" I brought my shaky hand to his neck and tried to feel for a pulse, but my fingers were numb and the leather-like material ensconcing them, thick. "Don't leave me," I whispered desperately.

Before my stinging eyes, his body turned gray and then exploded into ash.

"NO!" I hunched over the spot where his body had lain, where only his blood remained, running in rivulets through his ashes and into the fabric of my torn suit. I cried until my voice was hoarse and my eyes burned as violently as my elbow. Even though I welcomed my own death, no glass tore through my vital organs. "Why?" I shrieked at the white sky and the hailing shrapnel, which was probably butchering my face and neck.

I was too numb to feel anything.

Too numb to care.

I rested my torso onto my trembling thighs and my head on the bed of glass. "Why?" I cried. "Why?"

Why did you follow me inside the portal?

Why did I go after the damn apple?

Why didn't you run away when the ground rumbled?

Why did you sacrifice yourself to save me, a girl you hated?

And why does my heart feel as broken as this glass city?

14

THE RUBBLE

The ground stopped shaking at some point. The glass stopped falling. And my tears dried on my chilled cheeks, salting the little wounds.

I'd stopped crying.

I'd also stopped yelling and pounding my fist at the white sky.

I felt empty and crushed, the gashes on my skin as deep as the ones on my heart and mind.

I tried to cradle my smarting arm against me, but my elbow would neither fully bend, nor would it fully extend. It was stuck somewhere in between and throbbing as though my heart had slid into it. I pressed myself up, then stumbled over the grains of glitter like a *lupa* pup. The dome over the chrome train had crumbled too. Unlike the buildings which were only half-ruined, jagged edges gleaming like brandished swords, nothing remained of the station, except for the train.

The train which had led Remo and me to this nightmare of glass and concrete, now the repository of his ashes.

I glared down at the spot still stained by his blood. The viscous puddle blurred, then sharpened like the shard that had snuffed out his life. I bent over and grabbed the murder weapon, and then I

121

hurled it at the wrecked skyscraper, yelling my anger and pain at the top of my lungs. Breathing hard, I surveyed the destruction and then lifted my gaze to the ice garden, my black hair whipping in the relentless breeze. I pushed the strands that weren't clumped together by mud and blood off my face and evaluated the steepness of the mountain. There was no way I could climb it with only one arm. I wasn't even sure there was a way to climb it with two.

I needed to get out of here, back to Frontier Land, because there was nothing in this world except debris and memories that would forever haunt me. I'd never held my breath that our families would make peace, but now that Remo had died because of me—

I shuddered, my lids crimping over my swollen eyes. And then I tilted my face toward the bright sky, wishing sunshine would breach the clouds and sear away my grief.

"Oh, Great Gejaiwe, why?" I croaked. "*Why?*"

My tribe's Great Spirit didn't send any answer. Not that She'd ever talked to me before, but at that moment, I would've given anything to hear Her voice. Or anyone's voice. But who could survive these machiavellian cells? I didn't see how I would. Maybe I'd make it back to Frontier Land and die there. Unless Josh told someone where I was, but that would imply he cared about my welfare, and the Daneelie wasn't known for his selflessness.

I turned and trudged through the wreckage, crunching over the translucent crust, the glare of light hurting my eyes. When I reached the mirrored train platform, I froze. Was that—Was that *me*? I twisted my face from side to side, and the girl with the clumped and snarled black hair, and pallid skin speckled in blood and trails of mascara also turned her face.

I wasn't a vain person, but never had I looked so . . . so . . . I couldn't even find words to describe my appearance. Sickly and unkempt were too weak.

Frightening.

Frightened.

I kneeled to sweep away the shards strewed over the polished metal platform. I'd sensed my face had been hit but hadn't realized how hard. It looked as though I'd rubbed myself against a cheese grater. I removed my right glove with my teeth, then spit it out and patted my chin and the underside of my jaw, picking out pieces of glass. A streak of blood on my neck made my fingers spiral down. I dug out a nail-sized shard and flicked it away.

Again, I thanked the Skies I'd changed out of my dress. Not that this suit would keep me safe in the long run. The seam above my left shoulder had ripped. Lightly I touched the exposed flesh, finding nothing sharp or sticky.

I remained stooped on the mirrored platform, gaping at my slasher-flick doppelganger for a long time. At some point, I spit on my fingers and used the saliva to scrub away the bloody tracks. I wondered if some had belonged to Remo. The thought made my stomach seize, and my temperature drop down to Arctic-levels. I shivered, and the tiny shake sent a bolt of pain into my sore elbow.

Wincing, I sat back on my heels and glanced down at my arm. Was it broken or dislocated? And if I'd dislocated it, how could I set it? How I wished I'd listened to Nima when she'd encouraged me to take the medical course she taught over the summer in NU—Neverra's one and only university. To think I hadn't taken it because she'd taught it, because I'd cared what my peers would say if I earned poor grades, or worse, good ones.

If I got out of the Scourge, I swore to the Skies and Great Spirit that I'd stop caring about what anyone thought of me. My last name might destine me for the throne but that wouldn't be the reason I'd sit on it. I'd sit on it because I'd earn it.

Since moping wouldn't get me anywhere, I squirmed my fingers back into the glove, using my teeth to hold it in place, then rose to my feet and trudged toward the train, cocooning my arm. I tried to flex my elbow again, but the pain almost made my knees buckle. I let out a slew of shocking Gottwa words that I'd picked up from Sook over the years. I wasn't even sure what most of them meant, but they sounded as violent and awful as I felt.

I climbed onto the train and stood in front of the controls. Instead of levers, there were two buttons. One that read—*CLOSE*. The other that read—*START*. That was useful. If I started the train without closing the door, I would probably be ejected in some sort of limbo Scourge. I lowered my finger toward the shiny, domed *CLOSE* button just as a gust of wind whooshed around the metallic doorframe. It sounded like it was whispering *wait*, but the elements didn't talk. Besides, what I would wait for? Another earthquake?

"Amara!"

My hand shook, and the fine hairs on the back of my neck rose. Was my brain so starved for companionship that it had conjured up Remo's voice?

"Wait!"

The word was clearer.

"Amara!"

My fingertip slid off the smooth dome. It wasn't in my head.

Was it like the furniture in the buildings . . . another illusion? Or was his spirit back to haunt me. Gottwas believed in ghosts. I didn't, but I wouldn't put it past Gregor to add some inside his prison. What better way to obliterate his convicts' minds?

"Amara!"

I took a breath before turning around and peeking out the still-open train door. There, amidst the glittery rubble, walked a man who carried himself with the same straight spine as Remo. Who possessed the same proud gait and broad shoulders. When our gazes collided, he stopped walking. His chest heaved. His fingers twitched against his thighs.

He looked so real. "You're not gone." He *sounded* so real. But he couldn't *be* real. He'd died. "You didn't leave," he repeated, this time louder, clearer, stronger. He started up again, his boots crunching through the glass as though they, too, were real.

"Did you come to haunt me?" *Great.* Now I was conversing with dead faerie spirits.

Remo's ghost paused again. "Haunt you?"

"You. Died."

His mouth pressed into a grim line. "You sound angry about it."

"I *am* angry."

"At me?"

"No." I shook my head. "At Gregor. At myself. Not at you."

He advanced toward me again. "Phew."

"You're definitely an illusion, because Real Remo would never say *phew*."

He let out a soft, amused-sounding snort. "And yet I'm real."

"That's impossible. You bled and then exploded into dust!" Not only was I conversing with a ghost, but I was arguing with one. *Oh, Gregor, you're a sick, sick man.*

Remo stood a few feet away from me now, no longer smirking. "I'm guessing what you saw was another illusion."

"It looked *exceedingly* real."

He took a step closer. "Touch me, Amara. Touch me."

"Turn around." *Crack.* There went the last piece of my mind. "Why?"

"If you're real, then you'll have a gash between your shoulder blades, the same way I have cuts everywhere."

Remo's gaze stroked up my face as though just noticing the assortment of wounds I sported. A groove appeared between his brows. Skies, even his frown looked real. Slowly, he pivoted around. So much mud cloaked his back that I couldn't see the cut, but his tunic bore a rip.

Why was I checking for a wound anyway? Like bodiless Unseelies, ghosts were phantoms, the molecules of their flesh and bones as slack as air.

I huffed an annoyed breath and shook my head, trying to clear it of what was evidently a vision.

"What?" asked Remo's ghost.

"I'm chatting with spirits, that's what."

The specter glanced over his shoulder, eyes the same mossy

green as his real ones had been. "Why are you chatting with spirits?"

I cocked an eyebrow, then poked the air, expecting my finger to slide right through Remo's ghost, but it bumped against something solid. I reeled my hand back, the blood draining from my cheeks. "You're not . . . you're not . . . but—"

Remo pivoted to face me.

"How?" I whispered. "How are you not dead? You exploded into ashes. I *saw* you explode."

"Either you can't die in this place, or like I said, my death was an illusion."

"The mud on your tunic. It was on your front. Now it's . . . now it's only on your back. Why? How?"

Remo glanced sideways at the cliff topped with the ice garden. "When I came to, I was lying in the field of mud again."

My forehead grooved, which made the gazillion cuts on it sting. "The one under the portal?"

"Yes."

"Was the portal there?"

He swallowed, and his Adam's apple bobbed sharply. "It was."

"And was it still . . . far?" I wasn't sure why I asked. He'd made it clear earlier that if the portal was within reach, he wouldn't hang around. I was such a glutton for punishment. "You wouldn't be here if it wasn't."

His silence heightened the intensity of his scrutiny.

"We're never getting out of here, are we? At least not without some divine or royal intervention." I sighed, and then I did something so uncharacteristic that Gregor's grandson grew stiff as a *calimbor* . . . I gave the faerie a one-armed hug. "You might not believe this"—I inhaled the musky, mineral scent at the hollow of his collarbone—"but I'm glad you're alive."

He didn't hug me back. Didn't even pat my shoulder. "That is . . . hard to believe."

I absorbed his body's heat a moment longer before paring myself away. "Just as hard to believe as you saving my life."

"How is that difficult to comprehend?"

I raised an eyebrow.

"I obviously would rather be in bad company than alone."

Ouch. Supporting my aching arm with my gloved hand, I turned away from him and stepped back into the train. "We should get going," I said coolly.

He didn't move off the platform, and although I kept my gaze affixed to the *CLOSE* button, I sensed his eyes scraping across my profile.

Bad company. Because his company was oh-so-awesome. "In one second, your *bad company* will be on her way someplace else."

From the corner of my eye, I saw his brow twitch.

"Now or never." I rested the tip of my index finger atop the button.

Eyes still duct-taped to my face, he climbed aboard. "Amara..."

I pressed the button, and the doors snapped shut. His mouth, too. And then I pressed the second button and sat on the bench before the rattling carriage could break or dislocate another part of my beat-up body.

15

THE INN

During the entire magical train ride, I kept my lids cinched tight in exhaustion, in pain, and in annoyance. My bones rattled, awakening bruises I didn't even know I had—in my ankles, thighs, and abdomen. As for my elbow . . . the pain there was so raw it made sweat bead along my hairline and drip down the column of my neck.

"What's wrong with your arm?" Remo asked once the train stilled. "Is it broken?"

I tried to see if we were back in Frontier Land, but the windows were still obscured. "It feels like it might be."

He held out of his palm. "Let me see it."

When I made no move to show him my arm, he sighed and hoisted it up. I winced and tried to pull it away, but that simply angered the throbbing.

"Your elbow's swollen." His fingers trekked down to my wrist just as the train door let out a short squeal and slid open.

There was no brick station and no *lupa*, which meant we'd landed in another cell. Awesome. Just awesome. I couldn't wait to see what this one had in store for us.

"So, do we have a welcoming committee? Rabid wolves? Mutant mice?" Remo asked.

The only thing in my line of sight was a red bench and the white corner of a big sign painted with block letters. I made out an A and N.

"Is the sky still white?"

Pain radiated up my forearm. I shot my gaze back to my hand, which Remo had twisted so that my palm faced up.

"So? Is it?"

My breaths came out in ragged spurts. "What?"

"The sky? Is it white?"

I glanced outside. "Yes, it's—"

Remo thrust my hand toward my shoulder, and something popped. I screeched, snatching my arm out of his grasp. Breathing hard, I cradled my elbow against me. "What the hell's wrong with you?"

"You should be able to move it now." He dusted his hands together as though he'd just accomplished some filthy task and stepped off the train.

I sat there, stunned, and then I licked the sweat off my lips and eased my sore arm away from my chest. My range of movement had indeed returned, but Skies damn it, the pain was excruciating.

"You're going to have to lay off it for a while. We don't seem to heal as fast here."

I finally got up and, on legs that felt devoid of bones, walked off the train that was bulbous, with a silver body and red stripes, sleek but not quite as modern as the last one we'd been on. "You healed awfully quickly for a dead person."

Remo bobbed his head. "I suppose you could try to die and come back."

"Wouldn't you just love that? Especially if I didn't come back."

A sigh broadened his torso.

Before he could tell me again how he'd prefer bad company to no company, I read the word on the white sign out loud: "Rowan."

My eyes snapped so wide so fast my lashes knocked into my eyebrows. I sidestepped Remo and then trundled down a few metal stairs, boots clanking. I speed-walked down the sidewalk lining the station and came to an abrupt halt at the apex of a street lined with squat trees budding with new leaves, white-picket fences, and wooden boxes on poles. Metal numbers adorned their sides as well as an articulated red arm. Were those mailboxes? Clearly we'd gone back a century, since, nowadays, mail was beamed.

"Is this supposed to be Morgan Street?" I hadn't realized Remo was standing next to me until he spoke.

Morgan Street was Rowan's main street. Although I'd visited my maternal family's birthplace over the years, had fished in the Great Lakes with Pappy, and had wandered through my family's grave-yard with Nima, I'd never known it to look this way—alternating two-storied, pastel-painted houses and squat brick buildings—but perhaps, when Gregor and Linus established their prison, this was how Rowan had looked.

Shop awnings poked from the quaint buildings. One in partic-ular caught my eye—BEE'S PLACE. Nima and Neenee Cass had talked so often about it that even though it no longer existed in today's Rowan, it felt familiar.

Relief flooded me. Dread would've been more appropriate, because this town could be nothing like the real one I held dear to my heart and would tarnish its memory. Goosebumps sprouted over my skin even though it wasn't cold here. At least there was that.

Hugging myself, I asked, "You think everything will be fake here again?"

"Only one way to find out." He started walking.

The first building was made of red brick and read COUNTY JAIL. Remo pulled the door open, and we went in. There were desks, and behind them, a bulky metal door. Neat stacks of papers laid on the desks next to huge square gray things. I tried poking one but nothing happened. "What are these supposed to be?"

"Computers."

I blinked back toward the enormous box made of plastic and black glass. "You mean, like Holo-Screens?"

Remo twisted the knob on the metal door, and it opened with a beep. "Yeah." He stared into a dim corridor lined with metal grates.

"Jail cells?" I asked.

He nodded.

"Anyone in there?"

"Not that I can see."

He let the door go, and it clanged shut, and then he walked to the desk and slid open a drawer. It rolled right out, and objects rattled inside. Even though this world looked kinder than the last two, I sensed it was a front to lull us into a false sense of security. Evil undoubtedly lurked here, lying in wait like a *tigri*.

I leaned over a stack of papers and thumbed through them until I found a folder labeled Cruz Vega. My eyes widened. Was this the same Cruz Vega who'd helped Iba and Nima liberate Neverra and who'd died to save Neenee's life? The one who'd brought Pappy back to life after Stella had slit his throat? The fallen hero we paid our respects to each year on the anniversary of his death?

I flipped open the file and flicked through it until I came upon a mugshot of a handsome man with black hair and green eyes, the very same man Iba had a picture of in his office. Although I was grateful he'd sacrificed himself to allow my aunt back into Neverra, a piece of me had always wished he could've found a way to survive.

"What did you find?" Remo asked, spinning a pen he must've picked up in the drawer.

"Unless this is part of the decor, Cruz Vega seems to have been arrested for"—I skimmed the file until I found a sloppily hand-written note—"murdering and impersonating a medical examiner." I scanned the rest of the page, my gaze widening when I caught the bailee's name and signature. My father's. "Think this is real?"

Remo approached and peered over my shoulder. "Maybe. Too bad your dad can't bail *us* out of here."

"That would be convenient." I scraped my hair back and studied Cruz's picture again. The fae had been male-model gorgeous, not to mention kind, generous, intelligent, and selfless. If he'd survived and had been my age, or around my age, I would've fallen head-over-heels for him.

"You have some drool on your chin."

I lifted my gaze off the picture and set it on the fae who had, unfortunately, survived. "Funny."

He obviously thought it was funny since he was smirking. "While you were staring at the dead fae, I took inventory of the place, and besides this pen"—he twirled it again between his fingers—"there's nothing here."

I wanted to take the file with me, as a sort of memento for Nima and Iba, but had no bag and didn't want souvenirs of this place. Besides, this was all fake, or deepfakes, so it would probably not survive transportation through the portal. I set the file down and walked over to the door Remo propped open.

"After you, Trifecta."

Oh . . . the horrid nickname. "Why do the good men die but the bad ones persist?" I asked as I brushed past him.

"Just because he died heroically doesn't mean he was a good man."

"I beg to differ. That's exactly what it means."

"Then according to your logic, that makes me a good man."

I stopped walking and whirled to face him. Although the back of his body was coated in mud, his front was surprisingly clean and devoid of scrapes. "How does that make you a good man, Remo?"

"Well." He clicked the top of his pen, sliding the ink tip out, then clicked again, sliding the tip back in. "I saved you from breaking your neck in the last cell and died doing it."

"Except you didn't die."

"I beg to differ." He clicked his pen again. "I came back to life, but I most definitely died."

Even though he did have a point, calling me *bad company* canceled out any heroic act. "If you want to be a hero, stay dead next time."

He shot me a lopsided grin. "But then you'd be awfully lonely."

"Unlike you, I'd rather be alone than in *bad* company." I took off toward the next building, the one sandwiched between Bee's Place and the jail—a mint-green two-story house that read ANGEL SPA.

"You seem awfully bitter I called you bad company."

I spun around. "Was it supposed to be a compliment?"

His eyes darkened. I waited a couple seconds for him to apologize. When no apology came, I turned back toward the spa and shoved the door open. The bell over the door tinkled. I inhaled, expecting the scent of warmed candle wax and exotic oils. All I got was dry plaster and musty air. Glass jars lined the walls, but all were empty. I went up a set of carpeted stairs that creaked underfoot. The small landing gave onto three rooms—two had massage tables and empty cupboards, one had a small iridescent-tiled bathroom. Excitement tore through me at the sight of the sink. I twisted both the hot and cold knobs, but lo and behold, not even a rusty trickle spurted out. I turned to the toilet and lifted the lid to find the bowl as dry as the back of my mouth. *Damn.*

"Anything useful upstairs?" Remo called out.

Even though the massage tables were padded and thus looked relatively comfortable, we needed water and there was none. "Unfortunately not."

He looked up the stairwell.

"If you don't trust me, go check."

He returned his gaze to me. "I trust you."

"*Huh.* A Farrow trusting a Wood. That must surely be a first."

His jaw ticked as though he were working really hard to bite back a retort.

I pushed past him out the door, then walked toward the next

establishment—Bee's Place. Instead of barreling inside, I backed up into the road to take in the two-story brick inn with its big picture window. This place contained so much history that it somehow felt sacred. I had to remind myself that this wasn't the real Bee's Place. Just a pretty copy placed in a parallel universe. Still, my heart held steady as I crossed back toward it and pressed my fingertips into the glass door.

I froze on the threshold, the aroma of something sweet and flaky wafting into me. "Do you smell that?" I whispered, stepping inside.

Remo's nostrils flared. When his pupils dilated, I surmised the fragrance wasn't imaginary.

The glass door clapped shut behind us, and I jumped, but then I sniffed the air again and tracked the scent like a *lupa*. My nose led me to a square opening built into a wall beside a varnished bar. I peered inside, making out the gleam of metal countertops and the shine of upside-down pots—a kitchen!

Even though I could climb through the opening, I strode along the wall on the lookout for a door, stomach twisting in anticipation. The second I spotted it, I looked for a handle but found none. Remo, who'd trailed me down the dim hallway, pressed his palm into the wood, and the door swung on its hinges.

"I was about to do that," I said.

He shot me his usual arrogant smirk, the one that touted: *I am so much smarter than you.*

Instead of sinking to his level, I notched up my chin and entered the dim space that smelled so sweet, licking the air would surely candy my tongue. My nose guided me toward a large metal and glass box glowing with a light that enveloped the edges of a bubbling golden pie. I latched onto a long handle and tugged. A burst of hot air shot into my face. I was about to reach inside for the pan when Remo's voice stilled my hand.

"You're going to burn yourself."

"Burn myself? I'm made of fire."

I stuck my hand inside and grabbed the pan. Even through the glove, the heat of the metal scorched me. I didn't let go even though it felt like the material was melting and adhering to my skin. I all but tossed the pan onto the center island.

"You burned yourself, didn't you?" Remo followed the downward trajectory of my hand.

"Nope." My cheeks flamed, though. Hopefully, the obscurity would hide my blush.

He crossed the kitchen toward a sink and turned the knob. I was expecting it to be dry, but there was a groan followed by a familiar splash that made my heart catch and my throat tighten. I strode over to him so fast I thought I'd regained my Hunter speed. Remo didn't scoop out any water; he simply watched it fall. I grabbed a bowl from a shelf and shoved it underneath, terrified this was a fluke and any second the pipes would run dry.

I pulled off my gloves and laid them on the counter. My fingertips had reddened but thankfully not blistered. Although they felt funny—a little plasticky—I didn't complain, knowing Remo would get a kick out of my predicament.

I lifted the bowl out and carefully placed it aside. Then I cupped my hands and filled them with the water coming out of the spigot.

"Amara, maybe—"

The warning Remo had been about to utter died on his lips as I splashed the water on my face—a shot of pure bliss. I repeated the motion. The water dripping off my chin was laced with blood, yellow mud, and the remnants of my makeup.

"It's real." I grinned up at Remo. "Real water."

Remo's expression was as tight as the line of his shoulders, and the rest of his body, for that matter. When he didn't make any move to scoop some out, I tossed some in his face. He sputtered and spit as though I'd just lobbed toxic waste at him.

I laughed. "Relax. It didn't melt your skin off."

He grumbled something as he wiped his forehead on his sleeve.

I grabbed a glass off a shelf and filled it, and then I gulped down the contents hungrily. I felt like laughing again. Simple pleasures. I filled up the glass and fit it into Remo's hands. He reluctantly closed his fingers around the slick surface and then stared at it so long that I rolled my eyes. "I'm not dead."

"Yet."

My pulse quickened at that single word, and then my exhilaration waned. Would the water poison me? After what felt like an hour but was surely no more than a handful of seconds, Remo gave in and tipped the glass to his mouth, his Adam's apple bobbing as he drained it.

Once empty, he set the glass down and wiped his lips on the back of his hand. "At least, if we die, we'll die together."

"How romantic." I rolled my eyes and circled the island to reach the peach pie. I broke off a piece of crust and placed it inside my mouth. The flaky dough melted on my tongue and slid down my throat. I hummed in contentment, then broke off another piece, and another, thanking the Great Spirit for the offering. Maybe She hadn't had a hand in it, but regardless, thanking Her couldn't hurt.

"That good, huh?" Remo was watching me from across the island.

I pinched a gooey peach and laid it on my tongue. The explosion of flavors made my entire body quiver. "The best I've ever eaten." I pushed the pan toward him, metal scraping against metal.

He crossed his arms, making no move to tear off a piece of the divine dessert. "And it doesn't worry you that it was somehow baking when we walked in?"

My vertebrae jammed together as I swallowed the lump of peach. I raised my head higher, straining to hear any footfalls on the floor above before deciding that whoever could bake so well was not my enemy. Of course, this led me to a lightbulb moment.

"We aren't alone," I murmured in wonder.

Remo neither nodded nor shook his head. He watched the pie

and then he watched the oven behind me. "Did you turn the oven off?"

The oven? Of course, the oven. That was the name of the box from which I'd taken the pie. I swung around. The glass no longer glowed. "Could it have turned off automatically?"

He sighed and came around my side of the island. He popped the door down. Neither hot air nor light drifted out of the cooking box this time. "Maybe. Some of these had built-in timers."

"How do you know so much about ovens? Are antiquated electronics a prerequisite curriculum for becoming a *lucionaga*?"

A corner of his mouth curled. "Surprisingly, no. I learned about them through Mom. She used to run the bakery in this town."

Right. "What was it called again?"

"Astra's, but it's not on this street. It's by the harbor, and since these cells seem built on single streets, I don't think Grandfather included it."

I stretched and pulled the pan back toward me to snatch off another piece. Remo watched me eat. If he'd been a friend, I might've force-fed him, if only to prove how delectable it was, but he wasn't a friend. For all I cared, he could starve himself. More pie for me. I hummed around the bite of food.

"I was thinking of something . . ." Remo said.

"You? Think?"

He squeezed one of his eyes a little shut.

"Lighten up. I was just teasing you. I might not like you, but I know you're smart."

Even though only a trickle of daylight streamed over Remo's face, I caught his cheeks reddening. Was he not used to compliments? I was pretty sure he was praised every day of his life by his friends, family, and harem of women.

"So? What were you thinking?"

The big firefly's chest rose and fell a few times before he finally managed to squeeze out his answer. "I was thinking about Karsyn's dust."

I narrowed my eyes, wondering where he was going with this.

He nodded to my hand, to the dark whorls that stained my left palm and wrapped around each one of my fingers. "It's still on your hand."

"It is," I said slowly.

"Can you pull it out and use it like your mother?"

I dropped my gaze to my tattoo. "I don't know. I've never magnetized dust before." I wasn't even sure I knew how to get it out. I dug through my memories, trying to remember if I'd ever seen my mother do it, but couldn't think of a single time. She was always so cautious about her trapped dusts. Yes, plural. She hadn't only taken ownership of Remo's grandmother's dust. On the Day of Mist, she'd magnetized another Seelie's *wita*, and since he'd died after attacking her, it had become hers. Which wasn't usually the case, but Nima was unusual. Almost as unusual as I was.

"Never?"

I gnawed on my bottom lip.

The fact that I didn't have the slightest clue how to coax it from my skin must've shown on my face, because Remo asked, "So you don't know how to use it, do you?"

I shook my head.

He rolled his neck from side to side. There was a series of little pops. "Can't believe I'm about to teach you how to wield a weapon you could use on me—"

"Stop it."

"Stop what?"

"If I wanted you dead, you'd be dead. The same way that if you wanted me dead, I'd be dead." I leaned my hip against the cool island. "And I don't mean in this world, since death doesn't seem to be final."

He stared at me for a long time, as though dissecting my words, trying to find one that didn't ring true. "I saw your mother use it. She touched her tattoo, then slowly dragged her hand away, and the *wita* clung to her fingertips."

"When did you see her using it?" I wasn't jealous, but I was surprised *he*, of all people, had had a demonstration.

"In the elevator. It was one of my . . . *visions*."

Oh.

"She was arguing with Mom. It must've been right around the time she found out about what happened to my grandmother because she was asking your mother if it was true. If she'd really killed Stella."

"Is this the part when you tell me my mother brought out her dust to gas yours?"

He shot me a remarkable glare before averting his gaze and rubbing his earlobe. "Actually, it was my mother who brought out her *wita*." He said this so quietly I thought I misheard him. "Your mom stepped back and clutched her neck, yelling at mine to stop. That she didn't want it to come to this. My mother didn't put it away, so your mother brought hers out and crafted some sort of shield." His eyes seemed slightly unfocused, as though he was standing in the same room as our feuding mothers. "Your dad arrived then, shouted at my mother, threatening to throw her out of Neverra, and then grabbed yours and flew out of the *calimbor*."

If only Gregor hadn't opened his big mouth and blabbed to Faith that Nima had murdered his former flame. He insisted the information had slipped out, that he hadn't meant to cause a rift between my mother and Remo's. Though knowing the *wariff*'s fondness to have a finger in every pie, I betted his oversharing hadn't been accidental.

"It's hard to believe our mothers were friends, isn't it?" I kept expecting to see a younger version of Nima strut down Morgan Street. "It's sad that your mother can't forgive mine for the accident."

He stared to the side again, played with his lobe again.

"No: *It wasn't an accident, Trifecta*."

The vein under his birthmark throbbed.

"Gejaiwe . . . have you finally seen the light?"

He snapped his eyes back to mine. "What I saw was a scene that might've been fabricated for all I understand of this place!"

I crossed my arms. "Trust me, if you witnessed me calling your eyes poison-green and using flowery descriptors for your personality, everything you observed was very factual. As factual as everything I observed."

He gave his jaw a workout. "Except your grandfather's awfully lively for a dead person."

A growl vibrated at the back of my throat. "Because Cruz Vega brought him back to life."

"Your little hero."

My blood heated so fast I thought my fire might've come back, but when I tried to produce flames to char off Remo's eyebrows—apparently, I was spiteful like that—no fire lit up my tattooed palm, or my untattooed one. "What is your problem with him?"

"My problem is that everyone's so obsessed with him. He didn't single-handedly save Neverra. My grandfather was right there, helping him."

"Aw. Are you lacking recognition?"

"I don't give a shit about recognition, Trifecta."

I glowered at him, and he glowered right back. I tried to reconcile my heart breaking over his death with the way my heart felt at the moment. I wasn't sure how long we glared, but I suspected the pie was now as cold as the world we'd left behind.

I pushed off the island and shook my head. "Your family's so blinded by hatred for mine that you guys wouldn't see the truth if it smacked you in the face."

Remo pressed his lips together, almost making them vanish. Unlike mine, which took up way too much space on my face, his lips were on the thin side.

"And it *did* smack you in the face. And you still refuse to believe it."

I strode toward the swing door when he said, "My brother's dust. Can you use it?"

Even though I didn't feel like giving him an answer, I did feel like knowing, so I swept my fingertips to the sapphire whorls on my palm. Slowly, I tugged my hands apart.

Between them stretched three twinkling, golden strands. Their presence beamed some light onto my dark mood. I stared at them in awe and then in fear. What if I pulled the *wita* out completely, and it didn't return into my palm? The thought made my hands jerk away from each other. The ribbons of dust shriveled before slipping back underneath my skin.

Remo's sigh was audible. "Never thought I'd be glad that my brother attacked you."

I sought out the trapped dust again, stretching it out, before pressing it back into my palm like an accordion. I even began to shape it, managing to turn it into a rose, thorns and all. The flower bobbed in midair, resembling a real one, feeling like a real one, its petals velvet-soft.

I traced the edge of a green leaf. "You're such a hypocrite."

"A hypocrite?"

"You might not have wanted him to kill me, but I bet you enjoyed the show."

"If I'd enjoyed the show, I would've sat back and watched it play out. I wouldn't have intervened."

He'd only intervened so his brother wasn't offed on the spot. Instead of sharing my theory, I asked another question that had been on my mind. "Why did you say you pitied the man who'd stand beside me the next time the Cauldron showed up?"

A beat of silence stretched like *wita* between us. "Because I'm no fool, Amara. I know you're not planning on marrying me. And just so you know, you don't have to use your *gajoï* to get me away from you; I wasn't planning on going through with the charade."

I trusted he didn't want to plait his essence with mine, but *not wanting* and *doing* were two very different things.

"You think I'm lying." Not a question.

"I think I'll save my *gajoï* in case you don't feel like standing up to your granddaddy." The rose's petals fluttered as I spoke. I wrapped my fingers around the stem and squeezed it until the dust liquefied and retreated into my palm, then tipped my head toward the gloves on the sink top. "Your gloves. I hope I didn't ruin them when I took out the pie."

"They won't fit me anymore. Our hands aren't exactly the same size, and I doubt the fabric is adaptable in this place." He didn't make any move to retrieve them. He didn't make any move at all. He stood there like a giant piece of scowling granite.

I walked toward the gloves and picked them up. They'd kept my hands from getting sliced up in Deception Central and had proved a useful barrier against the cold. As I slid them back on, being all out of pockets, I cast a longing look at my Infinity. How I wished I could change out of my dirty jumpsuit. My gaze snagged on the bowl I'd filled. Although there was no soap on the countertop, water would get most of the dirt out, but doing laundry implied getting naked, which I obviously wasn't about to do in front of Remo.

I tipped my head toward the upper floor. "Shall we see what's upstairs?" *Or who...?*

The moody faerie finally shoved away from the island and lumbered over to me. "You shouldn't cover your tattoo."

In other words, what lay upstairs might go bump. *Ugh.* This prison sucked so much. "I don't have a bag or pockets."

With a sigh, Remo held out his palm. "I'll carry them."

My gaze slid down his mud-splattered tunic. "You don't have any pockets either."

"No, but I have a waistband." He hiked up his top, and the thin stream of daylight coming through the window edged the taut skin stretching over a neat stack of abdominal muscles.

Why was I stunned to discover the boy had a six-pack? *All lucionaga* had abs.

"Amara?"

I jerked my gaze off his stomach.

"The gloves."

I pulled them back off and dropped them into his open palm, careful not to graze his hand.

"Make a knife."

Fear slinked up my spine.

As he slid the gloves into his waistband, he added, "As a precaution." Was he trying to reassure me?

Swallowing, I touched my tattoo, hooking the threads. Unfortunately, I started trembling, and the threads snapped right back into my palm. I tried again. Failed again.

"Calm down."

"I'm trying." I tried again, and again, and again. At some point, I rolled my fingers into my palms and squeezed them until my nails bit into the dark whorls.

"Can I try something?" Remo asked.

I nodded warily.

He picked up my wrist from where it dangled at my side. "Open your palm."

Biting the inside of my cheek, I did as he asked. He pressed calloused fingertips against the trapped dust. Was he trying to extricate it?

"I don't think—" My dust seemed to rear in its tracks and pulse harder, wiping away my conviction *and* the end of my sentence. "It's responding to you," I whispered, stunned and worried that if I spoke any louder, it would scare off my dust. Not that dust was skittish, but maybe confiscated dust was . . .

Remo's eyebrows dipped in concentration. Slowly, he raised his fingers. Considering how strongly my palm tingled, I expected to see golden ribbons unspool.

But I was wrong.

The air between our hands stayed still and dark.

16

STANDARDS

"It was worth a try," Remo sighed as he pulled his hand back to his side.

I slid my lower lip through my teeth, partly relieved my dust couldn't be manipulated by another fae and partly confused as to why it was still swishing around in its tracks like a school of minnows. "It responded to your touch."

"That wasn't the dust, Amara."

I cranked my head up so fast my neck cracked. "What else could it have been?"

His eyes glowed like faceted emeralds. "Your pulse."

"My pulse? Why would my pulse respond to you? I'm not afraid of you."

The corners of his lips ticked up.

"I'm *not*," I said, stressing the *not* part.

"Well if it isn't fear, then that leaves attraction."

Like a wave, the blood drained from my face before flooding right back inside. "I'm definitely *not* attracted to you. I have standards."

The intensity of his smile turned up. "Oh yeah?"

"Yeah." Blood still pounded in my veins, but for a completely different reason now.

He was still smiling. "And what are those standards of yours?"

"Kindness."

"I'm kind."

"Not to me you aren't."

I didn't think his smile could get any wider, but it did.

"Humble."

Still smirking, he folded his arms, which somehow made his chest appear broader.

"Not redheads."

His smirk intensified.

"And not of Farrow descent."

"So, just not me?" He dipped his chin into his neck, grin intact. "Aren't you going to ask me about my standards?"

"I didn't think you had any."

His mouth unlatched, and he laughed, a deep throaty sound that made my already rapid pulse strike my neck harder.

I crossed my arms, matching his stance. "Fine. Tell me. What type of girl gets an invitation into your harem?"

He sobered up. "My harem?"

"Back in the Duciba, your grandfather mentioned you needed to break up with *all* your girlfriends."

"Right." Color crawled along the edge of his jaw. He rubbed his chin, as though trying to rub the blush out.

"So, Remo Farrow, what are your standards? Besides busty blondes."

His head jerked back, and his hand fell away from his chin. "Busty blondes? What on Neverra are you talking about?"

"Lydia." I wrinkled my nose at the memory of the waitress who'd all but thrown herself at Remo. "I think she drooled on my wine orb at our engagement revel."

"Lydia's a sweet girl, but nothing more."

I racked my mind for other women I'd seen Remo out and

about with but couldn't come up with any. "Have you ever dated anyone?"

"Dating isn't my style."

"What *is* your style?"

"No strings—or Cauldron—attached."

I bobbed my head. "Commitment-phobic, then?"

"It's not a phobia; it's a life choice."

I bobbed my head some more, not in understanding. On the contrary, I didn't understand his life choice at all. I'd always wanted what my parents had.

"Dating isn't your style either, is it?"

I stopped nodding. "Why would you assume that?"

"Because I've never seen you out with the same guy twice. Well, besides your cousin, but you're not dating him. Are you?"

"Um, *yuck*. And my not-dating isn't by choice."

He frowned.

"I'd like to have a boyfriend, but I have trouble relating to human men, and fae ones"—I lifted the hair off my neck and twisted it into a long rope . . . well, this was a weird conversation—"find me intimidating."

"Intimidating?"

"I know *you* don't think I'm intimidating, but my dust scares Unseelies, and my blood scares Seelies off, thanks to you."

He neither flinched nor apologized for his nasty rumor.

"And Daneelies, well there aren't many of them, and they're sort of a sect. They don't mix."

"Josh looked plenty happy to be around you."

"Not that I was ever attracted to him, but now that he sent me here"—I gestured to the kitchen even though I obviously meant the world outside this kitchen—"he's really at the bottom of my list of potential candidates."

His arms loosened from their tight knot. "Good. Because he's a scumbag." He turned and pushed open the flap door, then held it open for me to step through. "If we ever get out of here, I'll introduce you to a couple of guys who'd give up their dust to go out with you. And the only reason they haven't asked you on a date is because you're way out of their league, not because they're scared you'll inadvertently poison them with your blood."

I whirled around, and Remo bumped into me.

"Really?" I didn't even try to tamp down my enthusiasm even though the last thing I wanted was for Remo to think I was desperate.

Studying my parted lips and wide eyes, he said, "Really. Now can you create a sword or something useful out of Karsyn's dust, so we have a chance of getting *back* to Neverra?"

It was silly but knowing someone—several someones—wanted to date me steadied my hands. Not only did my *wita* respond this time, but I made one hell of a weapon—a dagger so sharp its tip gleamed lethally.

"A little motivation goes a long way," I said proudly.

"I see that." He shot me a wry grin, that instead of being cold, calculating, or disdainful, seemed genuine.

And sort of sweet.

I frowned because I didn't think Remo was capable of sweet.

He ticked his head toward the upper floor, and I lowered my dagger to my thigh, then followed him up the flight of stairs that creaked like old bones. The hallway on the landing was wide but dark. Still I could make out several doors. From the metal numbers nailed to each one, I was guessing this was where travelers spent the night back in the real inn.

Was one of these bedrooms presently occupied by the pie-baking person?

"Can you trade your butter knife for a gun?" Remo murmured.

I gaped at my dagger, then at him. "It's not a butter knife."

His expression, which had softened during our conversation in the hallway, narrowed again. "Well, can you turn it into a deadlier weapon?"

"Say please."

"Excuse me?"

"Asking nicely won't injure your masculinity."

He snorted, but his mouth curved. "Please, oh great Amara Wood, can you make a scary weapon out of your"—he gestured to my knife again—"what's it supposed to be?"

"A dagger."

He smiled, and I swore that for a minute, I felt like I was hanging out with Sook. "Can you turn your stunted dagger into a gun, *please*?"

"Stunted." I shook my head in indignation but squeezed my weapon's handle. A moment later, the blade transformed into a gun barrel, the rounded cylinder gleaming wickedly.

Side by side, we walked toward the first door. I raised my fist to knock, but Remo caught it before my knuckles could graze the wood.

"Why don't you hum them a little tune while you're at it?"

I glowered at him. "Surprising people isn't sm—" The *-art* died in my throat when Remo flung the door open.

I clapped my free hand on the gun's grip and swung my arms, directing the muzzle toward the bedroom. No one shrieked or raised their arms, because there was no occupant. The bed was done up with a flowery bedspread tucked around fluffy pillows, and the dresser surface was empty save for a white crocheted doily. Nana Vee was a huge fan of doilies and tried to teach me how to make them, but crocheting wasn't for me.

Remo ventured into an en suite bathroom. He flicked up the light switch, and although I didn't expect any bulbs to flare to life, the ceiling lights buzzed and flooded the white-tiled space. He thrust open the shower curtain, and I gasped. Tiny bottles of soap crowded a wire mesh holder. I shoved my gun into Remo's hands and unscrewed the lid off one of the bottles, almost purring when the scent of sun-warmed honeysuckle hit me.

I swung around toward him. "I call dibs on the shower."

"How about we go check out the rest of the place before you bathe?" He extended the weapon.

I eyed it, then eyed him, and it hit me that I trusted him. "You can keep it. For now."

His pupils pulsed in surprise.

"It's a better weapon than your pen," I added a touch mockingly.

As he trailed me back into the hallway, he said, "You'd be surprised the damage you could inflict with a well-placed pen."

I grimaced.

A light switch on the wall caught my attention, and I flipped it. When it flooded the dark space, I sighed. Audibly. Bee's Place felt like the eye of the storm, and I was planning on taking full advantage of the calm and comfort. We could even use it as our base while we built something to reach the portal.

As Remo opened the door to yet another empty bedroom, I spun to face him, which made him jerk the gun down and grumble, "Do you have a death wish?"

I rolled my eyes. "My own dust can't kill me."

He popped an eyebrow. "Except it isn't *your* dust."

I sucked in some air. Even though it felt like mine, he was right . . . it wasn't. How could it have slipped my mind? "For the time being, and quite possibly forever if we don't find a way out of here, it's mine." I didn't add that he was probably right about the killing-me part, because Remo Farrow didn't need any more strokes to the ego. "Which brings me back to what I was about to tell you. I was thinking that I could make a rope with it."

A groove furrowed his brow.

"To hook onto the portal."

His eyes widened, but then his tangible surprise vanished underneath a layer of caution. "First we'd need to scale the cliff, and it looked even steeper than in the last cell."

"I could make a tool out of my dust to help with that. A pick or something."

He bobbed his head. "We could try."

"After my bath."

"After your bath."

"Won't you take one?"

"Possibly. But first, I want to meet the person who baked the pie."

Hope had filed the baker into a recess of my brain. Sighing, I shadowed Remo as we entered the remaining bedrooms. All were unoccupied. The beds were made, and the bathrooms fully functional. On the way out of the last one, the largest on the floor, a wall of framed pictures caught my attention.

After we'd ascertained the bedroom was empty, I stepped closer to the still shots, unhooked one, and lifted it. Two women stood in front of the inn, one old, one Nima's age. Their eyes were squinted as though the sun was particularly bright. The younger one had her arm around the older one's shoulders, and her straight black hair was blowing sideways.

"I think that's my grandmother."

Remo frowned. "Milly?"

"No. The one who died when Gwenelda rose from her grave. Nima's birth mother."

From the stories Pappy and Nima regaled me with, I felt like I'd known Nova, the woman who'd cried during every showing of *Titanic* even though she knew how it ended; the friend who'd taken meticulous care of others, whether alive or dead (she'd been the town embalmer); the mother who'd painted the door to the basement morgue yellow so her daughter wouldn't look upon it with fear.

I also felt like I knew her thanks to Gwen. Giya and Sook's aunt still carried my grandmother's mind and memories within her. Although she didn't share them often, or freely, from time to time, over a tribal ritual that brought our families together, a reminiscence would trickle off Gwen's tongue, and I would lap it right up. If Pappy was in the vicinity when this happened, his lanky chest would swell with sorrow, which prompted Gwen to apologize, even though he always insisted it was a gift.

When I was younger, I always wondered if this made Nana Em jealous; after all, Pappy had never stopped loving his first wife. One day, while we were tending to the pink *drosas,* which had not only taken residence on one of her house's walls but crawled all over her roof, I found the courage to ask her. She'd set down her watering can, brushed my hair back, and said that it didn't make her jealous, that Pappy's fond recollections made her feel lucky.

Lucky? I'd asked her.

Lucky that such a good man decided I was worthy of his heart.

Neither one of my grandparents had magical brands on their hands or supernatural power in their veins, and yet they'd found true love. Perhaps I shouldn't discard the companionship of human men. Perhaps I should travel to Earth when we returned to Neverra and try harder to meet someone. Someone as good and kind as Pappy.

I replaced the picture on the little hook. "I wish I'd known my grandmother."

"I wish I'd known mine, too."

Even though Stella Sakar's fate wasn't my fault, guilt momentarily nipped at my conscience.

"Who knew we had anything in common, huh, Trifecta?" The tangible blame, coupled with the hateful nickname, eased my conscience.

I took my gun back and walked out, rewarding his malicious baiting with glacial silence.

"I was just stating a fact." He could choke on his facts.

"I think the inn has a basement. Good thing you still have that nifty pen," I called out before shutting myself inside the first bedroom.

I leaned against the door, half expecting him to grumble something about my family being a bunch of murderers before stomping down the stairs and out the inn.

Oh, Skies, what if he returned to the train and left me alone in this world?

I rushed to the window, but it gave onto a side alley, not the front door. I squeezed the gun, vanquishing its solid shape.

I didn't need Remo. I had dust *and* running water. And pie.

I'd survive just fine on my own.

17

THE BATHROBE

I drew myself a bath, kicked off my boots, then sank into it fully clothed. Dried blood and mud darkened the water, but I didn't drain it. I soaked inside without moving until the water became unpleasantly cold, then I sat up and scrubbed my suit with a handful of soap, before peeling it off my bruised body, being extra careful with my tender arm. How I missed the digital application and removal of clothing. So much simpler than getting dressed and undressed.

Casting a longing glance at my Infinity, wishing it would reactivate, I slung my suit over the shower rail. Droplets beaded out of the black fabric, plinking into the muddy bath. Even though I worried about draining the pipes, my long hair didn't feel clean yet, and neither did my body, so I turned on the shower head and lathered myself from top to bottom a second time.

My skin didn't morph into tiny copper scales here; didn't even glimmer like it did on Earth. How very strange . . .

What sort of dark magic blocked out fae powers? And could this magic be wielded on Neverra? I hoped that was impossible, because it would destroy our world.

When my black hair slid through my fingers like silk, I turned the tap off and stepped onto the cold tiles. For some reason, probably because the inn's amenities had made me forget where I was, I expected the water to steam off my skin and hair. Instead, a chill skittered over my fire-less body, and I shivered. I searched the bathroom for a towel, but all the racks were bare. *Damn.* I opened the door and tracked wet footprints over the white tiles and then over the navy runner.

Just as I remembered I could fashion a towel from my *wita*, I spotted a bathrobe laid out on my bed. *Bingo.* It hit me that the spun-cotton garment hadn't been there before, which meant someone had come inside the room while I was in the tub. Even though I sort of hoped it was the pie-baking person, I imagined it was Remo. I imagined the fluffy robe was his version of an olive branch, and my heart softened a little.

I tied the robe around my body, then worked on unsnarling my hair with a *wita*-made comb. Once that was accomplished, I banished my dust back into its tracks and headed toward the door to find the mercurial fae.

"Remo?" I called out.

The bedroom doors were all ajar except the one across from mine. I crossed the hallway and knocked. No answer came. I stuck my ear against the wood to make out any sounds. When I didn't hear anything, not the creak of a floorboard or the groan of a mattress spring, my pulse ratcheted up.

What if he'd left the inn after dropping off the robe? Or what if *he* hadn't dropped it off and it *was* the pie person?

Instead of knocking a second time, I twisted the doorknob and barged in. There, lounging atop the bed, one arm slung under his head was a bootless, shirtless, and pantless Remo. He had a towel wrapped around his waist that covered just enough for me to stick around.

"Didn't you hear me knock?"

He was reading a book with a faded cover. The title read *Kiss the Girls* even though it didn't look remotely like a romance considering the man on the cover held a rifle. "I did." He flipped a page.

"Then why didn't you answer?"

"Maybe because I wanted to be left alone."

Oh. I shifted on the rug, which was navy like the one in my bedroom. "Well, I just wanted to say thank you for the robe."

He finally looked away from his book. "The robe?"

I pointed to it.

His frown deepened. "Why are you thanking me for it?"

"Because it was on my bed when I got out of the bath, and I assumed—" His frown told me I'd assumed wrong. So we were truly not alone in this inn. "Did you meet the other . . . prisoner?"

"Nope. Basement was just a wine storage and laundry room." He said this a tad bitterly. I supposed I deserved it since I'd left him to explore on his own.

"There has to be someone else here, though. The bathrobe didn't appear out of thin air."

"Are you sure you didn't lay it out?"

I gave him a pointed stare. I was tired but not delusional.

"Well they must've gotten back while I was showering, because I didn't run into anyone." He went back to reading.

The fine hairs on the back of my neck rose as I looked over my shoulder at the door I'd left open. I was about to return to the hallway and call out a *hello* when I turned back toward Remo. "Want to come with me to greet our new companion?"

"Nope." He popped the word out like a chewing gum bubble.

I put a hand on my hip. For some reason, I'd been certain he'd join me.

He flipped another page in his book, perfectly disinterested.

"You're just going to lie back and read?"

"Yep."

My fingers slid off the absorbent material. "Fine." I turned and stalked out of his room without closing the door, because I was certain it would annoy him, and because I wanted him to be able to hear me in case the bathrobe-and-pie provider wasn't entirely self-less and kind.

To steady my nerves, I sang as I went about poking my head into every bedroom. When I encountered no occupants, I went down to the restaurant, which was as empty and quiet as the first floor. After a quick sweep of the booths and tables, I returned to the kitchen. What I found there made me freeze on the threshold. The door banged into my backside and skull as it swung closed. An *oompf* fell out of my mouth.

I stared at the island, at the pie dish. The slice I'd carved out had been replaced, unless this was a brand-new pie. When steam eddied off its crisped dome, my stomach twisted, and not in hunger this time. I scanned the kitchen for a dirty bowl or a bag of flour that might've been left out by the baker. Everything was spotless. I backed into the door, which swung out to release me, and then climbed the stairs and burst into Remo's room on a single breath.

"The pie," I said, panting. "It's . . . it's . . . whole."

Remo glanced away from his book and cocked up a dark eyebrow.

"Someone baked a new one!"

His eyebrow slowly leveled back. "They must've heard you moan over the last one."

I blanched. That would mean they were somewhere in the inn, but where? And why were they hiding? And what did they do with the last pie?

"Or the house is haunted," he said matter-of-factly.

I didn't have to glimpse my reflection in the mirror over the dresser to know I matched my white bathrobe. "Haunted?"

Remo sighed and tossed the book on the bed. "We're not on vacation, Amara. We're still in prison, or the Scourge, or whatever the hell this place is called."

A full-body shiver went through me. "But there's soap and pie."

He rolled himself up and off the bed in one fluid motion, his firm pectorals rippling into firmer abdominals. He was unreasonably handsome and vexingly aware of it.

"Is there a rule those two things can't exist in jail?" He strolled past me, closer than necessary, so close the heat and scent of him assaulted me, adding extra beats to my already ramped up heart.

A smirk clung to the edge of his smile. I scowled to hide my deep swallow. He disappeared into his bathroom, coming back out with his clothes, which hung limp and heavy from his fingers.

When he began to unknot his towel, I said, "I'm right here."

"And?" He dropped the towel.

Cheeks glowing crimson, I whirled around. Unfortunately, the mirror gave me a direct line of sight on Remo's backside.

Naked backside.

Naked and sculpted.

Look away, I told myself. *Look. Away.* But I was terrible at taking orders. Even from myself.

His body was an intimidating weapon of toned muscle and buffed flesh. Thighs bloated with power framed by trim hips extending into a waist that smacked of rigor and lack of indulgence. A warrior's body. Deadly to rival men; deadlier to rival women, because how were we supposed to look away from so much male perfection? And on a personal note, how was I supposed to feel about my own soft flesh and slender muscles, by-products of my preferred way of life—indolence and immoderation?

I wanted to beg him to open his mouth and utter something crude and vicious, but my throat was currently too busy purging the excess saliva pooling at the back of it to produce any sound, so I did the only reasonable thing . . . I dropped my gaze to the doily on the dresser and counted the looped threads.

The slosh and scrape of fabric against skin had more of my skin heating. Why was I still standing here? *Oh, yeah* . . . because there might've been ghosts outside, and I preferred to be in the presence of an uninhibited faerie than a devious specter.

"Are you decent?" My voice sounded weird, thready and throaty.

"I believe I am, but I don't think you share my conviction."

"What are you talking about?" I lifted my gaze to the mirror, found Remo staring back at me in the glass, half-dressed. The good half. Had his chest been covered but not his legs, my internal combustion would've made me a pathetic target for that forked tongue of his.

"I'm talking about the fact that you clearly think me on par with your little Daneelie friend."

"We already went over this in the kitchen. Joshua Locklear is *not* my friend. Plus . . ." I licked my lips, the pillar of flawless masculinity behind me miring my brain's ability to form rational thoughts. Wringing the life out of the ends of my bathrobe's belt, I spent minutes sorting through my head, trying to retrieve the words I'd meant to add. It was only when he smirked that they came back in sharp focus. "Plus, why do you care what I think about you?"

Remo's eyebrows hugged his piercing green eyes. "I don't."

My fingers slid off the belt ends, and I turned toward him, feeling like I'd somehow regained the upper hand. "You clearly do. You keep bringing Joshua up."

"I bring him up, because he's the reason we're here."

That made zero sense. "He's the reason *I'm* here. I still don't know why *you're* here." I crossed my arms. "Why *are* you here? I know you claimed stupidity, but that doesn't explain why you followed me through a mysterious portal. Were you afraid I was headed somewhere *fun*, and you didn't want to miss out?"

He took a step toward me, a giant step that put him right in my face. I tilted my neck farther back so my glare was perfectly aligned with his.

"I followed you out of the pavilion because I thought you were going after my brother."

I tightened my arms. "Does your brother usually hide in the Duciba?"

Water dripped out of the tunic clenched in his fist and onto my bare toes. "I didn't know where he was. And then I saw you studying the painted circlet. And I got curious."

"So, curiosity made you go after me?"

A storm brewed in his eyes. "Like I said, it was stupidity that made me go after you."

"So, you consider yourself a stupid person, Remo Farrow?"

"Not usually"—his timbre was low and deep—"but you somehow bring out the worst in me, Amara Wood."

I stood my ground even though my heart was clocking my breastbone, and my good sense was telling me to add some space between myself and the bulky fae. "Or maybe I just bring out what's already there." Why was I provoking him? Did I want to get stabbed by a pen? Not especially.

"Your last name suits you. You are a piece of wood. A splinter."

I knew this wasn't a compliment, and I knew I was playing with fire, yet I countered, "Splinters only bother you if they get under your skin. When did I get under your skin?"

Remo's nostrils flared, and for a moment, I actually feared death by damp-tunic-strangulation, but then I reminded myself that he'd saved me twice, so he only figuratively wanted to kill me.

After another long round of eyeball jousting, Remo stepped back, thankfully taking his intoxicating heat with him. "Get dressed. We should try to reach the portal before night falls."

The sky was still blisteringly white, but he was right. We needed to get to the portal, and the sooner the better. My arms fell out of their knot, and I arrowed toward the door.

"Maybe the inn ghost left some ointment for your cuts in your bedroom."

I froze on the threshold of his bedroom.

I didn't have to look over my shoulder to know he was smirking.

I heard the lilt in his voice when he said, "Is the great Amara Wood afraid of ghosts?"

I steeled my spine. "Not the kind who bake pie." And then I walked out of the room, desperately trying to believe this was true.

I was in fact so scared that before shutting my door, humming at the top of my lungs, I performed a thorough search of the bedroom, going so far as to check under the bed and inside the dresser drawers. Only when I was certain I was alone did I quiet down, close my bedroom door, then my bathroom door, and shrug off my robe. My suit was nowhere near dry, so I rolled it up inside my robe to transfer some of the water over.

Fat lot of good that did.

When I pulled my scaled jumpsuit on, stretching the material up my legs, it was still soaked.

Ugh. Squirming into clothes really sucked. Especially wet ones.

Just as I got the suit past my navel, the door to the bathroom flew open. Shrieking a little, I squashed my arms over my breasts and flipped around to face the ghost.

Not a ghost.

"What the hell, Remo?"

He leaned against the doorframe, twirling his pen between his long fingers. "I was checking Casper hadn't killed you."

If I weren't such a prude, I would've pummeled his smug face with my fists. "Humming is usually a good indication of liveliness."

"How was I to know *you* were humming and not the ghost?"

Insufferable faerie. "Can you get out?"

"You stayed while I got dressed."

My blood simmered. "Well, I'd rather you didn't stay."

"Why?" His teeth flashed between his curved lips. "You don't have anything I haven't seen before."

I glared at him, until what he was doing clicked. "I rattled you, so you're trying to rattle me back."

"Rattled me? Please, Trifecta. You did *not* rattle me." Yet the vein beneath his birthmark throbbed.

Yep. I'd rattled him.

Well, I wouldn't let *him* rattle *me*. I uncrossed my arms, giving him an eyeful of my not-very-spectacular-but-perfectly-adequate breasts, and went back to hoisting my suit up.

Color streaked over his cheekbones, and the pen tumbled out of his hand. Clearly, he wasn't expecting me to partake in his twisted little game.

"Are you blushing, Remo? I thought the female anatomy held no more secrets for you."

His face reddened some more, but in annoyance this time, and he jerked his gaze to his pen, crouching to pick it up. "And here I thought the princess of Neverra possessed a modicum of modesty, but you're just like all the other Neverrian girls." He latched onto his pen and squeezed it between his fingers, not looking up at me.

The barb cut deep, and I combed my hair forward with my fingers until it hid my nipples. Faeries weren't particularly prudish. After all, Seelie women were accustomed to flying around in dresses, flashing ground-dwellers, and Daneelies, male and female, enjoyed skinny-dipping, not to mention selling your body was legal in certain taverns.

"I am *nothing* like the call girls you sleep with." My voice didn't waver but my pulse did. It beat erratically. I suddenly hated myself for having bared my breasts—breasts no one besides Giya, Nana Vee, and Nima had ever seen. "Now get out."

He looked up, his gaze skipping right over my torso, and stood. "How do you do it?"

"Do what?" I snapped.

"Manage to make me feel like the bad guy when I do nothing wrong." He tapped his pen against his open palm.

"Nothing wrong? You barged into my bathroom!"

"To make sure you were safe."

"You could've knocked and asked through the door." I shivered from the wet hair plastered to my chest and the damp material plastered to my legs.

I turned so that even in the mirror he couldn't catch another flash of my bare cleavage and tugged on the suit, managing to get one arm in. Spearing the other, the one I'd injured, proved trickier. I gritted my teeth, afraid my shoulder would pop out of its socket this time. At least the shallow ache and aggravating outfit took my mind off the fact that I'd just flashed Remo.

What in the Neverrian Skies had gotten into me?

Even though I was in no way warm, sweat broke out over my upper lip as I wriggled my hand down my sleeve. I had to stop to catch my breath, before pushing more of my limb through. When I stopped again because the fabric was forcing my arm to bend, I considered ripping off the sleeve which had begun to tear anyway but then decided against it. Who knew how long it would be until we got out? Bare skin was more fragile, and even though it had felt warmer in this world, what if nights were freezing?

The strain in my shoulder suddenly eased as the fabric stretched away from my skin and a warm breath pulsed against my lobe.

"I don't need your help," I grumbled.

"I know, but you're still getting it. Consider it an apology for coming in without your permission."

As I wormed my arm through the sleeve and got the material over my shoulder, I said, "We're never discussing what happened in here. With each other or with anyone else."

"What happens in the Scourge stays in the Scourge." His knuckles grazed my skin as he released the top of the suit, and goosebumps appeared. I prayed he hadn't felt them.

I gathered my hair and pulled it out of my suit, then tugged the zipper up, squashing my upper body back inside. I was never taking this outfit off again, not until my Infinity was functional and zapped it away. When I finally turned, my nerves were still behaving spastically.

"I need to get my boots on, and then I'll be ready." I spoke to his Adam's apple since there was no way I was staring any higher.

"Are you going to avoid looking at me from now on?"

"Yes."

"That's not going to be awkward."

Because looking him in the eye wasn't awkward? "I've never flashed anyone before, Remo. No one. But here I am flashing you of all people, and for what? To prove you don't intimidate me?" I lowered my gaze to the chipped red polish on my toes. Polish, on Neverra, never chipped. Here, everything chipped. Including egos. "All I've proved is that I'm insecure and idiotic."

A beat of uneasy silence passed before he said, "I didn't mean to make you feel insecure or idiotic."

"Oh, you didn't do that. I managed it all on my own." I tried to step around him, but he boxed me into the corner, the corner *I'd* put myself in. A pattern was emerging. "Can you back up?"

"For what it's worth, you have very nice breasts."

I shut my eyes. *Gejaiwe, strike me down.* "Please forget you saw them."

"Hey . . ." His breath pulsed against my forehead. "You saw my ass."

"Don't worry. I'm working on erasing it from my mind."

"Why? I have great glutes, or so I'm told." The smile in his voice plucked away a layer of my embarrassment.

I dared to lift my lids. "Where do you get your information? From your harem of women?"

"Exactly. And just so we're clear, I've never paid for sex. You mentioned call girls earlier. I have nothing against them, but they're not my thing."

I neither nodded nor apologized. I just waited for him to back up so I could slip past him. When he didn't, I said, "It's none of my business. If our engagement were real, it would've been, but since it's all fake, you don't owe me an explanation."

However, as long as we were considered betrothed, we weren't supposed to date other people. Unless I used my *gajoï* to make him dissolve our sham union, but locking Remo out of Neverra seemed suddenly unfair.

"We're going to have to be really discreet about seeing other people. We wouldn't want the Cauldron to punish us or kick either of us out."

His eyes lost their playful glimmer, and he pursed his lips. Had he not considered this? Had he forgotten what had happened to my aunt when she'd broken her engagement off to Cruz Vega?

"Did you find some ointment for your cuts?" He pivoted toward the sink and opened the cupboard, revealing empty shelves. "I'll go check the other bathrooms. Put your shoes on." He shut the doors harder than necessary and stalked out of the room.

Way to avoid a subject. Did he think I enjoyed bringing it up? Discussing solutions to our amorous dilemma was weird. And considering how weird the entire day had been, that was saying something.

Hopefully, it would all be over soon. Hopefully, my plan to swing us back into the portal would work, and Remo and I could finally go our separate ways.

18

LOCKED IN

A low grinding noise resounded around me as I finished pulling on my knee-high boots. I lunged toward the window, fear sprinting into my veins that we were about to be hit by another earthquake. Although my borrowed bedroom gave onto an alley and the white wooden siding of a neighboring house, there was a tree, a thick vibrant oak of sorts. I watched it for tremors, but no branch shivered and its leaves were so still they looked painted on.

"Amara!" The urgency in Remo's tone made me bang my head against the window frame.

Rubbing my forehead, I strode out of the bedroom.

He was standing on the bottom stair, gaze affixed to the front window, which was no longer see-through, or rather, was, but no longer gave onto the street.

"What the?" I whispered, staring at the sheet of dark metal that had risen behind the glass. "Did you press some kind of button?"

"Of course not." He sounded offended I'd dared to ask. "It just fucking came out of the ground."

The obscured glass made me think of the train. "You think the house is about to transport us somewhere?"

"Are the windows upstairs obstructed too?" The strain in his voice echoed throughout my body, scouring my already raw nerves.

"They weren't, but I'll check again . . ." I ran back to the bedroom, which was as black as a moonless night on Earth, as though the curtains had been drawn and the blinds lowered, but there were no blinds, and the navy curtains hung motionless on either side of the window.

I sprinted down the hallway, sticking my head into every bedroom, praying one of them gave onto the blindingly white sky I so hated. I'd have given anything for a glimpse of it. Although not a born claustrophobic, I was developing into one.

When I turned away from the last room, the one with all the pictures, Remo was standing at the end of the hall, ghost-white in the darkness. Fear ramped up my pulse and spread the taste of copper inside my mouth. I flicked on the light switch, which, thank Gejaiwe, made the row of ceiling bulbs fizz to life.

For a moment, we stood on either end of the hallway, looking at each other without really looking. Like me, his attention was turned inward. Was he also running through a list of scenarios of what the inn had in store for us?

I fisted my palms, felt my dust pulse against my skin. An idea sparked, and I opened my hands, then skimmed the whorls, coaxing the dust out. Once the threads clung to my fingertips, I fashioned an axe, a monstrously large one that could not be mistaken for a butter knife, then went back into the bedroom. I tried opening the window, but it was either painted shut or magically bolted, because it didn't even budge. I raised my arms, putting all my pent-up frustration and dread into the blow, turned my head, and swung. The blade banged against the glass before bouncing off. I gritted my teeth as the impact vibrated into my sore elbow.

"What part of laying off that arm didn't you get?" Remo stood a couple feet away from me, tucked safely behind a rocking chair, his fingers wrapped around the top rung. "Hand it over, Lara Croft."

I glared at him, then at my stupid joint, then at the armored window. "My arm isn't the problem. This glass—"

"Your arm isn't working the way it should."

I handed him the axe, then backed up and docked my hands on my hips. "Knock yourself out. Or at the very least, knock out a pane of glass," I said sweetly.

All the bones in his face clenched as he raised his arms and swung. The blade pinged against the glass, jolting his arms right back behind his head.

"Huh. Could *your* arms not be working properly?"

Letting out a low snarl, he gritted his teeth and tried again. Again he failed.

"Wait. Could the glass be magical?"

"Your sarcasm isn't helping, Trifecta." He took two steps to the side and thrust the axe into the wall. Just like the window, the blade clanged without causing a depression. Not even a blemish appeared in the plaster. He growled this time and spit out a litany of Faeli curse words.

"Is there a back door? Or a window in the basement?"

"No."

My hands glided off my hips. "So, how are we supposed to get out?"

"Maybe we're not."

That sent a chill through me. Not even the prospect of running water and working electricity made our predicament comforting. I sucked in a breath and found it lacking in oxygen, although that was probably my imagination.

"Maybe we just can't use a weapon made of *wita*. Maybe there's a knife in the kitchen—"

"You even having *wita* is a fluke, *prinsisa*. A fortunate one, but still a fluke. Trust me, when our grandfathers designed this place, they didn't take into account that Huntresses able to wield confiscated dust would be sojourning in their prison."

"I'm still going to try." I walked past Remo and out the door, then dashed down the stairs, skidding twice but catching myself on the handrail. I flicked on every light in the kitchen, then jostled open the drawers and flung open cupboards in search of knives or pans. I'd even have settled for a whisk at this point. I found nothing. Except for the bowl I'd filled earlier. Before emptying it out, I twisted the tap to make sure the pipes hadn't dried. The spout hissed and ejected a single drop of water, then nothing.

Well . . . crap.

There was a bar in the restaurant, which meant there were glasses. I was about to head out to grab some when I spotted the pie in the middle of the island. I glared at the steam curling off the top, sweet stupid steam that shouldn't be curling off the pastry anymore. Animated with a violent desire to dump it on the tiles and stomp all over it, I dragged the pan toward me, singeing my fingertips on the warmed metal—*again.*

"Are you really going to eat at a time like this?" The door flapped closed behind Remo.

I narrowed my eyes at him, and then zeroed in on the axe dangling from his fingers. *My* axe. I crossed the kitchen, grabbed it, then cleaved the taunting dessert in half, pan, filling, and all. The slimy peach slices slithered off the edge of my blade and dropped onto the floor like slugs.

"There isn't a freaking knife in this entire kitchen." My words came out calm as a gathering storm.

Remo stared between the mess and my rage-flushed face. "Well, you didn't have to portion it out; I'm not much of a pie person."

A chuckle fled out of me. A slightly crazed chuckle. "By the way, the pipes are dry, so that bowl contains all the water we have left."

Remo's eyes widened a notch.

I recalled my dust. The axe crumbled like chalk, then flickered like starlight, before turning liquid and flowing back into my palm.

He opened his mouth to speak just as something began to beep.

"Do you hear that?" I was hoping he didn't.

He nodded, jaw flexing.

Beeping never heralded good things, although why was I still expecting anything good to happen in the Scourge? The pie and soapy bath had been flukes. As I shuffled toward the door, the globs of peach and smashed crust flickered as though made of dust, except they couldn't be, since food made of *wita* was inedible. And then the divvied pan scraped across the island and welded back together.

"Remo," I murmured as a new crust materialized, puffy and steaming. I swallowed saliva that felt as thick and slimy as the syrupy fruit. "To think I ate some earlier. What if it's making pie babies inside my stomach?" I blanched and peered down at my stomach, half expecting to find it bloating outward. It was flat, but that didn't mean the pie wasn't preparing to do damage.

"How do you feel?"

I looked up to find Remo's gaze locked on my abdomen. "Like my sweet tooth might end up killing me if whatever's beeping doesn't." I didn't eat quite as many chocolates as I used to, but if a box happened to find its way into my room, it never found its way out.

Remo's tensed lips quirked up.

Nothing like humor to deflect tension. That was Iba's mantra. How I missed him. Nothing bad ever touched me when he was around. My eyes stung, but I refused to cry. This wasn't the moment for tears. This was the moment for action.

"On the upside, no ghost baker. Nima's all about finding silver linings." My heart thumped hollowly. My strong and resilient mother would've known exactly what to do.

I was a such sorry excuse for a future queen. Seventeen and still completely reliant on her parents. I held on to that . . . the will to see them again—I was *not* dying in this damned place. I sidestepped Remo and went after the source of the beeping. Beside the front door, a red pinprick blinked in the corner of a bulky cream box containing an outdated keypad with ten rubbery buttons ranging from 0 to 9 set underneath a screen with four dashes.

"I'm guessing we're supposed to find a four-digit code." Remo's voice scraped across my temple, blowing against my damp hair. Did he have to stand so close?

"You think?" I squirmed to the side, so that his chin wasn't propped against the back of my skull.

He shot me a glare that would've made a lesser woman shrink, or at least one who wasn't inflated on adrenaline and enchanted pie. "Do you have any constructive input, *prinsisa*? Like perhaps an idea as to what numbers we should . . . *punch*."

I didn't think it was the keypad he wanted to punch. "This place's creation. In Earthly years." In Neverrian years, we were still celebrating new years in three digits.

Remo lifted his finger to the keypad. "What year was it created?"

"I don't know."

"Well, that's going to help." He started to lower his hand but then raised it again and hit: 1-7-7-5. The little light stopped blinking but stayed red. Was that a good sign?

"Why 1775?"

"It's my grandfather's Earthly year of bir—"

The box shrieked.

I slapped my palms over my ears as Remo let out a new string of expletives and tried two other combinations. His year of birth: 2018 —why he would think that could be the code was beyond me—and then the current Earthly year: 2124. And then he punched 2-0-3, his index hovering between the numbers five and six. "What's your birth year?" he yelled over the loud screeching.

"Five!"

He punched the five. The keyboard kept trilling and the light stayed red.

Remo struck it with his fist. The light neither magically turned off nor did it quiet. He growled and raised his fingers to the sides of the box, trying to pry it off the wall, but like the bricks behind it, the box was indestructible.

Panting hard, he lowered his hands and fisted them at his sides.

I racked my brain for combinations but there were too many to try out. I stared around the room, on the lookout for numbers. None had magically appeared on the walls, or on the tables. The only thing that had magically appeared in this room, which hadn't been there before, was the damn pie.

Remo must've followed my gaze because he muttered something—probably roared it, but since my palms were still sandwiched on either side of my head, it sounded unintelligible.

Suddenly, the high-pitched wailing stopped. We both spun back toward the box, hopeful to find the light off. It wasn't. It had simply gone back to blinking, and then the beeps started again. I lowered my hands, the sound bearable but most definitely not enjoyable.

"What's Linus's year of birth?" Remo asked gruffly.

"Um. At the start of the 1800s, but I don't know the exact date."

"Well that's gonna help."

I'd have stuck my tongue out at him if I weren't so busy gnawing on my bottom lip. "He was forty-four when he died." I remembered this because Iba had just turned forty-four, and he'd mentioned something about being the same age as his father had been on the Day of Mist.

"Did he ever live on Earth? Because if he did that would change the calculations."

"I don't know . . ."

Remo sighed. "Well he died the year I was born. And forty-four times five is . . ."

"Two-fifteen."

"So, that would mean he was born in . . ."

"1803," I said, almost without thinking.

Remo hiked up an eyebrow.

"What? I love math."

"I see that." He lifted his hand back to the keypad and punched in 1-8-0-3.

The light and sound went crazy again.

He tapped 1800 and all the other combinations until he got to 1810.

I clawed at my ears since clawing at the damn box was useless. I knew prison wasn't supposed to be fun, but come on . . . this was taking torture to a whole new level.

Concentrating on my breathing, I tried thinking of what four digits Gregor and Linus could've come up with in those scheming brains of theirs. I tapped Iba's year of birth—*wrong*—my paternal grandmother's birthdate—*wrong*—then 0000—*wrong*. I growled.

I walked to the bar, grabbed the freaking piping hot pan and lobbed it at the shrilling box. All that did was a big fat nothing. No, that wasn't true. It made a mess. Chunks of crust and gooey filling slithered down the bricks, darkening the mortar. When the pan hit the floor, its clang was barely audible over the pandemonium.

Heaving with fury, I molded my dust into a bat. Remo took a few steps back and crossed his arms. Apparently he wasn't going to stop me. Good, because I might've whacked him if he'd tried. Ears ringing, elbow smarting, I swung it into the brain-shredding box. It didn't break. Didn't even chip. Unlike my eardrums. *And* my sanity. *And* my elbow.

Skies, my elbow . . .

Sweat trickled down the nape of my neck, bled into my still-damp suit. To think I'd been reveling in a bath an hour ago, wondering why my skin didn't sparkle when wet. What petty, *petty* musings.

Snarling like a *tigri*, I took another swing. The bat flew out of my grip, hit the glass, and dropped before rolling toward Remo's boots.

He stepped on it but didn't bend over to pick it up. "Did you get it all out?"

I cradled my elbow. "No. Not even close. When I see Gregor—" I stopped talking. *When* . . . What a dangerous thing optimism was— it made you believe in miracles.

"Focus on that. On what you'll do to him *when* you see him."

The jarring ring turned into a staccato trill again, each beat like a nail scraping down a smooth piece of slate.

Scrape. Scrape. Scrape.

"I swear, this is why we haven't met any prisoners. They all went nuts and put an end to their miserable existences."

"You forget that death doesn't seem to be possible."

"Maybe in this cell, it is."

There was a bitter twist to his lips. "I say we don't find out."

I glared at the beeping box, then frowned when I noticed that over the dashes, letters had appeared. TRY. Then, LAST. Try last? *Last* what? Last day of the—

"You've got to be shitting me. *Last try?*" Remo's voice seemed amplified by the glass façade.

What happened if we failed? I didn't dare voice my concern. I didn't even want to speculate what could happen because knowing Gregor, it would be worse than death.

The rushing in my ears intensified, crashing against my temples. "I don't think it's a date."

Remo frowned.

"Your grandfather loves sick games. I think this is just another one of them. I think the four digits correspond to something in the inn." I was already behind the bar, lifting alcohol bottles, checking labels. "Look over the tables and chairs. Maybe a number's carved into one of them."

I wasn't sure if Remo would do it. He wasn't the type to take orders. Especially from me. He stared around the room at the dozen or so tables, and then, as though deciding my idea wasn't completely ridiculous, he walked toward the nearest one. After we'd scoured the entire restaurant, Remo announced he was heading to the second floor. Before leaving, I stared around the room one last time, noticing the pie had dematerialized. Although no greasy track mark remained on the bricks, its sweet, buttery scent clung to the air like smoke from a grease fire.

My stomach churned. When it didn't balloon outward, I breathed a little easier. Well, as easily as possible when the words LAST TRY kept flashing, punctuated by incessant beeping.

I tried the sink behind the bar before leaving, but not even a droplet of water splashed out. My mouth felt dry as the road in Frontier Land. I made a beeline for the kitchen, drank a few deep gulps from the bowl, thankful I'd had the foresight to fill it, then set it down carefully.

I'd already searched drawers and cupboards—all empty—but an etching by the cubby hole caught my attention. I walked over to it. Someone had carved a heart and placed the names BLAKE + CAT inside of it. A chill swept through me. Was this the Blake Geemee Kaji had absorbed when he rose from his grave? Had my mother and Blake been lovers? Had she drawn the heart? Had he? Was it even real?

My name sounded somewhere outside the kitchen. I left the markings on the wall and went up to find Remo. By the time I reached the landing, I was again out of breath.

"Found something?" I asked hopefully.

He walked out of the largest room toting the framed picture of two kids, one with black pigtails and black eyes, the other with light blue eyes and hair shorn so close to his scalp it was impossible to tell the color. The girl sat on the landing of a treehouse, stick-thin legs caught midswing, and the boy was climbing the ladder, looking over his shoulder at the camera.

"Is that my mother?"

"Possibly, but that's not why I unhooked it from the wall. Look." He pointed to the bottom of the picture where the date 2008 was scribbled in pen. "It's the only one with a date. I checked them all."

"Did you check every bedroom?"

"Yes."

"And you found nothing else?"

He shook his head, which made a piece of red hair fall into his eyes. "And you?"

I thought about the carving in the kitchen, but since it didn't bear any numbers, I didn't think I needed to share it with Remo.

"Should we try 2008?"

Goosebumps sprouted over my skin, awakening every little bruise and cut on my body. "What if we're wrong?"

"What if we're right?" He tucked the picture under his arm.

Gnawing the life out of my lip, I followed him back down the stairs. My gut churned and churned, as though trying to tell me something.

In six quick strides, he reached the alarm box whereas I froze on the threshold, gaze sticking to the table closest to me, or rather, to what lay on top. I clamped my hands around the back rungs of a chair and stared so hard at the damn pie its contours blurred. And then suddenly, they sharpened, and I whipped my gaze up. "Remo, wait!"

However much I wanted the beeping to stop, I sensed we needed to think this through a moment longer. I took a seat, and although it was icky, I raked my hand through the filling, looking for a clue.

On the anniversary of the *Caligo Dias*, it was Neverrian tradition that every ground-dwelling family be gifted a *Caligo Crosta*, a pie baked in the royal kitchens. Inside every pastry was a solid gold nugget. They all varied in size. For some families, the nugget could keep them afloat for an entire decade; for others, it would allow them to live like nobles for a month. It was Iba who'd established this tradition, inspiring himself from the *Galette des Rois* he'd sampled in France during one of his Earthly trips with Nima. Together, they'd come up with this compelling gift, a small token of appreciation for their less fortunate subjects.

I'd heard Gregor complain once that my parents were emptying the royal coffers faster than Linus had gone through women. I'd wrinkled my nose at the comparison, but Iba had smiled. For some reason, my father enjoyed riling up the *wariff*.

"What are you doing?" Remo asked, bringing me back to the inn with its shrilling box.

"Looking for a nugget."

"Not to burst your little bubble, *prinsisa,* but I don't think we can buy our way out of here."

I didn't react to his taunt. Simply spread the filling over the table, fingers brushing through the sticky fruit and chunky crust. "I'm hoping there's a number etched into the nugget." If there even was a nugget.

My heart palpitated when my fingers knocked into something solid. I squeezed it between my thumb and index finger only to find it was a morsel of peach pit.

"So? Anything?" he asked.

My eyesight blurred, and then a tear rolled off my cheek and plopped inside the emptied pan. I scrubbed my disappointment away with my knuckles.

Remo must've deduced my hunt had been fruitless.

The irony of a fruit-filled hunt being fruitless made me snort out a laugh. Oh, Skies, the demise of my mind was upon me. I tunneled my hand through my hair, streaking it with globs of pie. *Whatever.* They would just magick themselves out of existence, I thought with another dark laugh.

I laughed a minute longer, and then I stopped. Just stopped. Because it was really not funny.

Nothing about this was funny.

My hair smelled like freaking charmed peaches.

My elbow felt like it had been evicted from its socket.

My face was crosshatched with stinging cuts.

My eardrums were bruised from the beeping.

Not to mention that if we didn't figure out the correct four-digit code, we'd stay locked in this oversized tin box, drowning in warm pie.

Remo was watching me like I was one of those new animal specimens developed by human zoologists: a unicorn or a pompom. Probably more pompom than unicorn—horned horses made people gasp and coo, whereas poufy blue monkeys made people snicker and point.

"Why are you here?" I whispered to the pie. "Why? Why? Why?"

Great. Now I was talking to inanimate objects. Wait. Were objects that could materialize and dematerialize inanimate?

Grimly, I realized that in the end, inanimate or not, I was still chatting with a pie.

"Are you asking me?" Remo's voice stole my attention off the wrecked pastry.

"No."

He hefted a dark eyebrow, still clutching the framed picture. "You think the pie has something to do with it?"

"Don't you? I mean, if it was just about freaking us out, why not make other stuff appear? Why *peach pie*?" Just as it had done too many times before, the spilled contents evaporated and reformed.

Pie. Pie. Pie. Pie. Pie. Pie.

The word shrilled in time with the blasted alarm.

I stood up so fast my chair skidded and toppled. "Pi! Remo, it's pi!"

"We've established it's pie. We've even established it's magical and contains peaches."

I rolled my eyes. "No. I mean it's the *number* pi."

"As in 3.14? That's only three digits."

My astonishment that he knew the basic number when everyone relied on technology for everything these days subsided at his ignorance that pi was an infinite number. "It's actually 3.14159 . . ."

When his eyes grew as large as Gregor's paranormal pies, my voice dragged off. Uttering the ensuing numerals served no purpose besides showing off my love for math, which Remo would probably see as showing off since he thought the very worst of me.

"So, you want to try 3-1-4-1?" he said between two beeps.

I swallowed, suddenly unsure. What if the resurfacing pastry had nothing to do with the alarm box? "I don't know. I don't know anymore." I raked my hands through my hair again. My locks, although still a little damp, were pie-free. My fingers, too.

"I think it's smart." He put down the framed picture on a neighboring table. "I think we should try it."

I gaped at Remo. He thought something I'd said was smart? *Wow.*

"What?"

Before he could fathom how much his compliment affected me, I blurted out, "I don't want to get blown up, Remo."

He sighed, rough and deep. "Maybe we'll just get buried under peach pie."

"I don't want that either."

"It would make for a sweet death."

"I don't want to die."

"Then let's live."

As I stared at the blinking red dot, he turned toward the keypad and raised his index finger. And then he tapped in the sequence.

19

THE TORNADO

Red turned to green, and the inn fell silent even though my skull still beeped. The word WELL flashed on the screen followed by the word DONE.

The grinding sound from earlier erupted around us as the metal sheets retracted into the ground, letting in veins of bright light. I never thought I'd be happy to see the cloud-filled sky, but Great Gejaiwe, I was on the brink of prostrating myself toward it.

Until I noticed the shutters on the house across the street flapping as wildly as a *quila* drunk on faerie wine.

"Um. Is it me, or is the wind—"

A mailbox banged into the window, and I jumped. When the glass webbed, my blood turned to ice. *Now it breaks?*

I retreated so fast I knocked into a table and then into a chair. Suddenly, a tree—a full-grown, huge-ass tree—skidded down the street, its roots twisting like a *volitor's*. When the roots lifted, flipping it onto its leafy crown, Remo shot across the inn.

"We need to get to the basement!" His roar, combined with the impact of the trunk against the pavement outside, had my heart blasting against the zipper of my jumpsuit. "Amara!"

A segment of white-picket fence slammed into the window, crackling all the places the mailbox had spared.

I ripped around. "Shouldn't we try to get to the train?"

Remo's fiery red hair fluttered around as though the wind had somehow penetrated the cracks in the façade. Besides its deafening howl, the air was still quiet inside.

"Massive trees are flying around, and you want to go outside?"

"If we can't die—"

"What if we can? What if the last world just created illusions, and my death was one of them? We need to get to the basement. Now, Amara!"

I whirled around and headed toward the staircase I'd noticed earlier, then tore down the cement steps, Remo on my heels. The explosion of glass somewhere in the inn startled me, and I stumbled down the last three steps, shooting my hands forward. I officially detested stairs. Cinching my lids shut, I fell. My palms smacked into the concrete first and then my knees. Although my face didn't suffer from my clumsiness, my elbow shrieked in pain all over again.

I yanked back my injured arm but remained hunched even though all I wanted was to crawl into a ball and lick my wounds.

"Amara?"

Slowly, breathing through my pain, I opened my lids.

Remo was crouched in front of me. "Are you okay?"

No, I was *not* okay. We'd figured out the code just to get hit by a freaking tornado?

He lifted my face.

I twisted my head so that it slid off his roughened palm, not wanting to give him the satisfaction of seeing me in pain. "I'm fine." I rocked back onto my heels and glared at the shiny concrete under my bent legs.

Remo's concern clung to the air between us, charging it. Unless it wasn't concern. Unless it was smugness that I was so damn weak without my powers.

Wood splintered somewhere above us, and Remo jumped to his feet, then lunged toward the basement's entrance. A glance over my shoulder revealed a table tumbling down the stairs. I needed to get out of the way, but somehow, I couldn't locate the willpower or strength to get up and save myself. What was the point?

Remo groaned, and I thought he'd gotten hit but found him shouldering the door. The hinges groaned as he leaned all of his weight against it. Either it was the heaviest door, or it was stuck. The wood tabletop screeched as it got stuck between the walls of the staircase. Sweat glistened on Remo's brow as he pushed and pushed. I should've gotten up and helped him, but instead I sat there, my anger foaming like white caps. I wanted to scream like I'd done in the Cacti Desert, but all that had done was hurt my lungs.

A deafening crack sounded over the howling wind, and then the tabletop split in two like butterfly wings and flew straight at me. I squeezed my eyes shut, certain I was about to be struck, but the impact never came. And then the wind stopped blowing, and my hair stopped floating like Glade kelp around my face.

A latch clicked, followed by a booming thump.

I opened my eyes but could see nothing.

Either Remo had gotten the door shut, because there wasn't the faintest trickle of light, or I was dead.

I heard heavy panting. Mine but also someone else's.

I guessed I was still alive.

Something collided softly with my knee. I assumed it was Remo's boot until he spoke, and I realized he wasn't standing over me. "You think you can make a faelight out of *wita*?"

Swallowing, I pressed my palms together and extricated my dust. Its filaments glowed in the darkness as I stretched and weaved them into an orb which I tossed upward. It levitated toward the ceiling and spread light over the tight quarters, glinting against the shelves filled with stacked wine bottles and highlighting the edges of a countertop under which sat two large white boxes with portholes.

Remo was leaning against the door, breathing hard. His eyes ran over my still kneeling form. "Are you okay?"

No. I wasn't okay. I was a mess. A broken, useless mess. I bit my lip and averted my watery gaze. When I caught sight of what had bumped into the side of my knee, my molars clicked together. It wasn't pie, but it was almost as bad. I picked up the unblemished apple, and with my good arm, lobbed it against the wall of bottles. Its glossy red skin didn't tear, its white flesh didn't splatter. It simply bounced back down and rocked onto its side as though made of rubber.

I dragged my bad arm against my chest, trying to evaluate if the pain was the same as in Deception Central or if it felt different. Every inch of skin and bone hurt so damn badly that I imagined it was broken this time. How was I supposed to ascend a cliff with only one arm?

If we could even leave this basement, what with the windstorm raging outside.

"I thought I hated etiquette class, but faerie prison . . . it's officially the worst," I muttered.

"But it has soap and pie." Remo's voice nipped my nose.

I looked up so fast my neck cracked. He was again crouched before me.

"Show me your arm, Amara."

"It's fine," I gritted out.

"You're moodier than usual, so I'm guessing it's not fine."

"I have every right to be moody. I solved an impossible riddle, and for what? To activate a natural disaster?" The snort accompanying my pithy commentary froze on its way out of my nostrils, turning into a whimper when Remo tugged on my arm.

I tried to reel it in, but he held on firmly. His fingers climbed the length of it. Everywhere he touched elicited new whimpers.

Finally, he released it, his expression grim. "I don't think I can fix it this time."

I fluttered my lids, my lashes clumped with old and new tears.

He rose and walked around the cramped quarters, looking into one of the portholes before popping it open. He extricated a long length of fabric—a tablecloth or a bedsheet. As I wondered why it had been stored in the box, Remo twisted it, then looped it around my neck and knotted it.

"What are you doing?" I asked.

"Making a sling. Hopefully, it'll help." He lifted my elbow and placed it inside the white hammock. "Better?"

Surprisingly, it was. After a beat, I said, "I really miss flying."

Remo shot me a grim smile. "Think of how much you'll appreciate it once you're home."

"If we ever get home."

"We will." He picked up one end of my makeshift sling and wiped my cheeks with it.

There he was being nice again.

"Can I suggest something?" He let the fabric flutter back down. "Once we get back, you should train using the spirals. I can give you some pointers if you want."

I shook my head but smiled. "Oh . . . Remo." And then I was laughing but mixed into the laughter were giant sobs.

Like earlier, Remo didn't quite seem to know what to do with this insane version of me, but then his arms came around my back, and he pulled me against him, tucking my head under his chin, and even though his hug didn't magically heal my wounded arm, shredded face, or chipped ego, it dimmed my pain.

"Why can't we catch a break?" I murmured against his solid chest.

"Maybe because we're in a supernatural jail." His hand came up to the back of my head, and his fingers combed through my hair, causing a trail of worrisome goosebumps to strain against the compressive fabric of my suit.

Worrisome, not because he could feel them—the material was much too tight and thick—but because this wasn't the first time my body reacted to his touch.

Something banged against the door, and I jumped. When the latch didn't break, I asked, "Now what?"

"Now we wait out the tornado."

I swung my attention back to him. "You think it'll stop?"

He nodded as he climbed back up to his feet and walked over to the wall of wine. He scanned the labels, then selected one and blew dust off the dark glass. "What are your thoughts on Cabernet?"

"I'd be fine with moonshine at this point."

"Can you make a bottle opener, Amara?"

I frowned. "Is it just for me, or are you planning on drinking?"

"Don't feel like sharing?"

"I thought you didn't drink."

"I don't."

I touched my tattoo but remembered the dust was presently glowing on the ceiling. Tentatively, I stood up. My knees felt like they'd been stuffed with damp cotton, but surprisingly they held me upright. I directed my good arm toward the orb and snatched off a piece, then twisted it into a corkscrew that I handed over to Remo. He popped the cork out of the bottle, then tendered back the bottle opener, which I wadded up and tossed back toward the glowing orb.

He took a swig of the wine, then proffered it my way. The woodsy flavor coated my tongue and throat like velvet. I took another swig, then passed the wine back. We didn't talk as we drank, just plopped down beside each other with our backs to one of the brick walls. Every so often, the ceiling and door would groan, and my dust orb would shudder, but then all would settle and grow still again.

Halfway through the bottle, my blood began to fizz, sweeping away the ache in my arm. I leaned my head back against the bricks and watched the orb I'd created. "I'm glad you followed me through the portal, whatever your reason for doing so."

Remo coughed. He passed me the bottle and coughed some more.

I took a swig. "My grandfather was a really screwed-up man."

He wiped his mouth on his sleeve and side-eyed me. Since he hated my parents, he probably admired Linus. After all, Gregor had been a fan of the tyrant—before he'd switched camps on the Day of Mist, sensing the winds were changing—and Remo and his grandfather were almost the same person. *No.* That wasn't true. Gregor would never have crafted a sling for my arm.

Or hugged me.

"At least it never gets boring for prisoners in here," he ended up saying.

"Ha." My cheeks lifted with a cheerless smile. "Most creative correctional facility I've ever been to for sure." I took another drink, then passed the bottle back to Remo.

"You've been to others?"

"Sook loves virtual reality arcades, and some of the games we play take place in prisons."

"You two are close, huh?"

I bobbed my head. "He and Giya are my best friends. My *only* friends. Hard to trust people when you aren't certain of their intentions." Not that people had lined up to be my friend after Remo's rumor about my killer blood.

His gaze slid down my face. "I remember when that *dile* stung you. Sook was bawling when I got there."

I shivered at the memory of the sting, how frightened I'd been when I'd felt the venom coursing through my veins. I'd told Giya she could take the pearl earrings Nima had gifted me after her trip to the South Sea, and I'd told Sook he could take my roll-up TV— the first one on Neverra. The last thing I remembered before my heart had stopped was Giya telling me to shut up and that she hated pearls—she didn't.

Remo put the bottle back into my hands, and I upended it. "You know what I remember? How disappointed you looked that I'd survived."

There was a beat of silence. "Disappointed? I . . . I wasn't disappointed."

"Angry, then? Annoyed?" I glanced at the strong lines of his profile. "It's fine, Remo. Water under the bridge. Air under the portal."

"You're terrible at reading people."

"Oh, really?"

"Yes, really."

I sat up a little. "What were you, then?"

"Hand over the wine."

"Bottle's empty."

He got up and crossed the room to select a second bottle.

As he walked back toward me, I said, "We're going to get wasted."

"That's the plan. At least, *my* plan."

"I'm down with your plan." I stood, and the room spun a little. I was already well on my way to inebriation.

I grabbed a piece of my orb to fashion a corkscrew again, then handed it over to Remo. Once he'd yanked the cork out, I chucked the gob of dust back toward the orb and sat back down, bumping my tailbone against the wall because I'd miscalculated the drop.

Forget *on my way*, I'd reached my destination.

Remo tipped the bottle to his mouth and drank. And then drank some more. When he sat back next to me, he said, "Scared and relieved."

"What?"

"How I felt the day you got stung by a *dile*."

It took my befuddled brain a full minute to compute what he was admitting. "Why?"

"Because, Amara . . ." Was that a blush snaking over his jaw again? Instead of teasing him about it, I waited to see if he would add anything. *Because, Amara,* wasn't much of an explanation. "What good is a hero without a villain?"

My eyes widened, and then I blinked. And then I laughed. "I'm your villain?" In between waves of hilarity, I said, "What a villain I make. Scared of ghosts and a complete klutz on stairs." I wiped the corners of my eyes and elbowed him with my good arm. "No one would read that story."

Although he hadn't even cracked a smile, his eyes glittered. Even his lips seemed to shine. It was probably all the wine I'd ingested that made his features all glowy. When I lifted my eyes back to his, I found him staring at me with a disquieting intensity.

My breathing hitched, scattering too much oxygen throughout my body. My head felt light, my chest too. And then all of me felt too tight. I snatched the wine from his hands and drank. "Will I still be the villain in your story if we get out of here?"

"When."

I frowned.

"*When* we get out of here. Not *if*. And if you stop being the villain, then I stop being a hero."

"You saved the villain so many times that you've earned hero-status for life."

"Yeah?" His voice sounded funny, all at once hoarse and slightly high-pitched. He'd apparently had too much wine also.

I leaned my head on his shoulder. "You might've even become the villain's hero." I did not just say that. I clamped my lids shut, wishing I could incinerate the words. "That was the wine talking."

His shoulder shifted, and I thought he was pushing me away, but then his arm wound around my back, and his hand settled gently on my achy bicep. I must've grimaced, because he slid his fingers to my ribs. "Here I was hoping to ply you with alcohol to get a second free peepshow; instead I earn hero-status for life. Prison isn't half-bad."

I smiled, his humor deflating my ballooning mortification. "Oh come on, it's awful, but your cellmate *is* pretty awesome."

He chuckled, and the vibrations combined with his warmth made me sink into him a little more. "She's a handful, though."

After several breaths, I said, "Good thing you have such big hands." Wine-brain made my thoughts very slippery.

Said big hand gripped my side a little harder, and then Remo propped his bristly jaw on top of my forehead. "We should try to sleep."

"Yeah. We should." If only to stop spouting humiliating, drunken declarations. *Big hands? Seriously, Amara?*

Even though I didn't think I'd sleep, I'd obviously underestimated my level of exhaustion, because I fell down that rabbit hole as swiftly as I'd fallen through the portal.

20

THE WRECKAGE

I awakened slowly, my mouth vinegary, my palate fuzzy, my left arm leaden, and my ear numb from where it was still pressed against Remo's shoulder. I blinked around me, wondering if I'd been asleep for a minute or for several hours. My stirring must've awoken Remo, because his head rolled off of mine and his palm popped off my ribcage.

I shifted so he could pull his arm out from around me, and then I stood and stretched. Before the silence could grow awkward, I said, "Ready to go check if anything's left of our world, hero?"

That made him smile. And in turn, it made me smile.

Good. We were good.

He ran his palms down the sides of his face, then pressed himself to standing. "How's the arm? Is it swollen?"

Between the fabric sling, the compressive sleeve, and the weak lighting, I couldn't tell. "I don't know."

He peeled the white fabric away and prodded my flesh. It felt like he was touching my very bone. When I hissed, he stopped and tucked it back into the cloth.

"It's broken isn't it?" I asked.

"I'm not sure. But whatever you do, don't use it today."

"I don't think I could even if I wanted to. How's your head?" I'd had a slice of pie last night; Remo, to my knowledge, hadn't eaten anything, and wine on an empty stomach was a killer.

He rubbed his brow. "It's felt worse."

I was curious as to when it could've felt worse, because my brain personally felt like it was bobbing inside my skull.

"Grab the *wita*, and let's go."

I lifted my tattooed hand toward the orb, which landed like a feather inside my palm. Since it was our only source of light, I kept it aglow as we made our way toward the exit.

Before he unlatched the door, he said, "Stand behind me."

Since I didn't care to get more banged up, I did.

The latch clicked, and then Remo drew the door open, and it seemed like every piece of furniture and every brick of the inn converged inside the cellar. I swear, things kept coming, crashing, rolling. At some point, I thought we'd get buried alive under chairs, cracked ceramic, and broken mirrors, but fortunately, the influx stopped. Unfortunately, by the time it stopped, the pile we needed to scale was treacherously tall and loaded with jagged points.

"Have any advice on what sort of tool I could make with my dust? Besides a lighter . . . I don't think creating a pyre would be very safe considering there are no exits."

"A cast. You should make a cast."

"How will that help us?"

"It'll immobilize your arm and protect it."

That jammed my lips together and poked at my heart. Filing his kindness away to analyze later, I stared at the pile until an idea clicked. One that would help *us*. Not just me. "Stand back, Farrow."

"Why?"

"Because I want to try something."

"Should I be worried?"

"Always. I'm the Trifecta, after all."

His teeth flashed as he stepped back.

I turned my glowing orb into a bucket of glue, which I handed him, because it was darn heavy. "Can you toss it?"

His eyebrows hitched up. "What is it?"

"Glue. It'll lock the debris together and coat any sharp edges."

"You think there's enough?"

"*Duh.* It's magical glue."

I wasn't sure if he was convinced, but still, he threw my *wita* concoction onto the mound of twigs and glass. After a few minutes, I prodded the base of the pile with my boot. It was hard as concrete. Remo tested a higher spot in the pile. When there was no give, he climbed. The ceiling was so low he had to stay crouched.

"Smart little villain you are." He held out his hand.

I smiled, my heart lifting in time with my good arm. I seized his outstretched fingers, finding footholds in the stationary mound. Once on top, we crawled toward where the staircase should've been, the edges of broken things jabbing our knees and shins. Remo dug through a spot of loose debris until he uncovered one of the cement steps. Once he managed to stand, he nodded to the stationary mound.

"Grab your dust."

My dust? Had his tongue slipped?

I started to sweep my palm over the mound when he said, "Actually, wait."

I fisted my fingers and was about to ask what he'd forgotten down in the cellar, when his forearm snaked around my waist.

"Okay, go."

Stunned by his unceasing thoughtfulness, I spread my fingers slowly, and the golden strands of *wita* curled up like smoke. Things popped and rattled as though it was every stick for itself. Sure enough the knoll changed shape, sinking in spots, swelling in others, and its modifications affected the clutter in the stairwell. Everything rolled and tumbled anew, gushing like a mountain stream during snowmelt.

Remo's arm tightened around my middle, keeping me from

getting swept into the debris. Once things settled, he said, "Grab my hand."

I searched the wall for a rail but found none. Biting my lip, I slid my hand into his, then slowly pirouetted. My stomach churned, and not just from last night's winefest. Without meeting his gaze, I followed him up the stairs, the pressure on my fingers easing and hardening as we ascended. When we reached the opening, a pothole amidst a titanic field of rubble, I glided my fingers out of his and spun to take in the extent of the devastation.

The only thing that remained in the valley was the train. It gleamed red and silver in the brash light. I turned away from it to find Remo squinting at the steep bank that we needed to scale to reach the portal. It seemed somehow steeper and taller, as though the tornado hadn't only leveled out the town but excavated the valley.

"I wish I could make a hoverboard." Unfortunately, we couldn't craft electronics from *wita*.

"That would've been practical." He tipped his neck back, inspecting the magnitude of the rock wall, and then he took in the glittery field of wreckage, his eyes stilling on an uprooted tree. "If you make me an axe, I could try hacking at the trunk to make a ladder."

"Or I could make a ladder. A really thin one."

"You don't have enough dust for a ladder. Not even for a thin one."

I sighed. "We'd need more than one tree to make a tall enough ladder. And how would we stick all the trunks together?"

He shrugged. "With your magical glue."

"What about a rope with a hook?" I suggested.

"I couldn't swing it that high."

"Maybe I can float it up."

He exhaled long and deep. "Not if it has anything heavy attached to it."

I took a step, and glass crunched. A big, pointy piece that reminded me of the one which had jutted out of Remo's back.

I must've stared at it too long, because he said, "Don't even suggest it."

I wrinkled my nose. "I wasn't going to."

"We go back to the train."

"What if the next cell is worse?"

"What if it's better?"

"You're revoltingly optimistic."

That chiseled his hard expression into a softer one. "One of us has to be. Besides, have you ever met a pessimistic hero?"

I rolled my eyes as we started toward the train. When I skidded twice and almost face-planted into the rubble, my equilibrium impaired by the limb locked against my torso, Remo took my flailing hand and held it. I tried to squirm my fingers out of his, but he simply squeezed harder, sealing my palm against his calloused one.

"Stop fidgeting, Trifecta. I'm trying to help you, not seduce you."

His words made me grow hot all over. Even though I still wanted to put a mile between our bodies, I stopped fighting him.

"I didn't think you were seducing me," I grumbled. "I just don't like to be coddled."

A smile knocked into his lips. "I thought princesses loved to be coddled."

"You know nothing about princesses."

"How about you teach me about what it's like to grow up with a legion of faerie guards at your disposal and a brigade of servants at your beck and call?"

"Are you making fun of me?"

His smile collapsed, and he scratched a spot behind his ear. "No, Amara. I really am curious."

His edginess, combined with the use of my first name, made me relent. "It's overwhelming. Everyone's always judging you, evaluating your needs, jumping to attention when you enter a room. Not to mention the carousel of guards doesn't give me much time to build relationships with any of them."

His brows dipped. "Guards are appointed to protect you, not to chat with you."

"I got that."

After a beat, he ventured, "It can't be all bad, though."

"No. But it's not . . . it's not always easy to set the right example. To *be* the right example. I spent most of my childhood dreaming I didn't have so many powers, because power gets you attention, and sometimes"—I peered up at him—"denigrating nicknames."

An octagonal metal stop sign groaned and bowed under his boots. "Sometimes nicknames are born of jealousy."

"You're jealous of me?"

He peered down at me through his dark auburn lashes. "Who isn't? You have *everything*. You're even pretty. You could've at least been born with some facial warts or a weak chin."

I blinked at him. "You think I'm pretty?"

His forehead crinkled as though my question were causing him physical pain. "On the outside."

If both my hands hadn't been immobilized, I would've smacked him. "You're such an ass."

His eyes blazed greener. "I'm more than just a great body part."

I shook my head as we trampled over the station sign, the one printed with the town's name. It felt like we'd arrived here a week ago, and yet it couldn't have been more than a day since we got sucked through the portal. Maybe even less than a day.

"What does my grandfather have on your father?" Remo asked suddenly.

His question brought me to a stop, which in turn brought him to a stop. I released his hand, and he didn't protest because we'd reached the platform where my risk of nosediving was minimal. "What do you mean?"

"There's no way your father would've agreed to marry his only child off to the grandson of a man he barely tolerates if he has nothing to gain from the union."

I slid my bottom lip between my teeth. "I can't discuss it."

His stance shifted, his feet settling farther apart and his knees locking, and then he crossed his arms. "Why?"

"Because . . ." *Ugh.* How was I supposed to tell someone who'd saved my behind more than once that I didn't fully trust him?

"Because?"

I looked into the mossy depths of his eyes. "If I tell you, and we get out of here, and you use this against me—"

"I won't."

"How do I know you won't?"

"Because I give you my word."

"And I'm just supposed to trust your word?"

He drew his shoulders back. "You still don't trust me."

I was beginning to, but did I trust him enough? I fingered my sling, the weight of his attention making me extraordinarily uncomfortable. I steeled my spine and stopped twitching. "Do you trust me?"

His mouth flattened. "You're right. We haven't gotten there, have we?"

Would we ever get there, though? I scanned the crater filled with debris ringed with steep mountains. How many cells and how many days would it take to repair generations of distrust? Could it even be repaired? As the firm knot of his arms slackened, and he pivoted toward the train, I realized that Remo and I, we had nothing to repair because we'd never had anything to break in the first place. What we did have was the power to build something new.

Sighing, I decided to lay the groundwork. "Iba's convinced Gregor's harboring Kingston and grooming him for a second coup."

Remo's eyebrows almost kissed. "Kingston was executed four years ago."

The pressure on my heart eased. Even though I hadn't said this to test Remo's knowledge or affiliation, I was glad to find him perplexed by the news. If he hadn't been . . . Skies, I didn't want to think about the alternative. It was one thing to be related to a monster; it was another to be cavorting with one.

"Apparently, he wasn't executed."

"It was public."

"It was televised," I corrected.

"Are you saying it was staged?"

I waited for the information to settle.

"So, what? Your father thought that binding our essences would make my grandfather confess to some nefarious plan?"

"No. He thought it would keep him happy and *forget* about his nefarious plan." The episode of Gregor and Remo standing by my crib sprinted into my mind. "Getting his own flesh and blood on the throne beats getting a puppet there."

Remo lifted his hand to the back of his neck and kneaded it as though our conversation had given him a kink. "But you weren't going to go through with it."

Weren't? Did he think I'd somehow changed my mind? Instead of pointing out that I still wasn't going to, I said, "I'll be faithful to you and to our union as long as it takes to find out Kingston's whereabouts."

He snapped his hand off his neck. "This is so fucked up."

"Which part? The coup? The prison? Our betrothal? This conversation?"

"All of it!" He ran his hand through his hair, tugging at the roots. "Every fucking part of it."

For a long moment, the only sound was the breeze combing through the chunks of metal, glass, and brick.

He released his hair, his fist banging against his thigh. "I work with my grandfather. If he was training someone, I'd know."

"I understand your need to defend him, Remo. I understand that you'll always want and probably choose to believe your family over mine, but know that my father isn't alone in thinking this way."

His Adam's apple bobbed. "I suppose your mother thinks this, too."

"I wasn't talking about my mother. I was talking about someone who isn't related to my family."

"Who?" His voice rang out over the miles of flattened houses. "Who else thinks this way?"

Was I betraying my father's trust by sharing this information with Remo or was I helping our cause? What if we got out of here, and Remo went to his grandfather with all this knowledge—

"Amara? Who. Else?"

"Silas." His name fled my lips like an arrow springing off a bowstring.

Remo's mask of anger transformed into one of incredulity—his eyes grew wide and his mouth parted and rounded. The vein underneath his birthmark seemed to pump harder, fluttering the stained skin. I watched how he'd react next. It could go one of two ways: either the weight of his stepfather's allegiance would shift Remo's loyalty or he'd call me a liar.

The white light falling from the sky licked his mussed locks, making his head look ablaze. He kicked a piece of siding, which flipped before crashing down on the tracks, barely visible underneath all the wreckage. For the longest time, he stood stock-still and stared at the train.

The breeze caught in my hair and blew pieces of it in my eyes. I dragged my black locks away and tucked them behind my ears, but they slipped free. I neither turned nor took cover in the train. I waited, not wanting to miss the moment Remo picked his camp.

Finally, it happened. He looked toward me, and his eyes, although not the fiery shade of his hair, seared right into mine. "If Kingston's alive . . ." His voice was scratchy. "If he's alive, I'll find him."

I tipped my head to the side. "And what will you do once you find him?"

He pursed his lips before parting them once more. "I'll kill him."

I'd crept out onto a fragile limb. Instead of splintering, it had supported me. "Thank you."

"Don't thank me, Amara. I'm not doing this for you; I'm doing this because Kingston is a halfwit, and as much as I have trouble with your family on a personal level, your father is good king."

"Whether you want it or not, if you eliminate Kingston, you'll get my gratitude." My words did nothing to slacken his rigid stance or to calm the throbbing at his temples. "To think you could've milked this situation and didn't."

One of his eyebrows jolted. "How could I have milked this situation?"

"I would've paid a high price to protect my father. Perhaps even struck a *gajoï* or met you by the Cauldron a second time." My pulse picked up speed as I wondered what on Neverra had possessed me to add that last part. I could've stopped at the bargain. Why did I have to go and bring up marriage? Remo wasn't the devil I'd believed him to be, but he was also not the man I'd pictured at my side forever.

His eyebrow lowered. "A favor from you *would* have been nice, but I'll leave your hand to someone who deserves it."

My jaw slackened.

He chucked me under the chin. "Don't look so surprised. I'm not completely ill-intentioned."

He wasn't even a little ill-intentioned. I didn't know what to do with this new Remo. How to act around him. "What's your ultimate ambition, Remo? *Wariff* or *draca*?"

"Why do you assume my aspirations are political?"

I frowned.

"Maybe I'll uphold my family legacy and open a bakery."

"A bakery?"

His mouth curved into that signature half-smirk of his. "You can't see it?"

"Um. No. I mean, why not? I just . . . um."

"Peach pie can become the signature dish."

My jaw must've come completely unhinged, because the look that crossed Remo's face was wickedly bright.

"Relax. I'm just teasing you, Trifecta. I much prefer strategizing over baking." His teeth flashed and so did his eyes.

"But you like to bake?"

"Surprisingly, I do."

"Who are you, and what did you do with Remo Farrow?"

He grinned a little wider, then inclined his head toward the magical vessel. "Come on. We've got a train to catch." He started to turn but must've noticed I'd grown too stiff to move, because he grabbed my limp hand and all but dragged me into the glossy carriage.

"If you ever bake me a pie," I said, as he punched the two buttons, and the train began to rattle, "I'll unfriend you."

He leaned back against the console, closing his fingers around the edge and crossing his legs at the ankles. "Unfriending me implies you've friended me. Are we friends, Amara Wood?"

I studied him from my lower vantage point. I'd taken the precaution of sitting so as not to be tossed around. "Wouldn't that be an unexpected twist in your story? The hero and the villain becoming tight . . ."

"I draw the line at getting matching tattoos."

The smile, which had appeared on his lips earlier, didn't grow in size but in intensity. Slowly, it smoothed his roughened edges and dispelled the shadows from his face, and like mortar sealed the first brick to the foundation I'd lain out.

21

NEVERRA

Relief swept from my spine into my furthest extremities when we arrived inside the next world. "It's over," I murmured.

"What's over?"

"Our imprisonment. We're obviously home." The portals gleamed like miniature ponds beside the forest of *calimbors* whose crowns were drenched in a ribbon of mist so thick it obstructed the lavender sky.

"Don't you think there'd be more people if we were home? And what about the Pink Sea? I don't see it. Do you?"

I whirled around to find that Remo was right, even though he hadn't needed to be so snarky about it. There was no pink stretch of water; only tall cliffs frosted with mist. Disappointment flooded me, penetrating to my very marrow, washing away any lingering relief. "Cruel. So cruel." I didn't even want to leave the platform.

Remo hopped off the floating platform, which seemed to be woven from *volitor* fronds. He started walking but then backpedaled toward me and raised his arms to help me down.

"I'm not going."

He frowned.

"What's the point? A *calimbor* will surely squash us, because something shitty's bound to happen. It'll probably flatten a third of our bodies but spare our skulls, because what would be the fun in ending us *too* quickly?"

"No *calimbor* will fall over us, *prinsisa*."

I still didn't feel like jumping down and trotting around this poor replica.

"Maybe this is the cell in which we meet others."

I looked down at him, totally unconvinced.

"It seems hospitable enough."

I narrowed my eyes. "No, it doesn't." I realized then that the trees were lined up just like the houses had been in the last worlds, all tidy and symmetrical.

He didn't lower his arms. "We're partners."

"The villain wants to sit this one out."

"Fine." His arms began to drop. "Stay up there. If I die again . . ." He let his voice drift off.

"I promise not to board Train Hell until you resurrect."

"What if I don't resurrect?"

Ugh. I couldn't believe Remo was resorting to guilt tripping. He must've sensed me softening, because his arms arced back up. Even though I really wanted to get down on my own, I would probably fall face first at his boots. I chose the lesser of two mortifications, sat, then sprang toward him.

He caught me. "Can't believe you trusted me to catch you," he said as he unwrapped his fingers from my waist.

I whipped my gaze to his eyes, trying to surmise if he would've tricked me into a false sense of security. "You wouldn't have dared . . ."

"Are you sure? I'm a pretty daring person."

In truth, I wasn't sure. Allying ourselves to face this dimension didn't automatically make us best friends.

The green in his irises dimmed. "I wouldn't have dropped you,

Trifecta," he grumbled before carving a path through the soft moss, leaving me to stare at his straight back.

"I'm sorry, Remo, but it's going to take a little time for my mind to accept you're not Gregor's cruel heir who wants nothing more than to see me fail and fall."

He stopped walking but didn't turn around, his fingers balling into fists at his sides.

I made my way toward where he stood and circled his rigid body. "In real Neverra, you wouldn't have caught me."

"I would've caught you."

"Please. We were never friends, or allies, or partners." I cocked my head to the side. "Plus, we didn't only have each other; we had options. Right now, I'm your only option, so embarrassing me or hurting me wouldn't be wise. Especially considering you prefer bad company over no company."

"Can you let that go already? I only said it to piss you off."

My head jerked a little. "Why did you want to piss me off?"

He shoved his hand through his mussed red hair. "I don't know. Maybe because that's what we're best at. Pissing each other off."

My eyes grew wider; his did the exact opposite. "How have *I* ever pissed you off? I avoid you whenever I can. I rarely ever address you unless I have to."

His nostrils flared. "Just drop it, all right? And try not to hum or sing, so that, if there is anyone else around, we can spot them first."

"I wasn't going to sing," I muttered. "When was the last time I sang anyway?"

"When you were getting dressed back at the inn."

"Oh right. When you suspected I was dead and just *had* to check."

He kept walking, kept glowering. Not at me, even though I had no doubt he was visualizing my face on each patch of moss he stomped.

I picked up my pace; he accelerated. *Bagwa.*

We walked like that, me lagging behind, until we reached the

Gorge of Portals. He raised his arm to touch the lowest one. When his fingers cut right through it as though it were no more substantial than a cloud, my disenchantment with this bogus Neverra swelled. He raked his hand through a couple more illusory doors before abandoning his quest to uncover a real one. Where would it have led us anyway? Nowhere good, that was for sure.

Something glinted in the distance. I squinted trying to make out what it could be, but then a rattling sound I knew oh-so-well had my gaze dropping to my feet, to the tiny, quill-coated bodies writhing between them.

"Aw, crap," I heard Remo mutter.

Was he muttering because I'd just stepped on a nest of freshly-hatched *mikos*, or were some reptiles slithering around his boots, too? One of the snakes picked up its flat head and hissed at me, its forked purple tongue shooting out. Thankfully, it was a juvenile. Since *mikos'* tongues were as long as their bodies, an adult's would have reached me.

"How did you not see them, Trifecta?"

Now is so not the time to pick a fight. "Maybe because they're the exact same shade as the moss instead of black like on Neverra," I snapped, as a larger *mikos* slithered between my boots.

Since their tails resembled their heads to confuse their enemies, I watched for a hint of the tongue they never fully reeled in. Sure enough, it came at me, and I jolted backward, my boot rolling over a body. The creature hissed, then swiped the shell of my ear. Yelping, I whirled around and jumped, no longer worried about squashing the snakes, and man did I squash some. They were proliferating like bacteria, rising from the very soil.

Once I reached him, I stuck my back to his and stared at the slithering pit. Stupid power-blocking world. *Mikos* hated heat, so my *kalini* would've come in handy.

"Any bright ideas, Farrow? Because I'm all out fire."

"How about using your *wita*, Trifecta?"

My gaze dropped to my palm. *Crap.* Why hadn't I thought of

that? I tugged out my dust and fashioned it into a broadsword, which I swung around using my uninjured arm, chopping cleanly through the spike-coated bodies. Whenever I killed one, though, sixteen seemed to rise. "Any other ideas?"

"Run."

"Where?" They were literally everywhere. It was as though the very moss had morphed into snakes.

"To the *calimbor*."

"What if it's full of them?" I swung my sword, decapitating a *mikos* whose flat head was leveled with my throat. "We should get back to the train."

"The tree's closer."

It was closer. I still didn't love his plan, but there was no way I was running in a different direction than he was.

"On the count of three . . ."

As he counted, I sang softly. My nerves were fried, and the smoke from their frying needed an escape hatch.

"Two."

The rattling seemed to quiet, or maybe I had trouble hearing it over my frantic, throaty melody.

It was a song I'd heard in a human club a year ago. I'd thought it was super cool and had gone to gush to the droid DJ. My enthusiasm had him playing it so many times that night that by the time we'd left the club with Sook, Giya, and the legion of bodyguards assigned to me during my Earthly travels, I'd memorized every note.

The *mikos* swayed, and then their flat heads plopped right onto the ground. I stopped singing, worried we were in for something worse than a reptilian attack.

"Amara, keep singing."

I looked over my shoulder at Remo, realizing that my back was still pinned to his. Weren't we supposed to be running? Had he said one, and I'd missed it?

The rattling started anew.

"Please," he urged.

My mouth flew open, and I let out a loud sound that was in no way melodious. The flat heads, which had perked up, froze. I adjusted the amount of air rushing out of my mouth. The *mikos'* heads began to drift like clumps of mallow, settling on the ground or on a buddy's quills.

"What now, Remo Farrow?" I sang.

"We still run, but whatever you do, don't stop singing. Put the sword away first. I don't want you to lose it and have to dig for it in a snake pit."

Keeping up my frantic tune, I squeezed the hilt of my weapon until it dematerialized and melted back into my other palm.

"Ready?"

"Nope," I singsonged.

He snorted and then clapped my hand. We took off running, skating over the tubular bodies, quills crunching beneath our boots' sturdy soles. Miraculously, neither of us slid. Even more miraculously, none of the *mikos* reacted to being trampled. We reached the *calimbor* when I hit the chorus. Remo tugged open the turquoise door built into the base of the tree, and we burst inside the hull.

"Wait. Don't close it," I panted between two verses, fearing we might get locked in again.

He shut it.

"Remo! What if it never opens again?"

"I'd rather be stuck in here than out there. Besides, my grandfather is a creative man. I'm sure he'll have programmed a new method of torture into this cell."

Still, I extricated my hand from his and tried the door. The latch unclicked and the hinges worked. When a forked tongue darted through the small gap, I slammed the door shut. The strip of tongue fell onto the white and pink circle tiles, wriggling like a worm, before curling in on itself. I held my breath, praying it wouldn't morph into a snake. Or ten.

Remo caged the inert purple helix under a glass lid. I pivoted to see where he'd taken it from. A jar, now lidless, graced a wooden countertop built into the hollow trunk. It stood beside a dozen others, filled to the brim with rainbow-striped candy, gold-foil bonbons, floating pastel marshmallows, and garlands of candied *drosa* petals. Over the jars, on walls painted the same cheery turquoise as the front door, were scrawled names like "rainbow twists," "drops of sunshine," "morsels of cloud," and "blooming hearts." Was this candy shop modeled after the one which had been torn down to accommodate the Duciba? Was any of the candy edible or jeweled fakes meant to entice and disappoint?

I approached one of the jars, lifted the lid, and sniffed the contents. The sugary air made my mouth water. I plucked a marshmallow and placed it on the tip of my tongue where it melted into a delectable puddle.

"Obviously self-preservation isn't innate," Remo grumbled.

"Putting a horde of *mikos* to sleep worked up my appetite." Since the first marshmallow didn't make my stomach cramp or mouth foam, I snatched two more, then replaced the lid so they didn't float away. "I'm not sure what that says about my singing abilities, though," I added between scrumptious bites.

Remo didn't answer, his full attention on the red sphere bobbing on the thick russet waters of a crystal fountain sited in the middle of the shop. I sniffed the air, picking up notes of caramel and chocolate, then walked over to it and was about to dip my finger inside when Remo seized my wrist.

"I just ate some candy and didn't keel over, Remo."

He tipped his head toward the bronze ripples and the red sphere, which wasn't a ball but an apple, the same unblemished one that had appeared in every world. "That song you belted out, I despise it almost as much as this apple."

I tried to take the high road. Actually, I didn't. I contemplated the high road but chose to stay the course. "Must you always be so vindictive?"

"Vindictive?"

His underhanded criticism and the sight of the stupid apple spoiled the sweetness lingering on my tongue. "Never mind."

"I didn't say I hated your singing; I said I hated the song."

I stared at a bouquet of giant green lollipops spilling from a tall vase beside another turquoise door. "Where do you think that door leads? Back outside?"

A broad wall of navy fabric that smelled of sweat, loam, and man thwarted my sight of the door. "Don't change the subject."

"I'd rather not stay on the subject of my *mikos*-charming skill that obviously doesn't charm you."

"You really only hear what you want to hear. I repeat: I. Despise. The song." Did he hope his clipped tone would help me understand? I understood fine without him having to mimic a droid.

Borrowing his tone, I answered, "I. Don't. Like it. Either."

"Then why did you ask the damn DJ to play it all freaking night?"

I blinked. "You were there?"

His jaw reddened. I didn't think he was embarrassed as much as miffed I hadn't noticed he was part of my *lucionaga* entourage.

"I never asked him to play it all night. I just went to tell him it was good." I pushed a lock of hair behind my ear, flinching at the sting. "Until he played it over and over. Then I thought it was annoying." After a beat, I said, "Sorry for having missed your attendance."

"It's fine." He didn't sound fine about it.

"Were you at the club for fun or for work?"

"Fun. Until you came along."

"Wow. Thanks."

"That's not— What I meant was, if I'm off duty but in your presence, I keep an eye out for potential risks."

"Should've gone to another club the second you saw me arrive."

Silence beat loudly between us before he said, "Yeah. I should've."

"Why didn't you?"

His Adam's apple bobbed. "Your ear's bleeding."

I glanced down at my fingertips, red where I'd touched my wound, and rubbed them together. My blood turned ochre before flaking off. "So? Why did you stay?"

"Because it was a new club, and I wanted to see what all the rage was about."

Made sense. What didn't make sense was how disappointed his reason for hanging around made me feel.

Before he could sense my curious and confusing musings, I sidestepped him and headed toward the far door.

When I reached for the handle, he added, "And because I don't trust human men around you. They swarm you. And it's worse in clubs, under the influence of alcohol."

"They do *not* swarm me."

"Because your guards are tasked with keeping them away."

"Well, it would be nice if they stopped doing that," I huffed. "I'm not some helpless kid. I can take care of myself. Like you love to remind me, I'm the Trifecta." I opened the door a crack, enough to peek behind it and make sure the ground beyond—hardwood . . . *good*, we weren't back outside—wasn't crawling with snakes. It wasn't. "Seriously, Remo, I'd really appreciate it if you stopped alienating me from people."

"It's for your own safety."

"Is it?"

As he approached, his lips jammed together.

"Is it for my safety?" I repeated.

He wrapped his hand over the edge of the turquoise wood and drew it wider. "A spiral. Your favorite."

I guessed the topic of ostracizing Amara was closed. *For now.* "At least the stairs lead up." I didn't feel like spending any more time in a basement.

Slender openings had been carved into the coarse husk, acting as windows. As we plodded up the stairs, I glanced through one.

The mist, which had been high overhead when we'd arrived, was now draped over the land making it seem as though the *calimbors* were rooted in clouds.

"Do you think this is what Neverra looked like under my grandfather's reign?"

Remo peered out one of the openings. "It's exactly what it looked like. Have you never seen the paintings of our land from that time?"

"I saw some pencil sketches but never a painting. Where did you see one?"

"Grandfather has a couple in his home."

"He probably misses the mist."

I sensed Remo's eyes on the back of my neck even though I was giving the wooden stairs my full attention, desperate to avoid another tumble.

"Believe it or not, *prinsisa*, my grandfather was opposed to the creation of the mist. He told your grandfather it was a mistake."

I raised my gaze *and* an eyebrow.

"He said it would hurt the land, and it did. Crops took a hit. The *caligosubi* became poor, which sparked uprisings."

I knew our history as well as Remo. "Which were all squashed by the *wariff*. *Your* grandfather."

"Under Linus's orders."

"Just because he was following orders doesn't make it any less his fault. He gassed hundreds of men and women. Shut them in *cupolas*." Nima referred to them as the cage of nightmares. She would know since Gregor confined her into one to punish her after she'd been brought to Neverra. Even though for years, she hadn't wanted to speak of her experience inside, I finally forced her to tell me about it. I wanted to know how she'd survived when so many hadn't. "Probably shipped a bunch of them in here."

Unsurprisingly, Remo stayed mute on the subject as we climbed. He knew where I stood; I knew where he stood.

The second floor of the *calimbor* wasn't as fancy and modern as the apartments ground-dwellers now occupied in real Neverra, but it was nonetheless homey with its assortment of pale wooden furniture set against the same shade of turquoise as the shop. Iridescent seashells in all shapes and sizes decorated the walls of the bathroom. The sink was a ruffled clam and the bath shimmered as though made of crushed mother-of-pearl. I twisted the tap but didn't hold my breath for running water.

When it gushed through the pipes, I exhaled a gasp and cupped a hand to gather some to drink.

"I can't decide if you're fearless or clueless." Remo leaned against the doorframe, arms tied in a loose knot.

I drank whatever didn't slide through my fingers. When I didn't puff out of existence, I went for a refill. I used some to wash my face and rinse the blood off my ear. The scrape had already scabbed over. *Mikos* tongues were thankfully more sandpaper than cheese grater. I picked up a turquoise towel embroidered with conchs and patted myself dry.

"You might survive without food but not without water, Remo." There was no mirror in the bathroom, not that I truly wanted a glimpse of my face.

When I tucked the towel on the side of the sink, Remo pushed off the doorframe and walked to the still gushing water. I half expected him to turn off the tap and stride right back out, but he leaned over and placed his lips directly underneath it. I searched the bathroom for a container in case the pipes ran dry but abandoned my search because we'd undoubtedly be forced out of this world and into a new one by the time that happened.

I went back toward the window and surveyed the land carpeted with mist. "You think the snakes were the torment part of this world, and now we're safe?" I asked Remo as he came to stand beside me.

"No. In every cell, there's been two disruptive factors. In the first one, there was no food and everything was fake except the wolves."

"And my apple."

He slanted me a look. "And your apple. In the skyscraper city, there were deceptions and then the earthquake. In the inn, there was the peach pie and then the tornado."

"Do you think it's a way to chase us to the next world and keep up the torture?"

He bobbed his head noncommittally.

What would happen if we stayed on the train without hopping out? Would it take us to the next world without inflicting any horror and pain? And then I wondered about something else . . . "What do you think happens if we stay after the second event? Do you think the cell quiets and rebuilds?"

"I don't know."

"And what about the apple? You saw the red one downstairs? It's in every world."

"Yeah, I noticed it, but I have no clue what it does."

"Maybe we should try eating it."

"Maybe we shouldn't."

"What if it's our ticket out of here?"

"What if it's a trigger?"

"For what?"

"Who knows? A third form of torture." He returned his gaze to the wisps of mist glittering like stardust under the white sky. "My gut says to steer clear of it. Think you can do that?"

Even though I wasn't a fan of his cynicism, I nodded.

"Good. Now, what would you like to do?"

"Crawl into that bed over there and hide until someone breaks us out of here."

"By someone, you mean *me*?"

"No. I mean someone back home."

Remo's gaze flicked to the sky as though on the lookout for a flitting liberator, then to the tree across from us. "There are no spirals around the *calimbors* here."

He was right. On Neverra, stairs wrapped around the trunks like lianas. "Maybe all the stairs are indoors."

"Maybe." He backed up toward the front door. "I'll go see what I can find."

"Alone?"

"You wanted to rest."

I eyed the bed. Even though it called to me, it wouldn't be fair to let him venture off on his own. "What song doesn't make your ears bleed?"

His eyes flashed. I'd have said with relief but doubted Remo feared traipsing around alone. "How's your oldies repertoire?"

"How old are we talking? Last decade or last century?"

"Last century. There was this band my mother loved. Maroon 5. Ever heard of them?"

They were one of Nima's favorites but I doubted he wanted to hear our mothers had anything in common.

"Know any of their songs?"

I answered him by singing the opening verse of "Sunday Morning." He watched me, or rather my mouth, and it made me a little self-conscious, so I dipped my chin and started down the stairs ahead of him.

22

THE CONFESSION

The ground, obscured by the cloak of mist, was flat and spongy beneath my boots. It no longer wriggled with spiky reptilian bodies.

I stopped singing to ask, "You think the snakes are gone?"

"I think you should keep singing in case they're camped out somewhere else."

So I did. When we reached the next *calimbor*, we circled it, looking for a door, but the tree was solid bark. As Remo rapped on the trunk to see if it was hollow, I lumbered toward the next one. My boot caught on a jutting root, and I went sailing through the mist, landing hard on my knees and good hand. My elbow rocked in the sling but thankfully didn't connect with the ground. I grunted because damn, that hadn't felt nice.

"Amara?" Remo shouted.

"Down here."

Remo had offered to hold my hand when we'd exited the candy shop, and I'd refused, because I hadn't wanted to feel like a cripple. When he crouched beside me, concern edging his expression, I sensed he was about to duct-tape our palms together. Sure enough, he extended his hand.

I climbed back to my feet on my own. "I was just checking for *mikos*."

"Were you now?" He unfurled his tall body. "If I bring you back in parts to Neverra, your father will have me gassed, so give me your hand."

"Ugh." I slapped it into his. "I feel like a kid."

"You're acting like one."

"How am I acting like one?"

He closed his fingers around mine. "By making such a big deal about holding my hand."

As we circumnavigated yet another doorless tree, I said, "It's a well-known fact that boys have cooties."

Humor streaked across his face. "This might be part of the reason you don't have a boyfriend."

My cheeks warmed. Hopefully, my blush wasn't noticeable behind the rising tendrils of mist and the myriad of cuts and bruises I sported.

When his fingers flexed around my knuckles, I whispered, "What?" certain he'd spotted something in the fog and was trying to silently alert me.

"What, *what*?"

I scanned the heavy mist. "I thought you saw something."

"What made you think I saw something?"

My cheeks flared anew. "You squeezed my hand."

"That was me trying to keep your dead-fish hand from flopping out."

"Dead fish?"

He opened his hand, and my hand dropped. "You see. Dead fish."

"I just didn't want to cut off your circulation."

His teeth flashed as white as the mist. "How about you try cutting it off, so I can focus on our surroundings instead of on you?"

He wanted me to *try*? Bastard. I grabbed his hand and strangled it. "Firm enough?"

"Better." More teeth appeared.

I shook my head.

"By the way, you stopped singing."

"I thought I'd give your ears a break since the snakes are gone. I checked, remember."

He grinned this time. "At least hum."

"I'm starting to run out of songs."

"Know any songs by The Intrepids?"

"A few."

"Let's hear them."

So I sang the first all-droid band's greatest hit. And then their second hit. They pretty much only had hits since they created their music by tapping into the cloud and analyzing the most popular lyrics and melodies before weaving them together. The process was quite fascinating, having little to do with art and everything to do with artificial intelligence.

If I'd been free to choose my path, I would've gone to Earth and studied AI. Although Nima and Iba had allowed me to take some classes, I was never allowed to attend any full-time programs, and those were the ones where all the great things happened.

"How did you find yourself owing Joshua Locklear a *gajoï*?"

It had only been a matter of time until Remo brought it up. "Remember that pouch of Daneelie scales a squadron of *lucionaga* confiscated a couple months ago?"

"The ones Joshua sold to the Earthly army to use in biological warfare?"

I wrinkled my nose. Daneelie scales were an aphrodisiac, and yes, they'd been used in battle before—by my own parents on the Day of Mist—but since then, a law had been passed forbidding their sale on the Neverrian and Earthly black markets.

Remo pulled me to a stop, his expression wavering between shock and more shock. "You had something to do with that?"

I bit my lip. "I didn't know what they were going to be used for when I sold them to—"

"Wait. *You* sold them? They were *your* scales?"

My teeth sank deeper into my lip. I tried to collect my hand from his, but he tightened his grip, not even allowing any wiggle-room.

"Why?"

"Because I needed money."

He let out a dull chuckle. "The princess of Neverra needed money? Come on, Amara. At least make up a better lie."

"It's not a lie," I snapped. "I wanted to get my parents an anniversary gift."

"You have billions in Earthly banks, not to mention trunks of gold on Neverra."

"But those billions and gold aren't mine, and I wanted this present to be from *me*."

"So you clipped your scales and sold them to the most power-thirsty human general? How did you even meet him?"

"I didn't. I gave Josh my scales, and he arranged the whole thing."

"And that's why you owe him," he grumbled.

"No, I promised him a hefty commission on the sale." I locked my gaze on the mist, because at least the mist wasn't judging me. "I owe him because, when you guys busted him, he commed me to inform me he'd been compromised, and I begged him to take the blame for the scales."

"Damn, Trifecta, you're a real little villain. Not just my imaginary one."

I pursed my lips but still didn't look up, way too ashamed, but then another sentiment superseded my shame. Horror that I'd just confessed my crime to the *wariff*'s heir. The minute we were out of here, nothing would stop Remo from ratting me out.

I didn't know if the invisible tether that had formed between us the night his little brother had tried to kill me would be present in the Scourge, but I frantically combed for it. And then I felt it! "You will take my confession to the grave, Remo Farrow."

The strand between us vibrated like a plucked harp string, and then a knot tightened in my stomach. One must've tightened in his too, because his chin dipped into his neck, and his gaze dropped to his navel. "Did you just waste your *gajoï* on my silence?"

"I don't consider it a waste," I murmured.

Shadows fell over his expression. "I wouldn't have snitched, Amara."

My heart ratcheted up as I searched his face. Wouldn't he have? I'd gifted him ammunition to get me into a world of trouble. My parents loved me, that I had zero doubt about, but I'd infringed a law, so they would *have* to punish me.

He turned, and since he was still holding my hand, he jerked me back into movement. And then he walked so fast that for every stride he took, I had to take two. Oh, he wasn't hurt; he was furious. "I guess now you'll be stuck with me as a husband. Won't that be fun?" He popped the word out.

Dread rained goosebumps over my skin. "You said you weren't interested in my crown."

"I changed my mind."

I stopped walking and yanked my hand back. Or at least, tried to. The only thing I managed was to make him stop his crazy speed-walking. "You're not serious?"

"Till death do us part, sweetheart."

"Remo, that's not funny."

"Am I laughing?"

"No, you're not. You're acting strange and scary." Not to mention his fingers were crushing mine. "And you're hurting me."

He tossed my hand away as though it were a *mikos* and then he pivoted and stalked away, vanishing inside the mist.

23

THE CAGE

I didn't go after him, allowing him time to cool off, but I kept walking toward the cliff, hoping he hadn't decided to return to the train without me. The thick mist made it impossible to see more than a yard away, impossible to tell where he was. My trajectory was the cliff cresting over the white smog. Although I stepped carefully over the veiled terrain, I almost stumbled twice. By some miracle, that miracle probably being my snail's pace, I didn't come nose-to-moss with the ground.

As the steep wall of gray rock loomed closer, metal clanked and then a thunderous, human growl rent the air.

"Remo?" I yelled, hoping the sound had emanated from him and not some beast come to slurp me down.

My name was snarled, which all at once reassured me—not a wild creature since animals neither knew my name nor spoke— and spurred my legs to travel quicker—proud Remo was obviously in a heap of trouble if he was begging *me* for assistance.

As though some god had blown out a deep breath, the mist cloaking the prison cell dissipated. And not just a little but completely, giving me an unhindered view of Remo's predicament. His hands were wrapped around the golden bars of what looked like an oversized birdcage, his knuckles white from the strain. *Please let this not be a cupola.*

"Amara, behind you!"

My heart detonated as I twisted around. Since I was running, the momentum disrupted my precarious equilibrium. I tumbled, but at least I smacked down on my ass.

"It's coming for you! Get up!"

I jolted to my feet even though I hadn't seen anything coming for me, then backed up hesitantly, scanning the ground and air faster. When nothing moved, I called out, "What did you see, Remo?"

Metal clanked again. "The *lupa*. They're right in front of you! Skies dammit, run!"

I pivoted slowly toward him.

"Amara!" His face was as colorless as my sling. "NO!" he wailed.

Had the *lupa* torn me limb to limb in his mind's eye?

My doubt that the cage was infused with dark magic puffed away.

"It's not real," I said, keeping my voice calm because screaming at someone in the midst of a panic attack was surely not wise. "You're inside a *cupola*. Just open the door and get out." When it jounced off the ground, I sped up.

He blinked, but then he screamed again, at the wolves this time, his eyes glittering with fury, and I realized he hadn't heard me, or if he had, his mind was telling him I was dead or dying or had become a wolf myself.

The cage rose higher thanks to a pulley system tied to the top of the cliff. Had Remo thought this was an elevator? Didn't he know about *cupolas*? Maybe he hadn't understood what he was stepping into because the mist had hidden it.

Soon the cage would be too high to reach, so I ran, yelling at him to get the door open, hoping my words registered in his tormented mind. His gaze flicked to the sky. Whatever he saw made him jerk away from the bars and cower. I accelerated, reaching the *cupola* just as its floor leveled with my chin. I extended my arm and latched on to the door, giving it a firm yank.

It didn't open.

I yanked again.

The hinges didn't even creak.

Crap. Crap. Crap.

"Remo!"

He startled, his gaze whipping to mine.

"The door!"

He didn't move. Just stared.

The cage rose another inch. I fashioned a pair of heavy-duty snips from my dust and snagged the sharp blades around a bar. And then I heaved the handles together, sweat beading along my hairline. My sharp tool didn't even nick the metal. If only I had use of both my hands.

The cage drifted farther up. I tried again, failed again. What other tool could I make? An axe. As my dust morphed into one, the cage grazed the top of my head. I swung the axe, but it just pinged off the metal the same way it had pinged off the alarm box back in the last world.

Remo growled, upsetting my concentration. He punched the air, eyes slitted, muscles twisting underneath his tunic. "I will end you."

I wasn't sure whom he was going to end. I sort of hoped it wasn't fake-me, but then I remembered fake-me was dead, so it must've been someone else. I hoped it wasn't my mother.

He rammed one side of the cage like a bull, and it swung, its base clocking me square in the forehead. Stars brightened the edges of my vision, and I dropped my axe on my foot. The blade didn't go through my boot, but the weight made my breath catch and my toes curl in pain.

Remo rammed his cage again.

"It isn't real!" I screamed, trying to get through to him.

His eyes stayed glazed and unseeing. I grabbed my fallen

weapon and limped to the thick cord pulleying the cage up the steep wall, then batted it over and over. The heavy blade bounced like an arrow against taut string.

Ugh. Growling in frustration, I sponged my forehead on my arm and hobbled back toward the cage, my axe ribboning back underneath my skin.

What had my mother told me again about these cages? How had she defeated their magic?

The memory clicked. "Find the discrepancy, Remo! There's always a discrepancy. Hair color. Eye color. Size."

His nostrils pulsed. Were any of my words registering?

His gaze blasted back into mine.

Please see me. "Find. The. Discrepancy." *Please please please hear me.*

He blinked at me, then over his shoulder. His stance, which had slackened, cramped right back, and he ducked as though to avoid a hit. And then his leg streaked through the air as though he were sweeping someone off their feet.

I gripped a bottom rung and tugged, trying to drag the oversized birdcage down. "Remo!"

His concentration broke.

"His eyes! Or her eyes. Are they the right color?"

Again he blinked. "I . . . What—" His hushed voice told me his attacker must've vanished. "Amara, you're not dead." He gawped at me through the bars beneath his feet, the color, which had risen into his cheeks from his imaginary battle, draining. "Amara," he spoke my name again, incredibly gently this time, as though worried that if he spoke it any louder, I'd vanish back into the jaws of the *lupa*.

"The door, Remo. Open the door."

He raced across the cage, which lifted another inch, pulling me off the ground. "There's no handle!"

"Try kicking it open." Hopefully, my weight would keep the *cupola* from rising.

He raised his foot and snapped his leg, the sole of his boot hitting the door so hard my grip faltered and my fingers slid off the bar. I hopped but the cage was too high for me to reach now.

As he kicked again, I fashioned a hook with my dust and swung it, clipping it around a bar. The cage jerked up, and again my feet left the moss.

"Come on, Remo," I urged. I didn't want to stress him out, but I also didn't want to dangle from a spelled cage.

He froze midkick. Like literally, his boot was raised in the air but never made contact with the wall or with the floor. And then he fell, so hard his entire body thwacked the metal, making the cage dip then rise.

"Are you okay?"

He didn't move, and I noticed the back of his head had landed on the back of my hook.

Shit. "Remo!" I tried to slide it out from underneath him, but he was too heavy, and it wasn't like I had much leverage what with being suspended in midair from only one functioning arm. When blood spiraled down the metal and dripped onto my knuckles, I yelled his name again, then, "Wake up."

His lids reeled up.

Yes! "Remo. The door."

His head turned first, his cheek pressing into the hook, and then the rest of his body. He rose to his knees, muscles trembling. A bead of blood curved over his cheek before dripping off the tip of his nose. He palmed it away, smearing the blood.

I craned my neck back as far as it could go so I could keep my gaze affixed to his. "You need to get out of the cage. Open the door."

He stared at me, his pupils dilating then retracting as though his pulse were beating in his very eyes. His brow dipped, darkening his irises, and then his lips coiled into a sneer.

"Remo. I'm real. Whatever you're seeing isn't."

"What did you do with her, you sonofabitch?" he growled.

He was staring straight at me, but he was no longer seeing *me.*

His fingers dug around my hook, unclipped it. Teeth gritted, he pried it up.

"Remo, stop! It's me."

"Because of you, she's dead!" More blood dribbled off the tip of his nose, landing on my forehead.

"Remo, it's Amara, please."

His muscles strained his tunic, and his birthmark popped in fury. He growled, sending a look of such undiluted hatred my way that my heart shrank and slid into my clenched stomach. He agitated the hook as though trying to shake me off.

"Remo, stop! It's me! Trifecta! Your villain!"

He froze. Had one of my words registered?

"I'm trying to help you," I added, glancing downward. My heart crawled up, filling my throat and then my mouth. The ground was now so far below that slipping meant going *splat*. Swallowing, I tipped my head back and looked at him again. "Please, Remo. The door. You need to get the door open."

Unsealing the cage would stop the flux of magic. Once he was no longer possessed by his visions, he could give me a hand up and inside. Or at the very least, he could grab my arm through the bars and hold on to me until we reached the top of the cliff, because my arm was about to give out. I moved my bad arm to test if it had miraculously healed, but raising it an inch spilled acid inside my bones.

His eyes teemed with so much loathing that it iced my skin.

"Remo," I whispered. "I don't know who you're seeing, but that person's not real."

"Shut up," he snapped.

"Look for the—"

"I said, shut up!"

"Re—"

Before I could get the last syllable of his name out, he twisted the hook and let it slip through the bars of the cage, sending me hurtling into the ground. My tool shot out from my hand before I could turn it into anything that could save my life.

Falling couldn't kill faeries.

As my hair whipped around, I prayed these rules applied in the Scourge.

24
SECOND CHANCE

My fingers dragged through something sticky and cold that smelled of frost and earth. Had I survived my fall? I brushed my palms across the soil, expecting to feel clumps of moss, but no delicate plant tickled my skin. If I hadn't landed in Fake Neverra, where had I landed?

Slowly, I opened my eyes. Found myself staring up at the white sky and the portal that hung like a mirror fifty feet above me, reflecting a field of ochre mud and my sprawled body. We'd been right: there was no dying in this prison.

Relief warmed my body as I pressed both my palms into the ground and heaved myself into a sitting position. I realized two things at once: my sling was gone and my arm didn't hurt. I lifted my mud-soaked hands and marveled at the absence of pain. But then the memory of dropping my hook pinged into my mind, and I stopped marveling and started wiping my palms on my thighs, streaking my black suit russet-yellow. The filigree tattoo was still there, but was Karsyn's dust back inside its tracks? I brushed a shaky finger over the dark swirls. When a ribbon of dust sparkled out, I expelled a very deep breath.

I patted my face down for cuts and felt only smooth skin. *How incredible.* Still completely screwed up, but nevertheless incredible. As I stood, I inspected my suit, which unfortunately, hadn't mended like the rest of me.

A twig snapped behind me, and I spun, the mud impairing my speed. At the edge of the dense forest encircling the field stood a man with moon-pale skin and wild hair. Rigid as the trunks steeped in the leafy gloom, Remo took a step forward. The white light spread from his jagged contours, filling in his broad frame, painting his fiery locks redder and his wary eyes greener.

Chin to chest, he stared. Stared as though I were a stranger. *No . . .* not a stranger. A ghost. He'd died and come back to life, and yet shock and horror scored his features.

"I killed you." His voice was raspy and low, scraping through the cool air toward me.

Strangely enough, I was glad to see him, relieved he hadn't returned into the valley and boarded the train without me. "You made it out of the *cupola* alive. Most people don't." My hair swung like a leaden curtain as I approached him. "Congratulations are in order."

"I watched you turn to ash and die."

The memory of when he'd perished in my arms still haunted me, so I understood how shell-shocked he must've felt. Combing the mud out of my hair, I kept walking toward him. "Who were you picturing when you tossed me off?"

He shuddered as though reliving the moment. "Joshua Locklear."

"I'm relieved to hear it wasn't me."

His jaw clenched.

"So, how did you end up breaking out?"

"The door clicked open when I got to the top." He pointed to the bruise blackening the side of his neck. "I was in the middle of strangling myself."

"Eventful ride." I smiled.

"How can you be so . . . *smiley*? How can you even stomach to look at me right now? I killed you."

I tipped my head to the side. "Did you mean to kill me?"

"Of course not."

"Then stow away your guilt and help me reach the portal."

His reddened gaze raked over me. Was he looking for forgiveness? I'd already given it to him. Didn't he believe me?

"I promise, Remo, I'm not mad at you. *Cupolas* were famous for scrambling—"

He raised one hand to my cheek, grazing my mended skin. "You're really real."

I let his fingers roam over my hair and collarbone before spiraling down my neck, hoping the feel of me would reassure him that he hadn't murdered his princess. "I'm really real." My voice took on a strange, coarsened quality, as though goosebumps had risen inside my throat. Was that possible?

"I thought—" He swallowed and then he shuddered.

I knew what he thought. *Been there; thought that.* Sensing the weight of his guilt, I said, "You can stop imagining all the ways my father and mother will torture you for killing off their only daughter. I'm alive and well. Very well. No more broken bones or shredded skin. You, on the other hand, don't look too hot."

Shadows gathered over his blood-streaked face. "I watched you turn to smoke, Amara."

"And it didn't rate among the best moments of your life?"

"No!" His word was as violent as the look in his eyes, as brutal as the fingers gripping the back of my neck. "How can you even think that?" He shuddered, his lids falling over his eyes, his lashes shivering against his cheek. For a long moment, he stayed like that, with his eyes closed, his nostrils flaring, his jaw clenched.

My lips settled into a grim line, and I pressed my palms against his chest, right over where his heart banged like a Gottwa war drum. "I had a front row seat to your disintegration, so trust me, I know how horrifying it is, but look at me. I'm fine. You didn't hurt me."

His lids finally lifted. "I've never been more petrified in my entire life."

I shot him a sympathetic smile. "I can just imagine. I heard *cupolas* were quite the torture chamber."

His stare firmed and narrowed. "I wasn't talking about the effect of the cage, Amara. I was talking about the effect of watching you die. About *causing* your death."

"You weren't in your right mind."

His grip on my neck slackened and then his hand fell away from my body. "How can you be so forgiving with someone who's spent their entire life making yours hell?"

His admission stunned me into silence. Apparently, *cupolas* weren't only useful at causing nightmares; they were also useful for soul-searching.

Letting my hands slip off his torso, I sighed. "Don't give yourself *that* much credit. You didn't make my life easy, but you also didn't make it hell. Your grandfather, on the other hand . . ." I gestured to the land around us.

He craned his neck and glowered at the portal. "Let's not talk about my grandfather right now."

I dropped the subject of Gregor. "So, what tool should I make? A rope?" I pulled my dust out of my hand, the golden filaments gleaming like stretched gum.

"A spear gun."

"Wouldn't an arrow damage the portal?"

He returned his gaze to mine. "I planted a sword in one once. It suctioned the blade. Pulling it out was . . . *challenging*."

"Even for a big strong man like you?" I winked at him.

My teasing released some of the tightness between his eyes. "Did you snort some mud, *prinsisa*? You sound a lot like your grandmother."

He didn't have to clarify which one; only Addison existed in a constant mallow-haze.

A smile cracked across my lips. "I think I might be high." I shut my eyes and tipped my face to the white sky. "High on life." When I opened my eyes and leveled them back on Remo, I found him watching me, brows hugging. "What?"

His jaw flushed. "Nothing."

Instead of drawing out his discomfort, which was totally something Amara 1.0 would've done, I let him off the hook and concentrated on creating our ticket out of the Scourge. As I shaped my dust, I asked, "What's the first thing you're going to do once you get home?"

He didn't hesitate long. "Eat. And you?"

"Hmm…I'm going to fly and float around Neverra for hours." After I found Gregor and Joshua and made them both pay for what they'd done. Retaliation first, then indolence. "I really miss flying. Falling is much less fun." My reminder sparked a grimace on Remo's face. Before he started self-flagellating himself for sending me hurtling to the ground, I said, "You're welcome to accompany me on my excursion."

He froze.

His reaction made the spear gun feel as though it weighed a hundred pounds. We didn't need to be the best of friends, but we also didn't need to be sworn enemies.

"We'll be civil to each other once we're home, right?" His enduring silence made my raised arm arc down, the gun bumping against my hip. "Are you worried befriending me will hurt your rep and make your mother disown you?"

"Hurt my rep?" His tension finally eased, coiling off his face and shoulders as though he'd tossed aside some heavy boulder. "No, Amara. I'm neither worried about my reputation nor about my mother's feelings. I'm just surprised you'd want to spend time with me after what I said earlier."

I frowned. "What you said?"

He rubbed the back of his neck, gaze on the mud staining his black boots. "That I'd force you to marry me."

Oh. That. "Look, I know you're not interested in me or my crown. You were angry. We all say things we don't mean when we're angry." I slid my bottom lip between my teeth a few times, then released it to ask, "Right? You didn't actually mean it?"

His Adam's apple jostled as he raised his gaze back to mine. "I would never force your hand back into the Cauldron."

Was it a figment of my imagination or did he sound a little despondent? "No one's getting locked out of Neverra, Remo." I said this gently, assuming it was the source of his fretfulness. When the trench between his eyebrows deepened, I touched his bicep. "We'll just stay engaged until one of us finds our ideal partner." He flinched as though the idea sounded atrocious, which reminded me of his whole no-strings-attached lifestyle, so I amended, "Until *I* find someone to marry. I forgot marriage wasn't an ambition of yours. We'll just have to be extra discreet about dating other people."

The tendons in his arm roiled underneath my fingertips, taut as the mooring lines that bolted the Floating Garden to the Pink Sea.

"Actually. That's stupid. Unless we demand to end our engagement, the Cauldron can't kick us out." I slid my hand off his arm, eyebrows dipping in thought. "Right?"

"If the person has fae blood, and the . . . *dating* takes place on Neverra, the Cauldron will sense it and punish you."

My heart, which had begun to scud faster, missed a beat. "How?"

"I'm not entirely sure."

I sighed. "That sort of puts a dent in our matchmaking plans."

"*Our* matchmaking plans?"

"You were going to introduce me to potential candidates?"

His eyes tapered, and his pupils became pin-sized.

"You led me on," I murmured, hurt blooming in my chest. "There are no potential candidates. You just said that to"—I raked my hair back, the mud already caking my hair into dreads—"to placate me." I stared dejectedly at the spear gun.

It wasn't like I needed Remo to set me up. I could find someone on my own. For Skies' sake, I could even use *captis* to catch a man's eye. But finding someone wasn't what troubled me . . . it was the implication of his lie. Fae men didn't stay away because they feared my blood or were warned not to befriend me; they stayed away because they were simply not interested.

Tears stung my throat; I swallowed them back. And then I raised the spear gun and shot. My arrow went wide. Remo didn't comment on my awry aim, perhaps because he feared I might shoot him next, or perhaps he was attempting decency by not heaping criticism onto my squashed ego.

I tugged on the *wita* rope to reel the projectile back, feeling an acute kinship to it as it dragged unceremoniously through the mud. Discreetly, I scrubbed my blurry eyes on my forearm before aiming at the portal.

"Aaron." Remo's voice pierced the heavy silence.

I side-eyed him, found his arms tied firmly in front of his chest. "What about Aaron?" I tried to remember what he looked like from the brief episode in the elevator, but I'd been so focused on Remo that I'd paid the other *lucionaga* little attention.

"He's one of the guys who'd like an introduction to the *prinsisa*."

That stoppered my gloominess, but only for a second. It was surely a lie meant to improve my aim.

"Titus is another. Then there's Zane and Reid. Neither can shut up about your eyes and mouth, and Brooks is obsessed with your triple *aptitude*. Would you like me to go on? The list is quite long."

I wiped my eyes again, hoping he'd think I was brushing away sweat and not tears. "You're just saying that so I focus on the target instead of on my bruised ego."

"No. I'm saying that so you stop thinking I'm a liar."

I gave him a weak smile. "You must think me so pathetic."

A nerve jumped next to his eye. At least, he had the decency not to agree with me. As I raised the spear gun again, he said, "But I'm not setting you up with any of them."

That dragged my arm and mood right back down. "Why not?"

The tinged skin at his temple fluttered fiercely. "Do you still hate my guts, Amara?"

I cocked an eyebrow up. "What do my feelings for you have to do with dating your friends?"

"Everything." His arms fell from their knot, and he took a step forward. "So? Do you?"

Realization dawned on me. If the tables were turned, I would also worry about setting my friends up with someone who disliked me, because that would put a serious strain on the friendship. "I don't hate you, Remo, and I'm not saying that to have access to your fr—"

His palms settled on either side of my face, which had my mouth and heart screeching to a stop. A look of such deep concentration marred his features that if he'd been any other man, I might've assumed he was contemplating kissing me, but he was Remo. Gregor's heir was much more likely to snap my neck than to sully his mouth with mine.

I watched him watch me, thinking it might be wise to step back. When had I ever been wise, though? "I know I'll resuscitate if you kill me, but it'll put a real damper on our tenuous friendship."

The furrows on his forehead smoothed, and his mouth twitched around a low, slow chuckle. "Killing you isn't my intent, Trifecta."

"Then why are you holding my face so close, Farrow?"

His hold softened. "Because I was thinking about kissing you."

My quiet heart streaked back into movement, blasting against my ribs.

"But I was hesitating, because I wasn't sure if you'd appreciate it."

I swallowed, but it did nothing to moisten my dry throat. "I'd prefer it to death."

His lips twitched again, and he was so close that the slight realignment disrupted the air thickening between us. "I'm not sure how to take that."

My mind frantically scrambled to make sense of what was happening. Did I want him to kiss me? Did I want to kiss him?

His pupils shrank then bloomed. "Mind putting that spear gun away?"

My heart ratcheted up some more, stealing all the blood from my brain, which was terribly impractical, since without blood, there could be no rationality, and this situation demanded a modicum of level-headedness.

Expelling a tatty breath, I squeezed the handle of my portal-snaring tool to liquefy it. "How terrible a kisser are you?"

"I'm not even going to try to guess why you're asking that question . . ." I felt the curve of his smile against my lips even though our mouths weren't touching.

"You're obviously worried I might use the gun to put an end to our kiss."

The corners of his lips tipped higher. "I was actually worried the kiss would render you so limp your grip would loosen and your very heavy and very pointy weapon would end up lodged in my foot."

"Ha." I tried to roll my eyes, but the hefty mix of anticipation and adrenaline coursing through me prevented all tendons from shifting. "You should really learn to manage a girl's expectations."

His eyes flashed with amusement, and then with something else . . . something that made my pulse leap off the deep end. I darted my tongue out of my mouth and moistened my lips, my mind going blissfully blanker. His pupils danced, but no longer in amusement. Slowly, he tipped his head to the side and brushed his mouth over mine.

Once.

Twice.

Three times.

Tingles raced over my lips, radiated into my cheeks, before scurrying into my chin and down my neck.

"What a tease you are," I croaked.

Confidence dripped over him like my magic glue back at the inn, seeping into all the little cracks of his ego, raising an insufferably sexy smile that sparked another tingle, this time low in my belly.

The tips of his fingers edged into my hair, and he pressed me closer. "Good things come to those who wait, Trifecta."

"*Trifecta* . . . Any chance a kiss could earn me a better nickname?"

A ruddy lock of hair fell into his eyes, obscuring their vividness. "It's never been a disparagement."

"It always sounded like one."

He tipped my head up a little farther. "Trust me. It wasn't."

Did I trust him?

I thought about the wolves, the sling, our night spent in a dank basement with my head on his shoulder and his arm around my waist. Skies, not only was I beginning to trust him, but I was beginning to *like* him.

"Amara?"

How long had I just retreated inside my head? "I was just thinking about how far we've come, you and I. Mortal enemies to almost kissers."

His pupils throbbed with mock indignance. "Almost?"

"Um. Yeah. Kissing usually involves a little more pressure and a lot more tongue."

"How about I rectify the almost-part?"

My snark and voice left me. *Poof.* Gone like the fire in my veins. The only thing I managed was a thin swallow.

This time, when his mouth touched mine, it wasn't the gossamer brush of a butterfly wing. This time his lips molded against mine, opening me to him. In the haze of sensation, I managed a single coherent thought: I would totally have dropped my weapon on his foot.

His tongue stroked the seam of my mouth, coaxing my lips farther apart before penetrating a little deeper. I'd never been kissed like that before, with such measured skill. It shouldn't have surprised me considering Remo's extensive experience. I batted that thought away, not wanting to dwell on the number of girls he'd trained on.

When he pulled back, even though my eyes were lidded, I could taste his pleased smile.

"How was that?" The raspy quality of his voice made everything in me seesaw.

Slowly, I opened my eyes and fixed them on his. "Not bad."

"Not bad?"

Smiling, I raised my hands to his shoulders, finding purchase on the hard muscles, and initiated another kiss. Where his touch had been measured and firm, mine was chaotic. I liked slow and steady, but I also loved hard and wild. And, I soon learned, he did too. He devoured the press of my lips, the slide of my tongue. Our teeth scraped, and our fingers dented, filling the ridges of his body with the supple curves of mine.

Our kiss was unbridled, delectable, and completely reckless, transmuting years of hatred into something else entirely. Something that would make Neverrians balk in surprise. After all, Remo and I were known for only two things: nasty barbs and nastier glares.

As his greedy mouth feasted on my hushed moans, a series of unwelcomed thoughts scrolled through my weakened brain, reinvigorating the organ which had switched off when his palms had cradled my cheeks. Remo didn't want any strings, and I wanted all the strings. His mother hated mine, and mine hated his. He was a Farrow, and I was a Wood. Even if our mouths were compatible, our lives and dreams weren't.

I ripped my mouth off his and bounced away, panting harder

than when I'd run from the wolf pack in Frontier Land. "I can't do this, Remo."

"I thought you were doing it quite well, actually." His voice was hoarse and his breathing labored.

"I meant this. Us. We don't want the same things." I pushed my hair behind my ears, the weight of the caked mud straining my neck, all but forcing my gaze up to the portal. "Well, besides getting out of here and wishing we'd known our grandmothers. We do have that much in common, but that's *all* we have in common."

His eyes darkened beneath the thick shadow of his lashes.

"Our attraction isn't real. It's just a consequence of there being no one else around."

"I disagree."

"You can't disagree with a fact."

"What *fact*?"

"Is there anyone else around?"

"No."

"Then it's a fact that our choice of partner is limited."

A sneer twisted his lips. "We didn't have to kiss at all. It isn't like we've been stranded in the Scourge for years and are slaves to our baser needs." He stalked toward me, then threaded his hand through my hair, tipping my face back up toward his. "Besides, I didn't kiss you because you were my only choice, Amara. I kissed you because when you died, I wanted to die, too."

I covered his hand with mine. "That's called guilt."

His eyes shone darkly. "I have *never* wanted to follow in the footsteps of the people I've killed."

I knew Remo wasn't angelic, but hearing him admit to having ended lives made me remember just how ruthless he was.

"When that cage let me out, I told myself that if you came back, I'd confess a whole bunch of things to you. Like how, ever since that *dile* stung you, I haven't been able to get you out of my damn head."

My eyebrows squished together. "I was twelve!"

His thumb stroked my bottom lip. "I know."

"You've . . . *not hated* me for five years?"

"Yes." No hesitation.

"That's ludicrous. You've never shown an ounce of interest in me. Or kindness, for that matter."

"I hunted and killed the *dile* that stung you."

Okay . . . I dragged his hand off my mouth, because his caresses were distracting, then folded my arms. "That doesn't change the fact that you've been a first-class *bagwa* to me. You told the entire school a drop of my blood would kill them if it got on their skin!"

"I was jealous. Guys were starting to notice you. They were starting to talk about you and your ridiculously gorgeous mouth and eyes, and it was the only way I found to efficiently detract them from buzzing around you. I'm sorry, but I didn't know how to deal with my attraction."

My eyes turned as round as the shell rafts that bobbed atop the Glades. "You destroyed my reputation because you *liked* me?"

"Yes." He linked his fingers together and cupped the back of his head, drawing his elbows close as though this were the most painful conversation he'd ever had. "Skies, Amara, I'm so fucking sorry. If I could go back in time and not act like a world-class, insecure jackass, I would. In a heartbeat, I would."

"Here I thought I was just loathed by the entire kingdom."

He squeezed his eyes shut.

A beat passed, its silence awkward and loud. "Is it also the reason my personal guards rotate so often and aren't allowed to speak to me?"

"No." His lids reeled up. "That's so they pay attention. I don't want them distracted. Distractions costs lives. And your life, it's . . ." His Adam's apple was so jagged it seemed about ready to cleave through his neck. "It's important."

"No more than anyone else's."

His emerald gaze grabbed me, held me. "One of the scenes I saw in the elevator back in the second cell was your mother crying."

"That's a . . . rare occurrence." I wasn't even sure I'd ever seen her cry.

He disconnected his fingers from the back of his skull and let his arms fall back to his sides. "She'd just had another miscarriage."

"She had many before I stuck around."

"Your parents wouldn't survive losing you, Amara."

I bit my lip. People survived insurmountable grief. As long as my parents had each other—

"I wouldn't either," he murmured.

"That's just your guilt over tossing me off the *cupola* rearing up."

His pupils pulsed.

I made the spear gun reappear, then held it out in front of him. "Here. You're surely better at shooting things than I am."

"Amara . . ."

When he cupped my cheek, I took a step back. I needed to get my head straight. In a rush of folly brought on by getting a second chance at life, I'd kissed him, but unless I was certain I wanted to do it again, I was keeping my lips to myself. "I'd really like to get home, Remo."

Lips thinning, he took the proffered weapon, then lifted it and shut one of his eyes. After a steadying breath, his finger flexed on the trigger, and the arrow soared, arcing through the cottony air, piercing the portal in its very heart before drifting past it and plummeting back into the squishy mud like a fallen star.

"It's an optical illusion," I murmured. "There's no way out of here."

"No, I think it's real, but I think we may need salt to turn it solid."

My eyes widened. "We left the bag in Frontier Land! We need to get back there. We'll just ride the train, without getting off until—"

"Even if we had salt, I doubt that'd be enough to unlock the door from the inside."

Despair crawled over my disappointment. I wanted to cry and

scream. Both. I wanted to do both but did neither. "So we're trapped."

He handed me the spear gun. "Just for a little while longer."

His optimism did nothing to improve my morale.

As I liquefied our tool, I started to shake so violently that my teeth chattered. "What if no one comes for us?"

He loosed another deep breath before raising a paltry smile, one I didn't think he was feeling. "I'm the grandson of the asshole who built this place. He's bound to figure out where I ended up." Remo, to my knowledge, had *never* insulted his grandfather. "I'll admit, I'm surprised he hasn't yet."

Still, I trembled. I was sick of Gregor's horrific playground and missed my parents and cousins. My grandparents and Nana Vee. I missed flying, swimming, fire. I missed getting dressed at the press of a button.

Remo stepped toward me and startled me with a hug, tucking my head underneath his chin and stroking my spine.

As I filled myself with his calm breaths and even heartbeats, I croaked, "I'm sorry you're stuck in here because of me."

His hands stilled on my back. "Not your fault."

Felt like it somehow was.

"And although the location isn't ideal, the company . . . I couldn't have wished for a better partner-in-crime." He pressed a kiss to the top of my head.

It took everything in me not to crane my neck and give him access to my heart again, but using him to feel something other than despair wouldn't have been fair. "Forced together because of treason, then stuck together because of a mistake. What a pair we make."

He didn't answer, just held me a little tighter, and I melted into him a little harder.

25

THE RETURN

Although we walked side by side, we kept to ourselves, both of us lost in thought. Several times, I felt his eyes on me but kept mine on the forest floor until the shadow of tangled branches and leaves receded.

When we reached the cliff where the golden *cupola* awaited, its door already propped open, Remo's fingers rolled into stiff fists. I peered over the ledge to evaluate the feasibility of downclimbing the mountain. Too steep. Would *wita*-made rappelling gear be solid enough to carry us down?

Even though my understanding of Gregor's prison was still limited, I didn't doubt for a second the mountain was infused with dark and terrible magic. The rock would surely crumble beneath our boots or rise higher. After all, Remo's grandfather loved nothing more than playing games.

"I fear the cage is our best option, Remo."

His jaw was clenched as hard as his fists, and his skin tone had greened. "I'm not going back inside."

"I'll be with you this time. And we'll keep the door open."

He huffed. "What if I kill you again?"

"I won't let you."

He shook his head, his red hair spiking like a wildfire around his wan forehead. "That cage turned me into a psychopath."

I wrapped my hand around his fist and dragged it away from his rigid thigh. Prying his fingers open, I said, "I know how to defeat the *cupola*."

"No."

I peered down again. "I suppose we could try to hang off of it . . ."

Remo's gaze flicked to the pulley system. "We'll climb down the rope."

I eyed the rope, not trusting it. "I know!" I released his hand and pulled my dust out, shaping it into a parachute. I didn't have enough *wita* to make a harness, but I had fashioned four sturdy handles along the sides. We'd have to hold on and hope it would keep us afloat, or at the very least slow down our fall.

Although my resourcefulness didn't magically reassure Remo, it did unstiffen his body. He picked up my creation and stared a long moment at it, and then he handed me one side and took the other. "Thank you."

"How about you don't thank me until we make it down?" The moss seemed much too far below us. Even the *calimbors* seemed stunted and *calimbors* were not small trees. "Ready?"

"When you are."

Knuckles whitening on my handles, I inhaled a deep, deep breath before nodding.

Eyes locked together, we jumped. The fabric flapped, and then it tangled and our bodies smacked together. Remo stretched his arms apart, and yelled at me to do the same. Skies only knew how, I managed to drive my arms apart. The fabric snapped, and we were yanked up so violently, both my shoulders almost popped out of their sockets.

Gravity took ahold of our makeshift vessel, and we drifted like a dandelion floret over the neat row of *calimbors*, all devoid of windows and doors, except for the one housing the candy shop.

When my boots bumped against solid ground, my knees bent, and I stumbled into Remo, who caught me.

His hand lingered on my body long after I'd regained my footing, doing all sorts of things to my already chaotic insides.

Lowering my gaze to the moss, I stepped aside and reeled in the parachute. "Do we head to the train?"

"I think we should rest the night here and board in the morning."

I stared up at the white sky. "You think night's about to fall?"

"I don't know how time works here. All I know is that we both could do with a bath and a warm bed."

The warm bed part reminded me of the one I'd wanted to crawl into earlier. It also reminded me that I'd seen only one. I didn't bring it up. Not yet.

As we made our way down the aisle of tall trees, tendrils of mist rose from the moss and curled around our boots. Even though the ground hadn't changed texture yet, in other words it hadn't sprouted thorny, tubular bodies, I sang softly. Remo's knuckles brushed against mine, sending bursts of heat up my arms. When the mist thickened, turning as dense as cotton, his fingers slid through mine.

We'd held hands before but never like this. Never with our palms flush and our fingers twined. My concentration was so focused on all the points of contact between our bodies that I almost walked right past the candy shop. Thankfully, Remo's awareness hadn't faltered, and he tugged me inside.

My pulse was so jumpy it impaired all of my senses. Besides touch. Touch was the one sense working entirely too well. So well that the minute the turquoise door clapped shut, I pulled my hand out of Remo's and spent the next few minutes it took to reach the first floor of the *calimbor* rubbing my tingling fingers and palm on the leg of my black suit.

While Remo vanished into the bathroom, I searched the small

apartment for a second bedroom but found only an empty closet. Water gushed, sounding a lot like my pressurized pulse.

"There's no soap, and the water is cold," he said.

I gazed up from the bed, biting down on my lip. "Better than no water."

He bobbed his head as he approached me. "Ladies first."

I ducked past him and entered the bathroom, closing the door. I thought about peeling off my suit and washing it, but in the end, I only kicked off my boots, then stepped into the frigid water fully clothed. However uncomfortable, the fabric would eventually dry. I laid back, letting the mud soften and melt off my long tresses, and then I scrubbed my scalp.

The water turned a muddy yellow. I drained it, rinsed off under fresh water, then stepped out of the bath and ran Remo a new one. Shivering, I grabbed one of the seashell-stitched towels and rubbed it against my body and hair before going to get Remo.

He frowned upon seeing me. "You bathed with your clothes on?"

"My suit was filthy, and removing it is a pain." I stared longingly at my deadened Infinity.

"You're going to catch cold."

Catching cold. Such a foreign concept for people made of fire. "It'll dry faster on my skin. Besides, imagine something happens, and we have to bolt for the train."

He pursed his lips. I was about to tell him that it wasn't because of him, but wasn't it? If there'd been two bedrooms, I might've considered stripping.

Before I could say anything more, the bathroom door clicked closed behind him. Unlike me, Remo stayed a long time in the bath. I couldn't imagine it was out of pleasure—how could one enjoy soaking in icy water?—but the privacy was surely welcome. Neither of us had had much of that in the last day . . . days? How long had we been gone? I was braiding my damp hair, wondering if the cloud cover would ever lift, when he finally came back out, a towel wrapped around his neck and his pants back on, even though his top wasn't.

"Are the snakes back?" Water dribbled off his hair and streamed into all the nooks and crannies of his chest.

I turned back toward the vista. "Can't see much of anything through this mist."

After a solid minute of silence, he said, "I thought you'd be sound asleep already."

Is that why he'd taken his time? To avoid the awkward moment of discussing sleeping arrangements? Had he been hoping I'd be conked out, and he could just slip under the sheets and reserve the awkwardness for the morning after?

He drew the curtains closed, all the while holding my gaze. "Get into bed. I'll sleep on the floor."

His gallantry blew my reservations away. "Don't be ridiculous. I'm sure you're perfectly capable of keeping your hands to yourself."

His expression changed slowly. "I am, but are you?"

I rolled my eyes. "It'll be tough, but I'll power through my lascivious fae urges."

He shot me a disarming half-smile.

"Besides, I'm so wet, you're not going to want to snuggle."

The smile vanished, and his jaw pinkened. He turned and rubbed the towel over his wet hair. Who would've thought snuggling would make Remo Farrow blush?

The boy was such a strange mix of smugness and timidity. I liked him all the more for it, which was a perplexing insight to have before getting into bed—albeit fully clothed—beside someone. Especially since the bed was half the size of mine back home, and Remo was neither short-limbed nor narrow-shouldered.

I hung the towel on the doorknob of the empty closet, then slipped under the covers in my uncomfortably damp suit. I considered removing it for all of a second, but good sense sparked and made me keep it on. A moment later, the mattress dipped.

"I'm sorry about having walked in on you back at the inn, Amara. I honestly thought you'd be dressed." Remo lay over the sheets, his gaze fixed to the timber ceiling.

"Getting dressed here takes a lot more time. That's another thing I'm going to do the minute we get back." I refused to wallow in the possibility that we wouldn't. "I'm going to change into *all* of my outfits just for the fun of it."

He smiled. "That'll take you a month."

"I don't have *that* many outfits."

"I've never seen you wear the same dress twice."

"That's because my aunt is the head designer of Neverra. I get new outfits beamed to my Infinity for every occasion." *Okay*, I did have an inordinate amount of outfits.

"Your naked gold dress is my personal favorite."

I arched an eyebrow. "My naked gold dress?"

His skin tone looked as though it had darkened, but it was hard to tell in the obscurity. "The one you wore for your mother's fortieth birthday."

"You mean the silk dress with the gold embroidery and sequins?"

"Yeah. That one."

I smirked at him. "The correct terminology is nude, not naked."

A gleam entered his eyes but failed to brighten them. If anything, the green darkened. "I wasn't referring to its color; I was referring to how it looked."

My breathing hitched. "It looked like I was naked?"

"From afar."

I blanched. "A lot of people saw me from afar that day."

"You look a little queasy, Trifecta."

"People thought I was wearing strategically-placed golden sequins . . ." I whispered in horror. "Of course I'm queasy. The second I get back, I'm deleting it from my Infinity."

"That would be a shame."

"If you love it so much, I'll beam it to you, and you can gift it to one of your many consorts."

"It looked good on *you*." His tone was sharp and a little angry. "And stop alluding to me having other girlfriends; I don't. You're it." He stared at the ceiling again. Glared at it. "Even if you don't want to be it."

I wasn't sure how to react to that, so I stayed quiet, picking apart every moment from our past, and analyzing them in a different light, one where I meant something to Remo Farrow other than *mortal enemy*. And then I thought of his last few words: *Even if you don't want to be it.*

I studied his sharp profile, his clasped lids, the tousled locks of hair that had tripped over his forehead, the purple skin ringing his neck, the rise and fall of his bare, hard chest. "I want to be someone's choice, not someone's obligation," I whispered.

I didn't know if he'd heard me. I wasn't even sure I'd wanted him to hear me.

Sighing, I rolled onto my other side and stared at the turquoise wall until sleep erased it from my sight.

26

THE NIGHTMARE

"No. No. No! Don't. No! Amara!"

I sprang awake, my heart in my throat, certain we were under attack. A quick sweep of the room showed me we were alone.

"Don't. No!" Remo writhed next to me, forehead glistening with sweat and lids clamped so snugly they were bracketed by tiny lines.

I sat, then placed a palm over his drumming heart. "Remo, *shh*. It's a nightmare."

His eyes whipped open, brimming with such panic that I repeated my soft words, coaxing him out of whatever horrid dream he was having. A nightmare about me apparently. I hoped I wasn't the villain in this one.

His nostrils flared and then his hands shot up to my face and cupped my cheeks so suddenly I almost lost my balance. "You're not dead. You're not dead."

Keeping myself up thanks to the hand still planted on his chest, I wrapped my other one around his wrist, not to tow it off, but to reassure him that I was made of flesh and not ether.

"I lost you. Again. I lost you again. The *dile*, it . . ." He shuddered so hard my bones vibrated with his trepidation. "The poison . . . you never woke up."

The memory of the *dile* usually made me scrunch up my nose, but I forced my fear away in order to reassure Remo that I was all right. That I wasn't afraid.

"That little sucker didn't get me. *You* got *it*, remember?"

As though to confirm I was solid, his thumbs grazed my cheekbones while his gaze traveled over my mouth, chin, neck, before returning to my eyes and resting there.

Their intensity made me swallow more than once. "Do you get nightmares often?"

"Not since I was a kid." His lashes fluttered again, as though to sweep away the hateful images.

I sighed. "It's probably a side effect of the *cupola*."

"Better wear off fast, or I'm quitting sleeping."

"Troubled sleep beats no sleep, Remo." I squeezed his wrist before releasing it.

He lowered his hands from my face, returning one to the sheets and the other to his abdomen, just over his navel and the trail of hair that began there and ended . . . someplace I had no right ogling. I laid back on my side next to him, pillowing my head on my bent arm. I started to remove the hand covering his heart when he anchored it with his palm.

A stillness fell over him. Over me, too.

"How long do you think we slept?" The thumping at my temples told me it hadn't been long enough.

His gaze cut to the brightness edging the drawn curtains. "I don't know."

"Do you want to head out or try to go back to sleep?"

His head turned toward mine. "Have you slept enough?"

"Probably not."

"How about you try to fall back asleep?"

"What about you?"

His pulse, although no longer erratic, beat fast. "I'd rather stay awake."

Was he worried something bad was about to happen? I was. Gregor's prison loved nothing more than offering its residents a false sense of security before knocking it down. "Want me to sing you back to sleep? It worked so well on the snakes."

The corners of his mouth rose. "Can I shelve that offer for later?"

Saving it for later implied we'd be sleeping next to each other again. I supposed it was preferable, while we were locked in prison, to sleep side by side rather than camp out on our own.

His smile faltered when silence stretched between us.

I sighed. "My offer is valid for the duration of our incarceration."

"What about after?"

After? I wasn't ready to go there yet. "You'll either have to self-soothe or crawl into your mother's lap."

"You do know I don't live with my mother, right?"

His index finger idled up the length of my arm to the ripped fabric at my shoulder, coaxing out goosebumps he thankfully couldn't see.

"I didn't know." My thick inflection revealed what my suit concealed.

"I share a room with three other *lucionaga* in the guard barracks."

"How very . . . mainstream of you."

He dragged his finger back down. "We can't all live in floating sea palaces."

Grated by his critical tone, I stole my hand off his body and nestled it against my own chest. "Because you think I have a choice?"

His eyebrows dipped. "You're not happy with your living arrangements?"

I liked my house but wished others had been built around it. "I live under a magnifying lens, Remo." I sighed. "I always wanted to live in a *calimbor* or in one of the smaller beach houses on stilts, or even in the Valley of the Five. Just somewhere more *normal*."

"You could move into the barracks. I'm sure there'd be no objections from my roommates."

A smile quirked over my lips. "How magnanimous of you, but I think I'll pass rooming with four men."

"Oh, you wouldn't be sharing with four of us. Just with me. I'd kick the others out."

My heart tripped. "For someone not in the market for a relationship, you're awfully possessive."

For several seconds, his jaw worked, as though his mouth were forming plenty of words but then obliterating them. "We're bound by the Cauldron," he finally said.

He'd obviously missed my whispered confession last night, so I rehashed it loudly, "Please don't feel an obligation to be with me because of a magical object, Remo." I sat, then swung my legs over the side of the bed, and got up.

"Amara—"

"We should head out." My braid had held, which was nice, since I was all out of hair ties.

As I made my way to the bathroom, Remo called out my name again, but I shut the door and dropped onto the closed toilet lid, and then I laid my face in my palms and shut my eyes. I hated how upset Gregor's grandson could make me one minute and how special he could make me feel the next. But I especially hated myself for allowing him to have so much pull over my mood.

I needed some distance, but how the hell was I supposed to find any in this magical jail cell?

Besides boarding the train alone . . .

I stared at the door and contemplated leaving before him. Fear won out. I might've been a little brave but most definitely not brave enough to face this world alone. That was the reason I waited for him once I'd let myself out of the bathroom and he'd gone inside.

The *only* reason.

27

THE EXPLOSION

When we set off toward the train, the mist belted the *calimbors*, masking their crowns.

Remo climbed onto the hovering platform with the ease of a gymnast. He offered me his hand, but I didn't take it, pretending not to have seen it. I was done holding his hand. With the grace of a steel rod, I hoisted myself up and over.

While Remo grazed the modern touchscreen, I settled on the curved bench and stared out the window until the outside world disappeared behind opaque barriers. And then I curled my palms around the lip of my seat and readied myself for the molar-shattering voyage. I wondered if we actually traveled or if the train was static and the world around us reorganized itself. If it was the latter, then the juddering was unnecessarily cruel.

Then again, this was prison, not some spa with coconuts fitted with striped straws and fuzzy rainbow loungers.

Remo turned around, pressing his palms into the ceiling to keep himself steady. I felt his eyes on me but still refused to look at him. He'd kissed me, confessed he'd liked me for years, and then he went and ruined everything by bringing up his sense of duty to the Cauldron. Most importantly, though, why was I so offended? It wasn't as though *I'd* harbored feelings for Gregor's grandson. I probably cared because I was drained, physically and mentally, and exhaustion made me slightly grouchy.

I thought about our kiss, wishing I hadn't felt anything. It would've made it all so much simpler. Feelings couldn't get hurt when none were involved. The train finally stopped shaking, but my skull didn't. I swiped my Infinity to release medication into my bloodstream when I remembered the damn thing didn't work in this damn world.

"Are you okay?" Remo asked as the windows and door retracted.

I really wished he could go back to being an ass, because that made not liking him way simpler. "Just my head, but it'll pass."

I got up. Because the compartment was small and he wasn't, my wedged-in breasts made contact with his firm chest. I chided my skin for tingling. It needed to stop doing that.

"I'd rather a punch than your silence, Amara."

I stared at his jostling Adam's apple, and not because I was contemplating punching it—his neck was bruised enough—but because it sat in my direct line of sight and Adam's apples didn't stare back in the hopes of excavating your soul.

"Do you think any of this is easy on me? I kiss you, I confess stuff to you that I assumed I'd take to my flowerbed grave, and then you give me the cold shoulder, because I reminded you that we're bound by the Cauldron—"

I whipped my gaze up to his. "You reminded me? Because you think I forgot?" I tried to step back but the backs of my knees hit the bench. "I'm not mad because of that."

His eyebrows went up. "Then why are you mad?"

"Because, Remo, I'm confused. *You're* confusing. Do you like me or not? Am I an obligation or a choice?"

"You were never a choice until the Cauldron bound us."

"The Cauldron shouldn't have changed anything."

"But it did. Just like this place did. Just like watching you die did." He tossed his hands in the air, disrupting the flyaways around my face, which had fallen out of my braid during the night. "Tell me something . . . did *you* ever consider making out with me before we were tossed together in the Scourge?"

My cheeks brightened. "No, but that's because you were hateful."

"And yet you kissed me back, Amara, so admit this place changed you, too."

I notched my chin a tad higher. "This place changed how I saw you but not what I want. And what I want is a real relationship, not an ordained one, and certainly not one with an expiration date because the other party isn't into long-lasting monogamy."

"You barely know me. Maybe you'd hate dating me."

"Maybe I wouldn't hate it." Was I still pink or had my complexion veered right to purple? "But dating isn't even a possibility, because dating means strings, and you don't want strings, Remo, so why are we even fighting about this?"

His eyes lowered to my lips.

I stepped to the side before he could kiss me. I suspected that would be a bad idea considering how much it had scrambled my brain back in the mud field, and I wanted . . . *needed* . . . to keep a level head. "Don't."

"Why does it have to be all or nothing? Why can't it just be *something*?"

"Because I want what my parents have. What my aunt and uncle have."

"What if what they all have is only due to their brands? Both Kajika and your mother were branded by their partners."

My ribs contracted. Giya had brought up the same point during one of our many discussions about boys and hearts. I'd hated her insinuation, because it meant magic was mixed into their love, and I didn't want magic to have anything to do with that feeling.

"My grandparents aren't branded, and they're crazy in love. And my mother was branded by Cruz Vega first, and she never loved him. Besides, those brands are used by faeries to track humans. Unlike *captis*, they're not used for seduction."

"But what if—"

"Then I'll find myself a human consort once I'm out of here and brand *him*!" Infuriated, I spun on my heels and bustled out of the train and onto a platform that was carved right into a giant gray boulder.

Huffing a little, I scanned our newest cell—spectacular rock formations, a dark cyan forest denser and more tropical than the one on Neverra, and a glittering waterfall.

My lips popped apart at the sight. "This isn't too bad."

Remo grumbled, "We can't even see the ground, Trifecta."

Even though I now knew the nickname wasn't pejorative, I still didn't love it. "It's undoubtedly full of creepy creatures, but there's a waterfall. I love waterfalls." Sure the sky was pasty white, and it was eerily silent, but I was still hopeful this world would be kindlier than all the others.

But then my hope vanished when a tinny voice erupted from the train: "Countdown to self-destruction will begin in ten ... nine . . . eight ..."

Self-destruction? What was about to self-destroy? This cell? The entire prison?

"Six ... five ..."

"The train's going to blow!" Remo said.

I blinked up at him.

"Jump!" He grabbed my hand and dropped into a crouch, and then we sprang off the boulder.

The ground came at me hard. So hard my teeth knocked together, and my bones juddered, but the metallic sound of "three" had me scrambling back upright.

As a rumbling began, Remo tugged on my hand. "Run!"

My legs windmilled so fast they were probably blurring. It must not have been fast enough to Remo's taste, though, because he hauled me forward.

The rumbling turned into a bang that sent us both sailing onto our stomachs. Hot, white sand cushioned our fall as a spray of rock and tongues of fire lapped at our backs. I clapped my hands over my ears and burrowed my face into the ground, trying to sink right through it. Unfortunately, I didn't sink, and the chunks of debris lashed my back.

As pain crosshatched my skin, I thought up new ways to torture Gregor Farrow, but then dismissed all of my ideas. I'd have him locked in here, then order the destruction of the portal. A heavy weight settled over my back, and I thought the entire train car must've come loose, but the weight had a heartbeat. Praying it wasn't a wild animal about to tear through my flesh, I twisted my face to see what or who had landed on me.

I caught a brassy flash of hair and a whiff of masculine sweat —Remo.

Another detonation. His body tensed over mine as fiery pellets hissed through the air. Even though I was glad for his protection, I worried for his safety. I tried to free my hands and access my dust but could barely squirm. I balled my fist, touching the tips of my fingers to my tattoo, but couldn't get my *wita* to adhere. As though I were swimming through drying cement, I spread my arms wide and raised them over my head. When my palms connected, I coaxed my dust out, then parted my hands, fashioning a transparent dome to cover our sandwiched bodies. I probably should've made it a tad larger so I could wriggle out from underneath Remo, but comfort hadn't been my first priority. A cacophony of pings and clangs layered itself over the ringing inside my ears as more pieces of the train hailed over our shield.

Remo slid off me, but had to stay on his side, and me on mine to fit under my egg-shaped dome. His face glistened with sweat and trails of black smoke, but at least there was no blood.

Sand coated my lips. "Remo?" I raised my hand to his arm.

He winced.

When I lifted my palm, it was stained red. I tried to glimpse the rest of his back without touching him. But besides rips in the navy fabric, I couldn't lever my head high enough to see anything in the cramped space.

"The shield"—his labored breaths struck the tip of my nose—"good call."

If only I'd brought it out sooner.

Another cloud of detritus fell over the curved glass. I curled my head into my neck and my arm over the exposed side of my face, worried our defenses might crack, but Karsyn's dust—Karsyn's incredible, amazing dust—held steady.

I didn't raise my head again until the banging and thumping came to a stop. And even then, I waited a dozen heartbeats before lowering my bent arm back alongside my body and peeking around.

Remo's complexion had gone as ashen as when he'd been imprisoned in the *cupola*, and his eyes were feverishly bright.

"Are you okay?" My voice sounded like it was coming from another planet.

"Yeah." His, too, sounded faint and distant. "You?"

I nodded. In spite of the confetti of tiny pulses beating in my eardrums, skull, waist, ankles, I was alive and conscious, so I was okay. Funny how standards changed when in survival mode.

"Do you think it's over?" The air beneath the dome was so balmy that fog blurred the glass.

He looked over his shoulder at what he could see of the boulder platform, and then, gritting his teeth, he pressed his palms into the rounded glass and heaved it up so he could sit. Although my blood felt like it had spilled out of my body, I pushed up too. For a moment, all was gray, and then color returned in splashes, and the fuming crater crenellating the rock came into soft focus.

"It's over," he said, "but unless a new train appears, so is cell-hopping."

A chill swept over my overheated body, icing the slickness on my skin. What if this world was the worst one yet?

"One down, one to go." I didn't think Remo was murmuring but it felt like he was.

"What?" I croaked.

"If this world works like the others, we only have one more *fun* occurrence in store."

I returned my gaze to Remo's, which was shadowed by the waving blue-green fronds above us. "Do you think it self-destructed by accident or did you press a button?"

His gaze tapered. "I didn't activate any dead-man's switch."

"If I'd been the one manipulating the touchscreen, you would've asked me, too."

His stony silence endured, pigheaded faerie that he was.

I pressed my lips into a thin line as I kneeled and reeled my dust back into my hand. "Let me see your back."

When my fingers crept to the hem of his tunic, he said, "If you think you can get me naked after blam—"

I growled, which made him chuckle. I edged the fabric up, revealing a patchwork of little cuts. None looked particularly deep even though they all dribbled blood, thickened by clumps of sand.

"So? What's the prognosis, doc?"

As gently as when I'd pulled the fabric up, I inched it back down his curved spine. "You'll live, but we should get to the waterfall to wash out the blood and sand. Can you walk?"

He unfurled his long body. "The princess of Neverra just offered to bathe me. You bet I can walk."

"If you weren't already in pain, I'd slap you."

"If I weren't already in pain, I'd enjoy it."

The temptation to roll my eyes took hold of me, but the heat still crisping the air made my eyes water and sting. I didn't think tearing up would give my eyeroll quite the same clout. Remo offered me his hand but I didn't take it, preferring to get up on my own. As I rose to my feet, my head swam, and my vision went so pixelated that I wondered if Remo had tossed a handful of sand into my face. I tried to take a step, but the graininess turned into blackness. I fell. Metal rods hit my abdomen, and my name was yelled, or maybe whispered, the rushing in my ears too strong, a current that made words bob.

When the world materialized again, I was leaning against Remo, wheezing lungfuls of scorching air. "I'm okay." I tried to push away from him.

"No you're not." He loosed the noose of his arm just enough to bring up his hands that were coated with so much blood I almost passed out a second time. His gaze dropped to my waist, to the protruding piece of metal.

"Pull it out."

"We don't know how deep it went."

"Just pull it out." It felt like a legion of ants were walking over every inch of my skin. "Please?" I murmured, resting my forehead against the knob of his shoulder.

"Amara . . ."

"If I bleed out, meet me at the waterfall."

His body turned to steel.

"Plea—"

I never got the last syllable out. A flash of heat and pain sliced into my waist, dimming the tropical prison cell all over, except this time, it stayed dark a long *long* time. When I finally reeled my lids up, I was expecting a mirrored portal would be floating over me.

Instead, I got shards of white sky peeking from behind swaying turquoise fronds, the scent of *panem* drifting into my nose, and a strong heartbeat pounding against my ear. I tipped my face as far as my neck would allow and found myself staring at the auburn stubble on the underside of Remo's jaw. I hadn't died, but the wet pain thrashing at my waist almost made me wish I had.

A fresh wave of fire slammed into me, and cold sweat gathered on my brow. In the branches above Remo's head, a set of eyes glittered. Human eyes set into a crouched human form.

I tried to utter Remo's name and warn him. I tried to lift my hand and point. I failed at both.

I blinked, and the world became whitewashed. When my gaze cleared, there was no one in the tree.

Then there was no tree.

No sky.

No Remo.

Nothing, but an inky, quiet void.

28

THE GIRL

Water splashed against my dry lips, curved down my cheeks, dribbled into my hair. I sputtered and coughed, my throat so parched the air traveling down into my lungs felt like a ball of fire. More water. I snapped my lips shut, but again they parted around a rattling cough.

"Amara?"

I twisted onto my side, but choked as my nose and mouth hit water.

"Easy there." Hands cupped my head and eased it up, helping the water I'd inhaled come back out.

I realized I was still in Hell because never had I choked on water. On Neverra and on Earth, the inside of my mouth and my scaly skin both acted like gills, separating the oxygen from the carbon dioxide before siphoning it inside my body.

"I wish I were dead," I whispered between coughing fits. Coughing fits that made my body feel as though it had been cleaved in half.

"Don't say that."

"But it's true." The corners of my eyes released a few tears that bled right into my hairline. "I'm sorry," I murmured, realizing how selfish I was being.

"You have nothing to be sorry about."

After inhaling a long breath through my nose, I finally dared to open my eyes. Remo's face was shadowed but pale, his eyes large and shiny. Water struck and gushed beside us. I turned my head, which he'd cocooned in his lap, and found he was sitting half-submerged in an iridescent pool.

"I was hoping the water would help heal you." His voice was all at once tenuous and rough. "But I don't know if it's helping. Your wound hasn't magically sealed up. Maybe it's making it worse."

I didn't know if it had made it worse. I couldn't feel an entire side of my body. Maybe I *was* cleaved in half...

"I didn't want to rip up your jumpsuit, and I didn't think you'd want me undressing you, but I think you need to take it off, so I can see the extent of the damage. Make sure no other piece of metal went through you."

"The lengths you'll go to catch another glimpse of my breasts..."

He shot me a gentle smile. "You think you can sit up?"

I tried but my upper body felt chained to an anvil. "I... can't." I allowed myself a full minute to sulk. "Just unzip my suit. I'm past the point of caring whether anyone sees me naked."

"Good thing there's just me around."

I sucked in a breath, my lids pulling up higher.

"What is it?"

"Before I passed out, I saw someone... in a tree."

He frowned, but then his forehead smoothed out. "You lost a lot of blood."

"I didn't hallucinate it. I really did see someone."

"I carried you through the entire jungle and then I've been sitting here for some time, and I've seen no one. I haven't even seen an animal. Haven't even heard any."

Which could've been because the crashing waterfall camouflaged all other sounds. Or maybe it was because his ears were still ringing from the explosion. Mine certainly were.

He gripped the zipper nestled in the hollow of my collarbone and gently tugged on it. A groove appeared between his eyebrows as though undressing me required extreme concentration. I would've smiled had I not felt so pitiful. He drew it all the way down, but before peeling the compressive fabric open, he shifted me off his lap. Although he handled my body with great care, it still felt as though I were being whipped by a hundred scourges.

He took off his top, which made my pain take a backseat to my surprise. "If you're trying to distract me from the pain . . . it's working."

A bigger smile brightened his face but faded when his eyes fell to the water lapping at my body. I followed his line of sight, noticing the red tint.

He raised my head, fitting it into his tunic, and then he pulled it all the way down to my navel before his hands slid under and climbed to my shoulders. He stretched the fabric down my arms, then lowered it delicately down my ribcage. Sweat salted my lips. I licked them, a pathetic whimper falling from my mouth when the compressive fabric brushed against my open wound.

Placing a firm palm on my spine, Remo jimmied my back off the wet sand and rolled me onto my side. And then he pushed the fabric of his tunic up, bunching it beneath my breasts. I kept my gaze on the golden stretch of skin connecting his shoulder to his neck. When it tensed, I surmised the damage was worse than anticipated. I neither asked whether I would live, nor begged to die. I just stared quietly at the frothing iridescence behind him.

If I hadn't been injured, I'd be swimming. But how different it would feel to swim without being able to stay under. I focused on that instead of on the fingertips prodding the skin around the deep cut.

"It looks clean, Amara. No metal seems to have stayed inside."

"My blood," I murmured. "Be careful."

A faint smile drew up his lips. "I know how your blood works."

I raised my gaze back to his. "*Bagwa.*"

His smile firmed up. "I deserve that." He smoothed the tunic back over my abdomen, then washed his hands.

"Too bad we didn't end up in a hospital or a haberdashery. A needle and some thread would've been convenient right about now."

He contemplated my tattooed palm.

"No," I said before he could suggest I make both with my dust. "I won't be able to use it if it's stitched into my skin. What if we need it for something else?"

"We'll use what's around us."

"No."

"Amara, you're bleeding out."

"If I were bleeding out, I'd be dead already." Or would I? How long did it take for a body to empty itself of blood? "Besides, it's not my dust. What if it poisons my blood? I might not resuscitate from death by *wita*, Remo."

His jaw seemed sharper. All of him seemed sharper. Even his gaze as it cycled around the dense copse of twisted gray trunks topped with palm-shaped blue leaves, set against taller, tawny trunks with midnight-blue fronds draped in lianas, and shorter tufts of a curly yellow specimen. When he brought his eyes back to mine, resolve hardened him some more.

He latched on to the sleeve of my suit, the one which had ripped in Deception Central, and tore it clean off the bodice. "Make some scissors then."

I crafted the tool and handed it to him. He sliced up the sleeve until he had two lengths, which he tied together, building a rope of sorts. He handed me back the scissors, then cupped some water to rinse out the wound, soaked the strip to divest it of sand, and slid it underneath me. After positioning it around my waist, he knotted it so tightly it rid me of breath.

"I'm sorry for being so selfish, Amara."

"Selfish?" I whispered, my throat throbbing as wickedly as my waist.

"I shouldn't be trying to keep you alive. Not if dying could just fix you and take away your pain." The indent between his eyebrows deepened.

I melted the scissors back into my palm, then lifted my index and touched the dip to iron it out. "You're a lot of things, but selfish is not one of them." My fingers trailed along the side of his face, against the rough stubble and taut skin. When they reached the edge of his jaw, the strength to keep them raised left me.

All of my strength left me, and the world faded quietly away.

This time, wherever it was that my mind went, there was color and sound. And warmth. Slow caresses from the sharp bone of my shoulder to the inside of my elbow. I felt as though I were sinking to the very deepest parts of the Pink Sea and languidly drifting there.

When I awoke, the sky was still white, the sand still velvety.

I stretched out, but it tugged on the wound beneath my belted bandage, and I winced. "Remo?" I croaked.

When he didn't answer, my pulse quickened. Had something happened to him? He'd probably just gone off to explore. I tried to push myself up, but fire spilled into my veins, and I collapsed right back down.

"I wouldn't try getting up if I were you."

My heart banged against my throat, and even though it felt like I was being quartered, I shifted to glimpse the speaker. A girl with hair so blonde it looked white stared down at my crumpled form. Her jaw was soft and rounded, her skin finely freckled, and her ears, which held back pale dreads, slightly prominent.

I tried to inch away from her but made zero progress. "Who are you, and where's—where's my friend?"

"The better question is, who are *you*?" She tipped her head to the side, her long locks springing out from behind her ears and frolicking around a long necklace made of sharp, golden claws.

Even though I wanted her to answer my questions first, I was in no position to act pushy, so I wet my lips and parted them. "My name is—"

"Amara Wood," a nasal voice finished for me.

I jolted from the familiar timbre.

"Ace and Catori Wood's daughter." The boy approached, his handsome but hateful, elongated face framed by curled wisps of honey-brown hair. "My niece."

Iba had been right.

Kingston wasn't dead.

29

THE SURVIVORS

It had been four years, and yet Kingston looked exactly as he had when he'd tried to assassinate Iba and steal his throne. No, that wasn't true. His sandy-brown hair was thicker and longer, chopped unevenly even though the curled ends hid the irregularities, and his jaw was coated by a beard which veiled the conspicuous chin dimple he'd always been so proud of because it tied him to Linus, who'd apparently sported one too. Neither Iba nor Neenee had inherited that trait, but Sook and Giya had, to my cousins' great regret, even though theirs were not as pronounced as Kingston's.

"You aren't dead," I said flatly.

My illegitimate uncle, who'd been born the same year as Remo, grinned nice and wide. "Surprise." He was leaning against a branch whittled down to a sharp point. Had he carried the weapon to scare me or to keep evil creatures at bay?

"Where is Remo?" I scanned the trees behind them.

"Wandering around the caves," Kingston replied. "They're not far, so he should be back any moment."

"You haven't hurt him?"

"Hurt him? Why would we hurt him?" The girl side-eyed Kingston. "Unless you came to finish us off . . ."

"They didn't come to kill us. Remo is Gregor's grandson. His *beloved* grandson. If anything, they came to free us. It must be time."

"Why would they send the king's daughter if it was time?" the girl snapped.

I surmised they were discussing the coup my father had warned me about.

"Why don't we ask her why they're here instead of assuming, Little King?"

Little King? Back on Neverra, Kingston had often been referred to as King for short. The last time anyone had called him *Little King*, the woman—a female *lucionaga* devoted to my father for granting women positions inside the army—had vanished. I'd always held out hope that she'd gone to Earth and lived out her life there, but Sook insisted the sparkling blue honeysuckle vine that twined around the railing of my uncle's balcony at the top of the *calimbor* had appeared the day she went missing.

Kingston gnashed his teeth. "I think you forget who has the apple."

The girl glared at him.

The apple? Were they talking about the one that showed up in all the worlds? Before I could formulate a question, the girl asked, "Why are you here?"

How I wished I could climb to my feet, or at the very least, sit, because my prostrate position made me look weak. "I'm here because I was looking for someone. A girl named Kiera Locklear."

The fringe of dark lashes framing her navy eyes lowered. "Why are you looking for her?"

It struck me then, the resemblance—the blue eyes, the pale hair, the freckles. I'd found Kiera.

I licked my lips. "Your brother told me about this place, told me he thought you might be in here." I left out the bit about having no choice. I thought it much wiser she believed me a heroine come to rescue her than sent against my wishes. "I didn't know if I'd find you. I didn't know if we'd find anyone. Especially after our prolonged visit inside," I added with a bitter twist of my lips.

Kiera crouched next to me, the stained khaki shorts that grazed her knobby knees bunching around her thighs. "Kingston told me everyone thought I was dead."

"Not Joshua." I remembered she also had a twin—Cole. He was almost forty while she looked what . . . fifteen? Sixteen? Josh had said time moved differently here, but he was wrong; time, here, didn't move at all. "Cole is also trying to find you," I lied, although maybe he'd held out hope his sister was alive.

I knew Cole in passing. He was a soft-spoken marine biologist who was helping introduce and acclimate Earthly flora and fauna to Neverrian waters. Since he was my mother's age, I'd never had much contact with him. Giya knew him better, what with having taken care of his kindergarten-aged daughter when she helped with summer camps.

"Cole?" Her narrowed eyes told me she wasn't convinced.

"Yes, Cole."

She rose from her crouch. "My twin gave up on me the day he moved to Neverra and left me behind. Josh was only seven, so I forgive him, but not Cole. Don't try to bullshit me here, princess, because I will make your life hell."

"You'll make my life hell?" I probably shouldn't have snorted but how could I not? I was already *in* Hell.

"Ever heard the story of Prometheus and the eagle, princess?"

Yeah, I knew the story of the eagle sent by Zeus to eat the mythical hero's liver every night. "If you torture me, then I can't help you get out."

"Help me get out?" Kiera's words smacked of acrimony. "If you'd come to get me out, you wouldn't be bleeding on a beach. You'd have come with a platoon of faerie guards *and* Gregor."

"Why do you think I brought his grandson?" I hoped I sounded confident.

"I don't know, but I plan on finding out. Kingston, your spear." She held out her hand, and he tossed it at her. She caught it with the dexterity of a girl used to wielding a weapon.

Pressing the tip to my throat, she said, "Tell me the truth. Why are you and the boy here?"

"You pierce her throat, and I will make sure you *never* climb out of the portal." Remo's voice made my attention snap beyond Kiera. He'd sneaked up on Kingston, whom he was presently holding in a chokehold, the tip of his pen poised against my uncle's throat.

Kiera's lips twitched, and although her pressure on the spear didn't lessen, she glanced over her shoulder. "We finally meet, Remo Farrow." Her necklace clinked and blinked in the white light. "I've heard *so* much about you."

The sinews in Remo's forearm tautened. Although Kingston's hands rose to the fleshy noose, he wasn't able to dislodge or break Remo's hold and then he just stopped grappling altogether.

Kiera shifted her eyes to the thinning lavender-gray steam. "Once the smoke from the explosion clears, the cats arrive."

My heart, which was already beating too fast, sped up.

"In the state she's in, she has zero chance of surviving. So either we leave her to get mauled, or I—"

"I'll protect her." Remo's forearm flexed.

Kingston was turning a satisfying shade of grape-purple.

"You guys don't understand what you're about to face," Kiera said. "Unlike in the other cells where you can jump on a train to get to the next one, there is no next cell, and unless all of the cats are hunted and killed, more will come. Trust me. I've been here long enough to understand a thing or two about your grandfather's prison."

"How will killing me help?" I whispered, the point of her spear digging into my neck.

"You'll heal, then be able to fight. Instead of being a burden, you'll become an asset." Under her breath, she added, "Hopefully. Unless you're too pampered to do any heavy-lifting."

The ache throbbing in my waist reminded me I had little choice. "Can you die an indefinite amount of times here?"

"Yeah. Unless you bite the—"

"Kiera," Kingston wheezed. "Smoke . . . Gone."

She flicked her gaze to the dregs of smoke puffing out of existence in the white sky. "Follow the river to the waterfall."

"Don't kill her," Remo growled.

"Sorry, Carrot-top, but it's survival of the fittest around here. I'm not dying again, because you don't have the balls to trim the fat. Besides, you'll see your girlfriend soon enough."

"Girlfriend?" Kingston rasped.

Really? That was the part that gave him pause?

Branches snapped. I expected to hear a litany of growls, but instead I heard a new voice. A man with a thick beard but no hair raced from the forest. Like Kiera and Kingston, he wore a tattered and stained undershirt and shorts with a hem so frayed and uneven they must've been pants at some point.

"I got the weapons." He brandished a handful of hand-whittled spears.

Remo pivoted toward the newcomer, lifting Kingston right off the ground. "How many of you are there?"

"Four." To me, she said, "Oh, and, princess, when you get up there"—she tipped her head to the plateau—"don't wake the vamp beetles."

Vamp beetles? The tip of her spear scraped my thrumming carotid.

"Don't!" Remo tossed away Kingston, who smacked down on the sand so hard, an *oompf* escaped from his lips.

"Now," I breathed.

Kiera's biceps tensed, and then the pain was gone, and so was I.

30

THE BEETLES

I awoke to a distant babble and cool stickiness. Before opening my eyes to face the white sky, I swallowed a steadying breath and took quick inventory of my body, relieved to note the absence of pain. This world was still despicable, but I was thankful for the strange loophole.

I flattened my palms and pressed my fingers into the squishy mud. Even though my body didn't ache, I rose to my feet slowly, my clothes soaked in mud.

I stared at the hem of Remo's tunic that skimmed the top of my thighs, sheltering my upper body like a poncho. I'd abandoned him shirtless down below. Our clothing wasn't armor, but it beat bare skin. I hoisted the shirt up to dig my fingers into the tight knot of the belt he'd fastened around my waist to staunch the blood oozing from my wound. Once I got it loose, I slid it off my waist and hooked it around my neck. The tinny smell clinging to the soiled black fabric made my nostrils flare.

I was about to pull my arms through the sleeves of my jumpsuit when I remembered Remo had cut one off. Although not stifling, the air was warm in this cell, so I made scissors out of my dust, clipped off the remaining sleeve, then magicked my nifty tool out of existence and hoisted my suit back on. After threading the belt Remo had made me through the newly-felled sleeve, I retied a knot and looped it around my neck, then fit my arms through his tunic sleeves, rolled the cuffs twice to free my hands, and eased one arm through the stretchy necklace of sleeves to secure it across my chest.

Calling on my *wita* again, I fashioned a rapier. I wasn't sure whether I would encounter the cats Kiera had mentioned up here, but I thought it prudent to be prepared. After a meaningful glare in the portal's direction, I raced toward the watery expanse sparkling behind another tropical forest. There were no *panem* trees up here, just tall palms with ruddy bark coated in bulbs the color and size of gladeberries. As I slalomed around them, I finally computed what I'd seen down in the valley.

Kiera.

And Kingston.

Alive and untouched by age.

I couldn't believe Joshua had been right.

I couldn't believe Iba had been right.

I couldn't believe Gregor had created a prison no one had any inkling about.

Except for Joshua's source. Who the hell was Joshua's source?

Soon the sound of flowing water superseded the swish of my needle-thin blade and the crunch of coarse sand beneath my stomping boots. Should I swim or run along the riverbank? As I contemplated both options, wishing I'd had the presence of mind to ask Kiera, my sword nicked the base of a tree. I didn't think much of it until a low drone erupted, and the berry-like barnacles separated from the trunk.

"Aw, *crap*." I joined my hands on the sword's handle and raised it as a dozen overgrown ladybugs descended on me.

What I needed was a paddle, not a sword as thin as a toothpick. Grip slickening, I backed up, my boots sinking into softer sand, and reshaped my weapon. I dared a glance over my shoulder at the water. I was probably better off jumping in.

The buzzing grew so loud I whipped my head back toward the fleet of vamp beetles and swung, knocking out the first wave. Instead of plopping to the ground, they dipped like pollinating bees before rising anew and soaring straight at me. I batted the air, then whirled, my racket bowling a ribbon of them over.

A violent sting on my collarbone had my chin dipping into my neck. One of the bulbous things had latched on to me. The droning grew anew, and I flailed backward, one hand going to the bug and the other wrapped firmly around my paddle.

What was Gregor's obsession with toothy flying things? Did he regret being born a faerie instead of a vampire?

Sweat pooled between my shoulder blades as I tore off the gelatinous bug and lobbed it at the tree it had come from, before whirling around to smash its incoming friends. My footing faltered, and I sailed backward, smacking into the stream. The momentum ripped the paddle from my hands.

The vamp beetles dove toward my floating body. Before any could dig their sharp teeth into my exposed flesh, I sank, and they hit the surface like toy balls. When one dipped below the rippling surf, alarm gripped me.

Please let them not be engineered to swim.

Like a buoy, the submerged bug rose back. Blood ribboned around the stream of bubbles escaping my nose. I parted my lips to take in air, forgetting I couldn't breathe underwater. I snapped my lips shut around a mouthful of silt. Reflexively, I blew it out, along with my reserve of oxygen.

When I returned to Neverra, I would use a meat mallet and pound Gregor's bones, and then I'd drag him to the very bottom of the Pink Sea and wait for his lungs to seize and his organs to fail. These heinous contemplations scared me, not in their atrocity, but in the lack of guilt and disgust I felt visualizing them.

My own lungs cramped, urging me to break the surface, but the red bugs droned inches from where my air bubbles popped, and where the hell was my racket? I extended my hand, summoning my dust. When no golden filaments shimmied toward me, my pulse ramped up. I kicked to go faster, scanning my blurry surroundings for an oblong shape, but the only thing I saw was the uniform layer of vamp beetles reddening the top of the river. Had they all congregated to keep me interred?

I finally understood why non-Daneelies described suffocation as feeling like your lungs had been set on fire. My insides teemed with searing heat that spread as though my veins had torn and were leaking *kalini* into the rest of my organs.

I'm done dying, Gregor Farrow.

Estimating I had a couple seconds of air left, I squinted harder. Fortunately, the stream dragging me toward the cliff was narrow, and the water sweet and clear—salt would probably have stung in this world.

Come on, come on, I urged my racket. *Come back to me. I need you.*

Unless it had gotten stuck in the sandy riverbed, it would go over the drop with me, but I couldn't even spot the drop yet, which meant I would be out of oxygen long before I went over. The edges of my vision began to fray, which couldn't possibly be a good sign.

Maybe I could break the surface for a quick breath. I stared up. The beetles were no longer hovering over the water. They were sitting atop it, bobbing like bloodied ducks.

Time for Plan B.

If only I had a Plan B.

Something bumped into my foot. I craned my neck, and although I felt like I was floating in a puddle of opaque glue, I made out the faintest, shimmering curve. Like a faulty pendulum, my arm arced toward my thigh, and then my cramping fingers curled around what had hit me. Hoping I wasn't hallucinating, I dragged the thing toward my face and almost wept at the sight of it.

Instead of returning the *wita* inside of me, I fashioned a snorkel so long and thin it poked through the net of vamp beetles. And then I sucked on it. Water surged inside my mouth. I was so stunned I choked and almost dropped my device. In a dusky recess of my mind, it struck me I should blow into it to clear it, but I didn't think I had a blow left in me. I tried, though. Not even a trickle of air drifted up the flooded tube.

Was night finally falling? The watery world around me had turned incredibly dark.

Although my grip was weakening, I gave my oversized snorkel a soft squeeze, making it solid, and then another to make it hollow. And then I pulled in a swallow, praying for air, praying I wouldn't return to the field of mud, because I needed to reach the others and help whatever fight had begun down in the valley.

Air—delicious, pure, and crisp—luffed my cheeks and snuck into my stiff lungs. I breathed in and out, in and out. Slowly, my vision cleared, the gray dots replaced by dabs of bright color— iridescent blue and gladeberry-red. I didn't even mind the sight of the beetles anymore. They couldn't hurt me anymore.

I dragged one hand through the velvety sand, the grains puffing and dancing around me, tangling around my unraveling braid.

Boredom, or perhaps an innate sense that their mission had become futile, made the vamp beetles rise in droves and drift away, back to their bark ports. Breathing calmly, I took advantage of the respite to relax before what awaited me in the valley. After a couple more minutes of idle drifting, I reeled my dust back into my palm, kicked my legs, and broke the surface.

The water foamed, wavelets rocking into my cheeks and nose, spraying into my eyes. I was getting close to the drop-off. I poked my head out a little higher to gauge the distance. Half a mile. Perhaps less. I fluttered my legs, carving across the expanse toward the shore, fearing that flopping over the ledge would result in undesired spinal realignment. My muscles hardened and stretched, the tendons and sinews coiling deliciously. How I'd missed swimming. Too soon, I reached the embankment and clawed my way to dry land on hands and knees, droplets of blood plopping into the sand beneath my face. *Damn bloodthirsty fiend.*

Waterlogged, I rose to my feet. My clothing stuck to my body, but there was no point wringing them out, not when I was about to dive head first off a cliff and into more water.

I shuddered as the memory of my last fall lit up my brain. Not even the knowledge that I'd resuscitate tempered the horror of dying. My aim, when I pushed off the cliff, needed to be true. Unless I created another parachute . . . *No.* I didn't want the other prisoners to see I had access to magic.

I hurried along the shore, kicking up clumps of sand, my feet squishing inside my boots. Ten heartbeats later, I stood on the edge of the cliff. Although the dense blue foliage obscured most of the valley, the crescent encasing the pool was perfectly visible—white dappled with so much red I imagined someone else had gotten injured or killed, because all that blood couldn't possibly have come from my waist wound.

As though the cell had heard my contemplations, a striped beast with paws the size of dinner plates and lavender fur matted with blood inched toward the water. It tottered. Once. Twice. And then it collapsed, half into the water, half out. A hoarse mewl turned the fine hairs on the back of my neck erect.

Oh, Great Gejaiwe. I pressed my knuckles against my gaping mouth.

"You just gonna stand there, princess, or actually get your feet wet?" someone yelled.

I jumped as the voice of the older man who'd been on the beach earlier drifted toward me. He was paddling with the current, bald head slick and shiny as a pearl.

"We already killed half of them off," he continued, his voice carrying over the rushing water.

"Half?"

"Three," he shouted. "They're always as many as we are."

I gulped. Were they all as big as the one on the beach? I looked back down at it. The animal was motionless, deep crimson blooming around its thick body, golden stripes shimmering as though made of foil instead of fur.

"Where do we jump from?" I asked loudly.

"You need to get back in the river, swim to the middle, then let it carry you down! You dive from anywhere else and you'll break your neck. Take it from someone who's tested a variety of dive spots."

My saliva thickened anew. "How many prisoners . . . have the *tigri* killed?" I asked, retreating back the way I'd come. Strong swimmer that I was, in this current, I'd never reach the heart of the river before toppling off if I didn't add a few more yards.

"Just me. Damn tiger carved up my chest with its metal claws!"

Metal claws . . . Like on Kiera's necklace. She must've plucked them off one of the beasts and strung them up on a cord. A battle trophy.

A growl followed by yelling down below made me wade into the frothy water. I pushed off the embankment and swam toward the center of the river, and then I turned toward the valley and let the current lasso me toward the fight below.

3I

THE FOURTH ONE

I closed my eyes as I tipped over, curling my body into a compact ball to avoid skeletal damage. I thought of Sook, my thrill-seeking cousin. Of how he'd probably have hollered an impassioned "cowabunga" like he did when he flew over the Pink Sea and divebombed me, one of his very favorite pastimes.

Hitting the pool was almost like hitting solid rock. My organs remained intact inside my body, but damn . . . my poor skull. It pounded and wobbled like the rest of my bones.

I suddenly remembered my swimming buddy, and my arms and legs sprang out and carved through the water just as he collided into it. While he dropped like a stone, I scissor-kicked to the surface.

"Is the cat dead?" I asked once he'd emerged.

"If it doesn't move, it's dead."

Treading water, I surveyed its ribcage. When it didn't expand, I headed toward the shore. Over the sound of my arms slapping water came a series of distant grunts followed by a non-human roar. My pulse faltered, and so did my desire to join the fight, but Remo was out there.

I pushed away my apprehension and swam faster, studying the

278

purple giant's serrated claws, peaked ears, and twin golden fangs that jutted from its jaw, reddened by—I gulped—blood. As my boots gained purchase on the sandy bottom, a succession of shivers zipped up my spine.

"Move!" Baldie shoved past me, running his palms down his face to whisk off the water. "They need our help."

I raced after him, Karsyn's dust tingling in my palm, reminding me it was there for the taking, and I *would* take it if push came to shove. "What about weapons?" I yelled as he kicked up sand that stuck to my wet suit.

"They should have extra on site. If not, we hit the caves."

I didn't ask where the caves were, just followed him. Movement to our right made him change course. He veered so sharply around a thick, peeling trunk I missed the liana hung between it and the next tree, and it whipped my forehead, snapping my head back. Miraculously, I didn't fall, but little stars spangled my vision. I shook my head to clear it just as a growl erupted so close I swore I could smell the creature's rank breath in the air.

My blood and breaths came quicker. Soon, I burst from a thicket of yellow plants with curled tentacular leaves that scraped at my shins.

Holy Skies above.

A *tigri* was standing on its hind legs, and in front of it, holding a spear as puny as a matchstick, was Remo, bare chest streaked in blood and sand.

Not seeing Baldie anywhere, I fashioned a spear of my own that resembled Remo's, only three times longer and sharper. And then I hollered at the beast to get its attention, which also got my fiancé's attention. The huge feline landed, its paws making the very ground shake. My knees softened and bent as I squatted into a battle stance.

The *tigri* pivoted toward me and sniffed the air. And then it licked its chops and bounded.

Remo shouted, but my thrashing pulse drowned out his voice.

A dose of adrenaline so potent shot through me that I thought I might rocket off the ground if I so much as hopped. Even though I would never own up to it, I did jump and got a whole whopping foot of air between me and the ground before thumping right back down.

Since flying was a no-go, I reeled my arm back, preparing to throw my spear, but even if my aim was true and my velocity stellar, my pointy stick would probably glance off the compact wall of muscle coming at me. When I was younger, Iba had taught me that the best way to disarm your enemy, when outnumbered or outpowered, was by using the element of surprise. He'd demonstrated this when we'd jousted with reeds in place of swords. As I went for the final blow, Iba had dusted his face to look like Pappy, and although we weren't supposed to use any magic, and I *knew* it was a trick, it halted me long enough for him to sweep my legs out from underneath me and pin me under his play sword.

As my strategy firmed up, the *tigri* launched itself at me, gilded fur rippling around its protruding haunches. I flexed my fingers around my spear and transformed it into a net of barbed wire, which I tossed at the animal. It snarled as it made contact, then howled as it became so tangled in the spiky mesh that it smacked into the ground. Remo, who'd raced behind it, jumped and plunged the spear into the beast's neck. Right before my companion's body could land on the prickly metal, I summoned my dust back.

Scowling, he yanked his weapon out of the beast's neck, the flesh squishing wetly around the whittled wood. Remo's gaze was so full of anger and anguish and a hundred other murky emotions that I felt like I'd done something wrong even though my only wrong move had been displaying my magic.

Hopefully, no one had been privy to the little show.

"What the fuck was that?" Baldie asked, popping out from a yellow thicket with two spears and a machete.

Remo's lips were a thin line on his chiseled, blood-streaked face.

I feigned innocence. "What was what?"

"The fucking wire thingie. Where did you get it from?"

"What wire?" I asked.

"The thing that took down the cat!" Baldie's tall forehead glowed with exertion and annoyance.

I frowned. Although Nima could see right through my lies, this man didn't know me from Adam or Eve. Maybe he'd fall for my subpar acting skills. "Remo took down the cat with his spear."

Remo's biceps tightened as he readjusted his grip on his bloodied spear. "I'm not sure what you saw, Quinn. Besides my companion acting like a reckless child," he bit out under his breath as he turned away from me. "How many tigers left?"

"One. Next to the train site."

"Let's go." Without a backward glance at me, he stalked away, shoving past the leathery plants.

Stunned by his attitude, I stayed planted in my spot almost a full minute.

"I'm not crazy, little girl. I know I saw something," Quinn growled before going after Remo.

Grumbling, I took off after them, unhooking my sash before grappling with the edge of the tunic. That Quinn acted hateful was one thing; that Remo did . . . well that pissed me off.

"Remo, wait!"

He didn't.

I got in front of him, pulled off his sodden top, and slapped it into his arms. A muscle feathered his jaw as he flung it over his shoulder and brushed past me.

"Are you mad because I chose to die?" I wasn't one for letting things fester.

He halted, then slowly, turned. "I could've protected you," he gritted out.

More shouting rang through the jungle. Muttering under his breath, Baldie hastened, vanishing behind the dense vegetation.

Remo hinged around and took off again. Although his pace was hurried and he pointedly ignored me, he held up the tawny lianas longer than was necessary. Was it because he'd noticed the mark on my forehead and didn't trust me not to get walloped upside the head a second time?

At some point, I cinched his wrist, forcing him to stop again.

"This isn't the time, Trifecta. They need our help." He still wouldn't look at me, as though he'd looked his fill and could no longer stand the sight of me.

"You might've been able to protect me, but injured as I was, *I* couldn't protect *you*. So I apologize for leaving again, Remo, but I needed to heal."

His gaze finally slammed into mine, just as feral as the purple wildcat's. "Protect me?" His lips curled as though he found a princess protecting a faerie guard ridiculous.

Although I recoiled, I didn't let go of his wrist.

"What I need is for you to stop choosing death, Amara! What if the next time, you *don't* come back?"

"They said we always come back."

"Because you trust them?" he shouted.

I held his wild gaze a long minute, sensing many layers to his anger. Now wasn't the time to peel them apart, though.

"You would've healed. I would've found a way to keep you alive. To keep you safe!"

My hand slid down to his and squeezed his balled fingers. "In this world, it's not your job to keep me safe." And then I let go of his fist and headed in the direction of the tussle.

After a few silent strides, his fingers slid through mine. "Don't do that again, understood?"

I glanced over at him. "Die, or use Karsyn's *gift* in this cell?"

His gaze ran over my face again, stuck to the hollow of my collarbone. Was my puncture wound still bleeding? "Both. Don't do both. Either. Okay?" That tiny groove, which I was coming to understand was concern, marred the space between his brows.

"Okay."

A spine-hardening roar fanned through the valley. Without letting go of my hand, he tugged me forward, carving a path through the sagging lianas and compact undergrowth. My gaze pinged from the gray trunks of the *panem* to the peeling trunks of the exotic palms, on the lookout for red beetles. I saw none.

"Did you meet the fourth prisoner?" I asked between pants of sticky air.

His fingers stiffened around mine.

Before he could answer, a whine followed by a growl echoed so close it raised the fine hairs on the back of my neck. Through the thick copse of trees, I spotted dabs of purple and gold.

Even though I supposed I would find out soon enough, talking distracted me from the monstrous thing we were running towards. "So? Did you?"

"Yes." He snapped the word out, jaw as rigid as his fingers.

"And is it someone we know?"

He parted a yellow thicket with his spear, revealing a sight I truly wished I could forget. Sure, I detested Kingston, but seeing his body dangling from a *tigri*'s mouth like a ragdoll that had lost its stuffing made bile shoot up my throat. I spun away from Remo and evicted what little lay in my stomach.

When I straightened, Kingston puffed into gray ash, his blood still dripping from the beast's muzzle. The *tigri* roared its frustration, hopping over the debris of the train, closing in on Kiera and Quinn, who held spears up. The snap of a liana swinging over their heads had my gaze vaulting to the figure hugging the thick vine—a man with a head full of black curls and muscles that would put the proudest *lucionaga* to shame.

The man bent at the waist and leaped onto the fiend's back with the grit and confidence of someone used to hunting monsters. Hugging one arm around the animal's thick, striped neck, he plunged a knife into its cheek and drew his arm back, carving a line from jaw to shoulder. With a final, thin whine, the *tigri* collapsed, and the hunter climbed off his dead prey. He pulled out his knife, then wiped the blood and gore that lacquered the blade against the mountain of purple fur.

"Are they all slain?" His deep voice rang through the now-silent jungle.

Quinn nodded. "Yeah. The new kids finished up their cat right before we came here." He slanted a look my way that said he was going to demand answers about what he'd seen earlier.

I turned my attention back to the corded arms and built shoulders of the fourth prisoner, the only parts of him I could see from my vantage point.

"Look who's already back . . ." Kiera tossed me a smile full of teeth.

I'd heard stories of Neenee and Geemee's imprisonment in the Daneelie camp run by the Locklear matriarch. Kiera had chained and mistreated my aunt while her friends and family had tortured Kajika. To this day, my uncle hadn't forgiven them, even though Neenee, forever the kindhearted pacifist, had overcome her grudges. Which wasn't to say she wasn't still wary of Charlotte Locklear, but she could hold a conversation with her if need be.

"I'd been expecting you to die at least a few more times before making it back down to us, princess."

I wasn't sure if it was the hateful undercurrent in Kiera's tone or my label, but the fourth prisoner seemed to freeze. And then, slowly, he started to turn. Remo stepped closer to me. Not closer per se. Directly in front of me. My nose bumped the hard knob of his shoulder. Frowning, I touched his arm to shift him a little to the side, but with his feet planted wide, he proved as supple as a *calimbor*.

He was protective and possessive, but this was taking both to a whole new level.

Who was this fourth prisoner?

I stretched up on my tiptoes. When my gaze met the dark-haired prisoner's, my hand, which was still on Remo's bicep, popped off and smacked my parted lips.

32

THE REVENANT

I didn't think my heart had beat once since I'd laid eyes on the man standing beside the slaughtered *tigri*. I didn't think I'd blinked or breathed once either. All of my senses were suspended by the sight of a man who was supposed to be dead.

A ghost.

A hero whose memory Neverrians celebrated each year.

I inhaled so sharply my chest cramped. "How . . .?" My lids dragged up and down over my wide eyes as though to clear it of what was obviously an illusion. Every time my lashes whipped my brow bone, the man from the file back in Fake Rowan's sheriff station was still there.

Still staring straight back at me.

"Is he real?" I murmured.

Remo was so still he looked like he'd become one with the landscape. Only the fluttering at his temple gave away that he was still very much alive. "Yes."

"But *how*?" I thought of the mound of orange dandelion clovers that blanketed the gray rock atop one of the Five. "A plant grew from your ashes, Cruz Vega."

Cruz offered me a smile that made my heart lurch, because it was the same he wore in the picture Iba had of him. "They must not have been my ashes." Tucking the knife into his belt, he made his way toward where I still stood in Remo's shadow.

"You look so much like your mother, Amara, and yet so much like Ace, too. It's incredible." His eyes, the same vivid green as Remo's, shone with emotion. "How old are you?"

Remo stiffened, which was impressive considering there wasn't an ounce of softness anywhere on his body.

"Almost eighteen."

Cruz's Adam's apple bobbed in his corded throat. "Almost the age your mother was when I knew her." There was something heartbreakingly wistful in his tone.

"Since we aren't needed here," Kiera said, "Quinn and I are going to head to the fall and scrub some of the cat gunk off."

I couldn't believe I was standing in front of my father's best friend, speaking to him. This was insane. Almost as insane as the fact that he was still the exact same age he'd been when he'd vanished from our worlds.

Since Remo didn't shift a foot, not even an inch, I stepped around him, coming to stand at his side instead of behind him. "How are you alive, Cruz?"

"After Gregor . . ." His voice trailed off as he looked at Remo, shaking his head a little. "Sorry, but this is . . . it's—you were a baby when I was shipped to the Scourge, Remo. Now you're a man." He shook his head again, a black curl falling across his forehead and into his glistening eyes. He thrust one hand through his hair, then cleared his throat. "Gregor injected me with *dile* poison to get Lily back into Neverra. Next thing I knew, I was lying in mud below a portal. I thought I'd died and gone to Hell. Until I reached this cell, and found Kiera and Quinn and a few others."

"Others?" Remo narrowed his eyes.

"Yes. They've all passed on, but there were others."

My pulse stuttered. "I thought . . . I thought we couldn't die for good."

Cruz stared at his bloodied palms, then wiped both on his dark green cargo pants which bore a constellation of other stains. "You've encountered the apple, right? Each cell has one."

All of the blood drained from my body. "I almost ate it," I blurted out, glancing up at Remo in horror.

He slanted me an *I-told-you-chomping-on-it-was-a-bad-idea* look.

"I owe you my life, Remo Farrow," I breathed, and something poked my stomach. What the—

Remo's eyes, which had been pinched until now, snapped wide.

Oh . . . no. *Nonononononono*. I'd just struck a bargain with the faerie!

I could've been dead, so all in all, a bargain wasn't *so* bad. Besides, Remo was . . . *nice*. He wouldn't use his *gajoï* to hurt me.

"Amara . . ." Cruz rolled my name, completely oblivious to what had just happened between Remo and me. "*Love*. Who came up with your name? Your mother or father?"

I wet my lips and turned back toward Cruz. "It was my father's idea. So . . . so you landed here, and then what?"

"Then I understood Gregor hadn't killed me; he'd saved me. For the longest time, I believed he would come to get me out. But years passed, and no one came, and I realized he wasn't planning on letting me out. My only prayer was that he'd left me here to punish me for having awoken the Hunters and helped Ace take the crown, and not because he'd stolen it from your father. It was only when Kingston arrived that I learned no one was aware of this dimension." Anger stained his gaze, but it didn't linger. Soon, his expression gentled. "I also learned that my dearest friends were all alive and well. That the Woods still ruled over Neverra, and even though I never gave up hope that Ace would find out about this place, I was content."

A tear curved down my cheek. And then another. I rubbed them away. I wasn't even sure why I was crying since, inside, I was screaming. Screaming at how evil Gregor was to have locked an innocent man away. How could he do this? To Cruz? To Neenee? To Iba?

"Don't cry, Amara." Cruz lifted his hand as though to touch my cheek, but something in Remo's expression made his fingers return to his hip without making contact. "I could've been dead."

"It's unforgivable, and so unfair," I croaked. "Cruel."

It wasn't Remo's fault, yet he flinched as though his grandfather's crimes were his own.

Cruz expelled a deep breath. "So now, can I hear how the two of you landed in here?"

"I owed Kiera's brother a *gajoï*. He told me about a portal that led into a supernatural prison, told me where to find it. I thought he'd lost his mind, but then I got sucked through." I laid one palm over my stomach as though expecting it to cramp again. "I damned him for sending me in here, but now that I've found you ... now I'm glad he claimed his bargain."

Cruz smiled.

My hand finally slipped off my abdomen, coming to rest on my necklace of torn sleeves. "I still can't believe you're real."

Remo grunted, which made Cruz's thick black brows lift a little. I was tempted to elbow my moody companion so he'd act more civil with the man his grandfather had sent away for life. Why was he behaving like this, anyway? Did he think we were ganging up on him?

It wasn't *his* fault Cruz was in here. *He* hadn't created this place.

"And you, Remo? How did you happen upon this place?"

"Amara's my fiancée." His voice was as taut as the rest of his body. "Couldn't exactly let her go through a ghost portal on her own."

My cheeks warmed at the way he flung this label over me. "It's an arranged engagement."

Remo sent me a chilling glower.

"What? It is . . ." I said.

"Why did you call it a ghost portal, Remo?"

"Because it's a portal that doesn't exist. A lot like you, Vega," he added under his breath.

Cruz gazed at him a long minute. Instead of commenting on Remo's tangible antipathy, he asked, "Your grandfather never told you about it?"

"Never."

Silence stretched between the three of us.

I wanted to reach out to Remo, tell him he didn't need to be on the defensive, but Cruz said, "Kingston mentioned you and Gregor were close."

A wall fell around Remo. "*Were*." His voice was ice.

Sensing how hard this was for him, I touched his arm. He moved it away from me.

Not again . . . We'd made up mere minutes ago and now we were back to being . . . what were we back to being? Embittered children with zero communication skills? "Remo—"

He backed away. "I'm going to the waterfall."

And then he turned and stalked through the brush, leaving me behind with the ghost from my parents' past.

33

FORGIVENESS

Even though the jungle had swallowed Remo, the yellow underbrush still shivered from his brisk retreat.

"He was very close to his grandfather, which has made our . . . *trip* especially hard on him." I sighed. "Before seeing this place, living in this place, he still held Gregor on an exceedingly high pedestal."

I turned back toward Cruz, found him examining me.

"I can't believe that Catori and Ace had a daughter, and that I'm speaking with her."

"And I can't believe you've been in here for two Neverrian decades."

An Earthly century . . .

He scraped back his dark curls. "Does anyone know you're here, Amara?"

"Just Joshua Locklear. I'm hoping he'll have told Iba and Nima by now." Then again, if he had, wouldn't they have made Gregor fish us out?

"Iba and Nima?"

"It means Mom and—"

"I know what it means." He smiled. "I studied Gottwa. I'm

290

surely a little rusty since I haven't had anyone to practice it with for a long time." After a second, he said, "I'm surprised Ace answers to anything said in Gottwa."

My lips quirked into a smile. "Only when it comes from my mouth, or Nima's. He pretends not to understand our extended family's language otherwise."

"Skies, even your smile is the same as your mother's. But your eyes . . ."

"I had to take something from my father."

He chuckled.

"I also got his superior sense of humor, in case you were wondering. Made surviving this damn place a little easier." My gaze chased the bushes that no longer shivered from Remo's hasty departure.

My sense of humor *had* helped, but it was Remo who'd kept me sane.

And safe.

And smiling.

And alive.

"You should go wash up," Cruz said, as though realizing where my mind had ventured. Or rather, *after whom.* "I need to take care of the cat. Get some meat and fur out of our hunt. We'll meet back at the caves."

Even though I was curious about these caves, I knew I would see them soon enough. "Thank you, Cruz."

"For what?"

"For saving Neverra. For saving my aunt."

"Your parents saved Neverra, Amara. As for saving Lily's life, I don't deserve any gratitude. Especially since it was my fault she was locked out of Neverra in the first place." Guilt veiled his easygoing expression, making him look older than his body's age.

What an adjustment it would be for him once we got him back to Neverra. Everyone he'd grown up with had aged whereas he'd remained frozen at—how old was he again? Twenty-four? Twenty-five?

"They'll come for me and Remo, Cruz. And when they come for us, you'll finally be free."

His mouth pressed into a fine line. Nodding sharply, he turned away and headed back toward the dead feline. "Hope's a dangerous feeling to harbor in this place, Amara," he called out over his shoulder. "Dangerous but vital. It's what's kept me alive, but it's also what's brought me the most pain."

My heart went out to him.

Decades of confinement in this place…

I stared around me, at the swaying cyan trees, the sugar-white sky, the slate rock walls. Out of all the worlds, it seemed the least horrible, but it remained a cell.

As he knelt beside the mound of purple and gold fur, I trailed the noise of crashing water. It took me a while to reach the beach, a while that gave me plenty of time to think about Cruz and Remo and Gregor and this supernatural jail. I'd resented Josh for sending me hurtling inside, but not anymore. Now I thanked him because what an extraordinary voyage it had been.

Still was.

I imagined Iba's face when he'd see Cruz. Imagined Neenee's and Nima's too. All of them would be overjoyed. I was still picturing the reunion when I came upon Quinn and Kiera crouched beside the fallen *tigri,* carving up its belly with the tips of their spears. They'd set out large fronds on which they were tossing pieces of pink meat. The smell of fresh blood and damp fur pulled me out of my reverie and flung me back into the lackluster reality that we had yet to be rescued.

Kiera pushed back her dreadlocks, streaking the white-blonde cords with red. "Come to help us gut the tiger, princess?"

I gritted my teeth, not at the smell or the sight, but at the label she insisted on using and her demeaning undertone. "I'll help, but first, I need to speak with Remo. Do you know where he went?"

Kiera stared steadily at me before tipping her head toward the liquid curtain. "Swam behind there a while ago. Didn't look too happy." As I stepped into the clear water, she asked, "How was your little reunion with the Neverrian hero?"

I didn't miss her innuendo. "It was great, thank you for asking."

Quinn tossed me a hostile glance as I dove under the rippling surf and stayed under until I'd passed the thundering line of foam. When I emerged, I found myself inside a small cave. Although little light penetrated through the curtain of water, I caught a flash of cinnamon in the dusky recess. From the way Remo was leaning against the rock, arms extended on either side of him, I took it he'd discovered a ledge to sit on.

I swam toward him until I felt the cave's rocky bottom underfoot. The water rippled around my shoulders and then my breasts as the ground swelled beneath my boots. He didn't utter a single word, just stared with those hardened emerald eyes of his as though trying to scare me away.

Once the water reached my waist, he said, "Is he everything you imagined he would be?"

Was he jealous? Because I was childish like that, I responded, "And more."

His bladed jaw turned as sharp as Quinn's machete.

"Why did you tell him I was your fiancée?"

"Because you are." His voice was low yet echoed around us.

"So you didn't say it because you wanted him to know I was off the market?" I was toying with a man who might not have been as lethal as a *tigri*, but who could hurt me just as much. Especially now that I owed him a favor.

He grunted a dark sound. "Like you said, *prinsisa*, our union is arranged."

I was so close to him that his kneecaps grazed my thighs. He jolted his legs apart.

"So, you're okay with him and me sharing a cave?"

He seemed to become steeped in even more shadows. "I'm not your keeper."

"No, but you are my betrothed."

"Like that means *anything* to you."

"You know"—I took a step closer to him, which forced him to tip back his neck—"it didn't mean anything to me before we got here, but now that I got to know the Remo underneath the uniform and spite, I've realized it does mean something to me." I took another step, one that made me bump into the stone bench. "I realize it means so much that the thought of you remaining with me because of a magical oath *hurts*." Even though I wanted to set my hands on his shoulders, I hovered my palms over the water. "Remo, if your only reasons to stay with me are duty and magic, please have the honesty to tell me now."

"Or what? You move on to Cruz Vega?"

I shook my head at his vindictiveness, and the step I'd taken forward, I took it back. How I wished I could take my declaration back too. I felt more exposed than when he'd stepped into the inn's bathroom. "That's not who I am. But perhaps *you* still haven't figured out who I am beneath my crown and scales."

I started to turn when his knees closed around my legs, snaring them.

"I know who you are. You're the girl who makes me fucking crazy. Who's made me fucking crazy for years."

I side-eyed him, and although I was no longer shaking my head, I was still upset.

"Who I hope will drive me crazy until I turn into a weed."

I let out a little snort. "A weed . . ."

"Yes. A weed." He circled my waist with his hands and tugged me closer. "The sort that's impossible to get rid of. The sort that'll grow among your *adamans*."

It was surely the strangest declaration of affection anyone had ever spoken, but damn if it didn't thaw me out. "What makes you think I'll turn into a glass flower? My sharp wit and sharper tongue?"

His eyes danced, and not from the rippling surface of the water surrounding us. "You do have a sharp wit and tongue, Amara Wood, but I actually said it because it's my favorite flower."

Goo. I was becoming goo. It was a wonder he still had anything solid to grip on to.

I pushed a lock of red hair off his brow. "No turning into weeds or *adamans* for a long time still, all right?"

"Avoid consuming apples then, Trifecta."

I flicked his nose. "And if you don't want to be turned into a weed, avoid calling me Trifecta. Then again, you'd finally be quiet."

His thumbs brushed up and down the base of my spine. "You hate it when I'm quiet."

I lowered my forehead to his, the pressure of his fingers on my sore back delicious. "I do hate it. Almost as much as I hate you assuming I'm so flighty that I'd head into a stranger's cave to spite you."

His fingers gripped me a little harder, a little closer. "I've never been the jealous type, Amara. Never thought I would be. But now I realize I just never desired something that could be taken from me."

"Don't let anyone take me from you, then. And *don't* give me a reason to walk, fly, or swim away."

"So many methods of leaving me." A smile tugged at his lips. How that smile transformed his face. "Believe me, if the train still existed, I might've whisked you to another cell, so it could be just the two of us again."

"How romantic."

He chuckled, and his laughter tickled my lips. On a mission to swallow every last vibration, I lowered my hands to his shoulders and gripped his slick skin to steady myself as I touched my mouth to his still curved one. His lips unbent instantly, and then a sound between a growl and a moan filled him, and then filled me.

His arms slid around my waist to pull me closer, fitting my body into the crook of his elbows, bones and muscles roiling against my electrified flesh. As he chased my tongue, I threaded my fingers through his hair and drew his face higher, closer, deepening the crush of our lips.

How I'd hated him.

How I'd wanted to cry when Iba suggested tying my essence to his.

How I'd yearned to scream when the Cauldron's magic had licked up my body and bound me to Gregor's heir.

And now . . .

I murmured my wonder against his lips. "My fiancé . . ."

He nipped the corner of my mouth, then kissed his way across my cheek, stopping right at my ear. "I hate that this is what my grandfather wanted. That we're playing right into his scheme."

"What he wanted was to get you on the throne. I highly doubt he had any hopes you and I would fall for each other."

"Is that what we're doing? Falling for each other?"

The beats of my heart intensified until I was sure they were the only reason the water rippled around our bodies. "That's what I'm doing. Can't speak for you, though."

He loosened the lasso of his arms but didn't release me. "Why do you think I followed you through that portal, Amara?"

"You've been very vague about that, Remo."

"Because I didn't want you to end up anywhere alone."

Oh. Heat spread and swirled through me, almost as though my fire had returned. "I don't think anyone's ever fallen so literally for someone else," I teased.

"They do say actions speak louder than words." He pulled my body down until I was perched on one muscled thigh.

"You do realize I come with lots of strings though? A whole net, for that matter."

"Hard not to when I'm already tangled up in them."

"Good." I nudged his mouth back open and kissed him until a loud splash made us spring apart.

Remo swallowed thickly. "That must be your uncle. Back from the dead."

I sighed. "I can't believe he's actually in here."

"Can't you? I can." His abrasive tone revealed yet again the simmering anger Remo felt for his grandfather.

I curled my hand around the back of his neck. "You know how I feel about your grandfather, right?"

"You mean, about my entire family?"

I expelled a long breath. I didn't even want to wonder what it would be like once we returned to Neverra. Would Faith and Karsyn try to keep us apart? Would we be strong enough to stay together if they did? Would our union be the balm that would finally heal the relations between our families? "Just remember that although your grandfather cares little for people, he cares a whole lot for you, Remo."

"So, what? I should just forgive him?" He grunted. "He might care a whole lot for me, but he's lost my respect. And there is no love without respect."

I stroked the vee of hair at his nape, kissed his hardened mouth one last time before shimmying off his thigh. "Come on. You need to teach me how to skin a *tigri*."

"Hmm." He stood, spearing his fingers through mine. "I'd rather teach you other things."

The ground dipped and made me lose my footing. "I'm sure you would, and I'm sure I'd like all of them a heck of a lot more than butchering a dead animal, but I have to pull my weight around here, or Kiera and Quinn will keep looking down their noses at me."

He stared at their blurred bodies beyond the thundering sheet of water. "Noses are easy to break."

"You sound like Geemee. He's all about peace through physical mutilation. Not that Neenee allows him to enact Gottwa reprimands."

"I've always held your uncle in high esteem, but I might actually like him more for it now."

I rolled my eyes. "Let's forget about breaking noses for now and concentrate on making me look capable."

Remo reeled me back into his body. "Make you look capable? Amara, you're not some delicate, prissy courtier."

"You used to think I was."

"No. I never thought that." His irises darkened. "I knew you could hold your own against any fae or human. I protected you, because—"

"It was your job." I fluttered my feet to stay afloat.

"Because I could."

Sighing, I palmed the slope of his shoulder and bumped my nose into his. "You can't seal me in a box for my protection. You have to learn to trust me. To trust that that I can take care of myself."

"I do trust you. It's everyone else I don't trust."

"Trust me to hold my own against those you don't trust."

"Fine. But if I'm around—"

"You're always around."

A smile started on his lips. "If I'm around, I'm intervening."

"Fine." We sealed our deal with a quick peck on the lips, then glided through the waterfall toward the strange assortment of prisoners waiting for us.

34

THE APPLE

I wasn't sure if I would ever be able to get rid of the smell of raw meat and sickly-sweet hide. The reek of it was on my clothes and skin, inside my nose and on my tongue. Although it no longer made my stomach clench, I hoped I would never again need to scrape a pelt clean or hew through bone and sinew.

Although Remo had been hesitant to let me work on the *tigri*, saying the others weren't around, that I didn't have to prove anything to anyone, I insisted, threatening to create my own knife from my dust if he didn't share the machete.

"Brought you guys something to tie up the meat." Kingston emerged from a yellow thicket, brandishing a liana. He'd shed his undershirt and had replaced his shorts with a pair of black ones that were discolored in places but which seemed dry. Lucky him . . .

Scratch that. I didn't envy him. He'd gotten devoured by the vamp beetles.

Although his stings weren't dribbling blood, they'd left welts on one side of his face and along one of his arms. When we'd emerged from the waterfall, he was sprawled on the beach like a starfish. Kiera had kicked a spear his way, but he told her he was in too much pain to help. Sure, I'd only suffered *one* bite, and sure, it hurt, but he was being awfully dramatic. Not that I expected anything more from the faerie who'd only ever lifted a finger to shoot his dust into the face of people who bored him.

He dropped the liana beside me.

Here I'd hoped this place might've changed him for the better but apparently not. "Still can't help out?"

"I'm in too much pain." Kingston's brown eyes roved over the navy tunic top Remo had set to dry on a branch beside us. "You should hang up that catsuit of yours, Amara. You don't want to catch a cold."

I wiggled my wrist where the black Infinity gleamed uselessly. "The rest of my wardrobe's not exactly accessible right now."

He stared at the bracelet, which reminded me that he'd died before Neverrians were outfitted with them.

"I'm sure no one would mind if you walked around naked. Especially now that you're all grown up." The way he looked me over turned my insides to ice.

"The fuck is wrong with you?" Remo growled. "She's your niece!"

"Slim pickings." He stuck a piece of twine in his mouth. "I've tried thawing out Kiera, but to my incredible regret, she's not interested in men."

"Maybe she's not interested in *you*," I said.

His mouth lifted in that mallow-sweet grin of his. "Sugar, when in confinement, you do what you can with what you have. And frankly, between me and Cruz, the little Daneelie's spoiled rotten." He removed the twine from his mouth and waved it at me. "However, if you're completely opposed to walking around naked—"

"I'm completely opposed to it."

"—then we have some extra clothing in the caves. Not the Neverrian finery you're used to, but it'll beat a damp suit." He pushed off the tree. "Come. I'll take you to our walk-in wardrobe while Remo finishes up with the tiger."

Remo rose, rolling his bloodstained knuckles into fists. "She's not going anywhere with you, Kingston."

I got to my feet and gripped Remo's taut forearm before he could swing it toward my uncle. Not because I cared about Kingston—I absolutely didn't—but Iba had taught me to choose my battles, and this one wasn't the right one to wage.

Kingston hitched up one of his eyebrows, the one that wasn't riddled with welts. "Is that jealousy coloring your tone, Farrow Junior? Could what Kiera have said on the beach actually be true? A Farrow and a Wood, romantically entangled? *Oh* . . . the court intrigue I've missed out on." He twirled his little vine. "How did you end up dating the help, Amara? Actually, let me guess . . . My dearest brother is worried about Gregor stealing his throne, so he outright gave it to him? Am I right?" He looked from me to Remo and back, then clapped. "Ooh, I am."

A nerve ticked in Remo's jaw.

"How have the others not forced the apple down your throat?" I asked.

"Simple. I took it from Cruz's cave the first week I was here and hid it." He tapped his little vine against his thigh.

A surge of lethal animosity shot through me. "Would it be wrong to gas him?"

"I have no objections," Remo said.

"Gas me?" Kingston laughed. He actually laughed with tears in his eyes and everything. "With what exactly? A handful of sand? Oh, sweet little niece, your powers don't work in here, in case you haven't realized."

When he flicked my nose with his liana strand, Remo grabbed him around the throat and dangled him in the air.

"I'll just come back." His hair fluttered around his purpling face. "And when I do . . . I'll be very grumpy."

Remo set him down so roughly my uncle stumbled backward.

Still flushed, he added, "Has it already slipped your puny caveman brain that I have the apple, Farrow?"

"Nothing slips my puny caveman brain, Little King."

"Call me that again, and—"

"You'll run to your cave and grab your fucking apple?" Remo spit. "Good luck trying to shove it down my throat."

I laid my palm at the base of Remo's taut spine. "He's your ticket out of here, Kingston. You feed him the apple, you will never see the outside of this prison."

A pulse point in Kingston's neck throbbed. "I call *dile*shit. If Remo had come to free me, we wouldn't have had to fight off *tigri*."

Remo's mouth curled in that signature smirk of his, the one he used to toss my way. "Is that what you were doing? Fighting?"

Kingston rubbed his mottled neck. "To think I was going to make you *wariff*. You can forget about having any position in my government after this."

I stuck one hand on my hip. "Your government? And which government is that, Kingston?"

Kingston shot me another syrupy smile. "Why, the one I'll inherit from your father, Amara. Why do you think I was kept alive?"

"Except Remo's my fiancé, which means Gregor has no use for his puppet."

His smile flickered like a faulty faelight as he absorbed my news. In the end, he spit out, "I'm no one's *puppet*, niece."

"That's not the rumor circulating around Neverra."

"Because rumors are always true?" He tsked. "I thought you a tad smarter than the *caligosubi*, Amara."

Caligosubi was a term used to mean those who lived below the mist. Now that the mist was gone, it was considered slanderous, and faeries who used it were either fined or their dust was confiscated by the Hunters. Not that Kingston cared about decorum or political correctness; he was as vile and malicious as they came.

"If you weren't his puppet, then why did Gregor lock you inside this place?"

"Because I asked him to."

I frowned. "You mean to tell us you knew about this place?"

"Can't call yourself a leader if you don't know what your subordinates are up to."

Was that a jab at my father?

Remo picked up the machete and tossed it from hand to hand. "No leader would ever voluntarily enter a place they can't exit. At least, not a smart one."

Kingston's Adam's apple slid up and down his throat. "Maybe I can exit. Maybe I've chosen to stay."

Remo raised a brutal grin. "You're *choosing* to remain in prison? *Please* . . . You're under my grandfather's thumb, Kingston. Even if the idea to elude death was yours, you obviously didn't think your plan through real well."

"What part of me having the apple did you not get, Farrow?"

"Will you be threatening me with your little fruit for the duration of our visit? Because it's already getting old."

Should we be pressing my uncle's buttons? *I have dust,* I reminded myself. Dust he'd either failed to notice or deemed useless.

Annoyance contorted Kingston's face, accentuating the welts. "Fine. Don't take me seriously. It's your funeral." A smile formed at the edges of his mouth. "Or Amara's."

"You touch her, and you'll wish for a taste of your fucking apple."

Kingston's smile was still turning into a grin when Remo's machete flew through the air, handle over blade, and struck his skull. His eyeballs flared in shock right before bursting into dust along with the rest of his body.

As the blood-soaked weapon thudded against the sand, Remo said, "We need to find that apple."

"Or I can gas him when he comes back."

Remo's bare, sweat-slickened chest puffed with heavy breaths. "What if you can't asphyxiate him down here?"

"*Then* we'll find the apple."

He pillowed my cheeks between his bloodied palms, and even though they smelled like death, I leaned into his touch. "I won't let anything happen to you, Amara. I promise."

"I know."

He brought his mouth down hard on mine as though to stamp that promise into my flesh.

35
NEW CLOTHES

We'd finished hanging the various cuts of *tigri* meat on the nearest tree when Kiera came to tell us dinner was ready.

"Dinner?" I flicked my gaze to the bright sky. "What time does the sun set?"

"It doesn't." Her eyebrows drew together. "How have you not noticed this? You've been through other cells, right?"

"We have." I glanced at Remo. "But we were locked in the windowless basement of an inn—"

"An inn? How fancy . . ." Her dreadlocks bled water into her top, which looked clean-ish.

Remo frowned. "Did you not go through the cell that looked like Rowan?"

"No one goes through the same cells."

"What sort of cells did you go through?" I asked.

"Quinn and I got a *Jurassic Park* themed one. Then there was the frozen lake cell." Her mouth hooked to the side in thought. "The *Honey I Shrunk the Kids* one where we were the size of ants. Oh, and the landmine one. That one was especially annoying. I think Quinn got blown up six times and me four before we made it to the train."

She shuddered. "Oh, and the cell with the shipping crates that fell from the sky was quite memorable."

"So five cells?" That was one more than us.

"Five?" She snorted. "More like fifteen. How many did you go through?"

"Four."

"Lucky you. Almost as lucky as Cruz. He reached this one in three."

"How is this number determined?" Remo asked.

"Your grandfathers built this place. How is it you guys don't know how it's rigged up?" Her suspicious gaze raked over us.

"Neither of us even knew it existed until we got here," I admitted.

"So you didn't come to break us out." It wasn't a question. "I knew you two were lying."

I displayed the bracelet on my wrist. "These are called Infinities. They're powered by our pulse and used for everything, including tracking. However, whatever jams our powers here jams the band's electromagnetism."

"So, what you're saying is: it's useless?"

I looked toward Remo. "Not useless, per se. The only reason for the band to stop broadcasting is if the wearer dies. We're hoping our parents won't jump to that conclusion and will launch an investigation." I sighed. "And if that fails, your brother knows where we are. Hopefully, he'll tell someone he sent me here."

Although the lines of her body remained hard as ice, her sapphire eyes seemed to glow a little brighter. "The number of cells is determined by how you cope with the tests thrown at you and how many times you die." Was answering Remo's question a peace offering to thank us for giving her hope?

"How come neither you nor Quinn ever ate the apple?" he asked.

She stared at the jungle, her eyes a little unfocused. "Gregor warned us about it before tossing us in here. It was his only warning."

"A practical one, at least," Remo said.

Her dark blue eyes slammed into Remo. "I really *really* don't like your grandfather, Remo, so if you're going to be defending him—"

Remo raised his palms. "That wasn't me defending him, Locklear; that was me stating a fact."

"Uh-huh." She didn't look convinced. "Anyway, you might want to get cleaned up before dinner. You both stink."

Frank, much?

"Kingston mentioned extra clothing in the caves we could borrow," Remo said.

She nodded. "I'll drop some off at the beach for you."

As she turned, Remo asked, "Is Kingston back?"

"He is. And with more bites." A diminutive smile tugged at her lips. But as fast as it had appeared, it was gone. "He has the apple, so be careful."

"He mentioned it a few times," I said.

She drummed her fingers against a trunk the color of wet clay from which hung the chops of *tigri*, swinging among the odorous *panem* leaves. Even though I'd always enjoyed the doughy taste of the leaves, the mere smell was turning my stomach.

Remo jolted his chin to the pelt strung up to a vine. "What should we do with the fur?"

"You killed the tiger, so it's yours to keep, just like its claws and fangs." She stared toward the heap of bones. "Oh, and chop off a piece of yellow aloe." She patted one of the curly yellow plants. "The sap makes for great soap."

I walked over to one and snapped a stalk. A golden, gel-like substance oozed between the leathery skin. "Thanks, Kiera."

My gratitude gave her pause. She didn't acknowledge it, though, simply ducked beneath a liana and left.

We took turns bathing. I sensed that until Kingston was dealt with, and by dealt with, I meant killed, we'd be taking turns doing a lot of things.

While Remo rinsed the pelt, using some of the golden gel to wash it, his gaze roved over the curve of tropical plants rimming the beach, over the tree from which hung another chopped-up carcass. On the summer and winter solstices, it was a Neverrian tradition to tie glass ornaments and ribbons to *calimbor* branches. If I squinted hard, I could almost mistake the slick, dangling meat for solstice decorations.

I squeezed some aloe from a stalk and walked until my body was submerged to my chin, then dipped my head back and rubbed the gel into my hair. The smell of sunshine and honey curled around me, soothing and sweet. I returned to the beach for more aloe that I slicked over my suit and arms, then dove in, unzipped my suit and peeled it off. After a thorough scrub, I tossed it on the beach, then attacked the rest of my skin.

"Remo, can you hand me the clothes Kiera dropped off?"

He strolled toward the low branch from which drooped a gray T-shirt and shorts for me, and a cream top with a pair of dark jeans for him. He slung his pelt to dry, then grabbed the clothes, dumping his on the beach before fording into the water with mine. Pressing one arm over my boobs, I rose.

His Adam's apple jumped as his darkened gaze dipped to the glistening swells of my breasts. I pried the T-shirt from his locked fingers and single-handedly pulled it over my head. Once the fabric covered my torso, I lifted my hair out of the neck hole.

His eyes slowly returned to mine. "You don't have scales here." His voice was so hoarse it raised goosebumps on my damp skin.

"Is that what you were looking for so intently? My scales?"

His jaw flared with heat, and he rubbed the back of his neck. "Yes?"

I grinned. "Your lying skills need some improvement."

He shot me a rueful smile, then extended the shorts. Once I took them, he turned around and treaded to the beach. The smattering of stains on the faded denim made me sigh. It was either that or my wet suit, though, and dry won over appealing. I walked out of the water, then quickly speared my legs through and buttoned them up. They hung dangerously low. Although wet, I grabbed my makeshift belt, wrung it out, and stuffed it through the belt loops.

"Can't believe you didn't even peek," I said as I circled him.

He smiled down at me, his jaw still a little pink under a streak of feline gore. "I was afraid you might punch me."

Even though he smelled of sweat and blood, I stood on tiptoe and kissed the corner of his crooked mouth. "I wouldn't have."

"*Now* you tell me?"

For a moment, as he gazed down at me, I forgot about Kingston, about the Scourge, about our useless Infinities. But then his gaze snapped to the tree line, and his arm hooked around my waist, twirling me behind him. The reminder that this wasn't a vacation crashed through me as thunderously as the curtain of water at my back.

Hidden behind his broad body, I pulled my dust out and shaped a weapon, then whispered, "I made a *wita* knife."

He reached one hand behind his back, and I slipped the golden hilt into his palm.

A man finally emerged from the dense shrubs, and it wasn't Kingston.

Cruz froze at the sight of us. "Hope I'm not interrupting anything, but I was hoping for a bath before dinner."

The sigh I expelled raised goosebumps along Remo's shoulders. I extracted my knife from his fingers and made it vanish. "You're not interrupting anything," I called out, stepping around Remo.

"Amara, go sit on the rocks over there. I don't want you out in the open." He nodded to the jumble of boulders at the base of the rock wall.

"Can't exactly guard you from all the way over there."

He stroked the inside of my wrist. "Kingston would have to swim to get to me."

"Not if he dips an arrow inside the apple and shoots it at you."

His eyebrows folded over his eyes. "I don't think . . ." He swung toward Cruz, who was walking into the water fully clothed. I wasn't sure if he'd kept his pants and shirt on for my sake or because it made doing laundry swifter. "Hey, Vega, how does the apple work?"

Cruz juggled his stalk of yellow aloe between his hands. "What do you mean?"

"Do you have to bite into it and swallow a chunk or can the juice kill you?" I asked.

He clutched the curled stalk so hard a drop of golden gel hit the surface of the pool. "A piece has to get into your system. Juice alone can't kill you."

Remo turned back toward me, relief ironing his brow. "Feel better?"

"I'll feel better once he's gone," I whispered.

"Soon." His thumb drifted to the middle of my tattooed palm and gave it a light squeeze. "Now go. And if you see your uncle, yell and jump into the water, okay?"

Nibbling on my bottom lip, I nodded and then treaded around the foaming crescent until I reached the boulders, climbing over one and onto another. When I felt perched high enough, I pressed my back against the smooth stone and finger-combed my hair, then plaited it while Cruz and Remo spoke in low tones, drowned out by the waterfall.

When I caught both glancing my way and the edges of Kingston's name on Remo's lips, I deduced Cruz was being filled in on what had happened earlier. Maybe Remo was looking for an ally, or maybe he was just warning my father's best friend about our plan for my traitorous uncle.

Whatever they discussed was done surreptitiously and quickly. Before the wet patches on my new clothes had even dried, they were both stalking out of the water, naked. I flung my gaze down onto my pebbled thighs and picked at a thread in the hem of my shorts until large veined hands set on the stone, on either side of my bare feet.

"Just so you're aware, I *never* mind if you feel like staring. As long as it's at me, and not at Cruz."

The tips of my ears burned.

Remo took a step back from the boulder and extended his arms. "Come, fiancée."

I stood up, and although I could get down on my own, I braced myself on his shoulders to hop off. "Does he have any idea where Kingston hid the apple?"

"No. But he said he'd help me keep him away from you."

I stared up into his bright green eyes. "And from you."

"I'm your uncle's ticket out of here, Amara. He might try to hurt me, but he won't try to end me."

I wanted his words to reassure me, but Kingston was a slippery man-child with a massive chip on his shoulder. To think I'd all but landed in his lap by coming here. "Did you tell Cruz about my dust?"

"No."

"Because you don't trust him?"

"Because he'd already noticed it. He asked if you could use it."

"And you said yes?" We were standing so close that when he nodded, the tip of his nose grazed my forehead. "And?"

"He said asphyxiating him *might* work."

I liked the sound of might, even though Remo's inflection told me he didn't.

"He also speculated that your blood might poison him if we manage to get some in his heart," he murmured.

I shivered from his suggestion. "I'm scared, Remo."

He pressed me against him. "I'm here, Amara. Right here with you."

I nestled my chin in the crook of his shoulder. "I'm not scared of Kingston," I murmured against his honeyed skin. "I'm scared of failing. I don't want him to end up in the mud field. I want him gone. For good. Forever."

His hand threaded through my hair, tugging on my plaited strands, before he pressed a kiss to my temple. "When have you ever failed?"

I snorted. "If you want the full list of my failures, Sook knows each by heart. Just ask. He'll be more than happy to share them with you."

Sook. My heart thumped hollowly. How I missed him. Giya. Iba. Nima. Pappy. Nana Em. Nana Vee. I didn't tell Remo how homesick I was, but I clutched him a little harder, because until someone came for us, he was my only piece of home.

36

THE CAVES

Our four cellmates were sitting around a campfire when Remo and I reached the caves—an elongated grotto bracketed by two parallel rows of shadowy recesses. Pockets of light beamed through crevices in the vaulted ceiling, illuminating a series of bone-and-soot sketches.

Unlike the simplistic images early humans had painted in their caverns, these drawings had been executed by someone of extraordinary talent. Someone, judging by the landscapes, who'd lived on Neverra. I stopped in front of the one depicting the Glades, admiring the intricate details of the *stams* that bobbed like giant lily pads atop the water and the tentacular roots of the *volitors* which dipped into the gleaming expanse.

Although Remo stayed by my side while I admired the murals, his attention was on the group, or more precisely, on the scowling brown-haired fae. Even through the pale smoke of the roasting leg of *tigri*, I could make out the mountains and valleys on Kingston's skin. Kiera hadn't been exaggerating when she said his welts were more abundant. His entire forehead was covered in lumps, his nose was deformed, and his chin stuck out like the steel-capped toes on the two pairs of boots swinging from Remo's fingers.

"Cave one, six, seven, and eleven are taken." Kiera pointed to the carved etchings above the arched passageways.

"Who sleeps where?" Remo asked.

"One is Kingston. Six is me. Quinn's in seven. And Cruz sleeps all the way at the back."

That settled it then. To the back we'd go. "Ten?" I asked Remo softly.

He nodded, and we walked past the little circle of mismatched criminals.

Avoiding my uncle's glare, I said, "We'll just go set our stuff down. Be back in a minute."

The dark passageway beyond the arch curled in on itself like the inside of a conch. At its heart lay a circular room illuminated by pinpricks of light that streamed through tiny holes in the domed ceiling. The walls were rough, and the sandy floor cold beneath my bare feet. Save for a stack of purple pelts and a basket woven from cyan fronds filled with tiny shells, the space was entirely bare. I hadn't expected a bathroom or a feather bed, but both would've been welcomed. I gazed around me one last time, hoping I'd missed something during my first sweep of the room. To my great regret, I'd missed nothing.

I hung the damp pelt on a rock jutting from the wall. "This is taking minimalism to a whole new level."

Remo dropped the machete and two pairs of boots next to the hamper of shells. Did that mean he would stay with me? I raised my gaze toward him, found the beginnings of a blush staining the edge of his face, slowly coloring the whole of it.

"Sorry. I didn't mean to assume. I can head into—"

When he bent to pick up his boots, I stepped on the dusty toecap. "Stay. Please."

He straightened. Such a paradox this man—timid at times and yet so darn self-assured at others. He scraped his hand through his dark auburn locks, which unlike mine, had dried. How I missed my *kalini* . . . Since I'd landed in the Scourge, I was always either damp, cold, or soaked in mud.

His confidence ended up beating back his blush, and he cupped my head, lined up our mouths, then slowly backed me up against the curved wall. My heart pinballed around my ribs as I reached around his waist and hugged him. He nudged my mouth open, then swept his tongue against mine, all at once playful and not.

When a low rumble sounded between us, one that hadn't come from his throat, I tore my lips off his, adrenaline pushing through my lust-addled senses.

"That was just my stomach, Amara."

"Thank, Gejaiwe. Here I thought our new home was about to cave in."

His glistening lips bowed. "No more trials."

"Are we sure of that?"

"Yes."

I sighed. "If only we didn't have my uncle to deal with, I'd be partying it up right now."

"Soon." His stomach rumbled again, momentarily distracting me from Kingston and his poisonous apple.

Wasn't there a fairytale about a poisoned apple? Was that where Gregor or my grandfather had gotten their twisted idea?

I threaded my hand through his. "Let's get you fed."

When we emerged from our cave, only Quinn, Kiera, and Cruz sat by the fire. My uncle must've turned in for the night or gone to retrieve his fruit, because he was nowhere in sight. As I took a seat next to Kiera, my gaze traveled down the dusky cavern toward cave number one.

"Just grab a fork. The meat should tear right off," Kiera instructed, her chin glistening with a dribble of fat.

As I leaned toward the fire to grab a slender branch topped with two metal prongs secured by twine, I caught Quinn scrutinizing me. The flames bounced against his hazel irises, heightening his already suspicious air.

"What do you eat when your supply of *tigri* runs out?" I asked, taking a small bite. Although unseasoned, the meat was delicious, melting on my tongue before sliding into my empty stomach, which emitted its own little pleased rumble; nothing like the sound that had come from Remo earlier though.

"*Panem* leaves and mollusks." Kiera wrinkled her nose as she wiped her chin on the back of her hand. She'd probably eaten too much of both.

Remo finally sank down next to me, leaned over to grab a Scourge-made fork, and pierced the roasted leg of *tigri*. He gobbled the chunk of meat so fast I didn't think he even tasted it. His stomach grumbled again, which spurred him into tearing through a second piece.

I thought of all the cuts of *tigri* dangling in the jungle. "How long will the meat keep?"

"Once it dries, we'll smoke it." Cruz carved himself another piece of browned roast. "And then, we bring it into the caves, dig up a hole in the sand, and layer *panem* leaves around it. It's not as effective as a freezer, but it'll keep a few weeks. Months even."

"What's your deal with Kingston? Why'd you two kill him?" Quinn's change of subject was so abrupt it made everyone fall quiet.

"Just keeping him in line," Remo finally said.

"*In line*? Who do you take yourselves for? The police?" Grease glossed Quinn's beard. He brushed the wiry hairs with blood-crusted fingernails.

Kiera shrugged. "He tried to assassinate her dad, Quinn."

"Are you just going to shrug when she comes after us seeking revenge for what we did to her aunt?"

Kiera's shoulders locked up tight. "We never tried to assassinate no one, Quinn. We were protecting our people." She slanted me a look. "You don't have any plans to off us, do you?"

"You're seriously asking them?" Quinn snorted, tore off a chunk of meat, then swallowed.

"Do you plan on hurting Amara's aunt when you get out of here?" Remo asked calmly.

"We don't care about her!" Quinn stared at Remo through slitted eyes. "But we plan on giving your granddaddy a piece of our minds."

"Quinn . . ." Kiera hissed.

Remo's grip tightened on his fork. "He'd deserve it."

"What he deserves is to be locked up in this fucking prison," Quinn huffed out. "I give him a week before he bites the apple. Fuck, even I was tempted. If Kiera hadn't knocked it out of my hand, I would've given up. What sort of life is this?"

A sorry one.

"And you, Cruz?" I asked. "Were you ever tempted to *bite the apple*?"

He swirled the prongs of his fork in the sand, shaping an image that looked so much like Lily's face it made my heart miss a beat. When he caught me staring, he swept his palm across the sand. "Yes." The muscles in his arms flexed as he pressed his hands against his knees as though to rise. He didn't, though, just stared at me from across the flames. "She's happy right? With Kajika?"

"She is, but she'll be happier once she sees you still exist."

Cruz's jaw stiffened, then relaxed, then stiffened again. "I heard she had twins."

I found myself smiling. "Giya and Adsookin. They're a couple months older than I am. They're both"—my voice caught—"they're both amazing."

Remo's hand landed on my thigh, stayed there.

"Kingston told us the Farrows and the Woods hated each other's guts," Kiera said, not missing Remo's grip on me.

My heart felt as though it were ballooning a little. "They do."

"But not your generation?" she asked.

"Oh, no," I said, with a smile. "Our generation hates each other."

"Then why are you two so"—she wrinkled her nose—"touchy-feely?"

"Because he's my fiancé."

Her eyebrows, which were a few shades darker than her white-blonde hair, jolted up. "Your fiancé?"

"Yeah. My father wanted to appease Gregor, so they agreed on tying me to this one." I nodded to Remo, whose fingers traveled to my waist and pinched the skin, which just made my smile broaden. "It was the worst day of my life. Well, until I went through the portal your brother told me about." I looked back at her, saw so much of Josh, the same blue eyes and smattering of freckles, although he had a thicker spray. "Then again, it was the same day." I tipped my face toward one of the holes in the ceiling. "Maybe it's still the same day."

"Not if you went through four cells, it's not," Kiera commented.

"Feels like one endless day."

"So now, you don't hate each other anymore?" Quinn asked.

"Something like that," Remo said, his fingers no longer teasing my waist. Or rather teasing it differently. His nails raked across the skin he'd pinched, raising bands of goosebumps.

"I can't believe Ace agreed to an arranged marriage." Cruz's quiet proclamation made Remo's fingers still. "I was certain he'd abolish them."

Remo's face became an assortment of angles and edges. "Massin Wood thought my grandfather was about to orchestrate another coup." He swallowed jaggedly, his hand drifting away from me. "He looked miserable about giving me his daughter. Almost as miserable as Amara."

"I wasn't miserable; I was furious. And you didn't exactly look happy."

He held my gaze before staring back at the fire.

"I'm beat," Quinn announced.

Kiera rose, too, stretching her arms over her head. "I'll see you guys tomorrow. Don't forget to put out the fire." She trailed Quinn toward their caves.

"Cat, is your—" Cruz's eyes grew wide as he realized by what name he'd just called me. "I'm sorry."

"It's okay."

"You just look so much like her. Though she probably doesn't look like you anymore."

"Don't tell *her* that. Neenee Cass and Nima are all about forty-one being the new twenty."

"Forty-one? Wow." Cruz stuck his fork inside the sand, right where Lily's face had been. "Skies, how strange it will be—seeing everyone again."

Silence draped over us, interrupted only by the snapping flames.

Sighing, Cruz stood. "I'm going to call it a night, also. If you need to . . . relieve yourself, there's a designated area fenced by a wall of fronds. Just circle the outside wall of the cave. Can't miss it. As for drinkable water, you can find some in there." He tipped his head toward the wall behind him, or rather toward a piece of scrap metal fashioned into a squat barrel. "The blown-up train comes in handy. If you two feel like it in the morning, I'm planning on heading back to the explosion site to gather usable pieces before they fade."

"Fade?" I frowned at the barrel.

"If you don't pick them up within a certain timeframe, they vanish. Once you touch them, you lock them into this cell."

Why anything still surprised me was beyond me. "What happens now that there are no more trials?"

"Unless Gregor's changed the rules, it's all dreadful peace and quiet until someone new shows up." He rubbed his hands down his jeans that were a few inches too short on him. "To turn off the fire, just kick sand over it."

"And the meat?"

"Leave it. No animals roam around here except the vamp beetles, and they don't come down into the valley."

I looked at his retreating figure until the archway of his cave gobbled him up. When I turned back around, I found Remo poking at the blackened, sputtering logs. I held my palms out to the flames, relishing the heat. Although not cold, the air inside the cave system carried the mustiness of a basement and the chill of a place in dire need of sunlight.

I propped my chin on my shoulder and studied Remo. "Are you okay?"

He blinked at me, then at the dancing blaze. "Yeah. Fine."

"I made you mad again, didn't I?"

His eyebrows scooted a little closer to his nose.

"I'm sorry I blabbed about our engagement. I didn't think it was a secret since you told Cruz—"

"That's not it, Amara."

"Then what is . . . *it*?"

"Getting engaged shocked and confused me, but I was neither miserable nor angry," he said without glancing away from the fire. "I guess it just hurts to hear how upset it made you."

"You scowled at me throughout dinner."

"Because you had your back to me, Amara. You didn't even attempt to be civil."

A startled breath escaped me.

He ran one hand down his face. "Forget it. I'm just tired."

"You can't say something like that, then tell me to forget it." I lowered my palms and leaned back. "I'm sorry. I promise not to turn my back on you, or bite your head off for holding my hand during the binding ceremony next time the Cauldron appears."

His rigid posture finally softened under his borrowed cream Henley. "Next time, huh?"

I circled my finger in the air as though I were trussing him up. "Strings. Everywhere."

His face broke into a heartbreakingly sweet smile that heated my blood quicker than the little fire in front of me, quicker than all of his crooked grins and promises to keep me safe. Was this lust or love? How did one know the difference?

As the feeling strengthened, I decided it had to be lust, because how could I love him after such a short period of time? Yes, we'd lived intensely, but did intensity speed up feelings?

As though my thoughts were scrolling across my forehead, his smile vanished in increments and then completely. He jerked up to his feet, kicked sand over the fire, then extended his hand, and just like the dozens of times he'd offered it to me since we'd arrived in the Scourge, I took it.

As we walked to our newest nest, I ran my thumb over every crease and callous, the shape and feel of his palm as familiar to me now as my own. Once inside the round cavern, he lifted my knuckles to his mouth and kissed them chastely.

"I'll take first watch. You sleep." He let go, grabbed a few pelts from the pile, shook them out, then layered them over the sand, adding a rolled one at the top of the makeshift bed.

My nerves jangled as though I'd drunk an entire gallon of coffee. "I don't think I can. Why don't you sleep, and I take first watch?"

He grabbed his machete and dropped a kiss on the tip of my nose. "I'm used to night watches; you're not."

"But—"

"No, buts. Rest."

"Remo . . ."

He backed out of the cave, and then his footfalls whispered across the sand. Sighing, I laid out on my furred pallet and stared at the pinpricks of white light, which through my lashes almost resembled the *lustriums* that lit up the Neverrian night sky.

Even though they weren't stars, I wished on them.

I wished Josh had told someone about our *gajoï* and then I wished Kingston would choke on his apple and be gone forever.

37

THE TREMOR

"Amara, get up!"

I grumbled, attempting to twist away from the hands shaking me.

They shook harder. "Amara! Someone just arrived. You have to get up."

My lids flipped open, and I found that no one was even holding me. Remo stood at the entrance of my stone chamber, eyes gleaming wildly.

Another hard tremor dynamited the ground.

Great Gejaiwe, someone was here? Was it to get us out? I vaulted to my feet, adrenaline hemorrhaging through me. I lunged toward Remo, then past him. We took off running down the center aisle just as Kiera and Quinn emerged bleary-eyed, spears in hand.

Soon, they were running alongside us. And then Cruz was there, kicking up sand next to Remo. The only one missing was Kingston. He was probably hiding, sensing the death bells tolling for him, because if we were on our way home, he'd be judged and executed, this time by my father.

When we burst through the tree line, thick smoke clogged the sky and shards of metal and glass already littered the sand. A groan rose from beneath a curved sheet of metal. I ran toward it and heaved it up.

My grip faltered, and the piece of metal, which had shielded the new arrival, flipped over and seesawed at my bare feet. Shock spooled in my chest, and a gasp filled my mouth. I dropped to my knees, my hands scrabbling over the prostrate body.

"Giya? Giya!" A thin cut along her cheekbone wept blood. "Giya?" My voice rattled with shock.

Her lashes fluttered, and then her beautiful, gray eyes alighted on me, and her trembling lips parted around my name. She rose onto her forearms, and then she was sitting, and we were hugging. And although I should've been horrified by what it meant that she was here, I was too damn happy that she'd come.

I smoothed out her long brown hair, the locks so crusted with salt and tangled they almost resembled Kiera's dreads.

"Great Gejaiwe, Amara, I thought I'd never find you." Her torso hardened suddenly, and she pushed me away. "Wait. Am I dead? Is that why—"

I smiled, a wobbly smile so full of emotion my body shook even though the world around us had finally stilled. "You're not dead. I promise." I combed back a lock of hair that stuck to her weeping cut. "This is the final cell. It's why the train exploded."

Shock rippled over her drawn face. Even though she had never been pale a day in her life, her skin became bone-white.

"Giya, how did you find this place?"

"Josh. He commed me. Asked if I had any news from you." She gulped in air. "We didn't know what had happened to you. We thought . . . we thought Gregor made Remo kidnap you and destroy both your Infinities, so we couldn't track you, but Gregor . . . he said . . . he said he never ordered his grandson to do that. He said that if Remo took you . . . it wasn't on his orders." Again she gulped in air.

I rubbed the spot between her shoulder blades, trying to soothe her. "Does anyone know you're here?"

"Sook." Her lower lip rose over her upper one the way it always did when her heart was about to break. "B-but that *bagwa* decided to follow me inside." She shuddered.

"He's here?" I swung my gaze around the mishmash of sand and train parts, looking for another body, but located none. Had he died on impact? Was he waking in the field of mud?

"Oh, Amara . . ." Tears tracked down her cheeks, thinning her blood. "He didn't make it. He—" She choked, then let out a heart-shattering wail.

My blood became ice. "He ate the apple?" My tone sounded clinical.

She sniffled, then squeaked, "The apple?" She palmed her cheeks, making a mess of the blood. "No. He's allergic to apples. The *pistri* got him."

A smile knocked into my mouth, soon turning into an irrepressible giggle.

"A giant, three-headed—Why are you laughing? He's dead, Amara. Sook is dead."

"No, he's not." I tried to calm down. Really, I did, but my nerves were so shot that I couldn't get a handle on them. "And I'm laughing because I'm never going to let Sook live down the fact that he got munched on by a shark."

She frowned, her eyebrows almost colliding over her smooth forehead. "I saw him turn into smoke!"

"When you die in this place, you resuscitate. Interminably. Trust me. Been there, done that, came back." I sobered up. "Unless you eat the apple. Then . . ." My gaze rose to the loose circle of cell mates. Kingston was still not among them.

Giya cranked her neck, finally noticing we weren't alone. Her lips pressed into a tight line at the sight of Remo. At the sight of Cruz, though, they parted extra-wide. She whipped around and gaped at me, her gray eyes cartoonishly large in spite of her eyelids being puffy from crying. "Did I just see . . .? Am I . . .? Is that . . .?"

"Cruz Vega?" I supplied.

Her jaw unhinged farther. "Are you kidding?" she hissed.

"Nope."

"Is he real?"

"Cruz?" I crooked a finger, calling him toward us.

At first, he didn't even react to his name, but then he blinked out of his daze and strolled toward us in that slow, measured way of his.

"Can you say something to Giya, so she can come to terms with the fact that you're not a figment of her imagination?"

He squatted, then extended his hand toward her. "Hi, Giya. I'm not a figment of your imagination. And it's really nice to meet you."

She stared between his proffered hand and his open face.

"I think she's in a little too much shock to shake hands," I told him.

She slammed her eyes back to mine, then back to his. "Why do you look like you're . . . like you're—like us?"

Sighing, he said, "I'm guessing magic."

Her eyes widened, which I honestly thought was impossible considering their current width. "Nima is going to—oh, Great Gejaiwe, she's going to . . ." She couldn't seem to find the words to finish her sentence. "And my uncle. Oh, Skies . . ."

Cruz's green eyes glided over her face, smiling even though it looked painful for him to do so. Was it talk of Lily, or the fact that, in spite of having inherited her father's more chiseled features, darker hair, and honeyed skin tone, her eyes and bow-shaped lips were the same as her mother's?

"How many cells ago did your brother die?" he asked.

Her eyebrows writhed as though she were about to break down again. "Two."

I tucked a lock of hair behind her ear. "You went through an entire world on your own?"

Her bloated lids closed, and she shuddered. "Oh, Amara." When her lids swept back up, her eyes gleamed silver. "It was so horrible. Plus, I thought . . . I thought Sook was gone. Forever. And I didn't think I'd ever find you, and—" She bawled again, so I hugged her to me, nestling her head under my chin.

"You should take her to the waterfall. Get her cleaned up, and then bring her to the caves. The . . ." Cruz went silent as though to spare my cousin the news of the furred monsters that were about to descend upon us. "They don't fit inside the individual caves."

I nodded, then stood and helped her up, but her balance teetered, and although thin, she weighed more than my tired arms could carry. Remo, who was standing close, lunged toward us and caught her arm before she could tumble.

Thank you, I mouthed.

When she realized whose hands were on her, she spooked and bounced away, stumbling right into Cruz.

"Easy there, Giya," Cruz said gently.

"How come Remo's here, too?" My usually soft-spoken cousin wasn't speaking all that softly. "Did he force you inside his grandfather's prison?"

A small smile tipped my mouth. "Believe it or not, that *bagwa* followed me in."

"Again with the *bagwa*," Remo chided, even though his expression was amused.

"Do you even know what it means?" Giya snapped.

"Your brother called me a jackass in Gottwa enough times for me to look it up."

I grinned. "Oh, he's called you a lot worse."

A corner of his mouth hooked up. "I don't doubt it."

Giya's head ping-ponged between us, so absorbed by our easy banter she seemed to have forgotten she was being held up by a ghost. "Are you two"—her nose scrunched up—"friends now?"

Remo draped his arm around my shoulders and tucked me into his side. "Trifecta finally came to her senses and realized what a catch I am."

I rolled my eyes but wove my hand through the one dangling over my shoulder.

Giya's gaze fastened on our locked fingers. There had been times where I'd been happy in the Scourge, but having my cousin here, knowing my other one was on his way, and holding Remo's hand, I felt borderline giddy.

I craned my neck to look up at my fiancé. Although exhausted, he, too, looked somewhat happy.

"Not to interrupt your sappy reunion, but the smoke's getting thin." Kiera lifted her chin to the crater. "And there's meat hanging everywhere. It'll drive the *tigri* feral."

I gave Remo's hand one last squeeze, then released it and walked out from under his arm. "Hand her over," I told Cruz.

"Are you sure?"

I nodded, then snuck my arm under Giya's as she whispered, "*Tigri?*"

"Second trial. But don't worry. You can rest while—"

"I hate this place. I mean, I'm so happy to see you, but I really *hate* prison."

I shot her grim smile. "You and I both." As we slalomed through the train debris, I asked, "Does anything hurt?"

"My head."

Worry made me push her hair around, hunting for hidden gashes. "I don't see any blood. Besides the one coming from the cut on your cheek."

"It hurts because I've spent the last few days—hours?"—she looked up at the sky—"awake and alert and fucking terrified."

"Giya Geemiwa, did you just curse?"

"Oh, shut up. After what I went through, I get to curse. I also get to rant if I feel like it." Her voice was unnaturally high-pitched. "What is wrong with you? Why are you still smiling?"

"I'm just really happy to see you."

She shot me a befuddled look.

"Does anyone else know where we are?" Remo asked, slowing his strides to keep up with our snail pace.

"Josh."

"I meant, besides him?"

She shook her head.

"Hey, Farrow!" Kiera called out. "You're needed to collect the meat."

His gaze surfed past Giya and locked on mine.

"Go. I'm rested. *And* armed. We'll be okay."

A muscle ticked in his jaw.

"Let him accompany the girls," Cruz said. "We have enough time to gather all the meat."

"Why don't we dump it all in one place?" Quinn suggested. "The *tigri* will converge there and be easier to pick off."

Kiera chewed on her lip, clenching her fingers around her spear. I wondered if she slept with it. "Seven of them in the same place doesn't sound like such great odds to me."

"She looks familiar?" Giya whispered. "Why does she look familiar?"

"Because you're looking at Cole's twin."

"And the man with the beard is their uncle, Quinn," Remo added.

Giya's pupils shrank, which made her irises look impossibly wide. "Kiera Locklear and Quinn Thompson?" she hissed. "Iba and Nima's torturers?"

I nodded, glancing over my shoulder at the fine-boned, skinny blonde with the tousled dreads who was at present scanning the darkened expanse of thick palms, squat *panem*, and curled aloe.

"Where the hell is Little King?" she barked.

Giya faltered, and I tightened my grip on her.

As we scraped past a yellow thicket, I said, "Did I forget to mention our dear, dead uncle is here?"

"He's alive?" She came to such a sudden halt that she almost slipped from my hold.

"Yeah." With a sigh, I looked toward Remo, whose expression turned even graver. "He's the reason Remo and I had to tie the Cauldron knot. Iba was afraid Gregor was grooming him for a coup."

Giya stared between us, then all around. "Wow," was all she

said, but her writhing eyebrows told me she was thinking a heck of a lot more as we took off again. Ducking beneath a liana, she asked, "Any other dead fae lurking around these parts I should know about?"

I shook my head. I hesitated to tell her that Kingston not only harbored the apple but also an intense desire to turn me into ether. I thought she'd had enough craziness lobbed at her and didn't need more to process, but I wanted her prepared in case we ran into his deranged ass. "He has the apple and is intent on feeding it to me."

She gaped at me, then at Remo, whose knuckles were clenched around his machete, and whose gaze was on the shadows cast by the swaying blue canopy. "He'll be dead—and I don't mean *field-of-mud* dead—before he can even try."

She docked her mouth against my ear and murmured, "Are you sure you can trust him, Amara?"

By *him*, I assumed she meant Remo. "Yes." I smiled at my fiancé, but he neither caught my smile or her words, too busy scouring the land for danger, or rather, for Kingston. "I'm sure."

"Wait . . . so you guys are like, *actually* friends?"

"Believe it or not."

"When did that happen?"

"Somewhere between Fake Rowan and Fake Neverra."

She frowned.

Remo tsked, then volleyed, "In the city with skyscrapers."

"No, I did *not* like you then."

He side-eyed me. "You cried when I died."

"Because I didn't want to be all alone."

"Uh-huh." He winked at me, which made Giya's brows jolt back up.

One more shock, and she would get a kink in her forehead from all the eyebrow squirming. "This is so weird," she ended up saying.

"You're telling me." I smiled at Remo, thinking: *Wait till you hear the whole of it.*

After a beat, my ever-perceptive cousin leaned in and spilled a shocked whisper that threatened to blow out my eardrum, "You *like him* like him!"

I whispered back, "Maybe."

"I didn't quite catch your answer, Trifecta."

"Eavesdropping is beneath you, Farrow."

"You think too highly of me." His accompanying smirk hit me square in the heart.

"Wow," was all Giya said, again, but her eyes never stopped traveling between us as we escorted her to the waterfall.

38

THE AMBUSH

Giya scanned the depths of the frothing pool. "Please tell me there are no sharks."

"No. No fish either for that matter. Just mollusks." I waded up to my knees, not wanting to wet my clothes, and leaned over to scoop up some water. I drank my fill, then splashed the rest on my face. And then, because I was still a kid at heart, I splashed Remo, who was standing vigil on the beach.

He whirled around. "Oh no you didn't, Trifecta . . ."

When he came at me, I took off laughing. He caught up way too fast, grabbing me around the waist, locking my back against his front.

"Don't throw me in," I begged, between giggles.

I could feel him smile against my hair. "Give me one good reason?"

"Because then I'd be wet." I tried to wriggle away from him, but his arms were steel bands around my middle.

"And?" His voice brushed up the shell of my ear.

"And this fabric isn't half as concealing as my suit."

"Not a convincing argument, Trifecta."

"You're not the only man around."

He grunted, and his arms loosened. "Fine. Consider yourself spared." He dropped his mouth to my ear again. "But next time . . ."

I turned in Remo's arms and stole a kiss.

"You guys are seriously not some weird hallucination? 'Cause there was this cell where"—she shuddered—"where no one was real." Her body gave another hard shake, which made the water around her submerged calves tremble.

What had my poor cousin endured? "We're real. I promise."

She waded in to midthigh, soaking her brown suede leggings while her long, cream chiffon top billowed atop the surface. For some reason, I was only noticing now what she wore and how stained it all was. "So I need to get used to"—she orbited her finger in the air, wrapping us in an imaginary circle—"this?"

I glanced up at Remo.

"I'm going to go with a *yes* for fear of getting smacked."

I rolled my eyes. "So dramatic." As I splashed through the water toward her, I asked, "What's up with the outfit?"

She stared down as though she'd forgotten what she was wearing. "I was at Magena and Dawson's son's spirit ceremony when I got Josh's comm."

A spirit ceremony was performed when the child became a man or a woman. I'd celebrated mine at twelve. It was supposed to have been a small and intimate affair—only Unseelies—but Seelies had flown over the Valley of the Five to partake in the spectacle of me offering the Gottwas's Great Spirit a drop of my blood, thus sealing my fate with Hers. Thanks to Remo's warning about its toxicity, none of the Seelies had drifted too close, but still they'd watched. I wondered if he'd been among the hovering crowd of silk-and-leather spectators. I was about to ask him when a nasal voice skidded over the water toward us.

"Well, if it isn't the princess's little sidekick? All grown up, too. Four years does the Wood women wonders." Kingston stood beside an aloe thicket.

I stared at his hands, expecting to see the apple clutched in one of them, but his delicate, fisted fingers held only air.

"Is more of the family coming? Because I am *loving* this family reunion. Such fun to see everyone again."

"Amara mentioned Neverra's fool was still alive, but she forgot to mention how stylistically low he'd fallen." She whistled as she looked him up and down. "I really wish my Infinity was working, because that outfit deserves a picture. Are you trying to launch a new trend, Little King? Not sure this one will catch. And your face. Finally hit puberty, huh?"

Kingston's eyes blackened.

I caught Remo's mouth twitching even though mine stayed flat, too stressed to appreciate the moment. Giya was calm like Lily until you pissed her off. Then she became like Kajika—a cat with needle-sharp claws.

Which reminded me . . .

I glanced up at the sky, at the thin coil that remained on the horizon. "Remo, the smoke's almost gone."

I both felt and heard the weight of his sigh. "We need to get Giya to the caves."

"The caves?" Kingston, who'd snapped a piece of aloe off, waggled it at us. "Were you planning on hiding, nieces?"

Giya rolled her shoulders back and straightened her neck. "No one's hiding."

"But, Giya—"

"I'm fine, Amara. So how do we defeat them? Do we have to brew a potion with weird-ass ingredients again?"

I stared at her resolute profile, again wondering what sort of trials she'd gone through to get here.

"No potion-brewing," Kingston replied. "Just good-old-fashioned skewering."

"I'm guessing I'll need a spear then." Giya trod back toward the beach, splitting the clear water with her lean legs. "Where do we get weapons?"

Kingston stroked his hunk of aloe. "At the caves. I can take you girls since Remo's all set with his little machete."

Remo stalked out of the pool and caught up to Giya. "They're not going anywhere with you."

Even though Kingston stared steadily at Remo, the pulse point strained the skin of his neck, betraying his bogus sangfroid. "Amara has gotten you so well-trained. Bet she offers great treats."

My mouth opened to tell him off, but Remo beat me to it. "Were you hoping for another machete between the eyes to avoid becoming *tigri* lunch? Because, and I speak for everyone here, we'd much rather see you face off with the tigers."

Kingston shot him an oily smile that made the welts on his face writhe. "I was going to spare you, but you deserve the apple just as much as your master."

Vibrating with the need to shove my dust down his throat, I clenched my fingers and attempted to coax it out one-handedly. Like all of my previous attempts, it failed. Behind my back, I joined my fingers and fashioned a spear.

As I brought it in front of me, Giya cocked an eyebrow. Thankfully, she didn't ask where I'd found my weapon. Had she noticed my tattoo? She probably would've asked whose *wita* I carried beneath my skin if she had.

"Hey, Remo, can I trade you a spear for a machete?" I asked, coming to stand beside him. "I like smaller weapons."

"That must be a relief to your guard dog." Kingston shot Remo a wink that made me want to pop my bastard uncle's eye out of its socket. Both eyes for that matter. "Being on the small—"

Before we could trade weapons, Remo jumped on Kingston, smacking him into the sand. And then his hands were around his neck, both thumbs digging into the hollow at the traitor's collarbone.

"Remo, take the sp—"

A deep growl thundered over the waterfall, making my spine snap very straight. I spun just in time to see a purple beast emerge from a cluster of aloe across the horseshoe beach, golden eyes set on the four of us, lips hitched around its shiny fangs.

Giya took a small step back. "Holy ... spirit."

A snarl broke out of the mammoth cat as it kicked up clouds of white sand.

"Remo!" I yelled, raising my spear.

My palm slickened around the long handle, and my bicep trembled. Gritting my teeth, I nocked my arm farther back and then let the spear fly. It hit the *tigri*'s broad chest, bounced right off. The wild cat snarled. It was so close, its rancid breath tinged the air, overpowering the scent of *panem*. My heart catapulted into my ribs. The *tigri*'s hind legs bent and then uncoiled, and the furred monster was airborne.

Giya's hand clapped mine, wrenched me back. "Amara, run!"

I couldn't move.

Screeching something, she hauled me back, pulling so hard she almost dislocated my shoulder. My feet slid, and I flailed backward, just as the tiger hit the patch of sand I'd been standing on with an enraged whine, before crumpling like a tissue, silent and inert, the machete sticking out from between its eyes.

As Remo freed his weapon, he yelled something, but I couldn't make out a single word over the buzzing in my ears. Grasping I was out of commission, he trotted to where my spear lay on the ground, grabbed it, then raced back to us. I watched him scan the jungle, chest heaving. Was another *tigri* coming? Or was he looking for Kingston? Where had my cowardly uncle disappeared to?

Remo tilted his head in the direction of the caves. Giya's grip tightened on my hand as she followed Remo through the dense brush. In increments, my hearing began to return. I picked up the sound of shouts over the chorus of thunderous growls and snarls.

Had they managed to tempt the six other beasts with the butchered bodies of their brethren?

A branch snapped.

We halted. Even our labored panting quieted.

Remo pressed the spear back into my still shaking hand. "Can you make another net?"

Nodding erratically, I waited for the predator to show itself, not wanting to flay my palm and fingers on the prickly metal mesh. When two hulking beasts materialized in our line of sight at the very same time, my heart damn near exploded.

"Shit," Remo hissed.

"I don't think . . . I don't think my net can snag both."

"Just focus on the one coming up on your right side; I'll get the other." He widened his stance and raised his elbow, viscous crimson droplets of blood dribbling from the machete's blade.

As though a cannon had detonated, both mammoth cats sprang at us, their golden stripes glittering over their bloated muscles and their tails flogging the air.

"NOW!" Remo yelled.

I squeezed the spear, fashioning my barbed wire net, and hurled it over the cat. The animal howled as its front paws got tangled, which brought its huge body down right at Giya's feet. Squeaking, she hopped back. Unlike yesterdays' *tigri*, this one chewed through the wire, ripping it with its fangs. Muzzle and front legs wet with blood, it squirmed backward, managing to disentangle itself, licked its muzzle, then narrowed its gleaming eyes on us.

Crap. Crap. Crap. I needed to recall my dust and transform it into a weapon before it could chomp on one of us. "Giya, get behind me."

"Why? What are you thinking?"

"Just get back, please," I begged her.

She took a measly step back. I touched the part of the barbed wire net farthest from the tiger and liquefied it, molding it into a new weapon—a five-headed spear. Five, because accuracy wasn't my forte.

The second the net vanished, the *tigri*'s tail flicked up, its spine arched, and its haunches lowered. I lunged before it could become airborne, shoving my spear between its peaked ears. All five of my blades went in, and blood sloshed out in wet streams that spiraled over the handle of my spear, streaming down over my hand and wrist. When the hot, tinny scent hit my nose, I gagged.

"Amara!" Giya yelled, gesturing to Remo.

I gasped. The back of his T-shirt was shredded and red—four parallel grooves flapped while the rest of the fabric was glued to his skin.

The *tigri* limped back before growling and rearing onto its hind paws. I scaled the beast I'd killed and flung myself, spear first, at Remo's foe. I shut my eyes right before impact, but felt the blades sink into hide, heard the squelch of taut flesh, tasted the spray of hot blood on my face. Hands clamped around my ankles and dragged me back so fast the grains of sand rug-burned my chin. Since I was still gripping my weapon, the spear slipped wetly out of the beast's belly right before disintegrating and ribboning back into my palm. I tucked my arms in just as the ginormous feline collapsed, a hairsbreadth away from my head.

Heart rattling, I thought: *Three down, three down, three down.*

When I rolled onto my back, Remo crawled up my body, his palms cupping my cheeks. "Trifecta, are you okay?" His voice was as shrill with nerves as his gaze, which whipped over me, seeking wounds.

I inhaled deeply and nodded. Remo gently grabbed my hands and tugged me into a sitting position. A streak of blood on his temple reminded me of his lacerated back. "Turn. Let me see your back."

"My back's fine."

"It didn't look fine."

Inhuman yelps followed by human shouts had both our attention snapping to a spot beyond Remo's shoulder. When the ground shook, I inferred that another beast had fallen.

Remo stood, heaving me up. And then he hugged me to him,

and for a brief moment, the gore and jungle faded away. "Fuck, you saved my life."

Not really. I'd saved him from another mud-bath.

I nestled my face against his collarbone, feeling his heart kick against my cheek. It matched the tempo of the one presently lodged inside my throat.

Suddenly, I pressed away and my neck gyrated every which way. "Giya? Where did she go?"

He looked around, too. "I-I don't know. I was watching you." He rammed his hand through his wild red locks. "I'm sorry; I should've kept an eye on her."

"We have to find her. I have to find her."

He nodded just as an aloe thicket shivered.

"Giya?" I yelled.

Please let it not be another tigri. I'm not ready for another one.

Remo parted the leathery fronds.

What lay beyond made me wish it had been another furred behemoth.

39
BITE

"You fucking psychopath, let the girl go!" Remo growled.

Kingston had my cousin pinned to his front, one arm banded around her chest and both biceps, and the other hooked around her neck. The crimson apple gleamed like a mined heart inside his white-knuckled fist.

He pressed the fruit against Giya's lips, which were thankfully wedged so firmly they formed a line on her wan face. She shook her head from side to side and writhed. She even stomped down on Kingston's foot. He hurled curse words at her and lifted her a little higher, so that she was off balance, then whispered something in her ear that made her body still and her eyes brighten with fear.

"It's me you want!" My skin felt as though it had shrunk and stiffened, compressing my muscles like my discarded jumpsuit. "Let her go and take me."

"Show me your hands."

I raised both in the air. Indubitably, Kingston had seen my tattoo, but since he didn't fear it, I surmised he thought I couldn't access the confiscated dust.

"Turn." His slitted brown eyes followed my slow twirl.

"I have no weapon."

"You want Giya; you come to me."

Remo gripped my arm as I inched toward my uncle.

"You come alone, or I shove this apple down your cousin's lovely throat." When he nosed her neck, my fury turned into a raging ball of fire. Had I been able to access my *kalini*, all that would've been left of him would be cinders.

"Let me go, Remo," I murmured.

His fingers tightened on me. "Trifecta, no."

I glanced at him over my shoulder. "I can do this . . ."

His breathing had turned shallow and fast, fluttering his birthmark. Reluctantly, he freed me, and I walked toward them.

Kingston jutted his chin toward Remo. "Back up, Little Dog."

Remo vibrated with such rage that the leaves of the *panem* over his head frisked with it. He stood his ground, so Kingston backed up while keeping my cousin in a chokehold. I strode along with them, keeping my gaze on Giya's, trying to soothe her panic.

When we reached the beach, he said, "Closer, Amara."

I was trying to understand his strategy, which seemed hasty and ill-thought-out. To grab me, he'd have to release her, and the moment he let her go, he'd lose his advantage. Still, I approached. When I was within arm's length of them, I said, "I'm right where you want me."

His crazy eyes tipped at the corners, turning wildly mirthful. "You certainly are, *prinsisa*."

Giya's eyes widened. And then she started to shake her head. Kingston shoved the apple against her clasped lips with such violence he was going to bruise her face *or* the apple. As long as no juice leaked out . . .

What had Cruz told us? Could its juice kill us?

Her eyes widened and darted to a space over my shoulder. What was she trying to tell me? Was a *tigri*—

"Remo, behind you!" I screamed.

He spun just as Quinn ran at him with a spear. Remo released a snarl worthy of a *tigri* as he hopped to the side. The blade still nicked his waist, slicing right through his mangled shirt, reddening the cream fabric some more. Without missing a beat, he swung his machete into Quinn's neck, severing the man's bald, bearded head from the rest of his body.

Giya yelped and then retched, while Kingston grumbled a series of loud *fucks*.

The Daneelie disintegrated, darkening the sand. But that wasn't the only thing he left behind. A liana wrapped around a skinned piece of meat fell like a snake in the puddle of Quinn's blood. Confusion made the acid burning the lining of my throat recede. When gold and purple glinted in the shadows, I understood why Quinn had attached a piece of meat around his waist—to bait one of the monsters.

"Get Giya!" Remo grabbed the liana and hooked it around his wrist, and then he sprinted away from us, his wound making him falter over and over.

A crazed chuckle leaped out of my uncle's mouth. "How convenient, these little *tigri*. Maybe I'll bring one back with me as my pet. It'll become the new Wood crest."

Nails biting into my palms, I spun toward him and my cousin. "You are delusional."

Giya shook her head anew.

"Stop squirming, bitch!" he hissed, attempting to squash the apple against her mouth, but the remnants of vomit and spit on her cheek made the apple skid from side to side.

Using his distraction, I pressed my palms together behind my back to fashion a weapon when I heard a dull crack. My cousin went limp in his arms but didn't disintegrate. Had he broken her neck? Wouldn't she have disintegrated if he had? His smile became a grotesque, gleeful thing. He thumbed her chin down, and her jaw went slack.

When he ground the apple against her teeth, my heart all but leaped out of my ribcage, and my dust funneled back inside my palm. I couldn't risk flinging a handful of *wita* at Kingston when

Giya's mouth was wide open, so I rammed into them, sending both hurtling to the ground. The apple slid out of Kingston's grip, rolling and picking up grains of sand. I rushed toward it, but so did my uncle. As I bent to grab it, he smashed his foot into my jaw. I fell over, stars exploding in front of my eyes. Among those stars, I saw a headful of unkempt brown hair and vicious brown eyes. And then a heavy weight dropped onto my abdomen, knocking the wind from my lungs.

The edges of Kingston's body blurred and brightened as though he were wrapped in a string of lights. I blinked and blinked, until the lines of his body sharpened. I turned my eyes, looking for Giya, found her crumpled on the sand. Unmoving. She wasn't dead, but I almost wished she were. I wanted her out of the psychopath's reach.

Although my brain felt scrambled and sluggish, some primal survival instinct was screaming at me to get up. I writhed, trying to throw him off. He swore, and then he raised his arm and punched my mouth with the damn fruit. A trickle of warmth slid over my tongue—thick and coppery. I was guessing blood. Still I didn't swallow it. As he reeled his arm back, I spit into his face, speckling it with red droplets. He blinked. Hopefully, it was burning his eyes. How I wished it was as lethal as Remo had touted . . .

I squeezed my mouth shut just as Kingston roared, and his fist smashed down. This time, I managed to twist my face, and he caught my cheek. My brain swam and the little starlight edging Kingston's face became full-on *lustriums*. I heard my name tumbling on the breeze—raspy and deep. Was Remo coming back for me, or was I conjuring up his voice, wishing someone would save me?

Dust. I needed my dust.

I wriggled my fingers, desperately trying to coax it out one-handedly, but like every time before, the ribbons snapped right off my fingertips and cowered into their tracks. Without breaking eye contact with my irascible uncle, I raised my arms, dragging them over my head. When my palms met, his eyebrows jolted. He caught the wrist of my tattooed hand and ripped it off the other, severing the threads of magic.

He gasped. "Quinn was right. You can use your seized dust . . ."

I fought his grip, but his fingers felt made of solid bone. At least, he'd stopped smacking me with the damn apple. He shoved my tattooed palm under his knee, and then he punched me with the stupid apple again.

Anger rippled over my skin.

He thought my other hand useless. Well, he was about to learn that I hadn't only been taught to use my faerie powers in fights. Funneling all of my adrenaline into my fingers, I clawed his face, my nails coming away with strips of skin. He sneered as blood beaded over his cheeks and nose, shifting his weight off my trapped palm. I yanked it out from under his knee, and then, calling upon the Neverrian Skies and the Gottwas' Great Spirit and every Earthly god, I fisted my fingers. Karsyn's *wita* skittered and pulsed.

Please, please, please don't break.

Honeyed threads shimmered between my fingers and palm like harp strings. Fighting his hold on my other hand to keep him distracted, I lifted the sparkling dust and clapped it over his nose and mouth. He froze when he caught a whiff of magic and then lurched off of me, gagging.

Before my next heartbeat, I pressed my palms together and shaped the strands into a bat. I rolled myself up and swung it into his ribs, flipping him onto his back. And then I straddled him and shoved the fat stick into his mouth.

Tears leaked from the corners of his stunned eyes. I ground the bat deeper into his throat until his skin blued. And then I plugged his nose and liquefied the bat so all of it would slide down his throat and poison his lungs.

He tried to fight me, but he weakened fast. His hands flopped like dead fish on the side of his body. Before it could asphyxiate him, I recalled Karsyn's *wita*. Perhaps it could kill Kingston, but what if it simply sent him back into the field of mud? I wanted to be done with this fight.

While he was passed out, I reached over to grab the apple, but someone beat me to it. I raised my gaze, meeting Remo's brilliant green one.

"Looking for this?"

I wanted to throw my arms around his neck and never let go. Instead, I said, "Can you cut me a piece?"

Using the reddened blade of his machete, he sliced into the fruit, chopping off a bite-sized chunk. "Amara, let me do this. Killing someone, even someone who deserves—"

"No. I can do it."

"I have no doubt you *can*, Trifecta. I just—"

"I need to do it, Remo. For Iba. And for me." I got up. "Can you hold him? I'll be right back."

My legs felt made of wires and steel instead of cells and bone, moving of their own accord toward the glittery pool. Once I reached the water, I pressed my fingertips against my palm and crafted a watering can, then filled it to the brim.

Robotically, I returned to Remo and straddled my uncle, locking his arms under my shins. "Can you lift his head?"

Remo grabbed the back of Kingston's head, drove his blood-coated thumbs into my uncle's mandible, then chucked the piece of apple inside his mouth. I jammed the spout between the hateful fae's teeth, then Remo clapped Kingston's chin shut and shoved his head farther up.

Kingston's eyes, which had closed when he'd passed out, bulged open. I poured and poured, and although water dribbled down the sides of his mouth, his Adam's apple bobbed, which told me he was swallowing. But was it only water going down, or had the apple breached his throat?

His chest spasmed, but he stayed solid beneath me.

I kept pouring, draining the can, waiting, tears running down my cheeks, replacing the sight of Kingston's terrified eyes with flashes of Iba's body, limp, sinking through the lavender sky. With the smoke billowing out of the guards who'd survived the assault and the hill of ashes from the ones who'd given their lives so my father could rule another day.

I saw my mother, treading the Pink Sea beside me, the shine draining from her copper scales.

I saw my cousins laying down the oars of their canoe, faces turned heavenward, staring.

That day was the first time I understood that magic did not make us immortal.

For the past four years, I'd tried to keep the memories at bay, pushing them away as soon as one poked to the surface, but as I upended the can, I allowed them in.

I *welcomed* them in.

40
GOODBYES

A stillness settled over me as I set the empty watering can down beside my bent knee. Cool sweat beaded down my spine, but I didn't shiver. Remo's mouth spilled words, but none reached me.

Kingston was still alive, but he wouldn't stay alive. If the water failed its purpose, I'd find another way to execute the executioner. I was driven by a single thought: vengeance. It had steadied my arms and honed my focus.

His lashes fluttered and then his chest gave a violent shudder. He stared at me. I searched for repentance inside his eyes but found only terror.

I hated what he'd turned me into, but I hated *him* more.

So when his flesh finally turned as leaden as the cliffs choking the valley, I didn't gasp.

And when he exploded, I didn't flinch.

I sank through his dissolved body and into the ashen sand, completely and utterly numb.

I didn't feel Remo's hands cradling my face, skimming down my neck, going around me. I didn't hear what he was saying, just saw the edges of his words on his lips. He kneeled before me, crushing Kingston's remains under his legs, and pressed me into his chest.

The sharp beats of his heart finally brought me back.

I smelled the salt and steel of his fight.

I heard his tongue stroking my name, not the one he'd given me, but the one my parents had.

His callouses scraped my spine, and his breaths warmed my skin.

"Do you think he'll come back?" My tone was emotionless, the dam I'd erected still holding.

Remo pressed me away. "I'm going to go check."

"Check?"

"Turn around."

My heart stilled. "Why?"

"You know why, Trifecta."

When I finally shuddered, he stroked my jaw, careful not to graze the bruised flesh.

"I'll be right back." Another slow caress. "Wait for me here, okay?"

I looked at the ashen sand, not wanting Remo to leave. "If he's really dead, a plant will grow."

"Maybe it doesn't work like that here. Besides it would take time, and I don't want to waste another minute on Kingston."

I bit my lip, but it stung, so I released it. My uncle had broken my skin but hadn't broken me.

Remo called out Giya's name, and I turned toward where she now sat, silver eyes blinking from behind clumped locks.

She rose and took Remo's place next to me. And then she curled her arms around my back and held me as he vanished from my line of sight. He must've stayed in hers, though, because, a gasp pulsed from her mouth just as a wet grunt followed by a quiet thump sounded behind me. My chest tightened, and I shut my stinging eyes.

When I dared a glance over my shoulder, Remo was gone, and

in his place, was a mound of dust sprinkled through with drops of scarlet and topped with a soiled machete and a bloodied pen.

My lashes clumped, which was ridiculous, because I knew he was coming back.

"I don't think I'll ever get used to seeing someone die," Giya said, as she helped me stand. Her gaze skipped from one patch of gray sand to the next. When I shivered, she tightened her grip on my shoulders and tugged me closer to the water. "I don't know about you, but I'm going to steep in this little pool until I wrinkle like a dried gladeberry." She sniffed her arm and shuddered fiercely. "I reek of Kingston and of fish guts, although that may be one and the same. Gejaiwe, how did I not make the *tigri* flee?"

My teeth chattered behind a fleeting smile. "Aloe. S-Soap." I pointed an unsteady finger at the curly yellow plants.

When she slipped away from me, I locked my knees so I wouldn't fall. My hand thumped limply against my thigh, and my gaze, like my fist, drifted downward, landing on the red apple. On her way back, Giya crouched and picked it up. The carved flesh had filled in and the crimson skin reformed.

I wanted to smash it.

Burn it.

But Quinn would be back. And perhaps Kingston.

A flicker of the Daneelie shoving his dirty spear through Remo ignited a spark in my chest. Wordlessly, I reached out and took the tainted fruit from her.

A distant roar rose over the crush of water, and Giya's face whitened. I hoped it was the sound of the last *tigri* impaling itself on someone's spear.

"Are you planning on using the apple on Quinn?" Her voice cut through my throbbing temples.

"I don't know."

We stared at the apple for another long beat, then walked toward the frothing water, slipping inside its cool, cleansing depths until we were completely submerged. When I came back up for air, the concept of needing oxygen underwater still so foreign to me, I found Giya dripping yellow gel into her palm.

"It floats," I said.

She frowned, so I gestured to the aloe spear.

She set it on the water and watched it bob. As she lathered up, I returned to the beach and sat, knees bent into my chest, toes curled in the sand, apple stowed securely inside my palm. I shut my drained eyes, but the memory of all that had happened spooled behind my lids, so I fixed them to the boulder I'd sat on yesterday.

Was it yesterday?

How I hated the continual white sky.

"Whose dust did you magnetize, and when?" Giya worked her rope of hair into a lather.

"Karsyn's. The night of the betrothal revel. He attacked me. Tried to kill me."

Her eyes darkened like thunderclouds. "Why didn't you tell me?"

"Because I struck a bargain with Remo about keeping quiet."

She wrung her tresses so hard suds foamed between her knuckles. "I don't understand. I thought Karsyn attacked you . . ."

"Remo arrived mid-assassination-attempt. He helped me stop Karsyn."

The corners of her already bowed lips turned down some more. "I will *kill* the little twerp. Along with his grandfather and Joshua Locklear."

"I appreciate your savage compassion, cuz, but I don't want you going anywhere near them." I shot her a smile meant to ease her vengeful temperament, but it mustn't have been very effective, because her lips didn't unbend and her eyes didn't brighten. "Want some help with your hair?"

Her eyebrows stayed flat, unmoving, but her mood . . . it raged and writhed through her body. I wanted to reach out and steal her anger, lob it atop my own, let it fester inside me instead of inside her. The Farrows and the Locklears were my burden to carry, not hers.

"Giya . . . let it go."

"Would you let it go if someone hurt me?"

"No."

"Then don't expect me to let any of it go." Giya dipped her head back, rinsing out her hair before squeezing more soap into her palm and kneading the lengths anew. There was something cathartic about the spectacle, as though it wasn't only dreadlocks unraveling but also our collective tension.

As I watched new strands break free, a bolt of horror shattered the serenity. "How did Remo kill himself?"

The aloe spear jolted out of Giya's grasp. "What?"

"How did he take his life?"

"Amara—"

"How?"

She pursed her mouth. "I don't know. I was sort of trying not to look. With the machete, I think."

My palms became ice, and the back of my neck fire. He'd used the machete on the apple. I pressed a trembling hand to the organ beating too hard and too fast inside my chest, feeling as though it was about to detonate like the train.

Giya frowned and then she didn't. Then her eyebrows popped up. Both our gazes arrowed toward the top of the cliff. Quinn would come back, but would Remo? Cruz had said the apple needed to be ingested. What if a residue of apple had remained on the machete, and the blade had nicked his stomach?

"Where, Giya?" Foam danced around the cracked polish on my toes.

"Where what?"

"Where on his body did he . . . ?" I couldn't finish my sentence.

Again her expression turned guarded. Did she think I was asking because I wanted to torture myself with the details?

"I don't know," she confessed.

I closed my eyes and strengthened the dam, needing to keep myself together a while longer.

"Are you two having a relaxing bath?" Kiera's voice pierced the torpid air.

Slowly, I stared over my shoulder toward where Josh's sister stood, her outline unfocused, mere dabs of color—white, gray, red. Another person stood beside her. Although the contours of his body were as hazy as hers, Cruz was unmistakable. Then again, he was the only man left in the valley.

"Is that . . . the apple?" Her navy eyes gradually came into focus. They jumped between the fruit and my face.

Cruz froze. "Where are all the others?"

I couldn't get my breaths to coalesce into sounds.

Giya, suds still streaking her hair, strode out of the water. She sank to her knees in front of me and placed gentle, sunshine-scented palms on either side of my face. "He'll be back, Amara," she whispered softly but firmly. "He will."

Cruz and Kiera's shadows fell over us.

There was no sun and yet there were shadows. How strange.

Cruz crouched, spinning his grimy knife between bloodied fingers. "Can you tell us what happened?"

I swallowed, but the lump inside my throat was so thick that Giya had to explain. When she was done, a tightness appeared between Cruz's eyes.

Kiera turned away, silent and stiff, and dove into the water. I didn't know her well enough to read what was going through her mind, but I doubted her annoyance—or was it worry?—had anything to do with Kingston.

Cruz's knees clicked as he rose from his crouch. "I'm surprised Quinn sided with Kingston."

Giya sent a chilling glower his way. "Well he did. We're not liars."

He lifted both palms in the air, his knife's blade casting a stripe of light over my cousin's lethal expression. "I wasn't insinuating you were."

"He hates what I represent, Cruz." The volume of my voice dashed itself against the dam, sending the words up with little sound. "Who I remind him of . . ."

His chest expanded with a sigh. "Kingston must've convinced him you wouldn't have him freed."

Just as he emitted the hypothesis, a body plunged into the pool. My heart held still, hoping it was Remo, but the head that surfaced was bald.

"I guess we're about to get answers." Cruz turned toward Quinn. "I've just heard some disconcerting news about your alliances."

Quinn spit out a mouthful of water.

"Is it true?" Kiera, who'd vanished behind the iridescent curtain, reappeared and was staring at her uncle, her expression as harsh and unbridled as the Great Lakes of her childhood.

Quinn's gaze narrowed on me. Had he expected to find Kingston down here? Probably.

"Quinn? Your niece asked you a question." Unlike Kiera, Cruz's tone was placid.

"Yes! YES." He swam spastically toward the shore.

My lips parted. I'd imagined he would've tried to save his hide by painting me a liar.

"The enemy of our enemy is our friend, right?" he yelled, rising from the water.

"Kingston was never our friend!" Kiera said. "And Ace Wood isn't our enemy; Gregor Farrow is. He's the one who stuck us in here."

Quinn tossed a hand in the air. "And who do you think is screwing Gregor's grandson?" He pointed at me. "*She* is! So, I'm sorry if you're disappointed I chose to help him, but I don't trust her *or* her little fiancé. Did you know she has dust? She tried to lie to me about it, but I saw it!"

Kiera frowned at him, then at me. "You can use your powers?"

"No. But for some reason"—I displayed my tattooed palm—"I've been able to manipulate the dust I confiscated before coming here."

Her mouth thinned.

"Cruz was aware of it," I added.

"*I* wasn't," Kiera bit out.

"I don't know you, Kiera. I didn't know if I could trust you."

"You don't know Cruz either, princess."

"True, but I felt like I knew him because of Iba's stories. I apologize for not trusting you." Then again, had I trusted her, she might've told Quinn, and that might've changed the outcome of my battle.

Silence fell over us, silence punctuated by a gasp. Quinn's. "You have the apple."

When he cranked his neck back toward the top of the cliff, Kiera gritted out, "He's dead, Quinn." I wanted it to be true. "Your ally is *dead*. You bet on the wrong faerie."

The color leached from his whiskered cheeks. For a second, I thought he might try to run and hide, which, considering the scope of this cell, wouldn't have been efficient, albeit instinctual.

"I suppose you expect me to bite the apple now," he muttered.

I tipped my head to the side. "I murdered a man today because it was either him or me, and I chose me, but I have zero desire to murder another one." I turned my gaze back to the top of the cliff, willing Remo to hurry.

Quinn stalked toward me. "Give it to me."

Cruz stepped between us. "What do you want to do with it, Quinn?"

"I want to eat the fucking thing and be done with this sorry-ass life."

Cruz put a hand on the man's shoulder, but Quinn shrugged it off. "They're going to come—"

He snorted. "Yeah, and you'll be proclaimed a hero, but Kiera and I will forever be the villains . . . the traitors. And me, even more so now."

"Quinn," Kiera whispered his name as she stepped out of the water. "You promised not to leave me."

"You have all of them now. You don't need me."

"I do need you." A tremor shook the proud line of her shoulders, making the golden claws and fangs strung around her throat clink and cast riotous tinsels over the wet sand.

"I'm sorry, honey, but I'm tired."

She rushed into his arms, and he caught her, hugged her tight, and it reminded me that those capable of hatred were also capable of love.

Had Kingston ever been capable of the sentiment? Sure, he'd loved himself, but had he ever loved someone else? Maybe his mother . . .

"The apple, princess. Hand it over."

Cruz was still standing between us. "Are you certain, Quinn?"

"Yes."

"Please, Quinn . . . don't do this," Kiera croaked.

The bearded Daneelie shut his eyes. When he opened them, they were slick with tears but sharp with determination. "Go away, Kiera."

"Don't—"

"Go!"

She backed up. "You selfish asshole!" And then she twisted around and ran.

Quinn cringed but extended his hand, and Cruz shifted sideways to give him access to me. He stayed close, though, perhaps worried eating it wasn't Quinn's intent.

After handing him the apple, I pressed my palms together. I didn't extract my dust, but I readied it.

For a heartbeat, Quinn stared at the space between the *panem* and *aloe* where Kiera had taken refuge. "Cruz, you'll take care of her, right?"

"I will."

Quinn's Adam's apple bobbed. In slow motion, he brought the apple to his mouth, parted his lips, and sank his yellowed teeth into the crisp red skin.

His brows snapped together.

His body jerked.

The apple fell, the bitemark a small cloud floating in a crimson sky.

Like the water that flowed through his veins, the Daneelie liquefied, gliding into his watery grave.

41
THE WAIT

Cruz had jerked just as hard as Quinn in his final moment. But since then, he hadn't moved. Giya, on the other hand, had spun her head away, a fist clamped against her teeth. Her chest heaved, but she somehow managed not to be sick, the same way I somehow managed to feel nothing at the sight of another man dying.

I didn't wish to become anesthetized to death, because those who were took life for granted. But I hadn't known Quinn. Hadn't liked him. So how was I supposed to care that he was gone? I felt awful for Kiera and hoped she wouldn't hold his death against me. I felt bad for Cruz, because whether he'd been tight with Quinn or not, they'd coexisted in this cell since his own imprisonment.

"I'm—I'm going to go check on . . . Kiera." He shuddered. "Will you two be all right?"

We would be, in time. Giya was shocked and shaking. As for me, I existed but wasn't truly there. Raising my gaze back to the top of the cliff, I murmured, "Go."

He nodded, then strode away from the sandy graveyard. I'd always loved the beach, but today would blemish that love.

A wavelet lapped at the apple.

Whole again.

I didn't reach for it. I didn't want to touch it anymore, even though I probably would have to, if only to make sure no one else tried to take their lives or someone else's. After some time, Giya went to rinse the suds from her hair, then strode back out and dropped down next to me on the sand.

Since the sky didn't darken, it was impossible to tell how much time had gone by since Remo had . . . since he'd left. It felt entirely too long, though.

"You're shivering." Giya draped her arm around me.

I let my head drop against her shoulder. My sodden clothes stuck to my goosebumps, racking me with more tremors.

For a while, we were both quiet.

Then, "I can't believe you have feelings for Remo Farrow. The bully who made your childhood hell." She rested her cheek on the top of my head. "Faith and your mother are going to have to make peace. That'll be entertaining." I could hear her smile.

I was incapable of smiling.

She squeezed me against her. "He'll be back, Amara."

"What if—"

"He's a Farrow, *abiwoojin*. They're unkillable. Sook tried and failed spectacularly."

No one was unkillable. Instead of reminding her, I picked my head off the damp cream silk of her top. "Sook tried to kill Remo?"

"Not Remo. Gregor." Giya stared around her as though expecting to see her twin stroll out from the jungle, wearing his signature wily smile. "Thankfully, your father interceded. With Iba, they managed to bury the assassination attempt." She sighed, her worry so thick it glazed the air. "I hope he gets here soon."

I wasn't sure if she was talking about my father, hers, or her brother. Probably all three.

Even though Sook wasn't easily frightened, I couldn't imagine having to fend for myself in this prison. Couldn't imagine it, because I'd had a companion throughout every trial—an obstinate boy who'd followed me into Hell to keep me safe.

The dam fissured, and tears poked out from the corners of my eyes. "I'm sorry. I know how much you're hurting. I'm so sorry."

Giya's arm was back around my shoulders. "Sook is allergic to apples, so I'm not hurting. My brother will be fine. He's probably getting acquainted with more animal innards as we speak. But you know as well as I do that'll just give him more stories to tell. I bet he's secretly loving his adventures."

A chuckle broke over my sob, which turned into a loud honk.

"Oh, *abiwoojin* . . . Remo's coming back for you."

I tried to believe her, but with each heartbeat, my confidence frayed. What if he didn't return? How was I supposed to face a world in which he didn't exist? Anger welled inside of me at the girl who'd told him she wished he'd never been born. How could I have said such a thing? He'd always been such a huge part of my life back on Neverra. Hardly a day went by when we didn't have some form of interaction . . . mostly unpleasant, but the fact remained that we'd always orbited around each other. Now I wondered why. Was his presence deliberate or coincidental? Had *I* sought him out or had *he*?

Gottwas believed the Great Spirit placed souls within each other's paths for specific reasons. Had She placed Remo in mine so that he'd save my life in this world, or had She done it because we were meant to be together?

"Will you continue seeing each other once we get home, or is this some . . . *holiday* fling?"

"Holiday?" My lips quirked into a pitiful smile. "Some holiday we're all having." I drew a heart in the wet sand.

Giya laughed softly. "Yeah . . . next time I'm picking the destination."

A splash sent a wave hurtling over my sketch, erasing the curved lines. Holding my breath, I stumbled upright. And then I waited. When the popping bubbles were replaced by a head crowned with dark amber hair, my breath left me in a shallow burst.

Giya stood too, dusting the sand off her wet suede leggings. "Who's always right?"

My pulse scudded against the lining of my throat.

"What took you so long, Farrow?" she asked.

A smile made his eyes sparkle like the iridescent fall behind him. "Just being thorough."

I scrubbed the incessant flow of tears, but the act was pointless.

His shoulders broke the surface of the water, the cream fabric ensconcing them stretched as tight as my inhales. And then the pillar of his torso emerged, slabs of muscle visible behind knitted skin and torn fabric edged in the pinkish ochre of old blood. "Patience is a virtue."

Giya hooked her thumb toward me. "Not one of hers."

When the water cinched his trim waist, I finally moved. I sprinted toward him and threw myself into his arms, and like always, he caught me.

"Don't do that again," I growled, gorging on the mud-and-musk-scent of his skin. "Don't die and *don't* make me wait." My thunderous pulse lashed at my skin. At his, too.

The circle of his arms firmed. After dropping kisses along the frame of my face, he set me down. A fearsome scowl ripped away his smile as he took in my ruined face. "I almost wish he'd resuscitated." At my frown, he added, "So I could've gutted him—*slowly*—like the swine he was."

Instead of repulsing me, his evocative thirst for vengeance seduced me. Perhaps I should've mourned the death of my innocence. Perhaps I would, later.

He traced the edges of my bruise with his eyes, and then with his thumb. In a voice roughened by emotion, he asked, "Why were you worried I wouldn't come back?"

"You used the machete on the apple and then on yourself."

"Ah." He raised a brazen smile. "Remember what I told you about the effectiveness of pens?"

My breaths tangled, and I choked on my exhale, nausea battling with relief.

"Don't picture it." He leaned over and smoothed his mouth over my own as though to root out my distress. "I shouldn't have told you."

"No secrets. Ever."

He kissed me harder, and I answered him with a deep, debilitating hunger. When my split lip began to throb, sense knocked into me, and I jolted away, darting my tongue out on the hunt for fresh blood.

His chest turned to marble beneath my heaving one. "Did I hurt you?"

"No. I was just afraid to get blood—"

"Your blood doesn't scare me, Trifecta."

"My blood might not scare you, but it'll hurt you."

"You forget." A smile softened his body and expression. "I'm a big strong man."

A smile cracked my defenses as I recalled the moment I'd teased him with those words. "I forget nothing, and apparently, you don't either."

He nudged my nose aside before aligning his smirk with my smile. "Besides, you're no longer bleeding."

"Get a room. Or a cave, or whatever, but my last meal—which was days ago by the way—is starting to come up." Giya's voice eased our heads apart.

Remo and I smiled at each other, and then we smiled at her. She winked as she tossed the apple between her hands.

"Shall we go back to our cave, Trifecta?"

His hushed proposition tightened every nerve ending in my body. "I could use another nap," I said, bringing my eyes back onto his.

"A nap, huh?"

"Isn't that what you had in mind?" I tried to slide down the column of his torso, but he braced his arms beneath me, keeping me in place.

"We'll sleep. Eventually."

I tightened my koala grip on him as his long strides ate up water and sand. Once we breached the arc of *panem* and aloe, Giya falling into step beside Remo, I asked him to put me down; he didn't. He carried me through the jungle and over the threshold of the grotto as though I were his most delicate and prized possession. And perhaps I was, for he had certainly become mine.

42

FIRSTS

After Giya wished us a pleasant *nap* and vanished into the cave across from ours, Remo finally set me down and then proceeded to attack his damp locks, beautifully disheveling them. Even though a part of me found his distress both charming and fascinating, I clasped his fingers and towed them away.

"We don't have to"—the hand I didn't hold rose to his neck and rubbed the spot that had cleared of the bruise from the *cupola*—"do anything"—he cleared his throat—"you don't want to."

An onslaught of love—*yes,* love—rose in time with my smile. How could I not love this man who'd protected me fiercely before I'd become lawfully his to protect? "Although I'd terribly enjoy watching you try to make me do something I don't want to, Farrow, right now, I'm in the mood to do many things."

Shock and amusement stilled his distraught fingers, and then he squared his shoulders and laughed, the beautiful sound spooling over every stony crevasse, grain of sand, and cell inside my body.

"You are such a contradiction." I rose up on tiptoe, kissed his birthmark, then drew him through the coiled passageway that led into our little haven before I lost my own nerve.

"A contradiction?"

"So smug and so shy."

"Shy?"

Of course it wasn't the smug part that gave him pause. "Yeah. Shy."

He made a sound at the back of his throat, then smiled cockily and rolled the hem of his tattered Henley over the stacked bricks of his stomach. He shoved the fabric over his head and tossed it against the wall where it landed in a wet heap, and then he took my hands and set them on the hard planes of warm skin. "Still think I'm shy?"

I shook my head, trying to come up with something smart to say but failing spectacularly at the sight of so much whittled magnificence. I drew my fingertips into every dip and across each muscled hill. His nipples hardened under my tentative strokes, which had me leaning in and flicking one with my tongue, tasting brine, musk, man.

His eyes slid shut, and his breathing hitched. "Fuck, Amara . . . "

"Is that your plan?"

Shock made his lids snap up.

My cheeks warmed. "I can't believe I just said that."

I tried to avert my eyes, but he trapped my face with his palms and forced my gaze up to his. The way he stared at me made me feel like a fly caught in a spider's web. In a good way. I supposed that if I'd been a real fly, and he'd been a real spider, and his intentions were to eat me—

"I can't decide if you look frightened or excited." The raindrops of light seeping through the rock ceiling cast his intent expression in sharp relief.

Probably because I was a lot of both at that moment.

He skated his palms down my arms until he reached my wrists.

Slowly, he raised them over my head. When his fingers settled on the hem of my sopping gray T-shirt, he asked, "May I?"

I gave a jerky nod.

He peeled it up and up and up, his blistered knuckles scraping up the seam of my ribs, the knolls of my breasts, the hollow of my bones, raising pockets of fire over my damp skin. My shirt ended up on top of his.

His gaze, which had remained on mine, wandered low, taking me in one curve and goose bump at a time. "Perfect. Exquisite." He skated his calloused palms over my skin, and I shivered. Bringing his eyes back to mine, he rested his hands on my waist and drew me close, my nipples hard, his pecs harder. "Amara Wood."

"Yes?" I croaked.

His hands moved again, tracing each one of my fluttering ribs. "When we get out of here, will you go out on a proper date with me?"

Yes, I screamed but said, "It depends."

His thumbs perched on my nipples, and I let out a little mewl. "On what?" he shot out gruffly.

How I enjoyed incensing him. "On who breaks us out. If Joshua's the one—"

A storm blew across his face, lit him up with such animosity I worried Remo would seed the Neverrian soil with the Daneelie's ashes the second we made it home.

"I'm kidding."

He let out a low grunt like he wasn't sure that I was.

I kissed his sandwiched lips, pried them apart. Slowly, his anger receded, his lips softened, and his thumbs stopped pressing my nipples as though trying to turn them inside out. One of his hands spiraled up to the back of my head while his other ventured south, his fingers gliding under the waistband of my belted shorts, coming to rest on my bare ass.

He gave it a possessive squeeze. "Lawfully, you're already mine.

You do realize that, Trifecta? Mine," he repeated, walking me backward.

"You sound like a caveman."

"Perhaps because I am a man inside a cave." When we hit the wall, one hand cushioning the back of my skull while the other pillowed my tailbone, he asked, "May I get rid of your shorts?"

"I don't know, can you?"

His lips curled against mine, and then the hand on my lower back grabbed on to the stretchy sleeve stuffed through the belt-loops and shoved it, and my shorts, down.

A fevered rush of blood raced around my bared body, doing zilch to warm me up. "I guess you can."

Pleased, he took a step back. I started to cross my arms, but he caught them and pressed them apart. "Let me look at my wife."

My heart stopped. "I'm not your wife."

"You will be."

I hiked up an eyebrow and skewered him with a look. "Oh, really?"

"If you think I'm letting Josh or anyone else near that Cauldron when it reappears, you're highly delusional. There will be an electrified laser fence. *And* a fleet of armed guards, all of whom will answer to me."

"Sounds like a lovely ceremony."

That just made his eyes sparkle more wickedly.

"Are you sure you want this, Remo? That you want *me*?"

"I'm a thousand percent sure."

"You can't be a thousand percent sure. That doesn't make any mathematical sense."

"You really are a math fiend, aren't you?" His mouth lowered to one of my breasts, and he struck a peaked nipple with his tongue, causing pleasure to swell my veins.

"You swear you're not settling for me, because"—I gasped as he blew on my wet skin, before kissing his way to my other breast and flattening his tongue there—"because you feel like"—I held my breath, let it out, held it again, moaned—"like you should?"

He released my nipple with a pinch of teeth and rolled his neck until his head leveled on mine. "Like I should?"

"Out of duty to the Cauldron and your kingdom."

My reminder spirited away his wickedness, replacing it with stanch solemnity. "Amara Wood, I am not settling for you out of necessity or obligation. And I am a *hundred* percent sure I want you and will keep wanting you until you turn wrinkly and gray."

I grimaced. "Let's not talk about graying."

His eyes delved into mine. "Are you having second thoughts about us?"

"No."

"Are *you* a hundred percent certain?"

"I'm a thousand percent certain."

He grunted.

To prove my point, I shifted my hands to the only piece of clothing between us—his pants. I undid the button, then lowered the zipper, my pulse blasting from my boldness. After killing a man, undressing one surely shouldn't have been so terrifying, but damn if I wasn't one giant jumble of nerves. In timid increments, I swept my gaze over the buffed expanse of golden skin that tapered into an abdomen so ridged and trim it seemed soldered from sheets of metal. My fingers shook, which was all it took to nudge the waistband off the sharp indents at Remo's waist.

As the wet jeans tumbled, my fingertips jolted off his skin, and I blinked, first at his bared flesh, then at his hooded eyes. "Why did you—why did you assault Kingston when he ...?"

His forehead furrowed in confusion.

A blush crawled up my neck. "When he said you were ... um ... not—"

His frown smoothed, and his lips quirked. "Well-endowed?"

"Yes." I was tempted to fan myself. "That."

The small cave filled with his intoxicating laughter. I didn't know how long it lasted, but actual tears formed on his lash line by the time he sobered up.

Grin still intact, he said, "I punched him because he was an ass, and because, like you said yourself, I'm prideful. Not because my manhood felt threatened." His teeth flashed. "Were you worried?"

"No." *Hot.* Skies, I was so damn hot.

He caught my chin between thumb and forefinger and levered my face. "Thank you."

"For what?"

"For still wanting to be with me in spite of thinking I would be . . . underwhelming."

My nerves loosened, and my blush tempered. "It's your heart and mind I'm after."

"Good thing you'll get both, and so"—his hand fell from my face but didn't leave my body—"so *so* much more."

I tried to roll my eyes at his overwhelming confidence, but he stepped into me, his edges denting my curves, and my brain broke, ceasing all commands, reducing me to a single, highly receptive but uselessly static, nerve ending. His fingers began a slow voyage down the frame of my body, drawing tantalizing arabesques over my skin, coaxing whorls of goosebumps to the surface.

He lowered his face to mine, his tousled hair fluttering over his brow, and breathed my name against the tip of my nose and then again against my parted lips. I could still only stare, only feel, only gasp when his mouth dropped over mine, taking great care in not angering the tender skin. He licked and caressed, his tongue dancing into my mouth, lunging before withdrawing.

When his fingers stopped roaming my body, frustration welded onto my anticipation. I must've sounded my displeasure, because he released a low chuckle that vibrated against my teeth.

"You really are an impatient woman," he murmured, before pressing my lips apart and sheathing his tongue inside at the very same time he slipped a finger across my slippery folds.

I gasped, and he groaned, his kiss hardening along with the rest of his body. My limbs finally stirred, and my palms skated up the taut sinews of his arms to perch on his shoulders.

He stroked me slowly, and although I craved a faster pace, it was such exquisite torture that I let my head roll back against the wall and closed my eyes. In the back of my mind, it occurred to me that perhaps I should tell him I'd never been with anyone before, but his fingers magicked away my ability to speak. Besides, it didn't matter to me and shouldn't matter to him.

He nosed the side of my neck, peppering it with kisses that turned sloppier as he worked me harder, slickening me further. Seeking my pleasure turned him feral, the noises he made against my flushed skin more animal than man, fanning the gathering heat until my release sparked and set my entire body aflame. It wasn't my first orgasm, but it put all the ones I'd given myself to shame.

Before I'd even started to come down, he gripped my thighs and lifted me clear off the ground. My lids flipped open. I hooked my feet behind his back and my arms behind his neck.

"Trifecta . . ." My nickname was a rush of warmth against my neck.

I decided I didn't hate it anymore.

He banged a fist against the wall and let out a growl that startled the dregs of my orgasm right out of my system.

"What is it?"

"Our Infinities don't work!"

I frowned. "But your *manhood* does, right?"

He froze, and then his mouth twitched as though he couldn't decide whether to laugh or to roar some more. The smile won out. "My cock works fine." He pecked my lips. "But we don't have protection."

Before he could put me down, I did something completely reckless, which I supposed fit the girl I'd become. I slid my hand between our heaving chests and wrapped my fingers around him.

His breath caught. Held. And so did our eyes.

"Wouldn't be the first time we behaved irresponsibly, now

would it?" I kissed the corner of his mouth and stroked him, marveling at his silkiness and bulk, reveling in his ramping breaths. "But you don't need to worry. I had a shot a few months ago. It lasts two years." I didn't explain that it was because I had weird cycles and not because I was sexually active, although I did wonder if Nima suggested it for the latter.

The exhale that escaped him was so substantial Giya had probably felt its tailwind. "Thank fuck." His fingers crimped my ass, lifting me a little higher, until we were so perfectly aligned that when he lowered me back down, he slid right in. Well, the tip of him did; the rest of him encountered resistance that made him gasp my name, and not in a sexy, throaty way, but in a shocked and slightly horrified way.

I shut my eyes. Not so much because I was embarrassed, but because I was in pain, and I didn't want him to freak and pull out. When he didn't push in any farther, I rocked my hips, bearing down on him.

He hissed. So did I. Most probably not for the same reasons.

Sweat broke out over my upper lip. I licked it off.

"This was your first time?" His tone was full of something—regret, reproach. Definitely not smugness.

I opened my eyes to ascertain his mood: *not* happy. His jaw was getting a full workout from how unhappy he was.

Before my next breath, he pulled out and set me down.

Heat glided down my inner thigh. And then heat glided down my cheeks. I closed my eyes again, floundering in how very awkward it had all gotten.

His hands came up to my face, gentle and trembling. "Look at me, Trifecta."

I lifted my lids, sent him a death glare. "What?"

His brows drew together. "Whoa there."

I turned my face to the side. Well tried to anyway. Only my eyeballs managed to move.

His thumbs dragged across my cheekbones, skipping over the bruised skin. "Why didn't you tell me?"

"I assumed you knew."

"How could I have known?" His eyebrows slanted some more. "More importantly, though, why are you mad?"

"You looked horrified."

He snorted. "That was most definitely not horror, baby. Shock and worry, but trust me, zero horror."

"Then why did you stop?"

"Because your first time shouldn't be against a wall in a cave that smells of wet fur when you're feeling so emotional."

"I don't care about the *how* or the *where*. All I care about . . . all I've ever cared about is the *who*."

"I'd ask if you're certain you want me to be that person, but it's a little late now." His arms came around me and towed my stiff body into his. "I know it sounds pretentious, then again I *am* a pretentious ass, right . . . ?"

My snort was muffled by his satiny skin.

"But thank you for giving me that honor."

I rolled my eyes behind my lids.

"Now, let's start over," he said, pulling away from me.

"I'm pretty sure we can't." I gestured to the trickle of blood on my calf.

Remo towed me toward the laid-out pelts. "What I meant was, let's try this again. Let me make this . . . better." He let go of my hand, walked over to our balled T-shirts, picked one up at random, then returned to me. Before I could figure what he planned on doing with it, he crouched and wiped the blood off my leg before tossing it aside.

"I liked it, Remo." Sure the stabbing pain had put a tiny damper on how much I'd liked it, but the fact remained that I'd enjoyed the brief fullness, the quick slip and slide of flesh, the hiss of pleasure that had fallen from his lips. "You sounded like you liked it, too. Well, until . . ." I nibbled on the inside of my mouth.

"I did. Very much." He pushed long strands of hair off my face and tucked them behind my ear. "I promise you plenty of cavemen sex later, but let me make your first—"

"Second."

"I believe it still counts as your first—"

"Technically not."

He shot me a pointed look that shut me right up. "Lie down, woman. Unless you'd rather argue semantics."

I smiled; he smiled back. And just like that, all the awkwardness was gone, and my heart finally discarded all the different emotions that had beat within it, settling on a single one—joy.

43

THE WAKE-UP CALL

I woke up to Remo's nails gliding up and down the arm I'd slung over him last night and hadn't removed, afraid he might decide to leave while I slept. I'd never thought of myself as clingy but perhaps I'd be one of those girlfriends.

He must've heard my mind whirring, because his fingers stopped traipsing across my skin, and he turned to face me on our furred pallet. "Hey." He tucked a piece of hair behind my ear. "How do you feel?"

"I'm guessing the same way I look."

"Beautiful, then? Pleased to hear it."

I rolled my eyes, the prickly violet fur digging into my raw cheek. "I was thinking more along the lines of *giant bruise*."

Remo slid his arm under my neck and pulled me against him, pillowing my injured cheek on his bicep, which wasn't much softer than the fur but a lot smoother.

The way his eyes sank into mine made me forget all about my throbbing face. He leaned in, pressed a feather-light kiss to my mouth. "We should get up."

"We should."

Neither of us moved.

In truth, I wasn't sure I could. I really did feel like a massive hematoma. Although the main reason for my inaction was bliss. I flicked a lock of red hair out of his eyes, letting my fingers linger on his birthmark. "Can't believe I broke all my rules."

"What rules were those?" His words were so husky they sent a little thrill up my spine.

"Kissing redheads with the last name Farrow."

"Oh. Those."

I smiled at his evident contempt for my rules.

"You had too many standards to begin with."

I popped an eyebrow up. "Too many? Or none that pleased you?"

"Well, I did feel a little singled out. Redheads with the last name Farrow? We aren't many . . ." His mind must've wandered to the other redhead in his family, because his gaze turned somber.

"You'll see them again," I said, threading my fingers through the hand resting on his abdomen.

He didn't say anything for a while, then, "I can't believe Karsyn tried to kill you."

Felt like a million years ago. "Make sure to tell him you like me when we get back, so that he doesn't try to recoup his dust through murder."

His bicep flexed, curling around me as though to protect me from an invisible source of danger.

To dissolve the sudden dark cloud dangling over us, I said, "For someone who told everyone my blood was poisonous, you didn't seem too frightened by it last night."

A grunt rumbled through his chest. "Because my heart's thankfully nowhere near my cock."

I played with his fingers.

"My very *large* cock."

"You did *not* just say that."

"I didn't want you to forget."

"Like I could. I think you might've destroyed me."

"I tried my hardest."

"Tell me that pun wasn't planned."

His answering brazen smile made me swat him.

"Ouch," he whispered.

"Softie."

He rolled over me, bracketing my head between both his forearms. "There is nothing soft about me."

A grin threatened to cleave my cheeks in half.

"Amara!"

My smile warped off my face, and my eyelashes slammed against my browbone. I shoved Remo off and sat, and then I shot up to my feet, the pounding in my chest rivaling the one at the apex of my thighs.

I turned toward Remo. "You heard my mother's voice too, right?"

"Remo!" This time, Faith.

Remo grabbed me around the waist and twirled me.

"We're naked," I whispered in horror.

"And saved."

"But we're naked, and our mothers are here," I hissed, because . . . priorities. "Put me down."

"Giya!" Nima called out.

I scrambled for our clothes, before remembering the state they were in.

"Amara!" Nima's voice was so close I assumed she'd just entered the cave system.

My suit caught my eye, and although I'd sworn to never put it on without my Infinity, I grabbed it and yanked it up one leg.

Remo already had his tunic pants on, and since he was a guy, it wasn't like he needed anything else to look decent. *So. Unfair.*

My foot got jammed inside one pant-leg, and I fell. I whimpered from the ensuing series of aches and pains. Remo came to my rescue. Soon, he was stretching the maddening fabric up my legs.

Teeth gritted, I shoved one arm through, then the other. At least I no longer had sleeves to contend with.

"Can you try to run into another cave . . .?" I whispered as he zipped me up so fast most of my hair caught in the metal teeth.

"Remo?" Faith called out.

Although I didn't have a built-in sonar, if I had to hazard a guess, I'd say she was standing in front of the coiled entrance of our little cave. I brought the zipper back down, freed my hair, then tugged it back up.

"A bit late for that, Trifecta."

Here I'd thought all the blood had drained from my body, but nope . . . it had simply relocated into my cheeks. "What'll they think?"

"That prison had its perks." He waggled his brows.

I didn't smile, but that might've been because his mother was standing right in front of me, blue eyes as wide as her mouth.

My horror-stricken expression supersized Remo's grin. He swung around and crossed the very short distance toward his mother, whom he engulfed in a hug. She kept staring at me over his shoulder.

I dropped my gaze to a golden stripe in the rumpled fur pelts, ogled it so hard the gold blended with the purple.

"Amara?" my mother shouted.

"She's in here, Cat," Faith called out.

Cat? I glanced back over at Remo's mother, unable to read much of anything in her guarded eyes, but she'd called my mother Cat. She'd *never* called my mother Cat.

"Oh, thank Gejaiwe." Nima swung into the room and arrowed straight for me, then crushed me against her. "You're alive! Oh, Amara. Oh, baby." She shuddered. "My baby." Another shudder. "You're okay. You're okay."

"I am."

She didn't seem to have noticed Remo, but of course, my mother never missed a thing. Once she'd gotten her shuddering under control, she asked in a thankfully low voice, "Do I want to know why you're sharing a cave with Remo and not Giya?"

I was too choked and shocked to answer. Not that I especially wanted to answer her. I buried my face in her neck and sobbed like a big baby.

After a few more minutes of waterworks, I murmured, "I thought I'd never see you again."

Nima smoothed my hair back. "Oh, *abiwoojin . . .*" she croaked. "I'm so sorry it took us so long to find you."

I pulled away from her. "How did you . . . find us?"

Her lips were pressed into such a firm line they almost appeared thin. "Joshua Locklear finally came forward with the information." Her eyes tracked over my face, snagging on my cheek. "How did you get that bruise?"

When another sob tripped out of my trembling lips, she hugged me back against her, chest heaving. Was my hard-as-nails mother crying? My mother never cried. At least, never in front of me. She pressed away and cradled my cheeks, her thumbs stroking away my tears while so many rolled down her face.

"Is Iba here, too?"

Her fingers stilled, and she sniffed. "No. He stayed with *Gregor*." When I was a kid and did something naughty, Nima would pronounce my name the exact same way she'd just spoken Gregor's, which told me the *wariff* was in *big* trouble.

"Is it just the two of you?" I asked.

"Lily came too. As well as a handful of guards."

Had she seen Cruz, yet? Before I could ask, I said, "Sook! He's not here."

"We know. Kajika got him out a few minutes before we came in." Her eyes became incendiary. "If your father doesn't *kill* Gregor, I will. How could he have kept a place like this from us?"

I darted a worried glance toward Faith and Remo, whose hushed conversation had come to a standstill. I doubted either of them wanted to hear Nima discuss Gregor's execution.

"Did he know we were in here?" Remo's question made me suck in a breath.

I hadn't even considered Gregor *could* know and leave us inside. Why would he? Or rather, why would he leave the apple in play if it could actually kill us off?

"No. Dad swore he didn't know." Faith stared up at her boy, then at me. "I'm sorry, Amara."

I frowned.

"For what I said, and how I behaved the night the two of you—"

Remo draped an arm around her shaking shoulders, tucked her head under his chin before kissing the top of it. It was so darn sweet that if I hadn't already chosen him, I would have at that very moment.

Nima took my hand. "Let's go home."

Home . . . I considered pinching myself to make sure this was actually happening.

Remo slid me a gentle smile as we passed by him and Faith, one that made me want to reach out and take his hand. I didn't, though, since I was already holding my mother's. Plus his mom was right there . . .

Nima came to a brutal halt outside our cave as her gaze alighted on the body standing across the sandy aisle from us—Cruz. Neenee's fist was already shoved against her mouth, and her gray eyes shimmered with tears, the same tears that seemed to adorn everyone's faces. Well, everyone but Remo's, stoic man that he was.

"Cruz?" Nima whispered, his name rolling off her tongue. "Oh, Great Gejaiwe, Cruz!" She dropped my hand and covered the distance between them in three quick strides. She didn't touch him. Didn't hug him. Just stared unblinkingly, taking in the flash of green behind wayward black curls, the hardened lines of his face, the soft mouth, the cords of lean muscles stretching out from his neck like *calimbor* roots.

He smiled at her. "Hello, Catori."

She released a small, ragged peep, then finally touched his jaw.

Just for a second, as though to make sure he was made of matter and not air. Once she'd ascertained he wasn't a wandering spirit, she reeled her hand back and laid it over her heart.

Cruz tipped her a quiet smile, then directed his attention toward my aunt. "Lily."

As Giya circled an arm around her mother's waist, as though sensing Neenee would need the support to stay upright, she eyed me, then Remo, who stood beside me, so close that our hands grazed.

Remo's pinky hooked mine, and I swear, my entire body reacted as though I'd been electrocuted by a Glade eel. I thought I'd been happy before falling asleep, but it didn't come close to how I felt at that moment. Especially when I found him smiling down at me, that gorgeous, crooked smile I'd mistaken for smugness instead of what it truly was: a mix of bashfulness and heart.

A soft sob whispered over the walls of the cave, reminding me that we weren't alone. I found Cruz stepping toward Neenee, who was shaking as hard as a *panem* leaf during a windstorm. It was such a strange sight to behold: Cruz looking more like her son than an ex-fiancé. I couldn't imagine how strange it must've been for them to lay eyes on each other after so many years.

His hands came around her, and then his lips moved gently against her ear, pouring words that seemed to bring her more grief than comfort. Her arms snared him, too, and a spine-tingling rush of air splintered out of her mouth.

The lost one had been found, and yet the pain of loss lingered.

How long would it last? Forever? Could such agony ever be forgotten?

Remo hooked my fingers, and I crushed his palm, wishing nothing would tear us apart but knowing something or someone eventually would.

However united or magical, we remained two separate vulnerable beings.

44
HOME

"Where's Kiera?" Giya's question had me glancing around the dark space.

"Last I saw her, she was by the train crater, skinning one of the *tigri*," Cruz said.

I wrinkled my nose, imagining her elbow-deep in gore. I hoped it was helping her work through her grief.

"And Quinn?" Remo asked.

Cruz frowned. "Quinn bit the apple yesterday. Didn't Amara tell you?"

Remo's eyes, as well as everyone else's, fell on me. "No. She failed to mention that."

My cheeks flooded with heat, which worsened when their eyes fell to our clasped hands. My fingers froze and skidded from his. He tried to catch them, but I stepped away.

"Quinn?" Nima asked.

"Forest Press Quinn," Cruz said, and Nima gasped.

"If you think that's crazy, Neenee, wait till you learn who else was stashed in here," Giya added.

"Who?" Her question was a rush of breath.

"Good old Uncle Kingston."

379

"Kingston?" Nima's voice was so murderously sharp it would've sliced my traitorous uncle wide open had he still had a body to rip through.

"He's gone, though. Amara made him bite the apple." A hint of pride edged my cousin's proclamation.

"What are you all talking about, *biting apples*?" Faith asked.

Remo's brow furrowed. "Didn't Grandfather tell you anything before he let you in here?"

"He was . . . *indisposed* when we were shown through the portal." Faith's mouth pursed.

Indisposed? I wanted to know what that meant, but shouting erupted at the mouth of the cave as two *lucionaga* dragged in an indignant Kiera. "*Massina*, we've canvassed the cell and found one more prisoner. What would you like us to do with her?"

Nima and Lily spun around.

"Let her go." Startlingly, it was my voice which rang out.

Although Kiera stopped snarling at the thick-armed guards restraining her, she narrowed her red-rimmed eyes on me. She hated me. I hoped that in time, she would see I wasn't to blame for Quinn's suicide. The guards looked between Nima and me, and then they looked at Remo.

"You heard your *prinsisa*," Remo growled. "Unhand the girl!"

At least now I knew where I stood on the ladder of command—under Remo.

"Thank you," I murmured to him.

"They shouldn't defer to me." His jaw was so clenched it was a wonder he managed to produce words, much less entire sentences. He stalked toward his fellow guards, and the rest of us followed.

Kiera's eyes glinted as brashly as the strand of claws and fangs clinking around her neck.

"Kiera Locklear," Nima said in wonder. "You're alive."

"No thanks to any of you." She spit at Nima's sandaled feet.

Everyone froze. The *lucionaga*'s eyes jumped to my mother's fili-greed throat, probably assuming she would admonish the Daneelie for her slight with a handful of dust. My mother didn't raise her hand, didn't ball her fingers either. Calmly, she said, "Joshua's waiting for you beyond the portal, Kiera. He's very impatient to take you home. What do you say we get out of here?"

Kiera blinked. Because of Nima's calmness, or because of the storm of emotion rising within her? If we'd already been on Neverra, I had no doubt the girl's disquiet would've lacerated the sky with lightning. Nima looked over her shoulder at me and held out her hand. I took it, and together we walked out into the white light of the forever sunless, night-less sky.

I thought we would have to scale the cliff walls to reach the portal, but it had relocated itself, shimmering like a mirror right beyond the opening of the grotto. Lily and Giya slipped through first. Then Kiera and one of the guards. And then it was mine and Nima's turn.

I wanted to clutch Remo's hand, but sensed my mother wouldn't let me go. Not until I was safely home. As my fingertips touched the gelatinous surface, I turned my head.

"I'll be right behind you," he murmured, knowing exactly the direction of my thoughts.

I melted through the inky darkness between the worlds with my head still angled toward Remo and didn't look anywhere else until the broad lines of his body formed on a framed painting of Neverra cloaked in mist.

45
NEW REGIME

"**A**mara!" My father's voice made my attention whizz off the painting and the redheaded boy who'd just climbed out of it.

He stood beside Kajika, Lily, and my cousins by a bay window that gave onto the Gorge of Portals. So Joshua had been right about yet something else . . . the portal did relocate.

I raced toward my father and flung my arms around his neck. His answering hug was bone-crushing. "Oh, Iba." I thought I'd been done crying but nope. In seconds, my cheeks were damp again. Unlike in Gregor's prison, though, my tears evaporated almost as fast as they fell. "I missed you so much."

His chest gave a violent shudder. "Oh, *amoo*."

I closed my eyes, relishing the steel of his hug. "I found Kingston, Iba," I whispered. "You were right. Gregor didn't kill him."

He pressed me away, holding me at arm's length. "*Son of a . . .* Where's that scheming brother of mine?"

"Dead. He's dead."

"I thought—"

Giya draped her arm around my shoulder. "Amara fed him the apple."

"The apple?" My father's tired blue eyes roamed between us.

"If *wita* and beheading had a love child, it would come in the form of a red apple." Giya rubbed her stomach, then added under her breath, "Don't know about the rest of you, but I'm *never* eating apples again."

I smiled while Iba just blinked, first with shock, then with pride.

"I'm so sorry the task befell you, *amoo*," he finally said.

Sook's head bobbed above Iba's shoulder, and a small sound escaped my lips. "Sook!"

"Hey, cuz."

I jumped at his neck, hugging him tight. "Thank you for coming after me."

"Like I could let you have all the fun."

"Fun?" I barked out a laugh. "Yeah, *sooo* much fun. I'm still not sure what I liked best, the torture or that damn mud field."

"I'm pretty sure I know what you liked best," Giya said, and although I loved her unconditionally, I briefly considered strangling her.

I shot her a smile that promised retribution, then, before Sook or Iba could ask what she was insinuating, I blurted out, "Heard you were ingested by a shark, Sookie."

Instead of flinching, my cousin's grin grew and grew, eating up half his face. "But did you hear the part where I fileted the *pistri* using a rusted anchor?"

I wrinkled my nose whereas Giya shook her head and the adults' complexions went from pale to white.

"Ace?" Cruz's voice cut across the apartment, silencing every conversation, stilling every chest.

My father froze, and then slowly, slowly turned around. He looked first at Nima, then at his sister, as though questioning if they also saw him. When both women smiled, he finally unglued the soles of his leather boots and stalked toward the man who'd been more of a brother to him than Kingston.

His shoulders stiffened, then shook, and then they rolled forward. As he embraced his long-lost friend, I wondered if Iba was shedding tears or plotting Gregor's murder. Surely both.

My aunt broke away from my uncle and walked over to my mother, clutching her elbow. Where Neenee's cheeks still shone with tears, Nima's were finally dry, but her eyes belied her stoicism, their shine rivaling the sapphire-encrusted table next to me. Clearly, whoever owned the apartment was wealthy.

Smiling, I let my gaze drift over the little assembly until I found Remo sandwiched between Silas and his mother, no Karsyn or Gregor in sight. He'd traded his navy pants for his customary black *lucionaga* uniform, which made me feel particularly frumpy. Before I could scroll through my Infinity band, his eyes met mine over his stepfather's shoulder. He leaned over, whispered something in his ear, then cut across the room toward where I stood with Giya, Sook, and Geemee.

Out of everyone, my uncle looked the worst for wear, anxiety gnawing at his uncharacteristically wan features. Was he jealous? Did he fear he was about to lose Lily? I'd never doubted my aunt's affections, but I'd also heard Cruz and Lily had shared something special.

I watched Neenee, wondering if the life she'd built could crumble, because her old—or rather, young—flame was back, but suddenly Sook stepped in front of me, and I could no longer see her. When I realized why he'd done it, to block Remo, I shooed my worry for my aunt and uncle and bustled around my cousin.

"Sook, Remo's my . . ." I looked up into my fiancé's golden eyes trying to decide which term to use, but then became distracted by his irises. I missed the green, but not because it changed his appearance . . . because it was the color of the eyes that had watched over me during our imprisonment.

"Friend?" Sook supplied dubiously.

He was way more than that.

Giya squeezed my shoulder. "What Amara's trying to say is that we like Remo now."

"We do?" Sook asked, directing the question at me.

"Yeah, we do." I smiled. "Your eyes are gold."

Remo seemed to be drinking mine in, even though their color hadn't changed. The corner of his mouth tipped up. "And yours are blue. Shall we move on to hair?"

I laughed. Amidst all the awful memories of prison, that had been a good one. I reached for his hand even though I wanted to push up on tiptoe and reach for his mouth.

"Amara Wood, we meet again." The familiar voice made my gaze leap off Remo, who'd become as stiff as the buffed black marble beneath our feet. Joshua Locklear stood, one arm draped over his sister's shoulder. She seemed so slight and small beside him. "Looking a little bedraggled, but still hot."

Remo's fist crunched into the Daneelie's jaw, sending his face flying to the side.

As Josh pivoted back toward us, his brows slanted viciously beneath his sideswept blond bangs. "Back the fuck off, Farrow, or you'll be cleaning urinals for the rest of your *lucionaga* career."

Remo grunted. "Like you have any power."

"Actually, I do." Josh beamed. "You're looking at Neverra's brand-new *draca*."

"You're shitting me," Sook said.

That's when I realized that Josh's eyes were green instead of blue. "Wicked, huh?"

Wicked wasn't the first word that came to mind.

"Who the hell was cracked enough to make you *draca*?" Giya sputtered.

Kiera sent her a sharp glare.

"Why, Massin Wood. Apparently, our dearest king will do anything for his daughter." He tossed me a wink that vanished behind thickening eddies of sparkling smoke. The lines of his body changed, becoming almost too wide and tall for the high-ceilinged apartment, and then black scales slicked over his skin like an oil spill.

Kiera took in her brother's new form, from his long muzzle to his pointed horns, with a squeak of surprise. Chuffing, he extended his fibrous black wings and lowered his neck, an invitation for her to climb aboard.

It took her a minute to react, but as soon as she understood, she hurled herself onto him like Cruz had hurled himself atop the *tigri* the first time we'd met. Tucking his clawed paws into his abdomen, Josh took off, flying so fast toward the window that when his horns hit the curved glass, the entire pane shattered.

Outside the *calimbor*, lightning slashed the Neverrian firmament, weakening the glow of stars. I imagined I was responsible for the weather, although it was entirely possible Kiera and her dragon brother had provoked the storm.

Once my ears had stopped ringing from anger, broken glass, and thunder, I swung toward my father, bumping into Remo. "You made Joshua Locklear *draca*, Iba?"

I wasn't sure if I was shaking with anger or if Remo was, since his chest was flush with my shoulder blades. Maybe we both shook.

Iba stared out the broken window. "He was the only person who knew where you were and would only volunteer the information against a *gajoï*."

Had that been Josh's end goal all along? I doubted he was smart enough to have planned that far ahead, but damn, had my disappearance been convenient. Again, I lamented asking for his help. Sure it had brought me close to Remo, and we'd found Cruz, *and* killed Kingston, but now Joshua had an inordinate amount of power and weight. Skies only knew what he would do with it.

Iba approached me slowly. "It was either that or your hand. I chose not to sacrifice you a second and final time." His gaze darted to Remo, whose heart seemed to beat more violently against my tensed spine.

"You have no reason to apologize, Iba."

"I do, Amara. I should never—" He faltered and cleared his throat. "I should never have forced your hand into the Cauldron in the first place. I should never have told you about my suspicions about Kingston."

"It's not your fault I ended up in that prison, Iba." I wanted to add that I wasn't angry about the first part, but I didn't want to have this conversation in front of so many people. "Is Gregor still *wariff*?"

Iba dragged his palms down the length of his face. "No."

"Who is then?" Giya asked.

Silas crossed over to us, his shoulder-length hair unbound. More gray had threaded itself through the brown, our disappearance indubitably the source of these silvering strands. He stopped beside Iba. "I am."

Relief washed over me. "Thank Gejaiwe."

Remo sucked in a breath. I took it that was news to him, too. Good news, since his quaking had lessened.

"Joshua might be *draca*," Iba added, "but I am still king." His face was set with the confidence and calm of someone who knew how to do his job, and do it well.

"We'll keep him in line," Silas added.

"Where's Gregor?" I asked.

Silas stared around the apartment, and it struck me it might be Gregor's—so garishly fancy, and that painting of Neverra. Who else longed to immortalize Neverra with the mist? "Awaiting his trial," he finally said.

I peeked over my shoulder, found the vein at Remo's temple distending, found his fingers balled into fists.

"Now, I know you're all tired, but Silas and I would really like to hear what you kids have endured these last three weeks," Iba said.

Three weeks? We'd been gone three weeks?

Silas dismissed the *lucionaga* in attendance until only my family and Remo's remained. Oh, and Cruz. He was still there, arms crossed, standing on the outskirts of our tight-knit circle. He'd find his place eventually.

As my eyes swung back toward my father, they caught on my aunt, tucked into the crook of Geemee's tattooed arm, her cheek pressed into his chest. As I watched them, reassurance washed over me. What they shared, what they'd built was solid and beautiful and would withstand the return of Cruz Vega.

Nima threaded her fingers through Iba's. "It's just us. You can speak freely."

Where to begin?

Without missing a beat, Giya said, "Well, Sook was eaten by a shark."

Even though it wasn't really funny, I burst out laughing. She too laughed. Sook grinned but shoved his sister, which earned him a glower from his father. Finally, the tension on Remo's face dissipated. He didn't smile, but his golden eyes sparkled, and then his hand found the curve of my hip.

Which of course drew both our parents' attention and filled my face with so much heat I wanted to pierce my skin and let some steam out. In a way, though, I was glad for that tiny gesture. Glad that no-strings-attached Remo apparently came with strings of his own.

We detailed every trial, listened to Giya and Sook recount their own *adventures*, and then Cruz was put on the spot. His eyes sort of glazed over as he recounted his story. Once we were done talking, the silence that fell over the adults was thick and bleak.

"Oh, and Iba, none of our powers worked." I didn't mention Karsyn's dust, preferring to discuss him later and privately.

My father stared and stared, nerves feathering his jaw. "Silas, find out how that's possible."

The new *wariff* nodded, contempt and worry stamped into the furrows of his forehead.

He began to turn when Sook asked, "What will happen to Gregor?"

Silas and Iba exchanged a grave look.

"What do you suggest?" Iba asked.

Remo's hand tensed on my hip.

"Stick him inside his prison," Sook suggested.

Iba bobbed his head, storing that suggestion.

"He kept Kingston alive, *massin*." Remo's voice was as sharp as the dagger I'd produced the day we'd wandered through the inn . . . the one he'd called a butter knife. "That's treason."

Faith gasped, because we all knew how treason was punished.

Iba stared at Remo as though seeing him for the first time.

"But your grandfather also kept me alive, Remo," Cruz said slowly.

"He should've freed you as soon as Lily reentered Neverra!" Remo snapped.

Iba observed them both quietly.

"But then he would've had to reveal his prison." Cruz was so cool and collected.

I didn't get it. If I'd been him, I would've been incensed. I would've demanded Gregor's ashes. I would've requested to exact justice myself.

"If I may make a suggestion, Ace." Cruz stared at the golden circlet gleaming atop my father's head. "Have him erase his prison, then lock him out of Neverra. He was born on Earth, so once his fire burns out, his blood will sustain him a couple more years."

My father looked steadily at his friend. Even though he was two decades younger, he was clearly as wise as his biological age. "Does that seem fair to everyone?"

I placed a hand on top of Remo's. "I think he should be stripped of his dust."

"Agreed," my cousins said in unison.

"Remo? Faith?" my father asked. "Do you have any objections?"

I felt the torment swirling through Remo's body. Saw the little knots of tension forming in Faith's neck.

"No, *massin*," Remo said.

Faith flinched but ended up shaking her head.

"Then it is decided." Iba sighed and pressed himself away from the edge of the sparkling sapphire table he'd leaned against during our recounting. "Silas?"

"Yes, Ace?"

"Can you help Cruz settle in? I think he may like one of the stilt houses on the Pink Sea, but it's up to him." Iba stared at his friend again, then went to him and squeezed his shoulder. "I'm coming by to see you later. If that's all right with you?"

A black curl struck Cruz's eyes and tangled in his lashes. "When has answering in the negative kept you away? Do you respect people's wishes now?" His tone was playful, and yet I watched my father's face for a reaction.

When a smile crept over his mouth, followed by a bark of laughter, I released a short breath. "How would I have gotten Cat if I took no for an answer?"

He winked at Nima who shook her head but grinned.

As though remembering others were present, he shot all of us, but especially Remo, an eloquent stare. "No means no, children. Are we clear?"

Remo's fingers tensed, which made me smirk.

As my parents took off toward the door, they called out, "Amara?"

I sensed they wanted to have a little chat about the nature of the proprietary hand on my hip. To Remo, I murmured, "I'll comm you," then I hugged Sook and Giya. "Thank you for having my back. I love you guys."

"Shut up," Giya said, her tone distorted by emotion.

As she knuckled a tear from her eye, I caught Cruz staring at her, the smile gone from his mouth, replaced by some other look. Giya didn't notice. I didn't think anyone but me noticed. When our eyes met, his shot to the buffed marble beneath his bare, sandy feet. *Huh . . .*

Maybe Cruz *would* disrupt Lily and Kajika's future, just not in the way I'd imagined. Or maybe the romantic in me was reading way too much into the attention he'd paid Giya.

On the platform outside the front door, my mother hooked her hands around my father's neck as he cradled her and soared into the *lustrium*-flecked darkness. The brewing storm had receded and given way to a glorious violet sky. I'd always liked nighttime but had a new appreciation for it after the endless white.

As I stood on the overhanging deck, I gazed out at my kingdom with its reflective portals and dusty-rose ocean, its tall gray cliffs and swirls of starlight. Faeries were out tonight, like every night, but somehow there seemed to be more bodies crowding the sky. Many hovered around the *calimbor*, but none too close, kept back by a belt of bobbing *lucionaga*. I closed my eyes and took a long, deep breath of freedom, savoring the warmth flickering inside my veins, and then I dove.

And I didn't fall.

I flew.

46

THE TALK

I followed my parents into their glassed-in bungalow, drinking in the scent of brine and *drosas* that wafted off the sea and combed through the Floating Garden.

My pulse drummed inside my neck and skull, and my stomach was full of nerves. I tried to remind myself that I'd died—twice—faced innumerable monsters—most in fur, one in skin—and yet it felt like a thousand rockets had been set off inside of me at the very same time. And it all got worse when my father poured himself a whiskey before asking me to take a seat while Nima paced the plush beige carpet.

"*Amoo*"—Iba perched on the edge of the teal couch and swirled his drink—"you no longer have to pretend to be *nice* to Remo."

I cringed, the moment reminding me acutely of the birds-and-the-bees talk Nima had given me after my spirit ceremony. Except this was so much worse, because my father was present this time. "I know."

He took off his crown of golden leaves and placed it on the cushion beside him. "What we're saying is that you don't have to pursue the charade of your engagement."

"Iba, I understand." A small smile pierced through my nerves.

Nima thankfully stopped making tracks in the carpet. "Unless you want to."

I stared at her and then at my father. "I know this'll come as a surprise, but Remo and I . . . well . . . he saved my life. But that's not the reason I want to be with him." I toyed with the tip of my braid. "He makes me laugh, and he makes me feel safe."

Nima took a seat next to Iba, clasped his hand, and the small gesture made me acutely aware of the absence of Remo's hand in mine.

"I know what you're thinking. You're thinking this is a side effect of being locked up together, of having to rely on only each other, and now that we're safe and out, my feelings for him will fade and—"

"That's not what we're thinking at all, *abiwoojin*," Nima said.

"It's not?"

"No." She shot me a small smile. "I know you and Remo always had your differences, but we've always liked him."

"Really?"

"Who's my new *wariff*?"

"You might love Silas but you hate Faith."

"*Hated*." Nima sighed. "But that was more her than me. Then again, I did kill her mother."

"For a perfectly good reason." Iba eyed the tattoo girdling Nima's neck.

Her fingers tightened around his. "Anyway, the sins of Remo's grandparents shouldn't reflect on him. He was raised by a good man, and even though Faith has been difficult, she is a good mother."

Was she? One of her sons had tried to off me.

When I caught both my parents staring at my decorated palm, I slipped it underneath my thigh, worried they might change their mind about Remo if they found out whose dust pulsed under my skin.

Iba exhaled a protracted breath. "We heard how you got that."

"You did?" I squeaked.

"Believe it or not, Faith's the one who volunteered the information."

I sat up straighter.

"Karsyn's been severely reprimanded, by Silas *and* by Faith," my father said.

"Also, you are to keep his dust until his eighteenth birthday," my mother added.

Well, that wasn't going to earn me any brownie points with Remo's little brother. Not that I needed to ingratiate myself to the rascal, but if I wanted a future with his brother, I most definitely didn't want to be at war with another person in his family.

"Okay." I rubbed my palms against my thighs, about to get up, when I remembered something. "Iba, Josh said he had an informant. That's how he knew where the portal was and where it led. Did he by any chance tell you who it was?"

My father's jaw flexed. "Joshua *is* the informant. Gregor owed him a *gajoï*, and Locklear asked what had become of his sister. That's how he found out about the supernatural prison."

That weasel! "Why didn't he go get her himself then?"

"Because he didn't think Gregor would ever let him back out."

"Why didn't he ask *you* to help him?"

"Because he assumed I knew about the prison and would be plenty happy to lock him inside. Honestly, it would've been tempting."

To think he was the new *draca*. "Is he the one who told you about Kingston?"

"No." Nima sighed. "That was your grandmother. The one on your dad's side."

My father knocked his shoulder into hers. "We can't all have flawless relatives."

They might've surpassed the shock-factor of this revelation, but I most definitely hadn't. "Was Addison complicit with Gregor? She wanted you dead, Iba?"

"No, *amoo*." Iba rubbed his jaw, which was in dire need of a shave. "One of her maids heard her muttering while she was high about Gregor sending Kingston into a place called the Scourge, and she went to Silas with the information."

A wave of goosebumps washed over me. "I could go my entire life without hearing that word again."

"Sorry." Iba sent me an apologetic smile that deepened the little lines around his eyes and mouth.

Expelling a breath, I finally climbed to my feet. "Fire and dust may bring some rust, but words will never hurt me, right?"

Palpable worry tightened Nima's eyes.

"Well, if you guys don't mind, I'd like to go rest and change out of this outfit."

"One last thing, Amara," she said, and my father finished, "You're grounded."

"What? Are you serious?"

"Just because you're our daughter does not give you the right to break the law. Selling your scales on the human black market—"

"I did it to buy you guys an anniversary gift, Iba."

They exchanged a wordless but loaded look.

My father sighed. "Your motives might've been noble, but you still broke the law."

"But, Iba, haven't I been punished enough? I did go to actual jail." *Never thought I could play that card . . .*

Another look passed between them.

"I had to deactivate a bomb, and fight monster *tigri*, and—"

"Ace?" my mother said.

"Cat?"

When the corners of my mother's eyes tipped up in time with the corners of my father's mouth, I sensed they'd come to a mutual decision about my fate.

"You are forbidden from using portals," Nima said. "No traveling to Earth—"

"Or to anywhere else," my father interjected, to which I rolled my eyes, because I would never again hop through a creepy portal. "For a month."

"Deal!" I shouted before they could tack on some extra punishment.

"She took that much too well."

"Maybe we were too lenient," Nima agreed.

My gaze volleyed between them, praying they weren't reconsidering their decision. "You made me get engaged," I shot in.

Both their eyes narrowed.

"Clearly, you're *exceedingly* upset about that," Iba said.

I smiled; they smiled.

I walked over to them and leaned in for a group hug.

Nima sniffled loudly. "Never do that again, *abiwoojin*. Never go *anywhere* without telling one of us where, promise?"

"I promise." My arms tightened around their necks, and their arms tightened around my back. "I love you."

"Not as much as we do, Amara," they said at the very same time.

"*Ut Rowan e retri*," Iba added.

I swear, they shared a mind. Was that how Remo and I would be someday? Always surfing on the same wavelength?

As I stood, Iba turned to my mother. "Should I have that talk with Remo tonight or tomorrow?"

I coughed. "A talk?"

"If you two are planning on spending time together, *privately*," Nima said, "you can bet we're going to have a little chat with him."

"Weren't you on your way to see Cruz? Cruz who you thought was dead. Cruz—"

"You made your point, Amara." Iba shot back his whiskey. "But tomorrow . . ." He wagged his finger.

"I'll warn him."

"Because you're planning on seeing him tonight?" Nima asked.

Where was that field of mud when I needed it?

"You shouldn't keep Cruz waiting. He must be exhausted. I'm

exhausted." I feigned a huge yawn as I backed up toward their sliding glass door.

"Pappy and Nana are expecting you at breakfast tomorrow," Nima said.

"I'll be there."

One of her black eyebrows creeped up. "Alone?"

Although a blush stained my jaw, I asked, "If he's free, can I bring him along?"

"He probably won't want to after that talk—"

I cut off my father, "Please, don't scare him away."

"If he truly cares about you, nothing we do will scare him away." My father lifted my mother's hand to his mouth. The W on the back of her hand flared from her heightened heartbeats, and his palm glowed in return.

My cue to get out. "Goodnight, beloved parents."

I whirled and soared over the palatial gardens and then over the small bridge leading to my floating bungalow, landing on my *volitor* deck. With my mind, I slid open my window and walked past my billowy sheers, catching their silken hem and running it absent-mindedly through my fingers.

In the privacy of my bedroom, I sat on my bed and swiped my Infinity. Just for the pleasure of it, I scrolled through my entire closet, but of course that made me think of Remo. Especially when I landed on that dress he'd mentioned liking the day we were in Fake Neverra.

Smiling to myself, I fired off a quick message to his Infinity, swapped my tattered jumpsuit for a tiny red bikini, and then raced back across my deck and swan-dove into the ocean.

47
THE DRESS

When I emerged from the depths of the Pink Sea after a long and delicious swim, I found someone sitting on my deck, one long leg dangling over the ledge, the other bent and supporting his forearm. Although we had no use for pens in our digital age, my visitor held one, clicking the tip in, then out. A memento from the Scourge? Hadn't he left it on the beach with his machete?

"You're sparkling, Trifecta," Remo said, watching me levitate from the water and land beside him.

My copper scales had returned and so had my ability to breathe underwater. "Can't believe you actually came."

"You invited me." His eyes rappelled down my body, then climbed back up, gleaming like the pirate treasure I'd once found at the bottom of the Pink Sea—treasure I later learned had been planted by my parents to give me an adventure.

"I wasn't sure you'd be brave enough to show up, what with having to fly over the palace to get to my little abode."

"You must have me confused with some other faerie, because I'm the bravest one you'll ever meet."

"How about we revisit that tomorrow after your chat with my parents?"

"My . . . chat?"

"Oh yeah. I almost wish I could be there, but apparently they want to speak to you in private." My grin widened when he scratched his jaw. "I wonder what they want to discuss?"

Using his *kalini* to buoy himself up, he hopped to his feet and turned the pen to *wita* ribbons. "Probably my pie baking skills." He stroked the length of my neck, watching my scales, feeling them. I was guessing he'd never touched a Daneelie's skin, which brought me immense satisfaction.

"If you ever make me a peach pie, Farrow, or an apple one, you'll be standing by that Cauldron alone the next time it shows up."

"You've used that threat before, and haven't followed through with your *unfriending* menace." His eyes settled on mine, a smile—or was it my shimmering scales?—reflecting in them. "Besides, have you forgotten that you owe me a *gajoï*, Trifecta?"

I gaped at him. "You wouldn't dare use it to cement our essences."

"Wouldn't I? I am—what was it you called me again? Oh yes . . . *cruel.*"

My smile reappeared. "So very."

His smile strengthened. "But I just thought of a much better use for it."

"Really?"

"Amara Wood, how do you feel about me?"

How did I feel? Like a bottle of shaken faerie wine, pressurized and full of bubbles that were rising and popping against the walls of my chest, and then against the lining of my abdomen. And, oh crap—my stomach clenched.

I looked down at my belly button and then back into his face. "I can't believe—you used—your *gajoï* to . . ."

Concern made the smile warp off his face. "Sorry. I thought—I didn't mean to—"

"Extract the sentiment through brute force?" Since the cramps didn't lessen, I blurted out, "I love you, you *bagwa*." The violent pain ceased.

His hands wound around my waist, features still contorted in guilt. "That played out much more romantically in my mind."

Even though I was no longer in pain, I breathed in and out slowly. "Mm-hmm."

"I'm really sorry." His blush told me he was.

"The least you can do is tell me how you feel about me now."

Soon, his skin tone lost its red tint. "How about I show you instead?"

"You're good with words."

He brushed the edge of my sharp, no longer discolored cheekbone, my rapid healing having kicked in the moment I'd landed on Neverra. "I'm also good with my hands." As though to support that claim, he ran his fingers down my bare spine, bumping against the tie of my bikini top. "And my tongue."

He was. He was also good at changing the subject when it suited him. Instead of pushing him like he'd just pushed me, I said, "Forget I asked. I know you like me, and that's enough for now." I kissed his sinking smile.

He pressed away from me. "Amara, I've been away from you for an hour, and it's been the fucking loneliest hour of my life."

My heart performed a tiny somersault.

"I'm way past love. And the insecure fae that I am was afraid you weren't there, yet."

"When have we ever gotten off the train at different stops?"

His eyebrows quirked.

"Too soon for prison humor?"

He smiled and shook his head. "It's never too soon to turn something bad into something good." He finally leaned over, stopping an inch from my lips. "And just so we're clear, you and I are *never* getting out at different stops."

"What if I see a dragon on a platform, and I really want to stop?" Fire. I was playing with fire.

His scowl was quite formidable. "I'd kill Joshua, and then I'd make our fathers swear me in as the new *draca*." His arms curled around my back possessively. "Do you . . . have a thing for dragons?"

I smiled. "I have a thing for redheads with short tempers and soft hearts."

"Soft heart," he grumbled. "I thought we'd cleared this up already. Nothing about me is *soft*." He pulled me back into him, all but bruising my abdomen.

Smiling, I stretched my arms and hooked them around his neck, then pushed up on tiptoe—even though I could've levitated—and pressed my smile to the scudding throb beneath his birthmark before remembering we were out in the open where anyone and everyone could see us. I fell back on my heels and looked up. Sure enough, my new guards were right there, patrolling the airspace over my little house.

When Remo glanced up, their gazes flicked away. "Inside. Now." His hand moved to my lower back as we walked through the open sash doors of my bungalow.

When he reached for the handle to close them, I flicked the large pane of glass shut with my mind. He startled even though he knew my arsenal of powers as well as everyone else in the kingdom.

Perhaps even better.

"That one"—he tapped his temple to indicate my telekinesis—"that one will never cease to make me jealous."

He stepped toward me, but before he could touch me, I said, "I almost forgot something."

His brows slanted.

I swiped through my Infinity until I located the dress I'd favorited. With another sweep of my finger, I swapped my red bikini for the beaded nude gown. I wasn't sure if it was the reflection of the gilded beads or the fact that his eyes were no longer green, but they seemed almost molten as he took me in.

A ragged noise formed at the base of his throat and vibrated through the warm air. "I was quite a fan of the red bikini. In case you wanted to make a note of that."

Even though my feet were anchored to the ground, the way he looked at me made me feel as weightless as the stars outside my window. "Noted."

He stared at me some more before finally bridging the distance between us, flicking my dried hair over my shoulder and leaning in.

I pressed my palms into his chest. "Wait. I wanted to ask you something."

He straightened, one of his umber brows arching up. "Go ahead."

"First, is your mother disappointed that we—that you—"

"No. She told me to make sure not to step out of line, so that your mother doesn't gas me, but—"

My jaw slackened. "You're kidding?" I gasped. "Nima would never."

"Relax. I'm kidding."

I swatted his arm. "That wasn't funny."

"Sorry. It wasn't." He shot me a rueful look, pushing his red locks back. "The truth is Mom told me that I shouldn't lead you on if I wasn't sure. That she respected Cat and Ace and *you* enough not to subject their daughter to my philandering ways."

"Seriously?"

"I didn't even know she was aware of my philandering ways, but yes, seriously."

"And?"

"I told her that I loved you."

My jaw popped a little wider. "You told *her* but not me?"

He placed both palms on my face. "I love you, Trifecta. And I solemnly swear that until you grow tired of me, I will be at your side, and only yours. I will follow you through every damned portal, but if we can avoid visiting any more prisons, I'd really appreciate it."

My lips trembled. "How could I grow tired of you? You're much too infuriating."

"And handsome."

I rolled my heated eyes. When they landed on his again, my heart struck my throat harder, and I almost forgot about the other subject I wanted to discuss. But it was important, so I brought it up. "I know you don't want to discuss Gregor, but are you okay with the decision that was made tonight?"

His hands coasted off my face. I instantly missed their solid heat.

He gazed at his black boots, so dark against my pale carpet. His lids closed, and he inhaled deeply. "The outcome was unhoped for. I'm angry and not sure if I'll ever visit him, but the boy for whom he was such a hero is relieved he won't be put to death, however much he deserves it."

This time I was the one who cupped his jaw. "You'll visit him. Someday."

His eyes opened, but he stayed quiet on the subject. He wouldn't have long to visit him. Once on Earth, Gregor would age quickly, and since he was already in his late eighties, he could be gone in a matter of a few Neverrian months. Then again, the man was a force of nature, so perhaps he'd stick around longer.

I wished I hadn't brought up Gregor, but I cared about Remo. If I'd learned anything from observing my parents, it was that shouldering the weight of each other's grief was the only way to ensure the bearer wasn't crushed beneath it.

"And I'll go with you. If you want me there," I whispered.

He nodded. "Anything else, Trifecta?" His voice was roughened by emotion. "Your dress is making it extremely hard for me to concentrate."

Sensing he needed a distraction, and plenty happy to be that distraction, I said, "Is it? How about you take it off then?"

His hands were on me before I'd even finished talking. "Where's the zipper?"

I smiled. "Zipper? Oh, there's no zipper."

"Then how do you remove it?"

I tapped my Infinity, smiling a little wickedly, because I had no intention of making it that easy. "Actually, I was thinking we could talk a little more."

He grunted something unintelligible. "We can talk naked."

"You'll never be able to focus if I'm naked."

His nostrils flared. "Fine. What should we talk about?"

My smile grew at his mounting frustration. He crossed his arms in front of his chest, muscles bulging under the tight black fabric.

"You're regretting having used up your *gajoï* right now, aren't you?"

His eyes flashed. And then his mouth twitched. "I know what you're doing."

"What I'm doing?" I asked with mock innocence. "What am I doing?"

"Forcing me to be creative."

I frowned. "No, that's—" I squeaked when my dress went up in flames, flames that didn't burn my skin, just the pretty beaded fabric. "Remo Farrow! You can't use fire to undress me."

"I think I just did."

I hitched up a brow. He wanted to play . . . *Fine*. I sent my own wave of fire over his uniform and watched with great satisfaction as it chewed through the coated black fabric.

His grin became blinding. "My little villain." Wreathed only in smoke, he backed me up against the bed.

"Villain? I saved Neverra from Kingston."

He palmed my ass, yanked me up, and then tossed me on the bed. A moment later he was hovering over me, his warm breaths pulsing against the tip of my nose. "Fine, you can be the hero tonight."

Grinning, I circled his waist and towed his magnificent body down against mine. "What was it you were saying earlier about your hands? And mouth?"

Remo's knees and palms sank into the mattress, caging my body between his, and then his glistening lips curved. "I can't remember. What was it I was saying?"

"That you might be good with them."

"Might." He grunted. "I'll show you *might*."

I laughed, and then I stopped laughing, because he did show me. With deft fingers, he fastened the strings the Cauldron had cast around us weeks ago, binding them around our bodies and knotting them around our hearts.

EPILOGUE
CRUZ

Amara and Remo had decided to cement their essences in the Cauldron a month after our return from the Scourge. The ceremony was held on the wide strip of sand bordering the Pink Sea, sand that once upon a time had made up a desert that hid another prison—the *hareni*.

Although I'd seen the new-Neverra—had lived in it for several months before Gregor shipped me into his prison world—I'd spent the last month gazing at the sun-steeped land from the lilac sky I'd missed so much. I stared at it now, marveling at how it darkened with stars. For a century, I'd lived under a white sky that never deepened to black, that never shimmered with *lustriums*.

"Well, if it isn't my favorite cellmate." The familiar nasal voice had me glancing over my shoulder.

Kiera was advancing toward me, her necklace of *tigri* claws glinting fiercely against her all-black outfit.

Although I'd kept my distance the first few months she and Quinn had shown up in the final cell, confinement weaved intractable bonds between people. I wouldn't have gone so far as to call us friends, because we weren't—after all, she'd tortured Lily, and that was unforgivable—but we weren't enemies, either.

We were fellow detainees, fellow survivors, fellow ghosts.

I side-eyed her, remarking that she'd chopped off her dreadlocks into a bob that hit just below her earlobes. "Nice haircut."

She touched the blunt ends. "Thought it was time for a change."

The style made her look a decade older than the fifteen years she'd been frozen at for the past century. How strange it must've been for her to look upon her twin's face.

"Cole suggested I go spend some time on Earth to age . . ." Her tight tone made me wonder if he'd suggested she leave Neverra only for that reason. Where I'd been welcomed home with open arms, Kiera hadn't.

I found her twin standing on the edge of the crowd, chatting with Giya Geemiwa whose silvery-white dress was cut so low in the back, it revealed the delicate ladder of her spine. The few times Giya and I had crossed paths, I'd tried not to let my gaze roam over her sun-kissed skin or linger on her bowed upper lip, but Kajika's daughter—for reasons I didn't care to dissect, I preferred to think of Giya as his instead of Lily's—arrested my attention.

She arrested many people's attention. Everyone on Neverra seemed besotted by the girl, be they adults or children. Cole Locklear's daughter reached out to Giya, who didn't hesitate to pluck her out of his arms. She rubbed her nose against the child's, making the little one giggle hysterically, and the father grin wide.

As I watched them interact, my stomach churned, folding upon itself until it was as compact as a mosaic tile. "Are Cole and Giya . . . *together*?"

I couldn't imagine Kajika agreeing to such a match. Even if Cole hadn't been the one to torture him, the hunter loathed Daneelies more than he loathed Seelies, and from the many conversations Ace and I had had since my return, I'd learned that his brother-in-law was still not a fan of the *mishipeshu*.

Kiera smoothed her thumb over one of the *tigri* claws, a tic she'd picked up in the Scourge. "They're not." She wrinkled her nose. "But yeah, he's interested, which is gross if you ask me. He's a whole century older than she is." Her navy eyes swung toward my face and narrowed. "*Why?*"

I schooled my expression and tone, hoping to appear and sound utterly indifferent. "Because they seem close."

"She's your ex's daughter, Cruz." Kiera's disapproving tone scratched the air.

I crossed my arms over the white shirt I'd worn in honor of the bride and groom. "You read too much into my question."

Ever since Ace's and Catori's nuptials, Veroli had let on that wearing white to weddings had become a Neverrian custom. Apparently, Kiera hadn't gotten the memo. Unless she'd worn black *because* she'd gotten the memo. I supposed that was more Kiera's style.

"You seemed plenty fascinated with the girl when she landed in our cell."

"I was fascinated by the fact that she'd been created by people I knew and loved." Not because, even bloodied and coated in sand, Giya's silver gaze had momentarily made me forget how to breathe.

Kiera let out a soft snort. "Then I should encourage my brother?"

My spine stiffened. "I'm certain he doesn't need any encouragements."

Although I attempted to look anywhere than at the patch of sand upon which they stood, Giya suddenly tossed her head back and laughed, capturing my full attention. "I thought your brother was a marine biologist. I didn't know he moonlighted as a comedian."

Kiera grinned. "Oh, Cole doesn't have a funny bone in his body."

As a choir began to chant the melodious wedding march, Giya sobered and turned, then pointed out the procession of *runas* decorated in white blooms and faelights to the little girl propped on her hip.

When the first basket landed on the beach, Ace scooped up his queen and carried her to the ground. They were both resplendent in their white revel attire and matching proud smiles. The second their driver rose high, another *volitor* basket landed, this one carrying Faith, Silas, and their son, Karsyn. My childhood friend marrying Gregor's daughter was not a match I had anticipated, and yet, they worked.

Derek Price arrived next with his wife, Milly. Where her eyes glittered with joy, his glittered with unshed tears. Ace offered Milly his arm, while Catori took her father's hand. I expected Addison to show up, but no other *runa* landed. Had she become so despondent as to miss out on her granddaughter's nuptials or was she observing the nuptials from higher ground?

As the grandparents and parents took their places along the carpet of crushed shells and white petals to await their children, Kajika, who seemed to have grown wider and taller somehow, carved through the non-flying crowd toward his daughter. He must've signaled for her to accompany him, because she returned the child to the blond Daneelie and took her father's thick, tattooed arm.

Heads bent in conversation that brought a tender smile to the forever-grave man's face, they strolled unhurriedly toward Lily and the son who already towered over his mother. Though not quite as large as his father, Adsookin was gearing up to catch up. He was already a full head taller than his sister.

It struck me that while they'd lived, loved, and founded a family, I'd lain dormant in a cold world where the sky never darkened and the curses never quieted. I wondered if my fate hadn't somehow been more cruel than the lost clan's because I hadn't slept away the years. I'd felt them trickle by, eroding everything but my body.

A *lucionaga* tapped my shoulder. "Massin Wood has asked that you stand with the family, Cruz."

Sure enough, Ace's limpid stare found mine through the web of faeries, and he nodded. A jagged lump obstructed my throat as I approached this tightknit clan, who, in spite of all I'd put them through, still counted me as one of theirs.

I halted beside Veroli, whose puffy cheeks quivered with her uncontrollable sobbing.

Upon noticing me, she clasped my hand. "My boy. My beautiful boy. I am so happy tonight."

I smiled down at her, then raised her hand to my lips and kissed her roughened knuckles.

"Here they come!" Cassidy yipped, looping arms with an equally excited Aylen, and pointing at the sea that had become as smooth as a mirror.

A form glittered beneath it while another skimmed the surface. Both glided toward us.

A hush fell over the crowd, but the music . . . it grew and swelled.

Remo landed on the beach first, and then he turned toward the ocean and waited for Amara to rise from its briny depths. She did so slowly, luminous from scale to iris. She pressed on the black band around her wrist, and folds of red silk spilled from the ruby-encrusted belt of her bodysuit.

I caught Remo swallowing as he took in his betrothed, and it reminded me of the way Ace stared at Catori, the way Kajika stared at Lily—as though these women were their reason for breathing . . . their reason for existing.

"Amara and her love for grand entrances."

I jerked at the soft brush of Giya's voice. She stood on Veroli's other side, her arm wound around our nursemaid's juddering shoulders and her metallic gaze fastened to the cousin she'd followed into the unknown. Silver feathers and crystals had been embedded into her complicated braid, making the thick mass flash beneath the bobbing faelights.

She must've sensed my attention, because she met my stare and offered me a smile.

I didn't smile back.

I couldn't.

Her smile was too much.

It stirred something in me, something deep, something that shouldn't be stirred.

Not her.

Anyone but her.

Wanting Giya wasn't right. It could never *be* right.

Veroli inhaled a rickety breath. "My happiness will be complete the day you, my sweet Giya, and you, my dashing Cruz, marry."

Panic made my lungs seize and a cough rattle up my throat.

"Oh, and when Adsookin marries." Veroli patted Giya's elegant fingers that crimped the older woman's white tunic. "Although I'm not certain I'll still be around by the time that wild brother of yours decides to settle."

Grasping Veroli was merely listing the faeries she wanted to see stand beside the Cauldron—and not specifically together—did little to soothe my flustered heart.

As Giya, whose high cheekbones had grown as rosy as her lips, reassured Veroli that Sook would meet his match sooner rather than later, I turned to give Amara and Remo my full attention, but my eyes collided with another silver set—*Lily's*.

Had she caught me staring at the forbidden fruit of her womb?

Overcome with shame, I pried my hand from Veroli's and withdrew down the beach before I, once again, shattered this beautiful family.

ACKNOWLEDGMENTS

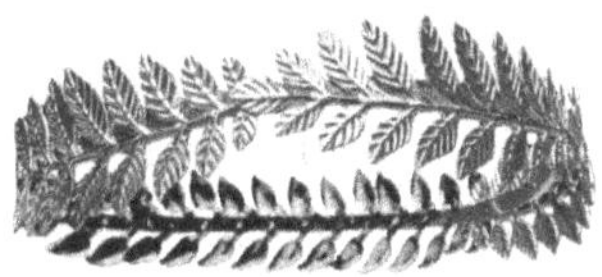

I hope you've enjoyed diving back into my faerie world with Amara and Remo; I certainly did. Writing about Ace, Cat, and the gang felt like hanging out with old friends. I hadn't realized how much I'd missed them until I set fingers to keyboard and traveled back to Neverra.

Thank you to all the lovers of *The Lost Clan*. I adore receiving your messages and comments. You wanted more Neverra, and I listened. This book was written entirely for you.

A sixth book will follow, and what a forbidden romance it'll be. After all, one main man still hasn't gotten his happily ever after, and if anyone deserves to find his other half, it's Cruz Vega.

I started writing *Reckless Cruel Heirs* back in December 2019 when the world wasn't yet ravaged by a pandemic that forced entire countries to close their borders and confine their citizens, and then I finished writing it during the first week of lockdown in Switzerland. For a while, I debated whether to change certain aspects of the story—shorten Amara's and Remo's confinement, add people in their jail cells earlier on so that it wasn't just the two of them. I was afraid that we'd been subjected to enough isolation in real life that no one would want to read an entire novel about isolation. In the end, I decided to tell my story as it was meant to be told. After all, fiction has always mirrored reality.

A huge thank you to my Facebook reader group. You guys are amazing and inspire me every day. As Amara and Remo's journey took shape, I asked for visuals pertaining to the different places my characters visited. So many of you took the time to scour the internet for outlandish tropical plants, old-timey frontier towns, and spectacular creatures.

Special thanks to Valeria Orlando for finding the Brazilian grape tree that led to the beetles in the last cell; to Amanda Curley for her torrent of visuals ranging from jungles to frontier towns to white-picket fences; to Julie Green Booth for all her peculiar flower finds; to Courtenay Oros and Amber Everett, whose vampiric flower specimen inspired my fluted, fanged fiends; to Rachel Theus Cass, for being my Neverrian boys' greatest ambassador. There are so many others from *Olivia's Darling Readers* who deserve my gratitude but listing them would take a whole chapter. Know that you are all deeply valued.

Thank you to my beta readers—Theresea Barrett, Katie Hayoz, Astrid Arditi, Joanne Milkins, and Celia McMahon—for poring over the long manuscript and helping me tighten the story and refine the characters.

To my phenomenal editor Jessica Nelson and hawk-eyed proofreader Katelyn Anderson. I so enjoyed working with you both on RCH. Special thanks to Rachel for buffing my epilogue.

To my three children, quarantining with you guys was eye-opening. I feel like I discovered something new about each one of you every day. Adam, Gabrielle and Estée, you are wonderful and smart, sweet and funny. You make me incredibly proud to be your mother.

To my husband, like Amara and Remo, we were stuck together because of this crazy pandemic. Is it wrong of me to say how much I enjoyed the time we spent in lockdown?

To my family abroad and the one in Switzerland where I live, thank you for your ceaseless support.

If you'd like to learn more about me and my books, visit http://oliviawildenstein.com and make sure to join my Facebook reader group, Olivia's Darling Readers, where so much magic happens. You can also find me on Instagram—I'm @olives21, the one with too many pictures of books.

ALSO BY OLIVIA WILDENSTEIN

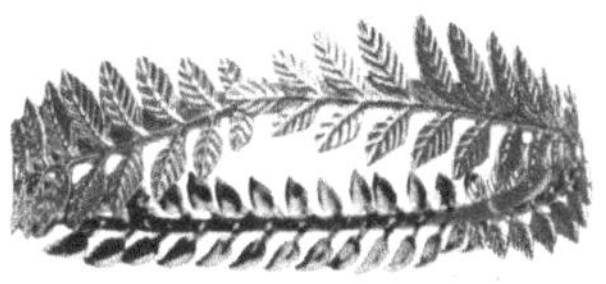

PARANORMAL ROMANCE

The Lost Clan series

ROSE PETAL GRAVES

ROWAN WOOD LEGENDS

RISING SILVER MIST

RAGING RIVAL HEARTS

RECKLESS CRUEL HEIRS

The Boulder Wolves series

A PACK OF BLOOD AND LIES

A PACK OF VOWS AND TEARS

A PACK OF LOVE AND HATE

A PACK OF STORMS AND STARS

Angels of Elysium series

FEATHER

CELESTIAL

STARLIGHT

The Kingdom of Crows series

HOUSE OF BEATING WINGS

HOUSE OF POUNDING HEARTS

HOUSE OF STRIKING OATHS

The Quatrefoil Chronicles series

OF WICKED BLOOD

OF TAINTED HEART

YA CONTEMPORARY ROMANCE

GHOSTBOY, CHAMELEON & THE DUKE OF GRAFFITI

NOT ANOTHER LOVE SONG

YA ROMANTIC SUSPENSE

Cold Little Games series

COLD LITTLE LIES

COLD LITTLE GAMES

COLD LITTLE HEARTS

ABOUT THE AUTHOR

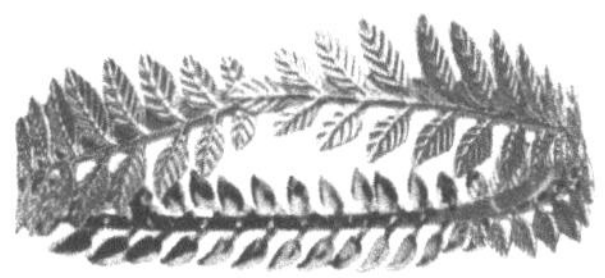

Olivia is the byproduct of a meet-rude in a Parisian discotheque that turned into an epic love story spanning several decades. Naturally, this shaped the way she viewed romance.

After meeting her own Prince Charming—in a Parisian discotheque of all places—she decided to put fingers to keyboard and craft love stories for a living.

None of her characters have ever met in a Parisian nightclub... as of yet.

WEBSITE

HTTP://OLIVIAWILDENSTEIN.COM

FACEBOOK READER GROUP

OLIVIA'S DARLING READERS

9 781948 463683